A Passion In Winter

Irene Landry Kelso

Canadian Cataloguing in Publication Data

Kelso, Irene Landry.
 A passion in winter

 ISBN 1-55212-414-2

 1. Canada--History--1713-1763 (New France)--Fiction.* I. Title.
PS3561.E39738P37 2000   813'.6   C00-910748-7

TRAFFORD

This book was published *on-demand* in cooperation with Trafford Publishing.
On-demand publishing is a unique process and service of making a book available for retail
sale to the public taking advantage of on-demand manufacturing and Internet marketing.
On-demand publishing includes promotions, retail sales, manufacturing, order fulfilment,
accounting and collecting royalties on behalf of the author.

Suite 6E, 2333 Government St., Victoria, B.C. V8T 4P4, CANADA
Phone   250-383-6864   Toll-free   1-888-232-4444 (Canada & US)
Fax   250-383-6804   E-mail   sales@trafford.com
Web site   www.trafford.com   TRAFFORD PUBLISHING IS A DIVISION OF TRAFFORD HOLDINGS LTD.
Trafford Catalogue #00-0078   www.trafford.com/robots/00-0078.html

10   9

To my son, Hugh, daughter-in-law, Julie,

and sisters, Theresa and Bertha.

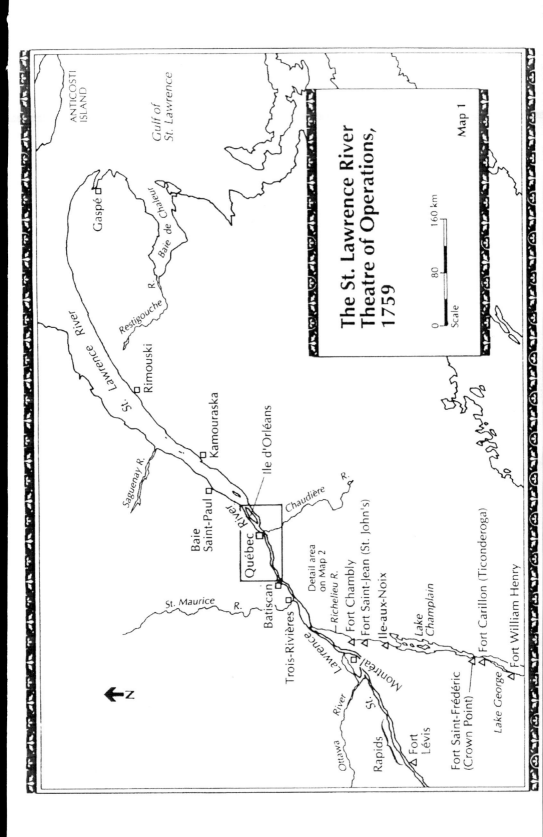

The St. Lawrence River
Theatre of Operations,
1759

Map 1

Scale

0   80   160 km

N

ANTICOSTI
ISLAND

Gulf of
St. Lawrence

Gaspé

Baie de Chaleur

Restigouche R.

St. Lawrence River

Rimouski

Saguenay R.

Kamouraska

Ile d'Orléans

Baie Saint-Paul

Chaudière R.

Québec

Detail area
on Map 2

St. Maurice R.

Batiscan

Trois-Rivières

St. Lawrence River

Richelieu R.

Fort Chambly

Fort Saint-Jean (St. John's)

Ile-aux-Noix

Lake Champlain

Fort Carillon (Ticonderoga)

Fort William Henry

Lake George

Fort Saint-Frédéric
(Crown Point)

Montréal

Ottawa River

Rapids

Fort Lévis

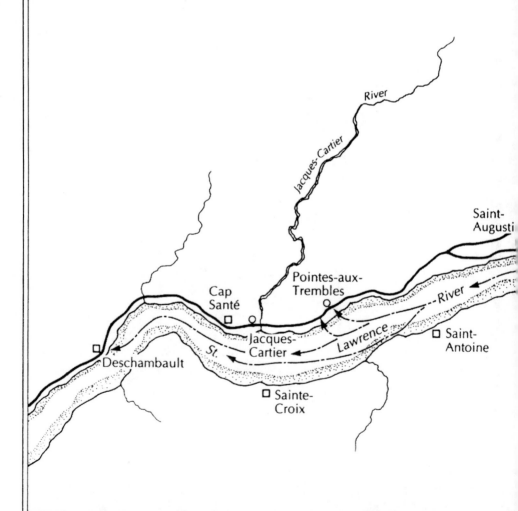

The Battle for Canada, 1759

- British encampments
- French encampments
- Troop advance
- Tidal flats
- Village
- Garrison
- Road

Map 2

Saint-Augusti

Jacques-Cartier River

Pointes-aux-Trembles

Cap Santé

Jacques-Cartier

St. Lawrence River

Saint-Antoine

Deschambault

Sainte-Croix

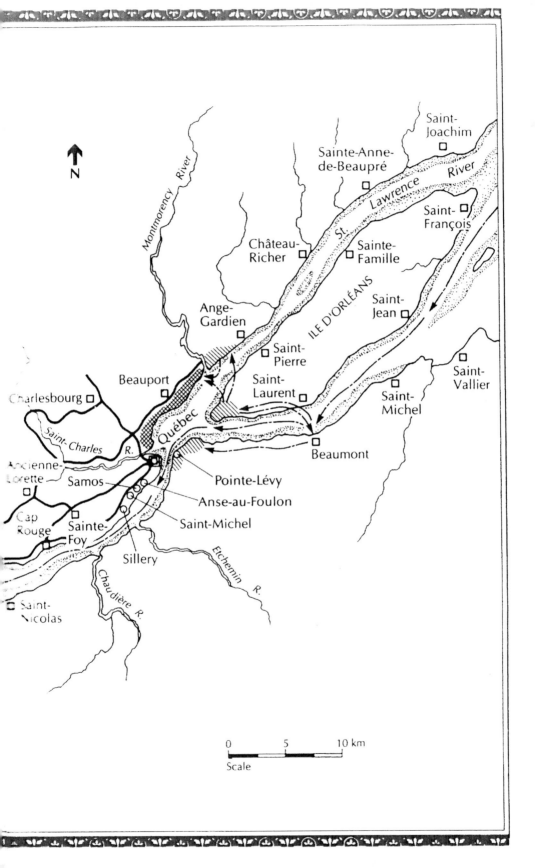

A special THANK YOU to all the people who helped with their input and support during the research and writing of this novel including but not limited to those listed below:

Laurier L. LaPierre, Author

Professor W. A. Douglas Jackson, Founder and Former Director of Canadian Studies Center, University of Washington, Seattle

Professor Fernand Harvey, INRS-Culture et Societé, Université du Québec

Deborah Daoust, Deputy Program Manager, Canadian Consulate General, Seattle, Washington

Sister Margaret O'Neill, Sisters of St. Joseph of Peace, Bellevue, Washington

Sister Gabrielle Daigneault, O. S. U., Ursulines de Québec

Sister Eliane Lachance, O. S. U., Ursulines de Québec

Sister Juliette Cloutier, A. M. J., Archivist, General Hospital, Québec City

Sister Marie-Paule Cauchon, A.M.J., Archivist, Hôtel Dieu, Québec City

Bruce D. Bolton, Adjutant, The Old 78th Fraser Highlanders, The David M. Stewart Museum, Montreal, Québec

Nancy Pearl, Director, Center for the Book, Seattle Public Library, Seattle

Marie-Noelle "Marino" Deseilligny, Reference Librarian, University of Washington Libraries, Seattle

Sydney Wright, Art Consultant, Seattle

Chapter One

"We are lucky to be alive," Jean-Paul Boisvert said aloud to himself. He nodded grimly and walked fast with long strides down Avenue Royale. The autumnal air was crisp and cool about the countryside of Beauport, along the King's road all the way to Quebec. Off in the distance a huge canopy of gray smoke hung over the city.

The September chill enveloped thirteen-year-old Jean-Paul. Would it be a severe winter? Not much left of 1759. He shivered in spite of his warm clothes. He pulled his woolen *toque* low over his brown curly hair. His dark brown eyes cautiously inspected the road ahead of and behind him. No one was in sight. A tall boy for his age, he quickened his pace and trudged on.

The mighty St. Lawrence River ran alongside of Avenue Royale. Jean-Paul never tired of looking at it. It was part of their lives. The snow geese had started to come down from the north and soon they would even leave this place to the ice and snow that would grip the broad river. Today, it looked like the whole British Navy out there. Since last June, British troop vessels had sailed in from their captured success, the Fortress Louisbourg on Ile Royale. They had established themselves on the evacuated Ile d'Orleans. Ever since, with bold certitude, their ships ran up and down the great river. British officers had viewed the coveted prize through their telescopes, the walled city of Quebec.

At mid afternoon, the sun still made a weak appearance. Jean-Paul walked against rumors. What was going on? He had taken all the short cuts. The Boisvert farm was near the forest, some distance away from General Montcalm's encampment in the plains of Beauport. He had skirted part of it before he hit the road. As he passed, he saw some tents still standing, silent batteries and trenches, some guns still pointed, kettles and food packs strewn about. A double sacrilege that he couldn't take time to stop and hide the abandoned food. Were they coming back? What had been the command? Had they rushed to the Plains of Abraham to do battle? Or had they escaped some thirty miles beyond to safety, to counter-attack from the back? Was Chevalier Gaston Francois de Levis there with reinforcements from Montreal?

Jumbled thoughts and fragments of villagers' conversations crowded Jean-Paul's young mind as he hurried down the road. Before the British had entered the St. Lawrence, Pierre Francois Rigaud, Marquis de Vaudreuil, now Governor Vaudreuil, had sent a circular letter to the militia captains of the parishes. It exhorted them to defend their religion, their wives, their children, and their goods from the fury of the heretics. It said that he, the Governor, would never yield Canada.

"Canada, our native land, shall bury us under its ruins before we surrender to the English!" The letter declared.

At a barn meeting the month before, Jean-Paul's father had commented with pride on Vaudreuil's words. "At least he said 'Canada', not 'New France'."

"The Governor is too jealous of General Montcalm!" Pierre Gagnon, the town's best carpenter, had shouted and waved his pipe.

"It could be our undoing, they don't see eye-to-eye those two, no communications." Louis Belanger had voiced his disgust. He was the town notary.

There were a lot of grumblings at that assembly. Jean-Paul had eavesdropped on part of the political gathering as he ran errands back and forth between house and barn. These bits of enlightenment made him fear along with the others that if the rivalry between Governor and General was not resolved it could pronounce the doom of them all.

They were lucky to be alive. A lot had happened throughout the summer. The British General had landed troops and occupied Point Levis across the river. There had been rain storms that prevented planned battles, resulting in skirmishes. The French had sent fireships to attack the British and had missed. From the river, bombardment of Quebec continued. In many areas some Canadians deserted to work on their farms but the French army aided by Canadian rangers and Indians won at Montmorency above Beauport.

"Ah, we won there!" Jean-Paul nodded. But his father was right, they had let a false confidence reign over the countryside after that victory.

He kicked the dust with his worn-out black boots. Would these boots last through the winter? He stopped abruptly to stuff the ends of his gray leggings into the boot tops. Last evening, messengers came from the battlefield to Beauport and surrounding villages with the wild news. They came on horseback, others walking, straggling, disheveled Canadian rangers, a few Hurons and Algonquins with hoarse cries. The city was besieged!

Incredible! It couldn't be? Jean-Paul didn't want to believe it. During the night of the twelfth, the British had climbed the cliffs at Anse au Foulon to the Plains of Abraham and met the French army. The rumor was that the battle had lasted less than one hour and the British general was dead! Well, he was walking to the city to find out the real truth. To see if his sister, Marie-Louise, was safe in the Ursuline convent.

The wonderful smell of freshly baked bread reached his nostrils. He had missed the aroma of pickling this morning, which was usual in the environs at this time of year, but this was even better. He also thought of the half sack of flour he had hidden to make a sugar cake for his bedridden mother's birthday. Food had been scarce; the people of Quebec had been put on rations of two ounces of bread a day. Yet, the Intendant, Francois Bigot and the Commissary General, Joseph Cadet lived in luxury. A great number of fowl had been fattened for their tables with the *habitants'* wheat. Jean-Paul wasn't quite sure how he was going to manage that cake yet. His mouth watered as he hurried. He had also put away a crockery jar of gooseberry preserves in a dark corner of the kitchen cupboard. They were fortunate to have some food preserved in clever caches.

How could the countryside still be so beautiful if war was clamoring in Quebec? It was his favorite time of year when the summer greens left the points of the maple leaves and turned to cardinal red, purple, brown, and russet. He liked the yellow tints. His mother loved autumn too. Would she recover yet another time. He said a prayer. He walked on. Who was that down the road?

"Jean-Paul! Jean-Paul, *viens prendre une bouchée.*" Mireille Le Conte was pulling hot bread from her outdoor oven by the roadside. "Come have a bite, you'll need it."

Jean-Paul came toward her. The world was falling apart but Mireille Le Conte was still baking bread. She must have more than a hidden sack of precious flour to be so flagrantly baking out in the open. There was hardly any bread anywhere. The best farmhouse larders had provided for General Montcalm's soldiers. A cold June last year, cold as winter, had blighted the harvest. Thank God, it was better this year, but not by that much after soldier raids. At the Boisvert farm, fortunately, there was still some harvest to be reaped this fall. And the French army had left them some of their cattle.

"You heard? The British are at the walls of the city! They climbed the cliffs at Anse au Foulon! So where are you going?"

Jean-Paul stopped. Mireille handed him a large slice of warm bread slathered with maple butter. He took it with a nod of thanks and devoured it instantly.

"You have flour?"

"A bit." She shrugged. "Where are you going?"

"To Quebec, to the convent if it's still standing, to find Marie-Louise."

"The nuns can take care of themselves. How is your poor mother?"

Jean-Paul shook his head. "Not good. She has good days and bad ones. I think she's dying." His voice was tearful. "We can't get the doctor to come. This damn war!"

Mireille put her arms around him. She had three sons of her own. If they were on the Plains, she didn't know whether they were dead or alive.

"Dr. Arnaux must be with the wounded. Go home, stay with your mother. Help your father put the food in proper caches. Who knows what we will go through this winter?"

"Uncle Guillaume is with Papa doing all that. He's wounded, he limps and spits blood. They sent him home."

"*Mon Dieu!*" Mireille rolled her eyes toward the sky.

A group of Canadian rangers, Indians and villagers on horseback clattered down the road.

"The city is besieged! Keep inside your houses." They shouted and grabbed at Mireille's warm bread as they thundered by. Pale brown dust rolled up from the road and followed them.

"Bolt all your doors and windows, Mireille. I will look in on you on my way back tomorrow."

"You are still going on into the city?"

"I must find my sister."

Mireille shook her head, gathered what was left of the freshly baked bread and walked up the path to her stone-built house.

Jean-Paul went on. He thought of Marie-Louise. The light-hearted Marie-Louise he had known as a small boy. Since his birth, their mother had never been well. Marie-Louise had practically raised him by herself. Now, she was an Ursuline nun. All was very serious. He was puzzled with all the rituals she must go through. Would she eventually lose her wide, happy smile? Everything was centered on prayers preparing for final vows. After that, would she be light-hearted again? He wondered.

He walked faster, then broke into a run toward the end of Avenue Royale. A new fear gripped him as he neared the St. Charles River. There was no sound of activity from the bridge of boats that crossed the stream. Was it unguarded? Had the British not reached this point yet? He ran across the foot bridge. He was stopped at the other end by Canadian civilians. Occasional bombings now rent the air.

"Then it's true? It's true!" Jean-Paul gasped and stated his business.

"*Quel malheur!* What a shame! Yes, it's true!" The man on watch said. "Hurry, we're leaving here to catch up to see if there are reinforcements back of the Heights. There may be a British guard here the next time you cross."

They let him pass. He entered the city by the Palace Gate. Gun powder stabbed at his lungs and made him cough. How could the battle have lasted only an hour? Why had General Montcalm waited so long? Where were Vaudreuil and Colonel Francois Charles Bourlamaque, Montcalm's third officer, all the promised French reinforcements ? How had the British gotten past the sentinel to gain the top of the Plains? What traitor slipped the password? How had they scaled those cliffs?

Billows of smoke rose up from a fallen wall, half of a house. Jean-Paul walked down *rue Sainte-Ursule* and crossed over to *rue Sainte-Anne*. Many buildings were still standing whole, parts of the city were left unscathed, a pocket here and there. All was confusion, people ran about with bulging bags, half-broken carts whipped around corners, children wailed and cried as they were hurried indoors. Civilian sentries were posted at the ends of each street. British soldiers were stationed outside the walls, waiting for the signing of the order of capitulation, waiting to get in. They were shouting orders, picking up their wounded, burying the dead.

No one stopped Jean-Paul. He turned into a familiar alley off *rue Desjardins* toward *Donnacona*.

"No!" He cried and ran. Part of a house wall lay across the alley.

In the debris, he saw two silent figures clasping each other protectively. They covered each other's heads with their hands.

"Don't move!" Jean-Paul yelled. "I'll get you out, I'll get you out."

Frantic, he pulled, lifted and swept stone, wood and earth out of the way. Fearfully, cautiously, he shook the elderly couple. Monsieur and Madame Couture of the little baker shop around the corner. They were still warm but they were quite dead.

"No! No!" Jean-Paul wept. He got up shakily, his hands were bleeding from cuts and splinters. Everyone knew the Coutures and their little bakery. Even now, in the chaos of the fallen wall, there was still something baking in their overturned oven. The smell of burnt sugar hung in the air. He thought of the Sunday he and his family had stopped at the shop after Mass at the *basilique*. It had been too busy to bake pastries at the Boisvert household that week. He could still taste that handful of sugared almonds, newly arrived from France, that Monsieur Couture had put in a paper cone for him.

Jean-Paul dragged himself to the stone wall of the house across the alley, he pressed his palms against the stone, retched and vomited. Then he threw his head back and yelled.

"*Au secours!* Help!" Someone had to come and get them out of there.

"We're coming, we're coming." Télesphore Couture, the dead couple's own son and Hector Langevin, their baker, lumbered down the alley with a cart.

Jean-Paul half limped then ran toward them. "Your parents! You already know?"

Télesphore nodded; tears streamed down his cheeks. "I'm taking them home, they'll be buried on my farm. My cart was taken at St. Louis Gate, I got this one at the tailor's and I just found Hector."

"*Que c'est triste,*" the baker mumbled as he cleared more debris.

"I'll help," Jean-Paul offered. He didn't know what to say. He didn't know what to do.

Télesphore Couture saw the pain and anguish on young Jean-Paul's face and it was he who comforted him.

"Jean-Paul, my parents are better off than we. They're with God." They embraced.

"I'll come with you."

"No, thank you Jean-Paul, I have Hector to help me. Pray for us. We must leave the city before dark. We'll go down Côte Ste-Geneviève, get past the wall, around by General Hospital back to Lorette."

In their shock and grief, Télesphore, Hector and Jean-Paul went through the necessary motions to extricate the Coutures from the destruction. Very tenderly they placed them in the cart and covered them. Télesphore and Hector carefully pulled and rolled the cart down the rest of the alley. Overwhelmed with sadness, Jean-Paul took another street to the convent.

His hands were rough and sore. "*Les maudits Anglais,*" he muttered as he wiped bile from the corner of his mouth. The few people out on the streets were dashing about, searching for havens of safety. Around the next corner, Jean-Paul bumped into a wild-eyed woman clutching a small gray velvet sack. She fell to the ground, the bag split open spilling out the most brilliant jewels Jean-Paul had ever seen and he had seen only the few encrusted in the Bishop's chalice and his mother's wedding brooch. He stooped to help the woman up.

"Are you hurt, Madame?"

"Young man, don't you dare touch a single one of those jewels," Still sprawled out, she grabbed at the stones and stuffed them back into the bag.

"Madame, I'm trying to help you up. . . ."

"A likely story," she screamed at him. Her hair was singed and she had a front tooth missing.

"Madame." Jean-Paul bowed stiffly, shrugged and left her. If she didn't live on a farm she would need those jewels this winter, he thought. She was probably some grande dame of the city, or a servant of the French nobility.

As he approached the convent he saw that the compound was still standing. Quietly, he entered the garden. Two elderly men hurried down the steps of the Ursuline chapel.

"He died at daybreak," one of them said.

"Who?" Jean-Paul stopped them.

"General Montcalm, Monseigneur de Pontbriand prepared him for death. Captain Marcel, his aide, was with him till he breathed his last."

"Where?"

"At Dr. Arnaux's residence," the other man answered. "And now, he will lie in state at the Chateau St. Louis until the funeral this evening."

"*Requiescat in pace,*" Jean-Paul made the sign of the cross and bowed his head.

"Come, we have a lot to do," the taller of the two prompted his companion. "Messengers will be sent around, such as we can." They hurried off.

A bell tolled as Jean-Paul came into the chapel. Here was an attempt at usual routine, a call to prayers. He was shocked to see the bombed-out hole in the middle of the floor. The debris had already been cleared for the evening service. He knelt in his usual place. He always visited the chapel and said a few prayers whenever he was in Quebec. On this tragic day, he said a few *Aves* for the Coutures and their family. He took a few moments to say prayers for General Montcalm too, before he made his presence known to his sister. He folded his painful hands, he needed bear grease, olive oil or lard to soothe them. Mother Philomène, the *cuisinière* in charge, had all of these in her cupboards in the convent kitchen. He would find her, if he didn't see Marie-Louise first.

Marie-Louise Boisvert, in religious life Sister Marie Madeleine, hurried out of the kitchen and floated down the hall into the convent's carpenter shop. Here, Bonhomme Michel was constructing a simple pine coffin for the illustrious French general. Tears rolled down his cheeks.

"*Que c'est triste!*" Marie-Louise murmured as she touched a smooth board. There were so many tasks to attend to in the midst of death and destruction.

"*Oui, Soeur Marie Madeleine*, very sad." A sob hooked in Michel's throat. "We have lost everything, not only the General, but the city! A sad day, a day of infamy for France, Sister. . . ." He sniffled.

Marie-Louise laid a comforting hand on his shoulder as she passed by him. Now, she must check the chapel to see that everything was in order for the *Libera* Mass. As best she could, she would have it ready. She felt as if she were performing duties in a half-dream. But it was all too real. She saw that the bombed-out hole in the chapel floor had been widened to receive General Montcalm's remains. That's where he would be laid to rest. It was close to the crypt of Mère Marie de l'Incarnation, founder of the Ursulines of Quebec.

For a moment, she thought of her parents. Please God, everyone must still be safe out there in the country. She checked the candelabra, candles, incense and what was left of the best altar linens. Abbé Jean Felix Recher, curé of Quebec, would sing the *Libera*. Her dusty veil fluttered as she went into the cloistered part of the chapel, to her own chair. The noises of war still thundered in the background with occasional flashes from exploding cannons and bombs. There was a whole city of confused people milling about in the streets. Their wounded were being brought in. When the hospital was filled to overflowing they would be brought here, she calculated.

Wolfe, the English General, had died too during that short battle yesterday. Father Joseph Resche, confessor of the Ursulines and Aide to Abbé Recher, told all the nuns at Hôtel-Dieu, at General Hospital and at their own convent that his remains were on the ship *Lowestoft*, in the St. Lawrence River, under special military guard.

Marie-Louise turned over her hourglass. Force of habit. Ah, well, she would not be able to pray, to meditate. There was no time. She would rest for a few moments; her head ached. There was fear and pain in her heart. Gone was the peace, tranquility and solitude she had known when she first came here fifteen months ago. All she could do now was cry out, "*Mon Dieu!*" Everything was chaos. Yet, she murmured a prayer for the two dead generals.

"Marie-Louise, *ma soeur?*" She heard Jean-Paul's whisper on the other side of the grille.

"Jean-Paul!" At once, she came to him in the main chapel.

"Marie-Louise!" He ignored her religious title when they were alone. "It's terrible. Terrible!" His eyes were haunted, he bunched his woolen *toque* in his big bruised hands. "I just found the Coutures crushed to death in the back of their shop. Télesphore just took them away. And Maman, is she going to die too? If only she could see you once more."

"Oh, the poor Coutures! God rest their souls. Your hands!"

"I need a little bear grease."

"*Mon p'tit frère*," Marie-Louise clasped him to her breast. "Come to the kitchen. Dear Maman, I wish I could see her too. And Papa?"

Jean-Paul shrugged. "Well enough, Papa is strong. Uncle Guillaume was sent home from the fighting, not too well. But we have most of the harvest in the barn. The soldiers didn't come up to our place, too far off the road. Who knows why? So far, we're lucky."

Marie-Louise nodded. She poured water into a large earthenware bowl and gently washed his hands. She had done it many times when he was a small child. Then she lathered a sweet-smelling oil over his bruises.

"The French left everything. Did they desert us?" Tears streaked his dirty cheeks. "Their tents and all the camp rations are strewn about in the plains of Beauport. . . . .

"The food! But we need food now, in the city."

"Well, the city will starve this winter for all they care. . . . I think they betrayed us, these French."

"Hush, you are French."

"No, I am a Canadian. Damn the English and damn the French. What's to become of us?

Marie-Louise sighed and shook her head. There was a tightness in her chest. Was this her little brother, Jean-Paul, now fierce, vehement, full of fear for them all?

"I don't know. Chevalier Roch de Ramezay, the King's Lieutenant will look after us. But first we must bury the General. We must do all these things quickly since this will be an open city. Until some order is restored, there are no rules or regulations inside or outside the walls until the British come in. Perhaps I could come back with you to see what I could do for Maman, but not till tomorrow. We could start at dawn, we might get through. . . ." The wild idea seized her. Already, she was planning.

"But how can you? Mother Superior. . . ."

"We will see. Ah, Noël," Marie-Louise greeted a tall Huron as he entered the kitchen. Here was a staunch friend to them all - - the Jesuits, the Augustinians and the Ursulines. He could put his hand to anything. "You come to share our tragedies. Thank you."

"Yes, Sister, to help." He looked about gravely. "The tapestries?"

"They are all well hidden, Noël. Sister Corinne put them in an underground cache with the vessels and vestments that won't be in service in the chapel this evening."

He nodded. He spoke French fluently; since childhood he had lived and worked at the Jesuit seminary when he was not on a long trek in the forest. "I'm here to help Father Resche or wherever I can. We'll make quarters in the kitchen for a few days. Clear the debris." A large, bronze, big-boned man with coarse black hair and dark flashing eyes, Noël looked like he could move a whole wall.

"Let's see if there's some kind of soup for supper before we all go to the funeral. Not much of a *pot de sagamité* today. And Jean-Paul, will you please run an errand, in spite of your poor hands. You have such good legs. Take some bed sheets and a note to our Superior at General Hospital. There'll be a bottle of brandy wrapped inside, so, careful."

Jean-Paul nodded. He sat at the refectory table with Noël while Marie-Louise ladled out what was at the bottom of a large cauldron that hung over the kitchen hearth. The pea soup had bubbled through the day's bombings.

"I keep the Reverend Mother informed on what's going on here and I can't send Bonhomme Michel today."

Jean-Paul nodded again. The ordinary life of the cloister was certainly shattered for him and Noël to be sitting at the Ursulines' table at this time of day. The hot soup soothed his empty stomach. It soothed all of them as they ate. There was no bread.

"Be cautious, hurry back," Marie-Louise touched Jean-Paul's cheek affectionately then gave him the package of sheets with the precious bottle of brandy wrapped in the middle. It would be needed for amputations. Whatever was available would be borrowed between the convent and the two hospitals.

Though the British had not entered the city yet, on the evening of the battle, Highlander regiments had made their way beyond city walls, across meadows of the countryside and had taken possession of General Hospital near the St. Charles River

When Jean-Paul arrived there, he found a tight British guard around the building. He was stopped and questioned. With only a few words of English and motions, he explained he was sent from the Ursuline Convent to deliver extra bed sheets.

"Captain MacDonald, sir," one of the guards called out. "Can't make out what this lad is trying to say?"

"*Qu'est-ce que vous avez là, mon jeune monsieur?* What do you have there?"

Jean-Paul, surprised at the imposing captain's fluent French, again explained his errand. His package was checked. The brandy was not taken. He was permitted to enter. More in awe now than fear, he surmised the special guard was posted around the hospital against possible attack from what was left of the returning French army, either from the Plains or Sillery.

Where were they all? Was there yet hope? His heart lifted for a moment as he went down a long hall filled with the transport of wounded soldiers, French and English, and some Indians. He found Mother Marie-Anne Migeon de Bransac of the Nativity in an improvised office. Piles of bandages were on all the chairs. He detected with quivering nostrils that even this room's floor had been freshly washed with vinegar to disinfect and repel all odors of sickness.

"We are prisoners of war, Jean-Paul, but the French army hasn't surrendered yet. General Murray has assured me that no harm will come to my nuns, or our dear sisters the Augustinians here at General Hospital, or the Hospitalières at Hôtel-Dieu, not to one hair on our heads. Soeur Marie Madeleine, your sister, has our thanks and our prayers to be with the vigil at our convent. How are they doing there, this terrible day?" She took the package and the note he had lugged across the tortured city. She looked tired but there was fierce, determined courage in her eyes.

"As well as can be, Reverend Mother. General Montcalm's funeral is at nine o'clock." He blew his nose. What kind of punishment, he wondered, would the Reverend Mother mete out to Marie-Louise if she knew his sister's plan to steal a day away from the end of the world in Quebec, before it even ended?

"It's nearly time now for the funeral. Some of us will be there. You must hurry back, then. Don't go near the Plains, there are still brutalized bodies lying around with their heads cut off. Pray for us all, Jean-Paul."

The guard let him through. Darkness descended on the city. Out on the great St. Lawrence River, lights glowed from all the British ships. A special vigil was being kept on board the *Lowestoft* where the body of General Wolfe lay in state.

In a sad silence, people gathered in the broken streets with torches to form the funeral cortège of General Montcalm. Solemnly, at its head the simple pine coffin enclosing his body was carried reverently. De Ramezay and his garrison officers walked behind, and the townspeople continued to join the procession as it went along.

There was no sound of *adieu* carillon from the bombed *basilique.* Nor was there sound of *adieu* from the bells of the Ursuline chapel for the most valiant of French soldiers. A priest led them all into the chapel in near darkness, lit only by wax tapers around the bier. Occasional flashes of shell-fire still appeared and glinted through the torn roof. Jean-Paul was at his usual place. He looked for his sister in the cloistered choir stall. He knew the exact location of her chair, kneeler and hourglass. He could make out that her head was bowed, her veil hid part of her face.

"Oh God!" Jean-Paul lifted his eyes to the torn roof, to the few stars in the dark sky. "Now that Montcalm's gone, what's to become of us all?"

Abbé Recher intoned the "*Libera me, Domine*" over the rough plank box that Bonhomme Michel had nailed together that morning. With a final blessing, Montcalm's body was lowered into the shell hole that had been widened for his grave. Instead of the honor of being laid in a proud mausoleum on his estate, Candiac, his final resting place was here in Quebec, so far from his native land. Sobs and tears broke out anew. To all of them gathered, it seemed that part of France descended into the bombed-out tomb. General Montcalm would never see his beloved family again, his olive trees, his chestnut trees that he had so often talked about. They were all attending the funeral of New France.

Silently, the townspeople left the chapel and returned to what was left of their households in the charred avenues. The nuns extinguished all the candles but the sanctuary lamp, the Repentigny lamp that never went out.

The gates of St. Louis and St. John were still guarded and closed. Final lingering noises of the British victory sounded over the walls from the newly built entrenchments on the Plains. Soldiers were still burying the dead, wounded strays were still being found and conveyed to General Hospital. Macabre echoes floated on the night air and enveloped the funereal solemnity of the besieged city.

Chapter Two

Jean-Paul dozed uneasily for a few hours crouched on a *paillasse* in a corner of the convent kitchen next to Noël. They had insisted Father Resche sleep on an improvised cot brought down from the nuns' dormitory. There had been some quiet during the night. Noël woke them at early dawn and served reheated porridge and strong herb tea. After Mass Father Resche prepared his small leather case with a quantity of hosts and holy oils and went off to the hospital. Noël and Jean-Paul went to the sacristy to help put away whatever was left from last night's funeral.

As he entered the sacristy Jean-Paul stepped back in shock. He saw his sister roll up her black habit, white novice veil, cross, wimple and coif into a burlap bag. "What are you doing?"

"I have decided to come back with you. For one day. To see Maman."

"But Rie-Ouise. . . ." the soft sobriquet he used to call her when he was a child always came out when he was surprised, happy or dejected. "What about Mother Superior?"

"I will deal with that when I come back. Since it's the end of our world, with the city in ruins. . . . What's one day away from the convent?"

"But. . . ," he protested in disbelief. At Marie-Louise's silent motioning, he put a huge candelabra in a chamois bag for safe keeping. The designated secret place was a cast-iron cabinet in the great wall that reached through the back of the sacristy armoire. At least, for the moment, it might be safe there within an enclosure that had withstood so much battering. Marie-Louise knew where it was.

"And I will come with you," Noël said reassuringly. He held the other candelabra that had been used for Montcalm's funeral.

"Ah, that's good." Jean-Paul gave him a relieved and grateful glance.

"Very sensible, Noël, but can you be spared?" Marie-Louise asked.

"Two Moose will help Father Resche until I return."

Francois, another Huron like Noël, was a trusted friend of the Ursulines and when he had a mind to he was Bonhomme Michel's right-hand man in the convent 's carpenter shop. He had won his new name last winter when he had triumphantly bagged two moose.

"Just one day," Noël said. "We must be back quickly. We will go above Beauport. We should go now."

Marie-Louise nodded. She no longer looked like Sister Marie Madeleine. In a pair of men's old trousers, a woolen cap over her short burnt-gold hair, a tattered jacket and ranger leggings, she looked like a gamine. Her brown eyes sparkled.

"Wherever did you get those clothes?" Jean-Paul shook his head. "Oops, Sister Philippe!" They were discovered.

"What is going on here? *Soeur Madeleine!* Marie-Louise. . . ." Sister Philippe, Geneviève Marcoux, had not seen her lifelong friend out of her nun's habit since they had taken the veil together. Bosom friends since childhood, their Beauport family farms side by side, they had gone to school and the novitiate together.

"Don't give me away, Geneviève. Maman is dying and I'm going home. For one day."

"But we are needed here! The wounded and the dead are all over the city, the French, the Indians, the English will be brought in, our own. We're setting up space in the monastery, making a hospital wing here, the hospitals can't hold them all. Oh! *Mon Dieu!* What are you thinking of? Mother Superior. . . ."

"She can chastise me when I get back. Do whatever she will with me. I'll do double the work. You'll see!"

"We're cloistered nuns!" They had both known when they entered the novitiate that they would never see their families again except on special visitation days, special granted permissions, and a few conversations through the grille. What craziness possessed Marie-Louise? War! Overnight, it changed all of their lives.

"I know that we are. Don't give me away, if you can help it." Marie-Louise embraced Geneviève. "Come," she beckoned to Noël and her brother. They went out of the chapel sacristy into the crisp September air.

Soeur Philippe stared after them with incredulous awe. Occasional faint echoes of gunshot, cannon and bombing could still be heard from Lower Town.

"*Soeur Philippe.*"

"*Oui, mon Père.*" Geneviève snapped to attention as Father Resche and Two Moose bustled in.

"First, I must tell you the very sad news that during the night two of our sisters died. . . ."

Geneviève gasped and felt a stab of pain. "Oh, no!"

"Mother Jeryan of St. Joseph and Mother Charlotte de Muy of St. Helen. Arrangements are being made for their burial in the garden cemetery of General Hospital this afternoon. Mother Superior thought it better than having them brought here."

"I'll be there." Her eyes brimmed over. "May they rest in peace." She made the sign of the cross.

Father Resche touched her shoulder comfortingly. "And Sister, wounded Highlanders, *des Ecossais,* and some of our own officers are being brought in here right now. An overflow from Hôtel-Dieu."

"Yes," Geneviève shook herself. "The *dortoir* on the second floor is still standing and safe. Some beds are all ready."

"Good. Let's put them there, Francois."

Two Moose signaled for Sister Philippe's attention. "I left some fish in the kitchen, *ma Soeur.*"

"I'll go cook it immediately and prepare a lot of bouillon for these people." She wiped tears from her face. She didn't even have time to mourn two of her favorite sisters. She knew that Mother Charlotte must have died of fright and a broken heart. Though assaulted with this new pain of loss, Geneviève told herself she must function. She passed out of the sacristy. What were they about next? There were now three Superiors at General Hospital, their own Mother de Bransac of the Nativity among them, so she was the only one in charge here with Mother Davanne. And Marie-Louise was traveling all over the countryside. What was she thinking of? Should she try to send a messenger after them to call them back? Her presence would be missed at this afternoon's funeral. She decided against it, there was too much to do.

At the refectory table she started to clean the fish. In the background, she heard noises of the wounded being brought in, the other sisters directing the traffic, assigning places. Another pain pressed her heart and she broke into uncontrollable sobs. After a few moments, she wiped her tears and continued her tasks.

Noël found an old horse in a wrecked carriage house on *rue St-Louis* that he cajoled into service for the journey to Beauport. He instantly baptized him Bijou.

For their exit from war-torn Quebec, Noël and Jean-Paul insisted that Marie-Louise be the first rider. In the saddle, in Bonhomme Michel's old clothes, Marie-Louise felt strange. She had not left the convent walls since she and Geneviève had become postulants together fifteen months ago. Her heart leapt at the thought of seeing her mother, her father, her old homestead at Beauport. But she was filled with sadness, disbelief, bewilderment as they traveled through debris-cluttered streets out of the besieged city. They feared being stopped by soldiers or civilians gathering the spoils of battle wherever they were found.

"Two boys and an Indian," a guard called out at the Palace Gate, the only safe entrance and exit from the town now that the English were camped before the Gates of St. Louis and St. John. "Going home to Beauport."

"Let them pass." A companion guard answered.

Their journey had started in a pale rose dawn. Now, full day was upon them with all the odors and colors of autumn. Even far off, at the edge of the forest, flashes of color could be seen from the turning of the leaves. For long stretches on Avenue Royale, no one bothered them. The little groups they did meet were like sad, silent ghosts, coming and going. One lone man followed them.

"*Je m'en vais chez Mireille*," he said. "To see if she's safe."

"I saw her yesterday." Jean-Paul told him. "She was baking bread. We'll all stop." The forlorn *habitant* fell in step with him.

"Leave it to Mireille to have a little flour stashed away. My farm above Charlesbourg, it's all pillaged," he shook his head. "They took everything. . . ., and left a lot of it strewn about. . . . *Toute gaspillée*, wasted. We will have to depend on whatever they give us from those British ships in the St. Lawrence this winter. We might starve!"

"Yes, Mireille managed to save and hide flour. I don't know where." Jean-Paul smiled.

"Maybe we'd still have flour if so many fowls hadn't been fattened with wheat for the Governor and French officials," the new arrival shook his head. "We were only allowed two ounces of bread a day in the city. I am Jerome Leduc, I know your father, Jean-Paul." They all shook hands. Noël led them on in silence.

At Mireille's house everything seemed to be locked up.

"Mireille, Mireille! *C'est moi*, Jean-Paul, let us in." The doors of the cellar cache opened. Mireille came out and blinked at them.

"Well, the sun's out, a beautiful day. And who is this?" Mireille approached the old horse timidly, not believing her eyes.

"Yes, it's me." Marie-Louise slid off Bijou and embraced Mireille.

"*Ma foi du bon Dieu!*" Mireille shrieked. "*C'est pas vrai!* Unbelievable!"

"Yes, it's really me. But we must go on. There are a few nuns at the convent keeping vigil and opening a hospital wing. Most of our nuns are at the General Hospital. The wounded are coming in from everywhere. I'm stealing a day to see Maman. . . ." her voice caught with emotion. There was no explaining her impulsive act.

Mireille nodded. "You poor dear, and in man's clothing. But come, have some hot cider. . . . And this *sauvage?*"

"Our friend, Noël, but we must not linger here now that we know you are all right."

"Yes, we must go. Are you secure in that cellar? Come with us." Jean-Paul and Jerome Leduc examined the huge boards she kept across the cellar doors from the inside when she hid herself.

Mireille shook her head. "I'm guarding this old house. You know what they did to your Uncle Guillaume's house at Orleans." Only a few months ago a British regiment had burned it to the ground.

"But what can you do alone?" Jean-Paul worried.

"But I am not alone. Jerome, my friend, has come for a visit here. And I will get caught up on what Charlesbourg is doing in this war."

"God be with you, Mireille. Jean-Paul you ride the rest of the way. I want to stretch my legs."

Jean-Paul protested but in vain. Noël pushed him up onto the horse. An hour later they turned off Avenue Royale.

"I never thought I would see my home again," Marie-Louise told Noël as they went up a private lane to the Boisverts' old stone manor that had once been part of a large seigneurie. Bright flowers were still in the window boxes, the lace curtains at the salon windows were a little limp, not as stiff and starchy as when her mother was well. She heard chickens clucking down the path to the garden, the sheep bleated by the north stone wall, and Pitou came running around the corner of the house barking loudly.

Marie-Louise broke into a run and flung open the heavy front door. It was still the same, hardly a blemish marked its age-old, smooth pine. There was her father lighting his pipe by the hearth.

"Papa! And Maman?" Her joyous cry and question filled the house.

"Marie-Louise, *chère enfant!*" Joseph Henri Boisvert dropped his pipe, rushed to his daughter and clasped her in his arms. "What are you doing here?" His voice shook with emotion as he beamed with happiness.

Ah, this was a high moment for them all, Jean-Paul thought. He motioned Noël to the barn with Bijou. This tired old horse had to be fed. While his father and sister went upstairs to his mother's chamber, he checked the soup pot hanging over the fire. He looked about for his Uncle

Guillaume. Where was he? Then he saw him limp into the kitchen with a basket of squash and turnips.

"What did you see in Quebec, Jean-Paul?"

"Don't you keep this soup pot filled when I am gone?" Jean-Paul scolded with affection. They both shared kitchen duties. "There is a big surprise here for you."

"Who has come to visit in times like these? We can hardly feed ourselves. Who's up in your mother's room?"

"Marie-Louise!" Aghast, Hortense Boisvert recognized her daughter instantly. She was sitting up in a huge bed against fluffed up pillows. She stretched out her arms. Marie-Louise ran to her embrace. Joseph Boisvert quietly left his wife and daughter as he wiped a tear.

"Maman, *chère* Maman." Marie-Louise stroked her mother's limp hair. How frail she looked, so pale, yet her eyes sparkled like fire-flies.

"What's happened at the convent?"

"It's still standing, most of it in bad shape. All but eight nuns are at the General Hospital. Father Resche makes his quarters in our kitchen for the moment. We will be housing some of the townspeople who have lost their homes. One floor will be a hospital wing." She smoothed the fold of blanket and sheet as she talked.

"How well you look, in spite of all our misfortunes. How kind of Mother Superior to let you come. . . . I don't understand?"

"Hush, I will make us a pot of hot chocolate. Do you know what day this is?"

"Of course, it's my birthday, *chère enfant.*"

"And I am here one day to celebrate it with you, Papa, Jean-Paul, Uncle Guillaume and our friend, Noël."

"In those clothes? Where is your habit?"

"At the convent. I must still have an old dress left here somewhere?"

Hortense shook her head. "I gave all your clothes away, to your cousins at Orleans."

"You must have something to fit me?"

"There's my cardinal red. I was just your size when your grandmother made it for me. Your father proposed to me the first time I wore it. We were dancing at Port Levis."

"Then it's perfect."

"Will the Ursulines forgive you this vanity? Ah, but *n'importe,* I am so happy to see you, dear child." Hortense lay back on the goose feather pillows. There was no doubt in her mind that her daughter would be returning to her bombarded convent. The Boisverts had given their daughter freely and lovingly to God.

"I am here for just one day, Maman." She pressed her mother's hand.

"I am happy."

"I'll go see about some supper for this *fête* to celebrate your birthday."

Their arrival was complete when Marie-Louise flew downstairs and was boisterously swung around by her astonished uncle, in spite of his injury. Then all was bustling activity in the kitchen. Everything they had in the larder was brought out and preparations began as if for the great meals of Christmas or *la Saint-Jean-Baptiste.*

Everyone had a special task and the moments flew. Marie-Louise threw open the windows to the clean September air. Jean-Paul brought in a bushel of apples in varied shades of greens, yellows and reds. He was grateful for the improvement over last year's meager harvest. He stoked a greater fire in the hearth, then helped to dress two chickens and put them on the spit.

Marie-Louise was flushed with culinary occupation. From the armoire she brought out linen and silver used only for special occasions, baptismals and weddings. She laid out silver goblets and plates of blue-and-white porcelain. With hoarded flour she made a quick soda bread, then a *paté.* She baked a maple-sugar cake and arranged a platter of greens with bits of salt pork. She mashed yellow turnips and heaped them in a huge serving bowl.

Joseph Boisvert put two flagons of white wine at each end of the table.

Rich spicy aromas spread through the whole house. Candles were lit and the hearth fire glowed on the woolen rug of primitive Canadian designs. Marie-Louise loved this room, she had taken the memory of it with her to Quebec. In her mind's eye, in the cloistered chapel, it had reappeared during some of her meditations when she prayed for her parents.

A cool evening descended on the countryside as she shut all the windows. A soft mauve and orange sunset lingered over Avenue Royale and the abandoned French camps. Greens and yellows covered the surrounding meadows and farms. It was quiet here in this upper back region, on the edge of the forest, where their old stone house stood. In this preparatory excitement for her mother's *fête* , Marie-Louise tried to shut out the thought of the besieged city only seven miles away, even the convent chapel.

She puffed up her mother's brown woolen shawl on the *tonneau* chair her father had made to protect his ailing wife from the severe cold and frigid winter that usually took hold over the lands of Beauport. They would carry her downstairs and seat her by the fire for the festivities. This would be an evening to remember. What would come next? Mother Superior, battlefields and wounded soldiers. How would she face the Reverend Mother? She would deal with that tomorrow.

The soup simmered. Noël and Jean-Paul brought in more wood. Marie-Louise put a bunch of marigolds in a faience bowl of fresh water.

"Voilà!" Her brown eyes sparkled. "Now, I must freshen up and see if Maman's dress fits me."

Hortense gasped with delight when she saw her daughter in the soft red wool dress. It was still a romantic garment. Marie-Louise's burnt gold hair was short and curly about her face. A three-fold cowl caressed her neck, a nipped-in sash circled her slender waist, yards of material puffed about her hips and fell to the floor in an elegant hem.

"Tiens! Look here!" Jean-Paul exclaimed with admiration. "If Mother Superior could see you now! You might be excommunicated!"

"We are celebrating Maman's *anniversaire.* Tomorrow is time enough to return to face the consequences with Mother Superior."

Marie-Louise took her mother's voluminous blue-and-white striped apron off the pine peg of the storeroom door and tied it about her waist.

Jean-Paul must still enjoy licking the bowl of whipped cream, she thought, as she started to swirl thick heavy cream. Ah, they still had good cows. The French army hadn't taken all of their stock. Would the British? She splashed brandy on the cake, then heaped mounds of whipped cream in its center. With a mischievous wink she slid the almost empty bowl across the table to her brother. He sat waiting with two spoons mimicking, licking his lips.

After dinner, though exhausted from the excitement, Hortense basked and lingered in the glow of the fire and surrounding love. Her pain and the next day were forgotten in the unexpected pleasures of the moment. As they all toasted her with another round of wine, they heard a great commotion outside. Who was approaching from down the road? Horses and the clashing of swords rent the calm evening air.

"*Mais, qui viens?* Who's out there?" Joseph Boisvert muttered. He took the lantern hanging by the fireplace, lit it and went out with Noël, closing the great front door.

Jean-Paul, Guillaume and the two women waited fearfully. They heard English voices. Joseph returned, leaving the door wide open.

"*Des Ecossais,* Highlanders, soldiers, from God knows where. I thought everybody was on the Plains. They took the wrong road. They're checking out the countryside. They're wandering about. They claim they're lost. I'll keep them out of the house. Jean-Paul, their horses need attention," he signaled his young son as he went out again.

Marie-Louise came and stood in the doorway. She held a small tray of goblets. The candlelight and soft glow of flames from the hearth fell on the path. Three men in bright-colored tartans, their claymores hanging at their belts, were talking to her father. One was very tall. Were they going to insist on coming in and spoil her *fête?* Her heart missed a beat. They were advancing toward the house. True, they must be tired and hungry and would want to avail themselves of hospitality whether it was offered or not. After all, they were not in a private world here from the aftermath of war that still raged only seven miles away. As quickly as the two more eager soldiers moved toward Marie-Louise, the arm of the tallest man shot out in front of them. He was in charge.

"We will not disturb these people," Captain Ian Bruce Lindsay said in distinct French. It was a command. A gut feeling of protection rose in him as he saw the young girl standing in the lighted doorway - - a very young girl, in a soft red dress and burnt-gold hair, holding a tray of wine goblets.

"But. . . . .," both his companions protested at once. Their nostrils quivered as the rich smells of food floated from the hearth on the September air. Their throats were parched. They knew there must be *eau-de-vie,* at least brandy, in this manor, as well as wine. They noticed the silver goblets on the girl's tray. They calculated these farmers must be very well-to-do.

"There's good hot food here, an Indian to take care of our horses," Lieutenant Leslie Hay insisted.

"Aye," Lieutenant Alexander MacAlister agreed as he crowded against the staying arm of his commanding officer. "We'll stay the night."

"Quebec's not that far. We'll go on." It was a second command. Captain Lindsay was adamant. Even if they had to ride all night, he thought, they would join Captain MacDonald at the hospital tonight. And there were other places down the road, according to their map, if they had to rest. What was the matter with him? He was suffused with a strange mixture of feelings. Under other circumstances it might be pleasant to linger a few moments with these people, this attractive girl. But he had already decided, he and his officers would not impose themselves upon them. Apparently this was a prosperous farm, far enough off the main road not to have been too disrupted so far, and he had no intention of doing so. This must be a private family gathering, a special occasion. He felt compelled to respect it.

"We will not disturb these people," he repeated. This time he spoke in English with a thick Scot brogue.

"Yes, Captain." Their reluctant compliance was filled with disappointment but revived when Joseph Boisvert went and took the tray from Marie-Louise, motioned her to shut the door, then came and offered it to the three officers.

Noël finished watering their horses. After they drank the wine, the Highlanders left with an exchange of civilities.

Joseph and Noël came back inside with the lantern and tray of empty goblets. Though their spirits were dampened by the intrusion, Jean-Paul went off to the winter kitchen to wash and wipe the goblets with a linen *serviette* and came back to the table to pour another serving.

"They're gone," Joseph said with a great sigh. He smiled at his wife. He came up to her by the fire and pulled the brown wool shawl about her shoulders with an affectionate pat. "They're gone."

"Marie-Louise, play something for us," Jean-Paul said as he handed Noël a piece of cake.

With a great sigh of relief and a prayer of thanksgiving, Marie-Louise went to the harpsichord. As fear, stress and tension left them, they all sang their favorite songs. But in these happy stolen moments, in the bosom of her family, Marie-Louise knew that after this reunion she might never see her mother again.

Chapter Three

Captain Ian Bruce Lindsay first saw the steeples and turrets of Quebec from the rail of *Racehorse*, the ship he arrived on. Then from the back of the Plains of Abraham at the end of the battle that brought death to the two generals, Montcalm and Wolfe. For him, the macabre scene was Culloden all over again. He had just turned fifteen when engaged in that fighting. Wolfe and Townshend fought there too. Wolfe's general had been the brute known as "Hangman" Hawley. The Cameron piper had shrilled his pibroch, "Ye sons of dogs, of dogs of the breed; O come, come here, on flesh to feed!" They had all rushed in a screaming, terrifying horde. At Culloden he had almost lost his right arm. He had seen gushing blood in his dreams ever since. And it was the same again, just a few days ago, on these blood-drenched Plains of Abraham.

The Fraser pipes had played "Lovat's March" as Simon Fraser had led them to join the redcoats in the bloody fray. When it was all over, about noon, those still able to stand were breathing hard, cursing and nursing their wounds against the wall of the city. Ian had piled some of the injured in carts taken from neighboring farms for transport to the General Hospital, across meadows, outside the wall. Miraculously, he had escaped serious injury. He was just roughly bruised and his bad arm still ached. As he had viewed the desolation on the blood-drenched Plains, the scattered dead of both armies, he thought they had all fed on flesh in the matter of a few hours. They had all labored in detachments to bury the dead quickly. There were always scavengers to steal loot from dead bodies.

New in command, General Townshend had dispatched all able-bodied men on emergency errands. Confusion reigned. With two of his officers, Ian had been sent to reconnoiter by way of back roads and across the Charles River to see if Montcalm's Beauport camp was really abandoned. And he had proceeded to get lost in the upper countryside of Beauport.

After their encounter at the Beauport manor, now they were coming near Quebec again across the Charles River by the upper countryside of Charlesbourg. It was after midnight when Ian and his lieutenants finally arrived at the General Hospital. They had seen its vigil lights from down the road.

He identified himself to the guard who awakened Captain MacDonald. They were all given a round of rum and Ian's officers were assigned sleeping quarters. They dropped their claymores and fell on the improvised cots in complete exhaustion.

The two captains went to a desk down the corridor to confer.

"Montcalm's camp is abandoned," Ian told MacDonald. "Where's Townshend?"

"On the *Lowestoft*. Aye, if it's confirmed that all is abandoned at Beauport, there's still a possibility of Levis' return. Vaudreuil or Bourlamaque and troops could still come in from the back, by Sillery."

An Augustinian nun returning from a crowded room of moaning wounded carried a small tray with two cups of steaming bouillon. She left it on the desk for the two captains.

"*Merci, ma Soeur,* that's very welcome." MacDonald gave one to Ian.

She nodded silently as she lowered her haunted eyes and noiselessly glided down the hall.

"Drink it," MacDonald commanded. "It will scald your stomach but do you good. Big day tomorrow. This is a map of sorts," he tapped a huge map draped over half of the desk. "Levis will probably station at Jacques Cartier. Sillery has to be checked next."

Ian sighed. He was weary in every bone. The bouillon warmed him.

"You'll share my quarters for tonight, Captain."

"Thank you, Captain."

"Let's get a few winks before the next hell breaks loose."

"Aye."

Before he closed his eyes, Ian thought of his home in Scotland, his French mother, Corinne Le Mire, and the hills of heather. He thought of a day long ago, during a summer vacation in France near the *brûlonnerie,* the glassblowing compound of his maternal grandparents, at the edge of the Vendôme forest. He and his mother had just returned from Mass at the nearby Ursuline convent. It was while the family was preparing a festive picnic on the lawn that he had wandered into the Records Room. There in the archives he found a century-old French explorer's journal. On a page yellowed with age, he had read the scrawled script.

"I have never seen anything as beautiful or as magnificent as Quebec. There could be no better site for the capital of a future empire."

He had smoothed the tattered cream vellum. He was twelve that summer.

And now, that very same capital hung in the hands of Britain. He was in the middle of it. Right here, in Quebec! He sighed, he was too tired, too wound up to sleep. He tossed back and forth. Yes, they had won the battle on the Plains but victory was bittersweet at this low moment. There might still be some stray bodies without heads out there, and other mangled bodies that would never rise again in this world. Had they really won more than a city that had not formally capitulated yet, a whole country, an empire? Not quite.

For what lurked in that back country by Beauport besides the Indians who crouched waiting, ready to leap, attack, scalp and scream triumphantly in bloody rage? They, the Highlanders, had been no less bloody at Culloden. That's where they had all learned to kill. He, Wolfe, Townshend, Monckton, Murray, the French and British regiments, they had all whirled their instruments of death anew on the Plains.

As he resettled on his good side, he thought of the farm manor at Beauport where he and his officers had stopped. Though he had just gulped

MacDonald's rum and the hot bouillon served by the *hospitalière*, he could still taste the wine offered by the proud seigneur of the manor. In drowsy imagery, he could still see the girl in the red dress standing in the golden glow of the open doorway.

Marie-Louise's stolen *séjour* at home was over. It was time to go back to her convent and face the consequences. She insisted Jean-Paul remain at the farm with the family and that she return to Quebec on horseback with Noël. Old Bijou served them well. They went by the back roads past Vaudreuil's encampment. They were stopped at the Charles River but were permitted to proceed.

Geneviève met her in the convent garden and told her the sad news of the loss of two sisters in her absence. Marie-Louise went directly to the chapel. In her choir chair she cried softly and prayed. Her heart ached. But now, her two sisters in Christ were in their new life, she tried to console herself. Ah, well, there were only a few moments to mourn in this chaos. With a great sigh, she left the chapel and went back to the garden. What was left of it?

In an untrammeled corner Marie-Louise found a few fall flowers. She divided them into two bouquets, mixed marigolds and plum colored asters. In the sewing hall she tied them with pieces of blue string discovered in one of the sewing baskets. The pain in her heart tightened. So now it was at their graves that she would meet these two dear friends again.

Marie-Louise's eyes were red and puffy. Geneviève helped her sponge her habit. In a few hours, as soon as she could get there, she would appear at the General Hospital and confront Mother Migeon de Bransac, the Reverend Mother Superior of the Ursulines. And visit the two new Ursuline graves.

Which sister had died of fright? Mother Jeryan of St. Joseph? She had been taken from her home in New England years ago by a band of Indians. She had been rescued from captivity and brought into Quebec. Forty years ago, she had been received among the daughters of St. Ursula.

Mother Charlotte de Muy of St. Helen had been their annalist. Her hand had traced all the details of the war up to the day of her death, just a few days ago.

In unison with Marie-Louise's suffering, Geneviève helped her dress in the freshly restored habit. The long black garment fell into place over her slim but well-rounded body.

Marie-Louise adjusted her bib, fitted a close cap over her short curls, tied the forehead-cloth almost down to her brows. The sleeves hung long.

Geneviève positioned the three-inch crucifix on a long black ribbon round Marie-Louise's neck. It fell to her girdle. She then pinned the final touch, the white veil of the novice over the forehead-cloth; it flew carelessly over Marie-Louise's shoulders down to a few inches below her waist.

"You'll do," Geneviève said approvingly as she inspected the appearance of her lifelong friend and colleague. "You'd even pass inspection for an audience with the Bishop or the Governor."

"Which Governor, French or English?"

Geneviève ignored the comment. "I'll say a little prayer. Maybe, it won't be so bad." She smiled encouragingly. "Here's Bonhomme Michel with the wagon." There was to be an exchange of provisions and at the same time he would accompany Marie-Louise to General Hospital.

Confusion reigned all over the city. Bonhomme Michel told her the rumors he knew. The British clung to the wall and the gates of the city waiting to get in. The capitulation had been demanded that morning over the strong protestations of Joannes, the town major. He swore Levis and French reinforcements were on the way from Jacques-Cartier. Where did he get his information? At least the *fleur-de-lis* still fluttered on top of Chateau St. Louis.

With a pang, Marie-Louise looked away from the insignia that waved over Quebec. How long would it be there? She looked straight ahead. The old cart lumbered through narrow cobbled streets. They were both silent as they traveled on toward the country, the General Hospital and the St. Charles River. What would Reverend Mother say to her? She threw her shoulders back, she was ready for whatever chastisement. Her dangerous escapade home had been well worth it. She really could not resent Mother Davanne of

St. Louis de Gonzague for reporting her absence in the daily note from convent to hospital. Mother Davanne was in charge until Mother Migeon's return to the Ursuline convent.

Marie-Louise sighed heavily. True, she was not the most volatile of the novices, but now she was guilty of breaking the most rigid rule. The war was no excuse.

They went through the guard. Inside the hospital, on the way to her audience, Marie-Louise was appalled at the number of wounded, French, English, Canadians and Indians. They were even squeezed closely together in the corridors. There was more work here than at her own convent. Finally, in the community room, she stood demurely before her Superior, eyes downcast.

"Dear child," Mother Migeon's voice was full of compassion. She always called her sisters children when they broke the rules.

Marie-Louise raised her eyes. Maybe she wasn't going to get a long lecture, punishment or outright banishment. "Reverend Mother," she began, she searched for the right words of contrition and humility.

Mother Migeon waved her hand. "We have no time for lectures. War is doing strange things to us all. I know you acted out of love. How is your dear mother?"

"She hangs on," Marie-Louise's lips trembled.

"She is in my prayers, child. And my other nuns at the convent?"

"We are doing our best."

"I have a special task for all of you."

Marie-Louise stood at attention with great relief. "Yes, Reverend Mother."

"I have just had a conference with Father Resche. I will be returning to our convent with all our other Ursulines who have been quartered here. . . ."

"When, Reverend Mother? We will be grateful to have you back."

"In a few days. Is our best altar cloth still intact?"

"Yes, Reverend Mother, it is. I checked the altar linens after General Montcalm's funeral." She had fingered the gold embroidered one after folding it neatly and placing it at the top shelf of the linen armoire.

"*Requiescat in pace,*" Mother Migeon crossed herself. "Since the *basilique* is in worse shape than our chapel, we are instructed to prepare the chapel for a wedding."

"A wedding!"

"Yes, Sister Madeleine. War or no war, Marie-Louise Pepin and Jean-Pierre Massal are going ahead with their wedding plans. No doubt, we will be having baptismals in our chapel too. If the city capitulates we may even be having Anglican services."

"Anglican services!" All Marie-Louise could do was exclaim in surprise at every announcement.

"Our chapel must make do."

"I will see to it that everything is ready." Marie-Louise had never been to a nuptial Mass in their chapel.

"Our chapel will be in use for our regular devotions and our townspeople who are bombed out of their homes. We'll house some of them as best we can and they will be attending Mass. I will make up some schedules with Father Resche."

"We are going to be busy, Reverend Mother."

"Indeed, child. So will you freshen up the ceremonial altar cloth for the wedding. And gather whoever will help. Bring out the gold vases for whatever flowers you find in our trampled garden."

"What time will the wedding take place?"

"At eleven o'clock. I'll send Sister Claire back with you. I hope the sun comes out on the twenty-first."

"I do too. After our sad funeral for Montcalm, this is a new leaf. They are courageous those two, I'll pray for them, the townspeople, all of us. . . ."

"Yes, it may give us all new faith, new energy, so see that everything is ready. We will be all together under our own roof, such as it is, in a few days. We must pray for de Ramezay and that there are enough supplies to hold the city."

"Yes, Reverend Mother." So instead of a lecture, chastisement and punishment, or banishment, which Marie-Louise had thought of as the worst that could befall her, she had been given a set of instructions. And in the midst of the fearful hurrying and scurrying in the troubled streets of Quebec, Marie-Louise returned to her convent with Bonhomme Michel and Sister Claire to prepare a wedding as if they were in ordinary times.

All the nuns were in the chapel praying for de Ramezay's decision. Would he capitulate? He was in a council of war now being held in the Chateau. It all hinged on whether there were enough supplies to hold out for the winter. Would Levis return or would the British crash through the gates from their encampment about the wall?

After Ian Bruce Lindsay left Captain MacDonald at General Hospital, he went to seek Townshend at the new entrenchments outside the gates of the city. There were still some stray wounded and their own dead to be cleared off the field. More trips were made to the General Hospital. More graves were dug. Ian gagged on the stench that hung over the Plains, over dead Indians, French officers, their white uniforms covered in dried blood, British officers and his own Highlanders with their scattered swords.

On the 17th, Ian helped the American Rangers and some of his own regiment to construct batteries to breach the fortifications on the weak land side of the town. On the ascent up the cliff, they had brought up sixty guns and fifty-eight howitzers and mortars.

General Townshend's next move was to force de Ramezay to firm his decision to capitulate. He directed the ships of the line to move up in a position to attack the lower town, as soon as he was ready to attack the upper town.

Eight great ships with their grinning rows of black guns moved up at midday. Ian watched grimly as they advanced. That should convince de Ramezay, he thought.

At three o'clock de Ramezay, over the protestations of most of the members of his council of war, sent Joannes to General Townshend to propose a capitulation. The excruciatingly painful fear that forced de Ramezay's hand was that he knew there was not enough food to feed the garrison for the winter. Not nearly enough even if Rochebeaucourt, commander of the French cavalry, came now in force with thundering hundreds and their bags of biscuits.

All was in readiness to take possession of the French fortress on the evening of the eighteenth. Fifty men of the Royal Artillery with a field piece were the first to enter. The British colors were hoisted on its carriage. The Louisbourg Grenadiers followed and mounted guard on the gates. The honor of hoisting the Union Jack on the walls of Quebec went to Colonel Williamson of the Artillery. At the same time, Captain Hugh Palliser of the navy with a body of seamen landed in Lower Town.

The French army, partly restored by Levis' efforts, had been ordered to go with Louis Antoine de Bougainville, at all speed to try to prevent the surrender. They were only half a league from Quebec when a messenger forewarned them the bitter news that the British were already in the city. Their hopes shattered, they fell back. Levis advised Vaudreuil to build a fort upstream at the mouth of the Jacques Cartier River to establish, for the moment, the "frontier" of the French territory.

Governor Vaudreuil left command of the army to Levis here and went on to Montreal to write his scalding reports and plan the next move.

From the top floor of the convent, Marie-Louise and Geneviève saw General Townshend march with his staff and two companies of grenadiers to the Chateau St. Louis. A line of French troops was drawn up before the ruined walls and wrecked gun batteries. Commandant de Ramezay stepped forward to hand Townshend the keys to the fort. The whitecoats turned smartly to file away and the grenadiers took their place. The *fleur-de-lis* standard was lowered and the lion of St. George was raised over the Chateau. From the river below came the crash of a victory salvo by the guns of the fleet. It rocked the whole city and even the three-decker *Royal William*, in whose stateroom lay the embalmed body of James Wolfe just transferred from the *Lowestoft*, waiting to leave for England.

Marie-Louise stifled a sob caught dry in her throat. "Thank God, Jean-Paul didn't come to town today." She pressed her hand over her heart.

"Yes." It was barely a whisper. Geneviève nodded. "Thank God for that." Silently, they went down to the chapel together.

In the next two days, in the midst of the noise and traffic of British occupation, Marie-Louise and her sister nuns prepared their chapel for the wedding to take place on the twenty-first. They also looked forward to the return of their Superior on that day. There was a lot to do.

In the laundry, she carefully pressed the altar cloths. She caressed the gold-threaded designs of wheat sheaves. Fertility, she prayed, we need fertility to replace the dead of this war. In the garden, all that was left of fall flowers were marigolds, small nasturtiums and a few dark purple chrysanthemums. She labored too long trying to arrange them to advantage, enlarging the bouquet with maple leaves and a few long-stemmed ferns. She polished the best chalice. There was a jewel missing in its stem, that beautiful amethyst. Gone! What had happened? It could be anywhere; the bombardment might have shaken it loose. She chased away the thought that someone had lifted it from its setting. She poured wine in the crystal cruets, made sure there were enough hosts. Then she rechecked everything.

With a dust-cloth, Marie-Louise went over all the benches and all the Ursulines' choir stalls in the cloister. "Why am I taking so many pains? We've been bombarded." She threw her shoulders back. "Because the time is now and I am here."

She thought of the wedding at Cana. Mary had not thought it was useless when the wine gave out. The mother of Christ had paved the way for the water to be changed into wine, a miracle. Well, they all needed a miracle, here and now! She smoothed the overhang of the altar cloth threaded with gold wheat sheaves and genuflected before the tabernacle.

"Dear God," she whispered. "Let these two young people be wed, Marie-Louise Pepin and Jean-Pierre Massal, be blessed in our chapel, walk out of here with their love and ours to raise a large family right in the face of this war. Let it be over, let the conditions of the transfer be favorable to all. Now, please God, let there be peace in our city. Let us survive the winter."

The return of Mother Migeon and all the other Ursulines who had been billeted at General Hospital since last July was marked with a special prayer of thanksgiving. The wedding of Marie-Louise Pepin and Jean-Pierre Massal followed immediately. It was well attended by the townspeople who had found refuge in a special wing of the convent.

The newlyweds just took enough time to be feted with soup and wine from Mother Philomène's kitchen. Then everyone fell to tasks for the newly improvised hospital wing that was taking up the overflow from the two hospitals.

A sharp September cold was already upon the countryside. Ian Lindsay hurried about with new orders. He was between the ships, the Chateau, the entrenchments about the wall and the main gates of the city. Proclamations were posted everywhere. The outposts were to take up all stragglers and marauders and bring them to the provost guard. All soldiers were to take care that there were no insults shown to any of the inhabitants who would be coming in from the suburbs, as requested, to take the oaths to the King of England. General Townshend's announcement assured the entire army that punishment would be death.

In the country, outside the wall, particular care was to be taken that no further harm be done to any of the houses. The Rangers were to advance on the roads leading to the river and St. Foy to the west. These areas were to be patrolled during the night and particularly before daybreak.

Conferences were held in the Chateau about the most immediate repairs necessary in the city and for procedures for the conveyance of food supplies to be brought from the ships to an appointed commissary. Momentarily, the commissary was to be the part of the Jesuit College that hadn't been bombed out.

In the turbulent hours of trying to establish order in town, the vision of the girl in the red dress standing in the doorway of the country manor with the lamplight on her golden hair never left Ian. Through every task, the image was always there in his mind. He could summon this reflection at any free moment and revel in it. He could fold it away tenderly, until it could be brought out again. It sustained him in his loneliest moments in the middle of the night if he had the watch.

A great deal was accomplished on the twenty-first. Ian hurried down *rue St. Louis* on his way to another meeting to help write reports and proclamations. One of them concerned General Robert Monckton's announcement to give leave to the Canadians to return to their parishes to reap their harvest, to repossess their lands. There were reports to be gotten out on munitions and hulks, and for the bridge of boats on the River Charles that needed repairs. A list of Commissions to be granted in the 28th, 35th, 47th, 58th and 45th regiments was needed. A list of Rangers' Commissions and a list had to be made of who was to stay and who would leave Quebec by October 5. That would lessen the drain on provisions. It was absolutely necessary that everyone whose presence was not required should leave Quebec. Disaster threatened both garrison and the fleet if it did not sail on that date due to the lateness of the season.

As he whipped around a corner to gain the mount of the hill, Ian heard warning cries.

"Look out! Look out, Captain!"

Too late, Ian looked up as part of a cracked wall came down on him.

He groaned in pain, crushed, sprawled on the side-walk. Soldiers were shouting all around him. Shoving the debris out of the way, they pulled him up carefully.

"Can you stand?" A soldier on each side held him up.

"Worse luck! Am I to be injured in an ordinary street accident now that the fighting is over?" He limped painfully. His right leg and right hand felt smashed. He thought his bad arm was going to fall off. There was blood all over his uniform and on the ground.

"Let's take him to the Ursulines, it's the closest. They've just opened a hospital wing." They continued to hold him up. Ian grimaced in excruciating pain.

Ian didn't know what kind of potion the nuns gave him after his injuries were dressed. He was propped up against a small pillow on a very narrow cot. During a long sleep, he dreamed of home in far-off Fyfe. In his thoughts, he composed a letter to his mother. He must get it written, he thought in a semi-daze. He must get it aboard the *Lowestoft* before it sailed. His dressing was soaked with blood. His leg and hand throbbed as he floated into another dream.

When he woke up, a nun who looked very much like the girl he had seen at Beauport was fluffing up a thin pillow. Strange dream or fantasy, she looked exactly like the girl in the red dress. His dressing had been changed.

He sat upright, then winced as an acute pain shot through him.

"*Doucement, Monsieur le Capitaine,* you are *blessé,* injured."

He addressed her in French. "You have a sister in Beauport?"

Marie-Louise's eyes widened. "You speak French, *Monsieur le Capitaine!*" She had recognized him instantly administering to him. She knew he was one of the Highlanders who had stopped at the Boisvert Manor during her short, stolen *séjour* home. He was the tall one who had ordered his officers not to go in, not to intrude on their family celebration.

"*Oui, ma Soeur. . . .*"

"I am being called down the hall. I'll be back." With a flurry of quick steps, her veil floating on the air, she was out of the room.

Ian lay back on the pillow and stared at the empty archway. Her sister, that's it! His imagery of the girl in the red dress and this nun, they must be sisters.

"Good Lord, Captain Lindsay, what happened to you?" A soldier on the next cot with his leg in a sling shifted uneasily.

"Not shot in battle, not stung with an Indian arrow, part of a wall just crumbled and fell on me. I have to get out of here."

"Not today. These little nuns will take good care of us. You'd think they'd tell us to go to bloody hell."

"What's her name?"

"The one who just left? Sister Marie Madeleine and she'll stand no nonsense from any of us. I'll bet she wants us out of here as fast as you want to go. There's a French soldier next to me, he's out. Not a peep out of him since I've been here."

"How long?"

"A couple of days. And across from us, there's a Huron, he's really cut up but doesn't believe it. They're trying to keep him strapped down."

Ian closed his eyes. How did one keep a Huron strapped down? Perhaps only an Ursuline nun could do that. He knew something about Ursulines. Again, he thought of the Ursuline Convent in Vendôme near the glassblowing factory of his grandparents. He had often gone to Mass in that convent's chapel with his mother in those summers when the family vacationed in France. He shifted to his good side. It was very quiet, for a few moments no one cried out in pain, no one moaned or groaned.

Ian stole out of bed. Very quietly, he limped and dragged himself to the window. Moonlight drenched the ruined city. It was achingly beautiful. Pain throbbed in his thigh and his right hand.

"Damn," he muttered. He had no time to be incapacitated. Everyone had too much to do, conquerors and conquered. First thing, he must get a letter dictated and written off to his mother on whatever ship was returning to England ahead of the fleet with news of their victory. Anew, he heard the stirring and groaning of other wounded patients as they tried to sleep.

Tomorrow, he would dictate the news to his mother through the kindness of one of these Ursulines, perhaps Sister Marie Madeleine. Uncanny how much she resembled that girl at the Beauport farm. He must not be too jubilant reporting the capture of Quebec. These people had lost everything and faced starvation this winter. They probably all faced the same privations, the food and supplies on the ships would have to be rationed. And what did the whole fleet know of a Quebec winter? Not much. But the whole fleet would not be here. Only a skeleton crew, at best, would be left to govern the prize. He prayed the generals would be wise with the kind of command that would be delegated to cope with the unknown. He thought of a million duties as he gazed at the moonlit city.

"But what are you doing here, Monsieur? You should be sleeping off your pain." Sister Madeleine was suddenly beside him.

"I am unable to sleep, Sister."

"Come, I will give you a stronger *tisane* that will help," she guided him back to his cot.

He caught her hand as he steadied himself. "I must dictate a letter to my mother before the first ship sails. And my hand. . . ."

"In the morning, Monsieur *le Capitaine*." She smoothed the blanket over him.

He peered at her in the semi-darkness.

"You must be part of that family in Beauport," he insisted. The vision came back. Perhaps she thought he was delirious.

"Shhh. . . . ," she pressed her fingers to her lips. "We will wake the others. I will send Gustave with a *tisane*, then try to sleep. In the morning, we will do your letter," she whispered. Then she quietly fluttered away.

Ian sighed. She must be a twin to that girl in Beauport. Yes, he must sleep, he must recuperate, get back to his duties. Get off a note to Lieutenant John Knox too. How was Knox's French? Before long, no doubt, they would all be speaking French. When he was better, he might go back to Beauport to verify his obsession. What else would he tell his mother, his family in Fyfe. He dozed off. But it was not the beautiful heather on the hills of his homeland that he saw in his dreams. It was the blood-drenched fields of Culloden and the Plains of Abraham. He woke up screaming.

He was hushed and soothed to calm by the *hospitalière* on duty. This time, it was not Sister Marie Madeleine. The *hospitalière's* hand was cool on his brow. She made him drink the rest of the *tisane* that had been brought earlier.

"Sister, I would like to receive Communion in the morning." Perhaps that would give him a little peace. Would he have to prove that he was one of the Catholic Highlanders? Murray had asked them to refrain from any open manifestation of their faith. Ah, well. . . . He fell back on the pillow and finally slept.

Chapter Four

The next morning after Mass, on the cloistered side of the chapel, Marie-Louise helped Father Resche in the sacristy. He was preparing to do the rounds and distribute communion to the sick.

"You have one Catholic among the Highlanders on your hospital ward, Sister, and our three very sick Hurons."

"*Quel Ecossais?*" Marie-Louise was surprised.

"Captain Lindsay."

She raised startled eyes.

"He has a French mother he tells me. I spoke with him briefly yesterday." Father Resche continued as he adjusted his purple stole. He counted the hosts in a little black silk pouch. Hosts he had just consecrated at Mass.

"Ah, that's why he speaks our language so well." Marie-Louise reminded herself she had promised to help him with his letter home today before part of the fleet sailed for England. "You have enough hosts, Father?"

"Yes, Sister."

All was bustle without ceremony. The usual silence was not observed. There was no altar boy with a ringing bell to announce the coming of the priest with Holy Communion. More than half of the ordinary rituals were now eliminated in the daily necessities of war.

A light rain fell on the gray city. Everyone helped bring in wood to the large covered bins outside the convent kitchen. Highlanders, sailors,

British soldiers, the townspeople living at the convent, all who were able were busy stacking logs to warm the huge building. Autumn had really set in. The colored oak and maple leaves still left on the trees glistened in the wet garden.

Marie-Louise shivered as she went to the kitchen. She heard the nuns who had remained in chapel after Mass drone the litanies. She was glad they were all back from General Hospital. The smell of incense wafted down the halls, it interlaced with the aroma of pea soup simmering in the throw all *pot de sagamité* over the kitchen hearth.

Jean-Paul had brought a large crock of molasses, also a crock of lard on his last trip from Beauport. Marie-Louise knew he would bring them something each time he came to town. He brought anything he laid his hand to. He was inventive in selecting from their still existing inventory on the Boisvert farm. He offered a strange but welcome variety to replenish the empty cupboards of Mother Philomène's pantry. And now, General Murray sent them supplies from the ships daily so that all could benefit, the officers, the sick and wounded and the care-takers of the Ursuline compound.

Marie-Louise thought of Madame Dulude breathing her last. She was being cared for by the remaining members of her family in the townspeople's wing. Widowed now, she would be leaving four of her six children. The other two had died in the last bombardment. Marie-Louise shook her head sadly, she doubted that Madame Dulude would last the week. She thought of her own mother waning away in Beauport. Strangely enough, she also thought of Captain Lindsay's mother. A French woman somewhere in Scotland who would soon be reading the news that Quebec had capitulated to the British. The Captain's family would be overjoyed to learn that their son had escaped more serious injuries. And Madame Seders, also widowed by the loss of her husband on the Plains, was due to deliver her baby at any moment.

She wondered if she could invade Sister Philomène's domain long enough to make a small molasses pie for Madame Dulude and Madame Seders. Certainly a luxury, and unfortunately not enough could be made for everyone. The spices, yes, the spices mixed in this delicacy traveling down the convent corridors would give her away. She abandoned her generous thought and steered herself back to austerity. Ah, but Geneviève would be all for it.

She smiled as she remembered their blueberrying outings when they were little girls. How greedy their eyes in those days, off with their small pails picking the luscious July fruit in the Beauport woods. On one outing they had lost their way. Their aprons and faces smeared with tears and the delicious purple juice, they had solemnly sworn that if their parents found them they would give themselves to God. They had sworn it, holding hands in that hot sun of long ago, they had promised to become nuns together. They had been found shortly after and been happily clasped to everyone's breast without even a scolding. Marie-Louise's smile grew wider at the memory. Of course, Sister Philomène would let her make that molasses pie.

The rain had stopped by the time she made the rounds of the wards. She went to Captain Lindsay last so he could dictate his letter. Her sister nuns had started to call him "*la Tête Rouge*." He was a big, impatient man among the sick. His foot was healing better than his hand. He might leave the crowded ward to hobble off to cautious duties by tomorrow. Yes, he could certainly leave his space to a more needy patient, Marie-Louise thought.

"Tell me about your home, Monsieur *le Capitaine*." She seated herself facing him with a lap escritoire.

Ian told her about Lindsay Hall, part of it still being repaired from ravages of Border wars, he described the moors, the heather, the chapel in his home, the road to town. Then he talked about his mother.

Marie-Louise could feel the beauty of this woman across the sea, Corinne Le Mire Lindsay. She laid her pen down on the vellum sheet and listened.

He reminisced about summer vacations in France, in Vendôme, the Ursuline convent near-by the *brulonnerie*, and the glass blowing. He talked about his brothers, his father.

"And your home, tell me about your home, Sister."

She raised her brown eyes. "My home is in Beauport." The rain was over. Birds chirped outside the rain-splattered window.

"I knew it." He was jubilant. "And you have a sister, a twin perhaps?"

Marie-Louise flushed a deep crimson. She would have to admit to this stranger, this Highlander, this conqueror of whom she knew hardly anything, the well-kept secret of her escapade.

"It was you!" Ian Lindsay fell back on his thin pillow happy, yet disappointed. Here before his eyes was the reality of the image in his heart. An image he had carried with him and yearned for since his stop in Beauport. And she was a nun!

"My mother is ill." She told him simply. "The day after the battle, my brother Jean-Paul came to see if we were safe here and I went home with him for one day." She put away the writing materials. "I will come back to finish this." She felt a great weight lift from her whole being.

"Sister," he caught her hand. He was filled with emotion, confusion, happiness but he wanted to keep her respect. She had chosen to tell him. She was the girl in the lighted door-way. He admired her honesty. Did she have sanction to leave her convent in the chaos of the besieged city or had she left without permission? And if so, she must have suffered some chastisement for this breach of their rules even under the circumstances. He didn't want to frighten her, this beautiful girl, this adventurous, courageous little nun. "You must have made your mother and your family very happy." His eyes held hers.

She read his compassion and understanding as she gently pulled her hand away and fled down the ward. She went directly to the chapel. Her face was aflame and she was perspiring.

"Why did I tell him?" She threw the question at the Tabernacle. *"Mon Dieu."* But how long could she have evaded the truth, camouflaged it with outright deceit. But it was none of his business. *"Bien sûr!"* She shook herself, the tip of her veil fell to the floor as she pulled the polished kneeler out from under her chair, she inverted her hour glass, closed her eyes and started to pray. A great sigh escaped her, she pressed her hand against her heart. She felt relieved.

Ian awakened from a deep sleep just as General Murray and Lieutenant John Knox were doing the rounds visiting the wounded. They stopped and chatted with him. Colleagues in arms, he and Knox had become friends on the sail out of Louisbourg to Quebec last May. After they had general exchange of amenities with everyone on the ward, Ian called out as they were leaving.

"Please stop by before you leave the building, Lieutenant Knox."

Knox waved and nodded. Then Ian cautiously got himself out of bed, limped down the ward to the hall and asked the *hospitalière* for Sister Madeleine.

"Ah, but she has been sent to General Hospital to help with emergencies of overload. More wounded are continually surfacing and being brought there."

Ian was beside himself. His hand throbbed. "Worse luck!" He muttered as he limped back the length of the ward. He was the less injured patient but he was stuck here for the moment. He wasn't much use to his commander with just one good hand. But he could go to the meetings held in Murray's headquarters here in the convent, he thought.

He certainly wasn't going to be pinned down to a bed. If his wounds were more serious perhaps he could have manipulated a transfer to General Hospital. His heart lifted. He could say he forgot something in the dictation of his letter. But he knew another nun here could finish it as well. He blessed his mother for having insisted that he learn French when he was growing up at Lindsay Hall. What was she doing now, he wondered? Weaving and humming those charming French songs, no doubt.

He sat on his bed weary from the limping walk. "Ah, the world was not that big after all." He looked out the huge window. The garden was still colorful with the last of the fall flowers. He sighed.

The fleet didn't have much time left to prepare for the sail back to England before winter set in. What would his orders be? To stay in the conquered city or to go home? His feelings were mixed. Whoever stayed on duty in Quebec this winter would have their work cut out for them.

So, how was he going to tell his mother whether in person or by letter that besides his military duties, it was a wisp of a nun who occupied his heart, his thoughts. A nun he had first seen as a golden girl in a red dress in the doorway of a country manor, at the end of the world. But no, of course, he could not. He had been away too long, he told himself.

"There you are, Ian. Feeling much better are you?" Lieutenant John Knox came up to him.

"Yes, much better. Get me out of here. At least, I would like to come to some meetings with you. My bed is needed for more serious cases."

Knox laid a gentle hand on his shoulder. "I'll pick you up tomorrow. Tomorrow's soon enough. There are a million left-handed things you can do. We are sending more food supplies to General Hospital as well as here and Hôtel Dieu."

Ian had been brought to the improvised hospital wing at the Ursuline convent on the twenty-first of September. It was now the twenty-third, he still hobbled but his hand was better and Doctor Russell found him well enough to be discharged. He was happy to give up his bed. An old nurse, Sister Marceline helped him dress. Sister Madeleine was nowhere to be seen. While he waited for John Knox, a subaltern came to the ward with the orders of the day.

Of special note, General Monckton desired that all the officers in the army would wear some mark of mourning for General Wolfe, "their late commander," as was usual in the field. He asked Sister Marceline for a piece of black cloth for his coat sleeve. He was embarrassed to ask, she was a very silent nun but she came back from the sewing hall with a worn swatch of habit cloth and she even stitched it on for him. He marvelled at her nimble fingers.

"I was not able to find the little nun, Sister Madeleine, who took care of me to properly thank her," Ian limped alongside of John Knox as they left the convent garden.

"You poor chap. You'll have to come back."

"That I will."

"When is the *Lowestoft* sailing?"

"Perhaps today. It's a beautiful day, the winds are fair. But we're still unloading food stuffs to the commissary and the hospitals. These people have been starving."

"Not in the country." Ian thought of the Beauport manor.

They walked on *rue St-Louis* past scenes of destruction that were being cleaned up by several crews in the devastated city. Before entering the chateau, they both took a moment to look down the St. Lawrence at a breathtaking panorama of Indian summer.

Lying in the basin between Orleans and Levis far below was the great fleet. Even the *Neptune* of 90 guns looked dwarfed. The trim and saucy frigates seemed miniature. The sound of great preparations for departure came from the ships. Ten thousand busy hands were getting ready for the rough voyage home which still had to be faced. Below in the Lower Town, the Church of Our Lady of Victory stood out in its ruins.

"A beautiful country, Ian."

"Aye, John."

They admired the lavish autumn colors spread out from the wooded banks of Orleans, of Beauport, of Levis, up and down the shores of the great river. The dark blue-green of the firs and spruces were thrown into sharp relief by the gold and yellow of the beeches and elms. The maples showed every shade of scarlet and crimson while in the far-off distance the hills themselves faded in ethereal blues.

A clear blue sky of Indian summer lingered over all, bright sunlight still comforted but exhilarating breezes announced a touch of forthcoming winter.

After a series of meetings at the Chateau, Ian was weary. With the help of a delegated subaltern he went aboard the *Sutherland* to pick up orders and do some paper work. His letter home would leave on the *Lowestoft*.

On the twenty-fifth, he helped to organize 500 men that were to be sent the next morning to Ile Madame. The party consisted of one file officer, two captains, four subalterns and one hundred and fifty men from the line, three hundred and fifty Rangers and officers in proportion. They were provided with grinding stones and felling axes from the King's stores.

One gill of rum each per day was to be allowed to the soldiers and five shillings for every cord of wood they would cut and put on board. The officers to oversee this work would receive three shillings per day each. All was prepared for departure for the next morning at eight o'clock, at the waterside in Lower Town.

On the twenty-sixth, at nine o'clock in the morning, Ian sat in at a court martial on the parade grounds. Colonel Young presided and the panel consisted of twelve captains of the line and one field officer. It was grim. Orders were issued for flogging every other day.

Special orders and patrols went about the town and the outskirts to see that none of the Canadians inhabitants were molested or interrupted. And in the environs, to make sure their canoes and other properties were not taken. The orders now proclaimed them subjects of His Britannic Majesty.

Ian slept badly now since he left the convent ward, two nights on board ship and one makeshift night in Lower Town.

At four o'clock on the twenty-sixth, he met with John Knox, other officers of the corps, and General Murray to draw for quarters. The happy outcome was that he was billeted with some of his fellow officers on the first floor of the Ursuline convent. They would occupy a whole wing and they were also alloted the official community room of the nuns for military counsel space. The nuns would now house themselves entirely on the third floor with their cloister. Strict rules, even on penalty of death, were to be observed about the cloister of their unexpected hostesses. Signs were posted and sentinels were on duty at indicated doors. The downstairs chapel continued to be in use for their usual devotions on the cloistered side and all who wanted to enter on the public side. Madame de la Peltrie's house in use for years for classes was heavily damaged and abandoned for the moment.

Ian moved his effects from the *Sutherland* into his new quarters and wondered when he would see Sister Madeleine again.

When Marie-Louise returned from her assignment at General Hospital she was pleased to learn that Captain Lindsay was among the Highlanders who were now billeted in the convent.

"If they have to be here at all," she murmured to herself in the middle of her prayers.

Yet, she looked forward to speaking with him again, to learn more about his French mother. She noticed that on a few mornings he attended Mass with the townspeople. He was usually with two of his fellow officers. Though they hung at the back of the chapel, it was difficult for them to be nondescript in their tartans. General Murray made it known that he preferred no great manifestations of faith from any of his Catholic Highlanders.

Marie-Louise's main tasks now were the care of Madame Dulude who was dying and Madame Seders who would deliver her baby at any moment. There were still mild enough days for the nuns to wash at the stream in the back of the garden but they were setting up to wash in large copper tubs inside for the winter. With the care of the sick and dying, the washings continued to be excessive. All of the Ursulines' hands were rough, red and chapped. There was no soothing rose water left. Now cut off from French trade they expected none, unless one of their benefactors like Anaïse Médard came by.

Anaïse Médard was an institution and a household word for hard to find articles. It was rumored that she had amassed quite a few treasures from the politician Joseph Cadet's warehouse before some of the nobility left. She had not been seen since the battle. The Reverend Mother had expressed concern and mentioned sending out an inquiry.

So now, the nuns smoothed their rough hands with oil and bear grease. When they washed outside, the officers were very gallant and helped them carry the heavy clothing baskets inside. Soldiers and officers continued to help wherever they could. They carried wood, water, supplies and the nuns were grateful for their assistance.

One day after Mass, Ian went straight to the sacristy to find Marie-Louise.

"Good morning, Sister Madeleine."

"Good morning, Captain Lindsay." She was putting vestments and vessels away in the armoire.

Father Resche gave him a nod. He was counting hosts for his usual distribution to the sick.

"I want to especially thank you for your good care of me, Sister."

She smiled at him as she gave the golden chalice a wipe with a chamois cloth. It caressed the jeweled stem gliding over the gaping hole of the missing amethyst.

"Our main work has been the education of young girls as you know, since you are familiar with our house in Vendôme. But now. . . ."

"Yes, now Sister, since we have come here. . . ." He bit his lip and looked at her with compassion. Yes, they had come and destroyed this beautiful city.

"Now," she continued, "we have no more students, we are assigned to take care of the sick, the wounded and bury the dead, God rest their souls. We are alive, our patients are recovering and you among them. That comprises our main work now, Captain."

"I wish there was something I could do besides help with menial tasks and errands. What a beautiful chalice!" The sunlight filtering through a high leaded window sparkled on the jeweled stem of the chalice.

"Yes, it is," Marie-Louise lifted it up for him to admire.

"Why, it has a jewel missing."

"We think it must have become undone in the bombardments. We don't know. . . ."

"Captain Lindsay, there you are." A subaltern entered the sacristy and saluted him. "Lieutenant Knox is waiting outside."

"I'm on my way. *A bientôt,* Sister Madeleine." He bowed to Marie-Louise and Father Resche.

Marie-Louise nodded and continued her duties as she watched them leave. Their frayed tartans swayed, their swords clanked. They stopped and spoke with the sentinel outside the chapel door.

Marie-Louise sighed. She was glad he was better this red-haired young man with the French mother but she longed for the quiet times of the convent before they came. Before they climbed up Anse au Foulon, before all the blood spilling on the Plains of Abraham. They were no more, those quiet busy routines of teaching classes to the little French, Canadian and Huron girls. *Mon Dieu,* why had they ever come? A tear slid down her cheek. Why did nations, tribes, people fight wars? Why did men kill each other, even women and children, to gain, to possess, to prove what?

She slid shut the last drawer of the pine armoire. Everything was put away till the next Mass. She clasped her hands fervently. It was Mother Migeon's opinion that the colony would not be destroyed. The British had decided to hold it for the winter. Thank God. They must make the best of it, all of them, to survive. As for one's work and vocation, there was only one little boarder left in the convent. All the nuns looked in on her every night. Her mother also lived in the convent.

"*Viens, vite!* Mother St. Etienne needs you. It's Madame Seders." A little novice called Marie-Louise to the infirmary.

Marie-Louise ran to help. In the drama of birth, she forgot the war. She felt like a warm woman, aflame, full of love not only for God but for the miracle of mankind. Never more so than after the delivery of Madame Seders' tiny son. Deftly, quickly she helped Mother St. Etienne clean up the blood and the after birth. At one moment she felt like throwing up but she gripped herself and followed all the directions of the older nun. As she held the newborn, the smooth little hands, legs and feet, and his small hungry mouth stole her heart. She wrapped him tenderly in a warm blanket after he had been washed and oiled. He was red, squealing and screaming until she put him to his mother's breast. Father Resche baptized him an hour later. He simmered down his lusty cries as a drop of holy oil glistened on his forehead. He was named Louis Joseph Montcalm Seders for their dead General.

Another little mouth to feed in desperate times. But in spite of the labor, the suffering, the trouble, the waiting, Marie-Louise thought what a joy it must be to become a mother. A joy to be in union with a man's love and God's love, to create a child in one's body. She wondered and marveled at this more now than when her own mother had tried to explain the wonders of a woman's body. Tired and overwhelmed she went to chapel to say a prayer for this new member of the Church. Would he become a general or a mason, this little Louis Joseph?

His father, Francois, had worked stone all his life. Alas, he had died on the Plains. He would never see his little son. Ah, but if God is everywhere, if souls never left us completely, then maybe his father does see him, maybe he does, Marie-Louise thought. Micheline Seders was not alone.

Marie-Louise also thought of the young couple who had married on the twenty-first. Several babies had been born in the last week right here in the convent. In spite of all the deaths since the fateful thirteenth of September, life went on. People married and babies were born. There were even a few mixed marriages to the consternation of General Murray and Monseigneur Pontbriand. Some had rushed into the enemies' arms. The principal question in everyone's mind, would they all survive the winter?

Ian still limped slightly but his hand was much better and he was now comfortably settled in one of the convent cells. Other fellow officers were not so lucky and had to find whatever lodgings they could in the half-demolished residences, carriage houses or shops along *rue St-Louis*. Most of the soldiers were still encamped at the wall and gates of the city.

And though he was in a space of his own in a well appointed quarter, he still woke up from nightmares in the middle of the night. Nightmares about the men he had killed. He sweated, his heart pounded in pain, and he saw the blood of the wounds he had inflicted in the rage of war, all that blood. He hoped most of his screams were stifled before he woke. He couldn't go on screaming in the middle of the night in this convent, this sacred place, where the sanctuary lamp glowed in the chapel.

"O God!" He prayed. There must be something he could do to make amends for his part in the tragedies about them.

His fellow officers were now accustomed to these recurring nightmares. One usually came to him to quiet him down. Was it the guilt that lay so tightly enclosed within him? Did other officers, soldiers, sailors, even generals conceal this better than he?

Tonight, he sipped his daily ration of rum silently by himself as he undressed. One day, he resolved to have a talk with Father Resche. He put his sword by the sconce on the wall and the sputtering candle caught a gleam of the garnet in its hilt. His father had given him that stone from a ring. He thought of the chalice with the missing jewel. Might he not offer his garnet to replace the stone now absent from the base of the chapel's chalice? And every morning part of him could be raised at Elevation. It was a good thought. He sighed wearily. But not now, there was too much to do. The days were not long enough to prepare the city for winter. Already tomorrow was October 1 and Lieutenant Seymour's effects would be sold at the Parade Ground.

"May he rest in peace," Ian murmured as he finished his rum.

He thought of home, of Fyfe, of Tain. It was now two years since he had left. One of the reasons some of his colleagues of Jacobite families had signed up to join Colonel Simon Fraser's newly formed regiment, the 78th of Foot, was permission to resume full Highland Dress without penalty of death or prison. Seymour had been one of them. And he himself had adopted the red brick tartan. Another friend James Thompson who had volunteered, had written him before they all left Scotland. Ian remembered his proud statement.

"After I had got myself rigged out in the uniform of the Company I had volunteered with, I marched alone from Tain, my native place to join my Company in Inverness. . . . We stayed some days at Inverness walking about the streets to show ourselves, for we were very proud of our looks."

Ian smiled as he recalled Thompson's pride. Was he still keeping a journal? John Knox certainly was. A lot had transpired in the last two years.

On July 1, 1757, Ian and his comrades had left in transport ships from Cork, under escort of the sloops *Falkland*, *Enterprise*, and the *Stork* for service "somewhere in North America." The destination was not disclosed to the troops until they were halfway across the Atlantic.

Since that date, they had crossed the Atlantic, debarked at Halifax on August 23rd. Then they were assigned to a mission in New England in October.

On June 28th of the next year, 1758, they took part in the capture of Louisbourg. Then they were newly assigned to New England from October to April of 1759.

On May 17, they left again for Louisbourg. In June, under the command of James Wolfe, they embarked on their expedition to Quebec. He remembered their landing on the island of Orleans to reconnoiter the countryside and gaze at Quebec.

On the first of August, they lost heavily at Montmorency Falls.

They kept an alert on Montcalm's and Vaudreuil's camps near Beauport and the Charles River.

On the fateful thirteenth of September, they followed bold Wolfe and climbed up Anse au Foulon for the battle on the Plains of Abraham.

They had been through hell and high water. And here he was billeted in a convent trying to organize and save a garrison with a skeleton crew against the possibility of a starving winter. They were still counting the dead, sorting out their effects, hurriedly writing letters to their families before most of the fleet left for England with Admiral Saunders. Ian thought of the grief and heartbreak these official letters would bring. He sighed with sadness as the Angelus tolled in the convent chapel.

Chapter Five

Members of all regiments read or had knowledge of General Murray's special announcements. He declared a time off from general orders, labors and duties, urging all officers, soldiers and sailors to attend a service of thanksgiving to signal the victory gained by His Majesty's arms on the thirteenth of September over the French, and for the surrender of Quebec on the eighteenth.

Everyone came at about eleven o'clock on Sunday, the fourth of October. All the military walked toward the chapel of the Ursulines and gathered inside. Murray had requisitioned the chapel for this first Anglican service in the captured city.

Mother de Bransac was working in her downstairs reception study and heard most of the victory sermon delivered by the Reverend Eli Dawson, chaplain of the *HMS Stirling Castle*.

Dawson stood over Montcalm's grave in the Ursuline chapel and rolled out his victorious words to the conquerors.

"Give thanks unto Thee, O Lord, among the Gentile. Ye Mountains of Abraham, decorated with his Trophies, tell how vainly ye opposed him when he mounted your lofty Heights with the strength and swiftness of an Eagle! Stand fixed forever your rocky base and speak his Name and Glory to all future Generations. Ye streams of Lawrence and propitious Gales! Speed the glad Tidings to his beloved country! Ye Heralds of Fame, already upon the Wing, stretch your Flight and swell your Trumpets with Glory of a Military Exploit through distant Worlds!"

Ian wondered how long it would take the "heralds of fame" to reach Portsmouth by fast frigate to set England aflame with triumph. The *Lowestoft* left on September twenty-third. And only a few days earlier, Captain Marcel had visited the chapel for a last farewell to the remains of his General Montcalm before he left for France with prisoners of war on a British ship. Ian's ears burned from the resounding words he had just heard. He wondered where Sister Madeleine was at the moment, all the nuns, and especially the Reverend Mother Superior? He knew that his double sensitivity arose from having a French mother and a Scot father. As a Highlander he felt the exhilaration of victory. They had captured the great prize, the city of Quebec. But he was divided, his sense of celebration was mixed. He felt the sad defeat of the Canadians, the shame and heartbreak of the French.

But every Englishman was an eagle today! Everyone in his regiment. They were all soaring on the wings of victory. He thought he must add another postscript to his mother's letter. It would not leave for London until most of the fleet left with Admiral Saunders. No doubt, General Townshend would accompany the Admiral. Ian knew that Townshend did not care to stay in Quebec any longer than necessary. What ships would be left behind to guard the garrison? Winter was just a few windswept weeks away according to the *habitants*. He knew he would be staying and already he was homesick. When would he see home again? And what were they in for here?

As he left the chapel, he was invited with fellow officers on board the *Sutherland* for a drink. He accepted and said he would join up after an errand at the Chateau.

The Ursuline chapel was empty now and all was silent.

"The good Lord preserve us all," Mother de Bransac muttered to herself as she shuffled her papers. "Hold us in the palm of your hand amongst all these soaring eagles."

She was glad she had asked Father Resche to leave the Blessed Sacrament exposed for twenty-four hours after Vespers today. They needed a special event now that even their chapel had been invaded. And the Anglican services would continue. For how long, every Sunday and Wednesday? As long as their own church needed rebuilding? And when would that be? If the British stayed and did not destroy the colony, when would Quebec's *basilique de Notre Dame* be repaired? Well, General Murray had certainly directed that the first priority would be the reconstruction of the convent chapel. She thanked God for that. But be still, she calmed herself. Levis would return.

Was it Vaudreuil or Montcalm who had remarked that Murray at thirty-nine was, "*un homme bouillant.*"

"Yes, he certainly is," Mother de Bransac sighed. A man on fire to get things done. She felt he would be just with her, at least, while her nuns were nursing all those wounded British soldiers.

For the rest of the day, there was great jubilation and toasting on all of the ships in the St. Lawrence. But the townspeople were quiet after attending Vespers. Those lodged in the convent returned to small Sunday pastimes, some returned to their half-bombed houses to continue tasks of clearing up debris, others went back into the country outside the wall to organize part of the harvest for the forthcoming week.

Late that night, Mother de Bransac dragged her feet to her cell. She took off her veil, the heaviest skirts of her habit, the sash and cross she laid on her escritoire, the coif still wrapped around her face, she sat on the edge of her bed. A great fatigue fell from her shoulders but tears flowed freely down her cheeks. Her heart ached. Ah, but all of her nuns were doing quite admirably. Except for Mother Monique who had a tomahawk under her bed. A tomahawk she had somehow managed to obtain from Two Moose. She would have to speak with her in the morning, very quietly, and give her renewed assurance that no harm would come to her. But how was she going to do that? She herself only had General Murray's word on it.

A soft tap sounded at the door.

"Who is it?"

"It is I, Reverend Mother, Mother Philomène, I thought you needed a special *tisane*, tonight." Mother Philomène wedged her way in carefully carrying a covered steaming porcelain cup on an oval tray. A fragrance of aromatic herbs filled the room.

"Yes, tonight of all nights. You are ever kind to us all."

Mother de Bransac accepted the offering. She knew it was laced with cognac. Cognac that was probably supplied by Anaïse Médard to the convent kitchen and Mother Philomène kept it well hidden. She used it sparingly enough in cooking but she had laced many a *tisane* for all of the nurses during the siege. She had little ways and treats that came up at the most unexpected moments. She nurtured them all, it was part of her survival plan, her stalwart personality. Her oft repeated motto was, "It takes imagination to survive."

"Thank you, Mother Philomène. Your *tisane* is very soothing."

"You will sleep. Reverend Mother, I'm worried about Mother Monique."

"Yes, I know. She's frightened poor thing. I will speak with her after Mass tomorrow morning. Ah, Anaïse is coming to see me in the afternoon. Perhaps you could send some little collation tray, well, at least herb tea to the Holy Family parlor about three o'clock."

"I'll see to it. Good night, Reverend Mother."

"Good night, Mother Philomène."

Mother de Bransac finished the hot *tisane*, said a few final prayers at her prie-dieu and slid into bed. They had to go on. And she had to get along with General Murray. Before complete drowsiness overtook her, she wondered about Anaïse.

Anaïse Médard on some days was a conniving politician and used every opportunity that presented itself. On other days, it seemed she wanted to nurture and mother everyone on earth. As if she were in competition with Mother Philomène. Would Anaïse make a mixed marriage with all this British manhood strutting around? No, somehow Mother de Bransac thought not. Even though she was never beyond using men to her advantage.

Anaïse was *pure laine*. Under that showy facade, the flounces, the silk flowers, feathers and ribbons, the coquettish smile, the beguiling, calculating eyes, it was all an act. In the moment of truth, Anaïse was sterling, Mother de Bransac had to admit, stouthearted and constant. She was devoted to any member of her family who needed her. She loved Quebec with a passion. She had her own rules and kept them in her own fashion. No one ever dared cross them.

Mother de Bransac knew that if some critical supplies were needed in future emergencies and it was within Anaïse's power and grasp to procure them, they would be packaged and routed to the convent steps immediately. She had a knack and a talent for meeting emergencies in difficult times. With her secret contacts, she had always known how to obtain money and it was rumored that she had affiliations with Cadet's illicit fur trade known as *La Friponne*. But the only accusation the town merchants could point at her was that she owned land by the warehouses Cadet had used and perhaps she had rented to him and his accomplices. It was also a known fact that her Uncle Alcide, now deceased, and Aunt José had made their fortune years ago with the fur trade and land grants.

On her way to the Holy Family parlor, the next afternoon, Mother de Bransac stopped on the mid stairway landing. Here, her favorite window overlooked the garden. Was that Sister Madeleine by the brook with Captain Lindsay?

Yes, and they were both in lively conversation. The Captain was helping Marie-Louise with a load of laundry. On good, warm enough days, they were still washing outside. Soon everything would have to be done inside. The washings were enormous now that part of the convent was a hospital. Mother de Bransac was sure that Hôtel Dieu and Hôpitale Général were coping much better than they were here. They were established hospitals with better equipment and facilities.

Mother de Bransac and all her Ursulines were grateful for the gallantry and help of the Highlanders billeted in her convent. It was certainly needed but she thought that it was turning the heads of her younger nuns. After all, this was suppose to be a cloistered convent. But not anymore, she reminded herself as she descended the last steps and steadied herself on the polished bannister. Not with all these officers coming and going on their first floor. For how long, she wondered?

"Ah, Anaïse, how are you? And your dear Aunt José? I'm afraid it's just plain tea that Mother Philomène brings us today."

"We are coping, Reverend Mother. Here, I found a little sack of *dragées* in Tante José's armoire." Anaïse emptied a small linen bag of pastel colored, sugar coated almonds. They rolled between the tea cups on the pewter tray, pale blue, pink, yellow and white ones.

"You are ever resourceful, Anaïse."

They drank the hot tea in silence for a few moments.

"I think you should urge your Aunt to move into the convent for the winter. Yourself as well. You know no matter how crowded we are, there's always a place for you here."

Anaïse nodded. "I know. I know." Tante José had made large donations to the convent and had supported Madame de la Peltrie's house for years. "But she won't budge, Reverend Mother. You know how stubborn she is."

"Ah, yes."

"I will be with her."

"I know you take good care of her."

"I'm thinking of repairing the Couture bake shop. This city is going to need whatever trade we can patch up this winter. I need a carpenter."

"You have a clever head, Anaïse."

"I can't find a carpenter. All our people are out in the country bringing in the rest of the harvest. What hasn't been ravaged by the army. And I know you can't spare Bonhomme Michel."

"*Hélas!*"

They continued sipping their tea. Mother de Bransac indulged herself with a pale pink *dragée*. It was delicious on her tongue with the hot tea.

"This is the last of the rose water, I'm afraid." Anaïse placed a package on the table next to the tea tray. "Tante José had an assortment of supplies in one of her armoires that fortunately was not crushed in the bombings."

"Then you must keep the last of these for her, dear child. We're using goose grease on our hands right now. It is no time to be vain."

But Anaïse would not hear of it. "I insist." She patted the package. "It's the preservation of all our healths I'm concerned with."

As Mother de Bransac walked Anaïse to the front vestibule, they collided with Captain Lindsay on his way to General Murray's office.

"*Pardon Madame, Révérende Mère.*" He bowed before them.

"*Un Ecossais qui parle si bien francais?*" Anaïse trilled.

"He has the privilege of a French mother. This is Anaïse Médard, Captain Lindsay."

Ian bowed again.

"Where is your mother from?"

"Vendôme."

"We have people there, the Médards. And also at Tours."

After a few more pleasantries, as if there was no war, Ian took his leave of the two women in the convent doorway.

"*Ah, il est beau cet Ecossais à la tête rouge.* Perhaps this handsome red-headed Scot can find me a carpenter off one of those ships."

"Anaïse! *Je vous en prie*, be careful. I understand right now they are trying to locate all the tinsmiths they can find in the fleet. General Murray has ordered lamp lights made for all street corners."

Anaïse nodded solemnly. "We need safety after all we have been through and a lot more to come this winter. I will give Tante José your love, Reverend Mother."

Mother de Bransac went down the long corridors to the kitchen in search of Mother Philomène clutching the package of rose water to her breast.

"Mother Philomène, here's another package of glycerine and rose water from Anaïse. Please dole it out sparingly as best you can to our hardworking sisters, especially those with the most chapped hands."

"*Certainement.* Bless Anaïse, she always comes through. Where does she get the stuff?"

"Who knows? Jean-Paul should be coming today. I wonder what he'll bring us."

"That dear boy, well quite a young man now! He doesn't forget us and Sister Madeleine. He always surprises us."

As Anaïse Médard hurried down Côte de la Montagne, she thought she had to find a way to approach Captain Lindsay. He looked like a man who got things done. About to turn a corner, she noticed Jean-Paul Boisvert lumbering up part of the hill with his old horse and cart. They waved to each other. "I must speak to Jean-Paul too, one day soon," she promised herself. "He would make a good tradesman, though he's going to be left the farm if the British don't take it first." She went on muttering to herself, her skirts swung about her legs. "Tante José, she's the worry."

Jean-Paul never ceased to be amazed at the panorama of the countryside in late September and early October when they were rewarded with Indian summer. Two years ago, he and his father had visited friends in the Huron village and they had spent lazy afternoons while hazy blue smoke rose from the wigwams and children ran and frolicked.

Today, he had admired the countryside down Avenue Royale, had made a delivery in Lower Town already, and now as he turned from Côte de la Montagne into *rue St-Louis*, he wondered what Anaïse Médard was up to. She was always dealing and trading, trafficking in something or other. From what he gathered from family talk he knew she was cunning, not to be outsmarted, she and her Tante José, but he hoped she would keep a level head in the occupation of the city. He lumbered on with his cart load of provisions. Today, he had cabbages, turnips, onions, squash and apples. He had even wrapped a bread in a dish towel. Bread that he and Uncle Guillaume had baked with the very last of the flour. So who was to get it? Of course, it would be divided into morsels to those who were the most ill and suffering. And if Mother Philomène had any flour left, Jean-Paul knew she certainly could bake bread better than they could at the Boisvert farm house.

Before leaving Beauport he had camouflaged his cart load well, lest he be stopped by soldiers and it be taken and confiscated. He had constructed a hidden compartment with his father, boards covered the better part of the produce. A negligible loose proportion on top was covered with a canvas and could be taken if he was stopped.

He had let Jerome Leduc off at the Palace Gate, he was on his way back to Charlesbourg. Mireille seemed to continue to manage by herself. She had given Jean-Paul a few sous to light candles in the convent chapel. She had also given him a jar of maple butter for the nuns. A huge one. Jean-

Paul accepted the coins to humor her. He wondered of what worth French money was now?

The day was beautiful and crisp. He pulled his *toque* over his ears as he directed his horse and load down *rue St-Louis*. Crews of soldiers all over town were still clearing up debris.

"Giddap," he commanded as he veered down a narrower street. The nuns would be happy to receive these vegetables and fruits. He thought of all the cabbage and pea soups they would make to feed their patients.

"Young man, would you lend a hand here?" An English officer called out in halting French.

Jean-Paul stopped. His heart plummeted. Now, his cargo would be taken from him.

"I'm Lieutenant John Knox."

"Jean-Paul Boisvert." They both nodded.

"What have you there?"

"Monsieur, I'm taking these provisions from our farm to the Ursulines."

"Good. They have need of it." John Knox lifted the canvas and examined the top layer of produce. "Could you help me haul these planks to that stable. My help is, no doubt, delayed doing more urgent tasks."

Jean-Paul hesitated then assented. What choice did he have? He pushed some of the produce to one side to make space and helped to load the planks.

They unloaded at a carriage house and stable around the corner from *rue de Buade*.

"My headquarters are going to be here, above this stable." Knox waved at the structure.

"You'll need a stove, Monsieur." And some solid carpentry, Jean-Paul thought.

"Aye, I've been told about the winter." Knox nodded. "Here," he placed a coin in Jean-Paul's hand. They were talking half French, half English and making a lot of signs with their hands.

"*Non, non, Monsieur, je vous en prie.*" Jean-Paul stared at the English coin in complete confusion. What was he going to do with English money? "Here," impulsively he gave the Lieutenant a small burlap sack containing four apples.

"Thank you, Jean-Paul. Better get to the convent, here comes my crew finally." He waved Jean-Paul on with a smile.

Jean-Paul continued on down the street with mixed emotions. He put the coin in his pocket with the French *sous*. Was he going to be a merchant now, as well as a farmer. He passed the enclosed convent garden and arrived at the kitchen door.

"You brought us all that!" Sister Philomène was ecstatic. "We'll make soup right away. I'll tell Mother Davanne and your sister that you're here."

Bonhomme Michel came out to help unload.

"I'll go to chapel," Jean-Paul said when they were finished. "Maybe, Sister Madeleine is there now." He would have a brief visit with his sister, her duties permitting, help the nuns with whatever chores were most pressing and in that case stay overnight and leave for Beauport early the next morning. He couldn't be away from home too long.

In General Murray's convent headquarters, Ian and the General conversed about the business of the day. Dr. Russell's order about patients not returning to duty too soon after leaving hospital care was one issue. They discussed that the Quarter-master of Corps had rounded up all the tinsmiths that could be found and they would be about the tasks of erecting lamps at every street corner. Many letters still had to be written before the fleet left with Admiral Saunders.

Murray expressed his worries that possibly only the *Porcupine*, the *Racehorse* and three small frigates would be left to guard the garrison for the winter. Part of the French fleet was still up the river. How to get them out in the open or just leave them there till spring was a good question. The immediate duties of fortifying the city were more pressing. They both wondered how long it would take the *Lowestoft* to get to Portsmouth with the victory news. It was one of the fastest frigates. With luck and good weather, it would probably get there in three or four weeks. It had left on the twenty-third of September.

Murray went over some of his thoughts and ideas about the establishment of a paper money currency and how he would emphasize that in his letter to William Pitt, the Prime Minister. They parted on the note that every service man must get his letters written before the fleet sailed.

A few days later, Anaïse hailed Ian on *rue St-Louis*. He was on his way to visit John Knox, to see how he was faring in his new living quarters.

"*Bonjour, Monsieur le Capitaine.*"

"*Bonjour, Mademoiselle.*"

"*S'il vous plai*t, could you take a moment to come and inspect the Couture's baker shop or the part of it that was not demolished. . . .?"

"And why, Mademoiselle? We are very busy with the emergency repairs."

"Well, this is one of them. The shop was left to me by the family. I mean to repair it. We will need some kind of trade here in the city this winter . . . ."

"That is true. General Murray is working on everything."

"Yes, the Reverend Mother tells me he is. Come, it will only take a moment."

Before he knew what was happening, Anaïse was leading him by the hand to the Couture location.

"I need a carpenter. You know everyone is out in the fields gathering the last of the harvest. General Townshend has even sent help for that."

Ian walked through the debris and the part of the Couture shop that was still standing as she talked.

"Are you going to use it as a bake shop? Or what else are you going to sell here?"

"Yes, a bake shop and whatever the traffic will bear. It could be anything that's needed and even "*fanfreluches*" if there are any about. A few baubles in the grip of winter is good for morale."

Was she going to sell her favors as well? Did she have a link with Montreal? Perhaps this entrepreneurial gesture of outfitting a destroyed shop was innocent enough. It would certainly benefit them all. Who knew? In all fairness, he could not misjudge this intriguing beauty with a calculating head.

But his military mind warned him, if this trade venture went into effect it necessitated surveillance.

Ian nodded. "I'll try to send you some help. . . ."

"I need a carpenter," she insisted.

"General Murray is issuing a regulation about selling rum to our officers." He needed to warn her.

"But I have no rum. Your sutlers' women who follow your army. . . ."

"The regulation will refer to anyone selling any kind of spirits. Do you understand?"

"I hear you, *Monsieur le Capitaine*." Her lower lip trembled.

Ian wondered if she was going to pay any heed to that regulation. What sensuous lips and those large brown eyes would melt anyone in the fleet, he thought. They would all be completely at her mercy, officers, soldiers, sailors, and he would not be the least of them even though he carried in his heart the image of a nun he had seen in a red dress only a few weeks ago.

She looked up at him and smiled. "Will you send me some help?"

"We'll see, Mademoiselle. We'll see," Ian repeated as he inspected the most destroyed corner of what had been the Couture *boulangerie*.

"The ovens will have to be repaired." Her voice rose strong, full of hope. "And lots of shelves will be needed."

"All possible with the proper craftsmen, Mademoiselle."

New confidence possessed Anaïse. "Then, we'll do it!" She nodded vigorously.

"I'll bring this to General Murray's attention." Ian smiled wryly but not unkindly. What had he wrought here in just a few moments.

After Anaïse left him, he examined further the sad scene of the shop. Even before Mother de Bransac had introduced him, he had heard of Anaïse Médard. Already, some of his officers called her, "la brune." What was she going to do here, exactly?

A subaltern appeared on the street on the other side of the debris to summon him to General Murray's headquarters.

It was only a few days after his encounter with Anaïse that Ian was able to renew his intent to visit John Knox in his new living quarters. The weather was crisp and cold.

"Well, you've made yourself quite cozy here John." Ian warmed his hands at a small stove and gave a sweeping glance of approval at the new carpentry just constructed inside the old stone cart-house and stable.

"*Mon hangar* as the *habitants* call it," Lieutenant John Knox poured hot rum into two tin cups. "Not bad. I have a closet, true it has no ceiling, save a parcel of boards laid loose and thereby forms the loft, a place for the hay."

"But the rack and manger stands at the other end. You're not bothered by the horses?"

"Not a bit, I'm separated by that stone partition. This will be my winter cantonment. Drink up." He raised his cup.

"Who knows what kind of winter we'll have here." Ian sipped the hot rum and sighed. He savored the liquid fire as it warmed his stomach. "Not bad, John."

"Well, there are a great many off the ships who, though they have more decent entrances to their houses, are much more indifferently lodged."

"Your habitation is tolerably comfortable, old chap."

"I think so. Of course, not as comfortable as where you are with all those women doing the cooking and all. . . ."

"Nuns, John."

"Yes, well I'm all right." He poured more rum. "And with an occasional visit to the French King's table by invitation to the General Hospital . . . ."

"And how is that?"

"I'm called to duty there on the eleventh by Madame Sainte Claude, the Mother Abbess."

"And that duty?"

"A week's command to the convent of the Augustinians, my orders will be to prevent soldiers and others from plundering or marauding in that neighborhood, to protect the house and whatever."

Ian nodded. "Well, I like your *hangar*."

"I wish my French was as good as yours. But then I'm not a Scot blessed with a French mother."

Ian smiled. He sat on a wooden bench by the stove and stretched his legs. The rum seeped through his veins. He felt warm and comfortable.

"You know Anaïse Médard? I saw you talking with her on the street the other day. I'll bet there's a bit of fluff under all those Laplander wraps."

"Yes, I met her. She wants the baker shop repaired to use as a general store. I warned her of what will happen to women who sell liquor to our officers."

"Surely that doesn't apply to the *habitant*s? Only sutlers."

"Who knows? We'd better find out pretty quick." Ian became annoyed at the mention of Anaïse. He hoped she wasn't going to skirt danger with clever tricks. "Where did you get the apples?" He noticed three lone red apples in a wooden bowl on a make-shift table by the stone wall.

"Ah, Jean-Paul, a boy from Beauport has been coming to the Ursuline convent with a few supplies. His sister is a nun there."

Ian sat up. "Her name? Do you happen to know her name, this nun?"

"I believe he calls her Sister Madeleine, also Marie-Louise."

"Marie-Louise," Ian repeated softly. He was stunned. So that was her name outside of religious life. A flame leapt inside him. He knew the rum had nothing to do with it.

"You know this nun? The rum's getting to you. You're all red, old boy. But here, have some more."

"No, thanks." He waived the offer aside. "You met her, the day you came in to see me. Sister Madeleine took care of me. She wrote my first letter home which reminds me, I must get the rest of them written now that I have use of my hand and before Admiral Saunders takes off for home. That could be any day now."

"And she took mighty good care of you. Your wound's all better if you can write."

"Well, only fairly. Yes, those poor nuns work night and day to save lives, not only the French, Canadians and Indians, but many of our own as well."

"And we certainly made a mess of their city!" John placed the two cups on the table and pushed the rum crock out of the way. "I, too, have many things to regulate before the fleet leaves the river."

"I'd like to meet Jean-Paul." Ian wrapped his mended tartan blanket about his shoulders.

"Perhaps you shall, the next time he comes 'round. And I'd like to meet Anaïse." John winked. "You going to the *Sutherland* now?"

"Yes, I'm chasing errands between Murray and Townshend. Monckton's sailing for New York to recuperate from his wounds. What about your journal, John?"

"Well, it's been neglected with the move but I have it here and mean to get back to it."

"It must be a *magnum opus* by now, since Louisbourg isn't it?"

"Yes, it's a bundle. Keep the faith."

"I wish I could go home."

"You can't bring that nun back with you."

Ian gripped the corner of the table. For a moment he glared at his friend. Was it that apparent that he thought of this nun constantly?

"Sorry, old chap. *Coup de foudre* is it? Can't pronounce it as well as you do. That bolt of lightning happens to some of us if we're lucky. But, aye, I wish I could go home too. Good man Monckton. Townshend can't wait to leave. Ian, what are we going to be left with here?"

"Murray, Carleton as his aide, and us blokes, our regiments and maybe only five ships of the fleet to stay. That's the plan so far. . . ."

"That's it? And we're going to guard a garrison against what's coming from Jacques Cartier, Montreal. . . . And keep guessing about Levis' next move?" John Knox threw up his hands.

"The river will freeze over and nobody moves till spring."

"Well, invoke all your respective deities against all those nuns praying in all three chapels that it'll be the British fleet that comes back first in May, better yet by next April. Keep the faith."

"Aye. Keep the faith."

Ian hunched into his collar as he left John Knox's *hangar*. It was colder as twilight descended on the city. A new lamp was lit at the corner of *rue St-Louis.* The tinsmiths had done their jobs. He went by the gardens of the Ursuline monastery, back to his headquarters before he went to Lower Town in search of a boat to take him on board the *Sutherland.* He thought of Jean-Paul Boisvert. He had helped with their horses that night he and his officers had stopped at the Boisvert manor. When would he meet this boy who was Sister Madeleine's brother?

Chapter Six

On the eighteenth of October, one month after the formal capitulation of the city of Quebec, Admiral Sir Charles Saunders with Brigadier-General George Townshend and most of the British fleet in the St. Lawrence River since June, lifted anchor and started the return to England. The citadel fired a farewell salute and the whole town shook. The three-decker *Royal William* carried Wolfe's embalmed body.

On the twenty-third, General Murray received orders by special runners from the Commander-in-Chief of the North American campaign, Brigadier-General Jeffrey Amherst, stationed in upper New York. The orders stated that he was to act as Governor of Quebec. Murray was left with seven thousand men, only five thousand of whom were fit. Sir Guy Carleton was appointed his aide.

Mother Marie Migeon de Bransac, thinking of the preservation of the colony, went to chapel with her nuns to say prayers for their new Governor. She felt he would be a fair man in all difficult dealings ahead and that he would be just. "Please God," she murmured.

Jean-Paul Boisvert watched the fleet leave. He stood alone on the highest rock overlooking Lower Town. He had not come to Quebec alone today. Juliette Duchaineau accompanied him. A neighbor and childhood friend, she brought hooked rugs to barter with Anaïse in the new shop. Juliette wanted to trade and exchange rugs for bed linens for her family's household. There was a quantity of linens left by a few of the nobility before their hurried return to France. At this very moment, she was negotiating with Anaïse.

Jean-Paul continued to gaze at the departing ships as the cannons boomed. They had done their work well. Quebec was a ruin. More than five thousand houses were gone. Lower Town was a maze of roofless walls, Côte de la Montagne a rubble-strewn path with the gaunt remains of the Bishop's palace clinging to its slope. The wind rippled through strands of hair that stuck out around his woolen *toque*. The cold swept up the river. He blew on his fingers then put on his woolen gloves.

"Why did they ever come here?" He spoke to the wind. There was no answer for his sad heart. The booming of the cannons grew fainter. Quebec would never be the same again. Well, there were some things he must do, steadily, faithfully, daily, he promised himself. At Beauport and in his heart, the fleur-de-lis would never fade away. He gritted his teeth. He promised.

He was glad Juliette came with him today with her errand of hooked rugs. He had brought eggs and a goose he was reluctant to part with. There was almost nothing left at their seigneurie that he could bring to the convent. And now, he thought, with General Murray supplying the nuns from the ships' stores and the commissary set up in what was left of the Jesuit College there was hardly any need of him juggling what he could bring and what he must leave on their farm for the winter. Now, the convent kitchen was in better state than most larders in Beauport and he was relieved. He hoped that whatever the departing fleet had left in supplies would see the garrison through the winter. Today, after he saw Marie-Louise, he and Juliette would go visit with Anaïse and Tante José and possibly stay overnight.

The Indian summer was gone. What was momentous for Jean-Paul today, most of the English fleet was leaving and Juliette was with him. For as long as he could remember they had played together as children. Now, in adolescence, they had started to observe reservations that had never existed before but, occasionally, he still permitted her to playfully pull his *toque* down over his ears. Her sense of humor always amused and entertained him.

In this past year, things had changed a lot between them. Now, he reddened in deep blushes when they were in a group and heard double-meaning jokes. His heart pounded when he sat close to her on the long trip from Beauport to Quebec, in the cart or the sleigh. Juliette, his family and the Duchaineau family, they were all part of his life. He felt awkward in his gangly, growing body but he felt strong. Juliette was strong too, she would make a good wife and mother. He thought of her hazel eyes, her long brown hair worn braided and wrapped round her head, the soft white collars she wore on dark homespun dresses. Her laughter always warmed him and she made the best ragoût in Beauport. He knew they were looked upon as a possible marriage when the time came. He sighed as he started down the hill. It would take many marriages to keep Quebec alive. It would take some kind of miracle. And first, they had to survive.

Jean-Paul wondered how many articles belonging to the city of Quebec were now on those ships going to England as souvenirs and trophies of war. He thought of his favorite plaque encrusted with the fleur-de-lis at the St. Louis Gate. He went straight to *rue St-Louis.* Last week, it had been his intention to bring it home, then he had thought better of it. Under either regime, it would be theft and desecration of city property. He hurried as a last boom from the ships' cannons echoed down the river. But when he got to the gate he saw that the plaque had already been ripped off.

His heart lurched. Who else had the same idea? Who took it? An Englishman? Or perhaps a Frenchmen? He hoped a Canadian had carted it off. Perhaps it was safe in some farm loft at Sillery. He made a fist and pounded on the wall. He gave way to a fit of sobbing.

"Mais Jean-Paul, qu'est-ce qui t'prend?" Juliette ran up to him. "Have you been to the convent yet? Tante José is waiting to see you. What's happened? What's the matter?" She folded him in her arms and rocked him back and forth.

Jean-Paul subsided, ashamed of his outburst. Juliette's body heat in the October cold made him feel warm and tender.

"The plaque! The plaque of the city, it's gone!"

"It's only a plaque, Jean-Paul. Quebec is in our hearts."

He nodded as he disentangled himself and pressed her hands.

"They'll never take Quebec out of our hearts, Jean-Paul."

"Let's go home. After I see Marie-Louise, let's go back, right away, today."

"But Tante José is counting on our visit. She and Anaïse prepared soup with extra salt pork, they even made *tarte au sucre.* Tante José's old, she went through a lot, she looks forward to seeing us. She'll tell us stories."

"*Mon Dieu!* All night if we let her." He hugged Juliette and looked deep into her eyes. "*Tu as raison.* You're right. We must listen to the old, love and respect them."

"They're all we've got." Juliette nodded. "Not many of them left."

"Tante José should move into the convent."

"She doesn't want to. She wants to die in her own house."

"She'll die in God's own time and who knows where? As for all of us, Juliette. Georges du Pont died on the Plains with his head sliced off."

"Enough. We don't have time to cry now, we're suppose to be working out the peace."

"The peace," Jean-Paul snorted. "To the advantage of the British."

"We are not going to be effaced, Jean-Paul."

"No, by God, we are not."

"We must be patient," she entreated and pressed his hand. "Go see Marie-Louise. Then join me at Tante José's for some of that hot soup. Then we'll see about when we go home."

After visiting his sister at the convent, Jean-Paul made his way to what was left of the Médard house on *rue St-Louis.*

Juliette welcomed him in the vestibule. "We have a pleasant surprise!"

Jean-Paul smelled the pea soup. His heart leapt for joy as he heard the voice of his hero, Hubert Carrier. But the moment dampened. The usual jovial voice he loved was now speaking softly, sadly, hooked on a sob. He had learned the sad fate of Quebec before entering the city.

"Hubert! When did you get in."

"Jean-Paul, *cher enfant!*" Hubert Carrier's huge frame rose from the fire side. "You've grown almost as big as I am." They embraced and clapped each other on the shoulder.

"*A table*, come now," Anaïse clapped her hands. "Let's eat while the soup is hot."

Jean-Paul and Juliette helped Tante José to the table. "Ah, Hubert you return to Quebec on a sad, black day. You missed it all. The battle on the Plains."

"All the days of Quebec are sad now." The returned *coureur de bois* bowed his head of thick, unruly black hair. He folded his large hands. "I thank God you are all safe and that we can still have a bit of soup together."

"And Levis? Where is Levis? How did you come in off the trail? What are the Indians doing?" Jean-Paul questioned as he sipped the hot *potag*e cautiously.

"Levis left a command at Jacques Cartier and went on to Montreal. He plans a come-back in the spring. All is not over."

"Pretty well over," Tante José muttered. She dribbled a spoonful of soup down her lace fichu.

Anaïse leaned over with an extra *serviett*e to sponge it.

"No, it isn't over ," Hubert boomed. "*Baptême!* I couldn't believe my eyes. I had to almost fight to get through the gate and identify myself."

"We can hardly expect a British guard to know who our famous *coureur de boi*s is. We are all broken hearted. . . ." Tante José said tearfully as she dribbled another spoonful of soup down her neck piece.

"Incredible! No time for broken hearts," Hubert finished his plate with the gusto of a man who has known starvation. "We have to survive this winter and help Levis' plan."

"You should all come to live at Beauport." Jean-Paul swept an inviting glance at all of them.

"I am not leaving Quebec! I am not leaving this house!" Tante José piped up shrilly.

Anaïse patted her hand. "We'll have the maple sugar pie now, Tante José. And you don't have to go anywhere." She served Hubert a goblet of cognac.

"Ah," he smacked his lips. "I see the *maudits Anglai*s didn't bomb out your entire cellar."

Anaïse smiled at him. It was a smile and a look that contained a secret.

Some of the shocked anger and sadness fell away from Hubert as he answered her smile with a wink.

"When there's no one left in the world, maybe, you'll marry me, Anaïse."

"Well, there's hardly any one left now. Certainly, hardly anyone French or any of us left in Quebec."

"Never mind," he said softly as the cognac warmed him. "*C'est pas fini.*"

"It's safer in Beauport," Jean-Paul insisted. He handed his plate to Juliette for a refill.

"Montcalm's former headquarters, the manoir de Salaberry, isn't that occupied?"

Jean-Paul lifted his shoulders. "We skirt around it."

"Who knows?" Tante José pushed her plate back. "They have their hands full with Quebec at the moment."

Hubert flashed Jean-Paul a wide smile. "*Ah, mon p'tit,*" he stroked his black beard. "Before I forget, I brought something back from Montreal for you."

"You did!"

Hubert went to his knapsack by the fire-place. "Here's a beaver hat, you should look very handsome in that."

Jean-Paul put it on instantly.

Juliette clapped her hands. "Bravo! A stylish change from that old woolen *toque.*"

"Merci, merci," Jean-Paul was jubilant.

Tante José and Anaïse laughed and admired him in his new finery. Hubert went to stoke up the fire.

"Could we sing a little, even though we have curfews and guards on every street corner. . . ." Tante José, now revived from her dribblings with a little anisette liqueur, was excited and in a party mood. It was not every day, even in normal times, that the renowned Hubert Carrier came by.

"*Par derrièr' chez mon père,*" Jean-Paul suggested still wearing his new hat. He got the mandolin from the top of a small armoire and handed it to Hubert.

Hubert's deft fingers strummed music from the instrument, sang softly and lulled them all into a reverie while Anaïse calculated how she was going to bed everybody down. As she swayed with the melody, she decided she would leave Tante José on the chaise longue by the fire with extra blankets. Juliette could share her bed and Hubert and Jean-Paul could share the only extra bedroom that had been saved from the bombings.

With that settled in her mind, Anaïse picked up the tune and hummed along as she gazed dreamily at the hearth's fire. The flames curled about the logs, flickered, crackled and threw a mellow warmth about the room. She regretted this night would be different. Before the capitulation, when Hubert came in from the forest and the house was intact, they would sit by the fire and talk till dawn.

Sometimes they took a walk down the moonlit street bundled up in zero weather, or in a soft late rain of Indian summer. A few times they made love. They understood each other, they respected each other's tragedy and asked nothing of one another. Both had been struck with great losses in the prime of their lives.

While still a very young girl, Anaïse had lost her intended, her fiance, to France. Albert de Vaillancourt, on a return voyage to visit his parents and conclude arrangements for their marriage, had sailed from Quebec never to be heard of again.

Hubert was an orphan from Mont Joli and he often sang about the Gaspésie. He was brought up by the Jesuits at the Petit Seminaire but he became a woodsman at an early age. Though he could read and write and might have been seriously interested in law, he preferred the wide open spaces of the great outdoors.

Before he was nineteen, he married a Huron girl, Thérèse, who was educated by the Ursulines. They had a son, Francois, and lived on a farm in Sillery. Thérèse worked with the farmers while Hubert was gone on his long *coureur de bois* journeys in the wilderness. Happiness with his small family was short lived. One day, Thérèse and little Francois went on a journey into the interior to her Huron village by Mont Ste-Anne to visit her people. While there, Thérèse, her son Francois and most of the people in the village were massacred by an Iroquois up-rising.

The Jesuits came to help Hubert in his great tragedy. They traveled with him to bring back the mutilated bodies of his wife and son from the Mont Ste-Anne region. Tenderly they buried them in the small cemetery by the church at Sillery. Hubert didn't speak for weeks. Then, silently he went back into the forest to assuage his grief, to find himself.

In the next few years, he gained a reputation as a hardy *coureur de bois*. He developed a trade exchange relation with Anaïse Médard whom he had known since his early days at the Jesuit College when she delivered supplies to the school's kitchen. Many of their friends thought they were a good pair, that some day they might marry.

In time, Hubert left his grief at the foot of the Virgin's altar in his favorite church, Notre Dame des Victoires. In the middle of the daily tasks of living on the trail or in the city, he thought of Anaïse. They were alike in many ways, he grew to love her from afar. He knew she was a coquette and clever with men. On some occasions, he thought he divined her secret heart. She belonged to no man but she knew how to play and connive around most men.

Anaïse had always admired Hubert, this "hulk of a man" she called him. They had negotiated profitable fur deals. Though they understood each other, she was coy with him. Over time she had helped to bring him back from his great chagrin. But she knew he slept with Indian women on some of his long treks. Each May, if Hubert had not returned from the forest, she would always visit the graves of his wife and child on the anniversary day of their deaths.

When Hubert finally admitted to himself that he loved Anaïse, he wanted her to know. He reasoned that could be a good thing for both of them. On his last two returns from nowhere, he started to press his attentions. In a humorous manner at first, he took whatever crumb she gave him. He would be patient, he would bide his time, he thought. Yet, he knew she did not measure time like the band of adventurers he travelled with. On his visits to Quebec City, he ate Anaïse's *crêpes* with relish. He pinched her behind and slapped his thigh and roared with laughter at her jokes.

He did have some moments of despair, in the quiet of the woods when he looked at a bright pale moon and thought of Anaïse. But there were always the distractions of women in the Indian villages. Suddenly, they were there in the cold grip of winter, or on hot summer nights, with their warm, silent, copper colored bodies. They stilled his roaring nature with the necessities of life in the forest.

"Ah, it's good that you come back to us, to civilization, Hubert. At least once in awhile, but this time it might have been better for you to stay away from this broken city. . . ." Tante José was tearful, the music of the mandolin and Hubert's voice engulfed her with emotion.

"Tante José we'll survive the winter, then we'll see, we'll see."

"I thank God, you always come back, Hubert." Jean-Paul straightened his new hat.

"Well, take that hat off Jean-Paul, you'll roast and breed lice, *des gros poux,*" Juliette scolded and grimaced.

"Now, sing '*A la claire fontaine*'." Jean-Paul asked for his favorite request, obediently took his new hat off, hooked it on a wooden rack by the door then stretched out on the floor by the fire.

Hubert complied and entertained them all.

Yes, Anaïse thought as she poured him another cognac, he always comes back to us, to civilization. He always came back to Quebec to make some men rich. He, himself, didn't care much for great wealth, she reminded herself. His pelts had sold and dressed some dandies, crafty politicians, as well as men of honor in the genteel courts of Europe.

She knew his brown wrists could wrestle with anything in the forest. He wielded an axe with strength, aimed usually on target with bow and arrow as well as his Huron, Abenaqui and Ottawa friends. He was swift and precise with his huntsman's knife.

Out there, in the wilderness, he blended with the forest like a huge tree. It was his home for eight months of the year. He went to great distances. There were times when his friends thought he was lost, or gone forever in the depths of some lake, or some Iroquois had his scalp, or he had been strangled on some lonely wood path for his pelts and his dirty pack of pemmican.

But he always came back from the vast wilderness with his smile, his treasures, his tales of far-away places in the lands of winter, that white world far above them. He came back from rivers in the south too, rivers with rapids that bore him in giddy swiftness through the unknown. He always came back though he was out of place on the streets of Quebec. He smiled and bowed to all the ladies. He drank his cognac, played the mandolin and violin. At soirées, he danced and sang.

He revived his strength in Quebec and Sillery so that he could hunt and fish with more vigor, more cunning. He restored his skills with rest and relaxation so that he could steer his canoe more cleverly, more silently past any crouching enemy. He fortified himself with hearty ragoûts so that he could withstand hunger when the hunt was scarce. He had long since learned how to live on berries for several days. When wounded and alone, he knew how to rely on the medicinal sap of secret trees until help came. He valued the tranquil companionship of missionaries and of Indians, their chiefs some times met on the trail.

To Jean-Paul, Hubert Carrier had almost no human faults and was a fearless hero who had mastered the art of living in every season with all the animals of the Nordic forest. He was in awe of *coureurs* who knew the camouflage of the woods. He asked many questions about medicine men, shamans who could watch and even drive away the evil spirits of long fevers from which some men and women never recovered.

Hubert Carrier blended his religion with that of the converted and unconverted Indians. All through his journeys, he prayed. And he danced to the sun with his native friends. By the camp fires they laughed together, ate, drank, told stories far into star-lit nights or inside wigwams protected from slashing rains or blowing snow storms. They washed their fatigue away with *eau-de-vie* as long as it lasted.

On some quiet mornings, at the end of a journey, in some little village by the St. Lawrence, Hubert often would find a lone missionary preparing to say Mass. He would confess all the riotous flaws in his nature and after absolution would humbly receive communion. He would sing the *Agnus Dei* loud and clear with whatever small congregation was present.

On his returns to the city, he always lit candles to his patron saint, St. Hubert, either at the *basilique* or at Notre Dame des Victoires. He carried a small, very old tattered book of "Lives of the Saints" given to him by one of his teachers and he often read part of the life of St. Hubert by the light of his many camp-fires.

He never tired of rereading that St. Hubert was the patron of hunters and trappers, that he became a bishop and replaced St. Lambert at Tongeres-Maestricht, a district of Belgium. He savored particular bits of information on St. Hubert's life, especially that he had done missionary service in the Forest of Ardenne. He liked the legend attributed to St. Hubert since the fifteenth century that while hunting on Good Friday, he had come upon a stag which displayed a crucifix between his antlers and that it was this imagery that had lead St. Hubert to a better life.

When Hubert finished the last notes of "*A la claire fontaine*" there was a contented silence.

"If only Maman could hear you play and sing, Hubert, and Papa and Uncle Guillaume," Jean-Paul sat up against the warm stone of the fire-place. "Come to Beauport and visit with us."

"Yes, I will come and see your dear Maman, Jean-Paul. After I visit Reverend Mother at the convent and take care of a few things here that need putting a hand to."

They all shared an instinctive feeling that he would have a lot to do with lines of communications between Quebec, Jacques Cartier and Montreal in the approaching winter. And what was to be done with the part of the French fleet that was still up the river? Anaïse wondered.

"You'll be bumping into a lot of British officers at the convent," Tante José said. "They're putting their hands to everything."

"They had no right to come here in the first place. I'll not be in their way, I assure you. It was bad enough trying to enter through the gate."

They heard the guard down the street. "Ten o'clock and all's well."

"All's well indeed!" Juliette snorted. "May we get to bed now, Anaïse? There'll be frost in the morning. Jean-Paul and I must leave not too late in the day."

Anaïse indicated where they were to sleep in the chambers *d'en haut*, the enclosed part of the second floor still standing. She threw an extra blanket over Tante José who was already dozing in the chaise longue.

Jean-Paul and Juliette went up the re-enforced staircase. They embraced in the hall.

"*Dors bien, Jean-Paul.* Sleep well. Never mind about the plaque."

He clasped her hard against his young body. "*Dors bien, Juliette.* If I listen to you, there'll be another plaque with the *fleur-de-lis* one day. It's good to see Hubert." He brushed her lips and released her. They separated to go to their appointed beds.

Hubert banked the fire for the night. "What about Tante José's jewels?" He asked as he stood up beside Anaïse to enjoy the last of the subdued warmth from the hearth.

"She hid them. She thinks she might have need of them this winter."

"Ah, she's still a tradesman."

"As we all will be. New Englanders will be coming up here. They might want to make us a fourteenth colony."

"Not if I can help it. " Hubert shook his head. "But never mind, enough for tonight. In the excitement of arrival, I forgot earlier that I brought Tant José a *p'tit cadeau* too, but it's a mere bagatelle along side some of her jewels."

Anaïse's eyes sparkled in the candle light. "What is it?"

"She can find it in the morning." Hubert placed a small purple velvet box next to the water carafe set on an oval table by the chaise longue. Tante José wrapped to the throat in her woolen blanket was snoring softly. "It's a gold *fleur-de-lis* pin. And did you think I had not brought you a little something?" He proudly gave Anaïse a thin red silk envelope.

"You come back to this war-torn city like *le Père Noël*, Hubert. Your heart is bigger than your body." In pleasant anticipation, Anaïse unfurled a long red silk scarf and twirled it about her neck. "It's beautiful!

What an exciting color.   Is this what fashionable Montreal women are wearing?"

"I don't see that many of them," he winked as he hugged her.

His beard was grizzly. Anaïse raised one of his big hands against her cheek.

"When I come back from Beauport. . . ."

"Yes," she whispered as she caressed the sensuous silk. "When you come back from Beauport. Now, go tell your tall woodsmen's tales to Jean-Paul. The two of you will be talking for the rest of the night."

Chapter Seven

"What are you reading, Sister?"

Startled, Marie-Louise dropped her book. A green felt bookmark embroidered with gold *fleur-de-lis* fluttered across the path.

"It's 'The Life of Marie de L'Incarnation', Captain."

Ian picked up the book and the thin strip of ornamented felt. At early November, the garden was somber and gray. A pale sun tried to break through a hovering mist swept up from the river. Her face seemed small and delicate today, swathed in her white coif. She wore a long black wool cloak against the chill. Her feet were shod in brown moccasins instead of the black regulation shoes. So, they were short of shoes as General Murray had noted.

"May I?" Ian bowed indicating he wanted to sit beside her on the stone bench. He placed the bookmark in the book and handed it to her.

She nodded solemnly. Her smile was weak. She moved over a little, still in some awe of him. This *Ecossais*, she thought, with the French mother from Vendôme, his courtly French retained a strange accent.

"My mother knew something of her and I certainly should while I am housed in this convent," he smiled.

"We have other books about Marie de l'Incarnation in our library, our archives. You could borrow one." Marie-Louise raised her strong little chin as she looked up at him and placed a work-worn, rough, chapped hand over the book he had just retrieved from the path.

His heart contracted. How hard they worked. And he and all the other Highlanders in his regiment were an extra burden in their house, their chapel. And all the sick and wounded who needed constant care. What atrocities had been brought in to them, all these nuns. Even some of the Indians came in scalped.

"Thank you, Sister Madeleine. I will avail myself of that kind offer."

"Your hand? How is your hand, Captain?"

"Much better, thanks to you, Sister. I even help the Adjutant with dispatches and do my own correspondence now."

She nodded approvingly.

"Are you getting extra help with the laundry, now that you are back to washing inside?"

"Yes, all the town families who are quartered with us help a lot. And Anaïse Médard has brought us rose water and glycerine for our hands," she placed her fingers to her lips with a little gasp. Too late, she realized that was information she probably should not reveal. Anaïse had secret stores of other commodities besides rose water, most probably contraband to the new regime.

"Well, at least that is one small comfort. I promised Sister Philomène to help stack some wood today. . . ."

"Is your hand well enough for that?"

"Well enough, Sister." In spite of the November chill, remnants of dead fall flowers, the hardened path bordered with frost-dried grass, a pale sun did come through and even cast a slight shadow on the convent's stone wall. Ian felt warm and happy in her presence.

A bell rang from the tower of the chapel.

"I must go, Captain. I was only out for a few moments of fresh air."

"And reading and meditation which I interrupted. Please say a prayer for me, for us all." He was asking her to pray for the enemy. That's what they were, all of them, the enemy. What were her thoughts? He wondered. He was full of compassion and bittersweet emotions. If she was not wearing a veil and he was in a salon paying court, he would tell her, probably with a foppish bow, that he was completely at her mercy. This slim girl with the soft eyes that he had already seen without her coif, in a red dress.

"Yes, for us all," she assented as she rose in a stately manner, trying not to lose her composure. She crushed the book against her breast. What was it about him? He suffused her with strange feelings. Feelings she could not explain. Well, there was work to do, a great deal of work and to sustain them all, a call to prayer. Her few moments of liberty were over.

Ian watched Marie-Louise hurry down the path, her veil floating on the November air.

They were all starting to feel the cold in his quarters and as a gesture for kindnesses received in the hospital wards, the officers volunteered part of their liberty hours to stack up more wood for the convent fire-places. He was on the work force to donate a few hours this morning. After posting the Order of the Day in the Place d'Armes, he had come to the garden nursing a secret hope that he would see Marie-Louise.

Two young Gautier boys whose family was housed in the basement of the convent were going to help him. For a long moment, Ian stood quietly by the stone bench savoring the few moments of exchange he had enjoyed with Marie-Louise. And they had been alone. There was a singing in his blood as he went to Sister Philomène's kitchen door. Strong odors of cabbage and carrot soup wafted over a partly open window transom.

It was late afternoon when Ian returned to his quarters. His uniform was messed up from the wood stacking. They needed work clothes, he thought grimly. He knew there was a detachment going through some things left behind by the French Army at Chateau St. Louis. They were going to be a motley looking crew in this ruined fortress before the winter was over. He loosened his collar to relax his fatigue, pulled off his boots, poured his rum ration, settled at his writing table and sipped leisurely.

As he shuffled through orders and dispatches, he thought of his encounter with Marie-Louise in the garden. In his heart and mind, she was Marie-Louise, now. When he spoke to her or of her, she was Sister Madeleine.

"What's this?" He muttered. "A meeting in General Murray's quarters at four thirty." He looked at the French clock. "Why, it's that time now!" He pulled his boots back on, freshened up from a bowl of water on his night stand, smoothed his hair, tied it at the back and hooked his military collar.

In the hall, he met two of his lieutenants, Leslie Hay and Alexander MacAlister and Captain Simon Rose.

"They call us "*les gens sans culottes,* you know." Leslie was chuckling.

"Who?" Ian asked.

"The nuns," MacAlister laughed.

"Well, it's better than being called *"les sauvages d'Ecosse".* Are we Scot savages?" Rose fell in stride with them.

"At times we are. At times, we are." Ian was serious but they were all laughing.

The soldier on duty lit the street lamp on the corner of *rue du Parloir* as they entered the General's headquarters. The soft murmuring of prayers from the chapel and the aromas of the evening meal from the kitchen receded as the Highlanders closed the heavy oak door. Most officers present were Black Watch.

"Gentlemen, I've called this meeting to check and execute a heavy agenda. It's going to be no light task to defend a ruined fortress in a hostile country without the aid of the full fleet and in the face of the rigors of a Canadian winter. And that I'm hearing a lot about. As you already know, the regiments left with us are the 15th, 28th, 35th, 43rd, 47th, 48th, 58th, 60th and 78th."

Captain Duncan MacNeil read from his notes. "In addition there are men of the Royal Artillery. The 60th Regiment contains two battalions of colonial troops, Royal Americans."

"There are also 100 Colonial Rangers." Captain Rose put in.

Murray pointed out, "Most of the officers are reasonably housed. Those of you not in the convent are at General Hospital, or in patched up housing on *rue St-Louis,* Lower Town or on board ship. I'm worried about my soldiers, not only do we have to fight off the cold, we have to fight off scurvy. To properly feed the common soldier will be a priority."

Guy Carleton, the General's Adjutant, also read from a sheaf of papers. "A part of the fleet is to remain at Halifax under Lord Colville for the winter. The two sloops of war, *Racehorse* and *Porcupine* and three armed vessels, that's what's left to us here at this garrison."

"I must say, gentlemen, puny evidence of Britain's might upon the sea." General Murray walked up and down in front of a large map of Quebec and the St. Lawrence River. "We'll be in a deadlock here. The French think they have us blocked for the winter with the cold, the Canadians and the Indians. And they plan to retake us in the spring."

The adjutant picked up from his notes. "To ensure the health of our troops, we require access to the supplies of fresh provisions in the neighboring villages. And a large quantity of fire-wood is necessary for the duration of the winter."

"Aye," Ian's voice was loud and clear. "We must control some areas of the forest."

Murray went to a map made by the chief engineer, Major Patrick MacKellar. It hung between two windows overlooking the convent garden now faintly outlined in a soft blue dusk. He addressed them all.

"To ensure safety, I find it necessary to occupy all approaches to the city. We will extend our outposts to keep the French army beyond the River Jacques Cartier." He pointed, then attached a red marker to the location. "The farthest out-post is Lorette," again he pinned a marker. "Not on the plateau. . . ."

"Yes, there in the valley, some eight miles to the west." MacKellar nodded.

"There we continue to fortify the church," Murray said. "By holding this place, we cut off the enemy from the most important road to Quebec, the one that leads through Charlesbourg."

"The church at St Foy?" Ian asked.

"We continue to fortify both, at Lorette and St. Foy," Murray pointed to the marked areas on the map. "We're stationing field pieces and surrounding the positions with entrenchments and stout picket work."

"We will continue to place a force at Cap Rouge," MacKellar stamped a red marker over Rouge. "That pretty well covers all approaches." The engineer and the general laid their pointers down on the table.

"These posts mean the control of the parishes in the immediate neighborhood of Quebec." Murray told the meeting of assembled officers. "And gentlemen, I think it would be wise to provide for the administration of justice in the parishes by appointing a Canadian magistrate."

"Hear, hear," they all nodded approval.

"Quebec is still really weak." The chief engineer was thinking of the return of the French.

"The danger comes from the landward side." Murray was also pensive for a moment. "This thin wall built for protection against attack from the Indians must be fortified, stretched inward from Cape Diamond, the cliff overlooking the St. Lawrence to the suburb of St. Roch."

"It would not stand vigorous cannonade," a young Highlander piped up from the back of the room.

"Aye." This they all knew and agreed unanimously.

"We must get hold of all the horses and sleighs to bring in wood. We could pay the *habitants*. Make friends for mutual exchanges, the people of the city are without fresh produce as well as we. So friendly terms are recommended for mutual exchanges. They still have fresh vegetables in the villages, in their cellar bins. They know how to farm and preserve. And we have an abundance of biscuit and salt meat, all the supplies we've transferred from the ships to the Commissary in the Jesuit College," Murray was getting hoarse. He refilled his glass with sherry and pushed the decanter down the length of the table to his officers.

"Even share your slender allowances of rum, gentlemen. I promised to take care of the nuns, provide for their kitchens. They have worked untiringly to restore everyone back to health, regardless of what creed or army the wounded belong to."

"That they have! That they have!" Lieutenant Leslie clapped. They all applauded.

Ian nodded and here they were, all of them, overrunning their Ursuline household.

"I'm issuing another manifesto to tell the *habitant*s that the British have come to give them mild and just government."

"With due respect, General Murray, they haven't accepted us as conquerors, they want us out of here. They haven't given up, they're planning the next coup. How do we know what the remnant of the French fleet still up the river will do? We must not get too generous, I suggest we control with firmness, strength, caution. . . . They are not all docile." This input was from Captain Alexander Fraser. There were five Frasers present. Not Simon, but two Johns, Bruce and Duncan besides Alexander.

"Yes, we have some atrocities on both sides we can't forget. But the Canadians themselves are not enchanted with Vaudreuil . . . . For the most part, I think they've decided to make the best of it." The General lapsed into serious reflection as he sipped his sherry. His glance embraced all of the officers present before it returned to the map on the wall.

"I hear they keep trickling in from the parishes to take the oath to be faithful to King George. . . ." This came from a very young voice, an officer at the back of the room who had arrived late and had not signed the attendance sheet.

"The Canadian women are especially vehement against Vaudreuil." One of the Frasers had heard this bit of information.

"Vaudreuil is capable of inciting the Indians to commit outrages on the Canadians who accept British rule." This was a prime concern in the plan of organization to rule. "I'm also issuing a proclamation denouncing the Canadian Governor's conduct and now that I have been appointed Governor of Quebec by our Commander-in-Chief, General Jefferey Amherst, I'm wearing two hats. I will impose all the rigors that the rules of war allow if the Canadians prove unfaithful to their new oath of allegiance. We're all holed up together in this garrison for the winter. What about the street lamps, Major MacKellar?"

"They're all lit on time, sir. The curfew patrol is on duty."

"Major MacKellar will pass out the assignments for reinforcement of the fortifications, gentlemen."

"About tomorrow's court-martial, Order of the Day?" Ian asked.

"Yes, I expect you all on the Parade Ground at nine o'clock. The court-martial committee will remain, the rest of the meeting is adjourned, gentlemen."

Ian sighed, he was not on the committee but he had made up the Order of the Day. There were two soldiers listed to receive 500 lashes at eleven o'clock for theft and drunkenness. He winced. They were all barbarians, he thought, as well as the offending soldiers. Even with nuns praying in their midst.

Another bell rang from the monastery, the last call to evening devotions. Marie-Louise must be going to chapel now. He loosened his collar on the way back to his quarters and to his unfinished rum.

Lieutenant Hay caught up to him.

"Ian, will you dine with us aboard ship tonight?"

"You talk as if the whole fleet was still with us. Which one?"

"The *Porcupine*, Captain Townley has gotten up a little party."

Ian hesitated, he needed to be alone, he had planned to go to the library to research a book about Marie de l'Incarnation. There was even at the back of his mind a poem coming on, a poem to be written and perhaps never to be seen by the eyes of the beloved.

"Oh, come on. Do you good, get rid of that love-sick look in your eyes. The steward has a deal with a Canadian brunette who's told him how to make *ragoût*."

"Now, that sounds palatable."

"And there's plenty of rum and sherry on that ship."

Ian smiled. Did he really have a love-sick look in his eyes? Well, he must get rid of it. Certainly, he would enjoy the camaraderie with his fellow officers. Why not?

"Delighted. I'll come."

"Be in Lower Town in half an hour. We'll pick you up in the dinghy. The mists have lifted, looks like it'll be a clear night."

After the last litany was said, Mother Marie-Anne Migeon de Bransac called a meeting of her own. She directed Mother Davanne of St. Louis to assemble all her nuns in the community room.

There was a hush after the usual invocation to the Holy Ghost.

"My dear daughters in Christ," Mother Migeon addressed them all. "We will continue to say prayers of thanksgiving for the decision of the

British not to destroy this colony. As you all know Brigadier-General James Murray has been appointed the new Governor of Quebec. He promises his protection to all of us. I believe he will be a fair and just man."

Mother Philomène and a novice came in carrying tea trays and placed them on the conference table in front of their Superior.

"Sisters," Mother Migeon continued, "we will go on as if they are not here. The Catholic Highlanders know who we are but some of the soldiers have never seen the likes of us." She poured the tea and Mother Philomène distributed the steaming cups to each nun. "They are curious. On penalty of death, they are not to appear on the third floor, Governor Murray has decreed." Silently, she hoped Governor Murray had received her compassionate letter interceding for that foolish man who had peeked through the half glass in the door barring the cloister. "But please, Sisters, no more hysterical screaming if some of them observe us at close range from the other side of the cloister while we go to chapel."

She threw a meaningful glance at Sister Alphonse who lowered her eyes over her tea cup. Then directed it to Mother Monique who also lowered her eyes. She must be tolerant, Mother Migeon reminded herself. Mother Monique must have been terribly frightened, as they all were, the night after the battle on the Plains. It was not too surprising that Mother Monique had bargained with Two Moose for a tomahawk and hid it under her bed. Two Moose should know better, but then they were more realistic than she, those two and they did not speak with a General turned Governor every day, as she did.

"I am proud of you all, I know you will be resourceful to defend yourselves if the need arises. But we are in the Governor's safekeeping," she used his new title, "and he has assured me that no harm will come to us. We will keep Quebec and Canada before our eyes in the good example of Marie de l'Incarnation," she went on. "Though we no longer have our students, our boarders, except our little four-year-old Constance, the work of educating our youth has been lifted from us with the return of our French families to France. But we have the continuing care of the sick and wounded and we are the unexpected hostesses to the military in our own house. True, nothing is normal. That's war. But we are alive. We will do the very best we can." She flung part of her veil over her shoulder and started to pour herself another cup of tea when Sister Philippe came to her assistance.

"We will continue our assignments of extra duties, we will continue with our devotions at the appointed hours and to keep our morale up in the face of winter. While waiting for the return of Levis, we will do something beautiful for God and Quebec." Then she presented her real surprise announcement. "You will all be assigned a commission according to your talents."

A fluttering, questioning gasp came up from all of them.

"We will have music concerts twice a week, organ, piano, harpsichord. Sister Eustace will co-ordinate these in the music room."

Several happy, "Ahs!" swept the room.

"Those of you who are artists, writers, weavers, lace-makers, engravers, tapestry embroiderers of bark art work will make special tableaux, write special poetry and stories depicting Quebec and the Huron Village with a theme representing Canada and our heritage."

"Reverend Mother," Marie-Louise spoke up. "You wanted to be reminded about the feast of St. Andrew on November 30, that we were going to do something special . . . ."

"Yes, thank you, Sister Madeleine. We are going to make honorary stoles for the Highlanders with crosses to show our appreciation for all their help with the cutting and stacking of the wood chores, with the carrying of the water for the laundry. . . ."

"But surely, Reverend Mother, only the Catholic Highlanders would appreciate that," Sister Catherine dared to comment her disapproval.

"Let me remind you, Sister Catherine, St. Andrew is the patron saint of all of Scotland." She knew Sister Catherine's thinking. It was her habit to be always mindful of extra pleasures if and when they meant extra expenditures. She was the most frugal nun of the community and she helped with the bookkeeping having come from a family of accountants in Montreal.

"They have no business here in our convent, in our city." Sister Catherine dared further.

"Nevertheless, Sister Catherine, they are here and we are captive. Though I've assured you otherwise, they could do what they like with us."

This time the community gasp was full of fright.

Mother Migeon raised a comforting hand. "It is wiser, dear Sisters, to keep an open exchange. We need each other to survive the winter. While we care for the wounded of both armies, the British are putting food in our mouths. Mother Philomène, how is your knitting brigade doing with the knitting of leggings for these '*sans culottes*'?"

"Very well, Reverend Mother, they'll be glad of them I'm sure after the first snow storm. They're not going to slide down Côte de la Montagne on their bare behinds, I hope."

Twitters and giggles gushed forth from the younger nuns.

"That will do, Sisters. We are all grateful to you, Mother Philomène and your delegation for keeping our feet warm too with woolen hose. We will be wearing moccasins as our shoes wear out now, the Huron Village will supply us. I have no idea when we will be able to order shoes from either a French or British merchant."

They were aware of the glow from the new street lamp outside as the early November dark enveloped the convent and they continued to pay serious attention to what their Superior was saying.

"I expect all of you who knit to be part of Mother Philomène's brigade too. We will be at chapel after you finish your tea. Bon courage." They adjourned the meeting with a prayer and signed themselves.

Mother Migeon accorded them a brief period of liberty and relaxation and bestowed a smile of love on all of them as she left the new improvised community room.

Later that evening after supper and Complines, a few more prayers were said to the Holy Ghost for inspiration on the special arts project. Mother Migeon's announcement had generated some excitement. As they left their choir stalls, most of the nuns were already planning what they were going to create according to their individual talents for this morale booster.

Marie-Louise noticed that Geneviève remained in her choir stall. She looked sad and withdrawn. Her hour glass was turned over for another hour of devotions. It was much too cold. Marie-Louise shivered and promised herself she would look in on her when she came back from checking patients in the townspeople's ward. When they were all together in their choir stalls their body warmth, at least, kept the unheated chapel at a comfortable level.

When she returned, they were the only two left in the chapel. Geneviève was sobbing softly. Marie-Louise came and sat beside her.

"*Mais, qu'est-ce qu'il y a, à part des Anglais et la guerre?*" She leaned toward her childhood friend, now her sister in Christ. "Your parents?"

Geneviève nodded. "Exactly, *les Anglais, la guerre!* I received a letter. Bolduc delivered it to the Reverend Mother. Half of our barn is burnt to the ground, some of our cattle were taken. My father refused to sign the oath at first but then he had to as security to keep the house intact."

"*Ah, mon Dieu!* And your parents, how are they?" Marie-Louise pressed Geneviève's hand. She feared for her own home and family but their farm had the advantage of being a good distance away from the main road.

"They're all right but they're angry, hurt, bereft, crushed. . . . I guess we all thought they were concentrating on Sillery, St. Foy, the area between here and Fort Jacques Cartier to force the signing of the oath. This is not according to the Articles of Capitulation. Not as I understood it."

"They keep vascillating to force the signing of the oath."

"My parents think they should move to the back country with some of Mireille's people."

"Oh, no! They can't leave Beauport. Jean-Paul, Papa, Uncle Guillaume, they would all help. They must stay in their home."

"And your father? He signed?"

"Right away. He didn't want my mother disturbed, it would kill her outright. It broke Jean-Paul's heart."

"I didn't know. What do we know of each other's family with all that's been going on? What can I do for my parents here, shut up in this monastery? What do we know? Nothing. Only what we see and hear over the convent wall every day."

"*C'est abominable!* I'm so sorry about your parents. They must stay in their home. The British are trying to make good subjects of us all. I'll talk to Reverend Mother, she has Murray's ear, some repairs should be made here, or to Captain Lindsay. . . ."

Geneviève raised her hand. "He's among those who write the orders and their brutes carry them out. We may need each other to survive the winter but we're at their mercy."

Marie-Louise bit her lip and fell back as if she been slapped. The truth was ugly. Oh, God! None of this could be justified. "They promised no harm would come to us but yes, our parents are at their mercy. We all are."

"What can I do for my parents here?" Geneviève repeated.

"We can pray."

Geneviève nodded tearfully. Marie-Louise had just reminded her who they were, where they were and why.

"Yes, I pray that we all hold out till spring, please God. Till Levis comes back. I pray my parents find the courage to stay in Beauport."

"Please God. But let us return to our cells now, Geneviève. It's too cold here at this hour. We are not praying for martyrdom. We have too many people to look after." Marie-Louise rose and helped Geneviève up from her knees. Ah, it was too much. On most days, she walked through reality half mesmerized. What were the inner inscriptions, the fine script of the Articles of Capitulation? Yes, an early spring would be welcome. Would there be some solutions? She thought of Sister Veronique who was already planning the convent garden. And who would plan the Boisvert garden in Beauport this year?

The two young nuns incanted their prayers fervently. That they knew how to do. Then they crossed themselves. As they left the chapel they noticed from one of the hallway windows that a light snow was falling on the city.

In her cold cell, Marie-Louise tossed and prayed all night. She promised herself that during her duties the next day she would avoid the areas where she might see Ian. It would not be easy. She felt torn apart with mixed emotions.

Chapter Eight

Bitter cold and a windy, gusty snow descended on the city the next day. Ian visited John Knox in the afternoon. While they talked and shared their rations of rum, neither noticed the storm accelerate into a blinding blizzard.

"And that's the gist of yesterday's meeting, old man. I must be off for some of that good convent soup before your whole stable is buried in snow here."

"Aye." John poured more rum in two tin cups. "Have another sip for the road."

"No thanks, friend. More paper work tonight. I hope they're well on the ships. The river may freeze over tonight."

"Aye. Listen to that wind, the fury of it. It's warm and cozy here. Stay the night, why don't you? Who'll know the difference?"

"Duty calls." Ian wrapped an old woolen scarf he had retrieved from the armoires of Chateau St. Louis along with other French soldiers' effects that were divided and passed out to his regiment only last week. He stumped out into the blizzard. He couldn't see the tower of the convent chapel. He couldn't even see the length of the street, or some of the half-gutted houses that were supposed to be close to John Knox's stable apartment. Was he lost, already, in some back lane? Incredible that he might be confused between *rue St-Louis* and Donnacona trying to find the garden gate to the convent and the entrance hall to his headquarters.

He bumped into a figure bundled and wrapped up to the eyelids. It was Anaïse Médard.

"What are you doing out in this *tempête*, Captain?" She pulled part of her scarf away from her mouth and gasped for breath.

"I'm trying to find the convent. . . ." They conversed in French.

"You probably can't see two feet ahead of you."

"And you can?"

"I'm used to this. I know where I am, if it's not too far off *rue St-Louis*." She puffed as they walked against the winds, already they were covered with snow.

"Here's my house," she took him by the arm. "Come in, catch your breath, I'll fix a hot *tisane*. No sense over-exerting yourself. This is going to last awhile." He was about to protest but a sharp wind cut his breath and took the words out of his mouth.

The warmth of the Médard foyer was a welcome relief. They shut the double doors, the wail of the wind receded and they shook the snow off themselves.

"I'll see if Tante José is sleeping. Then I'll warm some brandy."

"You have brandy?"

"A little," she gave no further explanation.

"*C'est toi, Anaïse?* Tante José called out in a sleepy voice.

"*Je viens, je viens.*" Anaïse flew up the stairs.

Ian dropped his wet coat, his sword, bonnet and scarf on the floor by the fire, then warmed his hands. He looked around the room and thought the Médard residence must have been elegant before it was half-gutted by bombardment. His glance lingered on the few paintings and objets d'art still left in place as he anticipated the brandy and continued to stretch his cold, stiff hands over the comforting flames. Scurvy and frostbite would be two of their main concerns this winter, he thought grimly. The military trick, the coup in any general's hat would be to outguess Levis' next move.

Anaïse came back with an arm load of towels and threw one at him.

"We'd best dry ourselves. Take off your boots. We're lucky to be inside. It's prudent not to go too far. Some people have perished trying to get home from Lower Town. A tragedy last year, Alcide Dubois perished only one street from his house. Found him the next morning, stiff as a board."

Ian shook his head. He dried himself and took off his boots. He acquiesced to her every command. He sensibly recognized that she knew a lot more about blinding snow storms than he did. Before leaving Scotland, he had heard that winter in Canada was a lot colder then in Europe.

With all her bulky wraps removed, Anaïse looked flush and rosy in a loose draw string blouse. Her round breasts were discernible through the thin, soft wool. She too had removed her boots. They both stretched their bare feet on the hot brick floor toward the crackling fire on the hearth. A fringed Indian skirt fell softly over her knees. With a small towel, she dried the ends of her long brown hair.

What a pretty woman, Ian thought. His fingers were beginning to thaw out. The warmth of the room enveloped him. He felt drowsy, lulled, like he was being rocked on the huge breast of mother earth.

"Where's that brandy," he murmured.

"In a moment," she smiled up at him as she stretched out on the warm bricks. "I closed Tante José's door so we won't hear her. Her snoring is terrible. And she won't hear us."

Ian liked Anaïse's Canadian accent. He closed his eyes. His mind was empty. As the storm swirled about the house, the shutters banged against the thick stone walls. He hung in a reverie of comfort.

After a while, Anaïse shot a plump arm toward a small cast iron door below the hearth's oven and withdrew a crystal flagon of amber brandy. It scintillated in the firelight. From the bottom shelf of a side table she withdrew two goblets and poured generous servings.

"So that's how you keep your brandy warm. . . ."

"Only in winter, otherwise it's in the liquor cabinet at room temperature."

They drank slowly with satisfied "Ah's."

All of Ian's senses awakened as Anaïse handed him a second serving. Her lips glistened with the warm brandy. Lights from the flickering flames in the fire-place danced in her hair. As she leaned toward him, one of her round breasts touched his cheek. Instinctively, he reached out to caress her with his free hand. He set down his brandy goblet as her voluptuous body slid into his embrace. Fire shot in his loins as their lips met.

"Come," she disentangled herself. But all the way up the stairs as Anaïse led the way with a fluttering night candle, they clung to each other.

Ian had an anxious moment as he thought of all the rums he had consumed with John Knox and now the brandy. Would he be of any use to this sensuous woman?

The candlelight drew shadows on a repaired bombed-out wall as they entered the cold bedroom. Outside, the storm raged. They quickly disrobed. Her hot body shivered against his. He reveled in the smoothness of her skin as they fell on the soft downy bed. He held her close as he pulled the huge comforter about them.

As they gave to each other, their passion mounted with swift movements to a high pinnacle. He cried out in ecstasy as they were swept into another world where he no longer heard the storm. All was calm. Then they slept.

When Ian opened his eyes the next morning, sunlight poured into the room. He was alone in the warm bed. His nostrils quivered as he stretched out. Could that be coffee he was smelling, coffee and salt pork? Or hot chocolate? Hot chocolate had sometimes been a rare treat back home in Fyfe. His mother imported it from France. Was he home? The curtains at the leaded windows looked like those in his mother's boudoir. A pair of Alencon lace curtains had been brought back to Scotland one summer on their return from the Vendôme *brûlonnerie.* But no, he was in Quebec. And the grim aftermath of the Battle on the Plains of Abraham shot back into his mind. The stage was reset.

He got up, dragging the huge comforter after him and looked out the window. The snow was up to all the roof tops. There were soldiers of his own regiment and townspeople in the street shoveling paths. A horse drawn sleigh was coming from the far end of the street. He could hear the jingle of the harness bells. There was a scarcity of horses in the city so it must be coming in from the country. Perhaps Jean-Paul Boisvert, Marie-Louise's brother. At the thought of her, a slight pain brushed his heart. He came back to reality. The reality of an aftermath of war in a capitulated city.

Though he had been obsessed over a few fleeting encounters with a nun in the last few months, last night he had been overpowered not only by the elements of a natural storm of the season but also the pent-up storm in his loins since he had left Louisbourg.   There, he had a few furtive and unsuccessful dalliances with Simone, a French innkeeper's daughter.   Still young in spite of service at Culloden, he knew his parents were proud to have seen him off to the great campaigns in North America.   He knew they expected to see him come back even more matured and were, no doubt, trying to arrange a successful marriage for him in Fyfe.

He sighed.   He was a lucky man according to any red-blooded soldier.   What red-blooded soldier would not have considered it an interlude of enormous good fortune to have been permitted to Anaïse's bed.   Yes, he was grateful, she had pulled him off the street, out of the storm, perhaps saved his life.   Now, was he going to be an amorous fool, a sensible lover or never darken the Médard door again?

All of his clothes were neatly piled on a rustic pine chair but his sword occupied a lone position on a gold gilt bench.   The garnet stone in its hilt sparkled in the morning sunshine.   On the night stand, steam rose from a huge bowl of hot water, a towel hung on the side bar.   Anaïse must have just come up to lay out these luxuries while he was still asleep.   From downstairs he heard voices and the clattering of dishes.   Then Anaïse was at the door.

"Bonjour," she smiled demurely.   Her hair was piled high on top of her head in a chignon, a long white apron draped over her wool dress.   She was beautiful.

Ian bowed.   "Bonjour."   Making love in a storm becomes her well, he thought.

She came up to him and caressed his bare shoulder.   He quivered as he pulled the comforter more securely about himself.   He placed a chaste kiss on her smooth forehead.

"Tante José wants you to have a bite of breakfast with us.   Now, mind, she hates the British but tolerates *'les Ecossais'*."

"I shouldn't be here at all."

"Shush. . . . We never leave people walking about in a storm.   And you're not leaving here without something in your stomach."   She leaned against him and the puffed comforter, she touched his chin. "You were wonderful last night. *Absolument merveilleux!* Some of you British are so stuffy and pent-up. . . ."

"Ah, but I'm a Scot. . . ."

"And a good thing too as far as Tante José is concerned."

He pressed to hold her fast but she slipped away and laughed all the way down the stairs.

Ian smiled to himself as he washed. If he was as wonderful as all that, they should be back in bed making love. Was he really *absolument merveilleux?* The convent bell rang and it sounded like tinkling crystal this morning. Again, he felt a little pain brush through him. Was that how some serious husbands felt when they had been unfaithful?

A fragrance of lavender hung in the room. Was it Anaïse's scent? He wondered as he hooked his collar. Or was it from that porcelain bowl of potpourri on the window sill. These homes had known more than a few subtle elegances before the British fleet had sent some of the affluent French families back to France. And had Anaïse negotiated with some of them before they went back? What supplies had she reserved from Cadet's great warehouse, and if part of her reputation was true, where had she hidden these treasures? Now that he had slept in her bed, he was really worried about her. She must move with extreme caution. What sort of trafficking would Murray permit, if any, from women who might set themselves up as merchants this winter? She must never be caught on any illegality. He adjusted his small sword to his belt with mixed feelings. He would go back to his headquarters by Place d'Armes and see what was going on there with all the snow.

He took a deep breath and again sniffed the lavender fragrance. He thought of the moist brown earth in the gardens of his home in the spring, the heather on the hills. Then he looked out the window. There was a lot a activity to get the snow off the street. He heard children laughing and calling out to each other. Well, he must move too. As he glanced at the rumpled bed on the way out the door, a thrill shot through his young body as he sensed again the velvet touch of Anaïse's voluptuous curves. He went down the stairs, ready to meet Tante José, a proud French woman whose niece considered herself a Canadienne. He was primed to be a courteous guest though he was really the enemy. He'd be lucky if she didn't spit in his face. He was more than a highly privileged guest, *fortune de guerre*, taken in out of a storm, he had shared her niece's bed but even though by mutual consent, he'd be luckier still if this Tante José didn't suspect rape. Though he was half French himself, he never ceased to marvel at the non-committal diplomacy of the French.

As he entered the sunlit dining area, he wondered what might be waiting for him in his military quarters at the convent.

"Bonjour, Madame. Thank you for your hospitality. I am Captain Ian Lindsay." He bowed over her hand.

Tante José grumbled haughtily. Done up in a fresh lace fichu caught at the throat with a small cameo pin, she had managed to dribble hot chocolate down its front. She motioned Ian to sit down in front of a faience plate heaped with hot pieces of salt pork and small wheat pancakes.

Ian remembered faience plates his mother had brought back from Quimper, yet another summer. There was coffee as well as hot chocolate. It was strong and delicious. Again, he wondered what kind of traffic Anaïse was into to have so many luxuries, so many commodities while they were still making military inventories for the winter. Where did she hide all these things that might at any moment become contraband?

"I would like you to bring a package to the Reverend Mother," Tante José told him arrogantly. It was a command not a request. She sipped her hot chocolate.

"I am at your service, Madame."

"You're part French, Captain, so I'm told."

"My mother is French. My maternal grandparents have a *brûlonnerie* on the outskirts of Vendôme, by the edge of the forest."

"Ah, I knew Vendôme once," Tante José reminisced. "You won't forget to give that package to Mother de la Nativité?"

"I will deliver it to her immediately upon arrival at the convent." Ian wondered what it contained. He hoped the guard wouldn't insist on inspecting it.

He took his leave of the two women, bowing over their hands. He stepped out of the Médard residence into a white world of snow and blinding sunshine.

A few boys were shoveling along with the soldiers on duty. Younger boys in ragged clothes made snowballs and threw them far down the street. They were shouting and laughing, they didn't seem to mind the cold. The snow made them forget the war. And there was the sound of sleigh bells again.

Jean-Paul Boisvert appeared down the street in his horse-drawn sleigh. All the smaller boys ran toward him clamoring for a ride. He stopped and helped them aboard.

In the excitement of their new divertissement, the boys flung their extra snowballs at random to get rid of them. One hard-packed ball whizzed by and knocked Ian's bonnet off.

Jean-Paul stopped the sleigh, got out and came toward Ian. He recognized him. One of the officers who had stopped at his home in September.

The boys quieted down in fearful apprehension.

"*Pardon, Monsieur*, that was not intentional, these small boys are very frisky after a snow fall." Jean-Paul searched for apologetic words in broken English.

Ian brushed his hat. "*Ce n'est rien*. No harm done."

"*Ah, vous parlez francais, Monsieur*."

"Where are you taking these mischievous boys?"

"Just as far as the convent."

"Delivering supplies to the nuns?"

"Yes, I'm Jean-Paul Boisvert."

"Captain Ian Lindsay."

They both nodded.

"Carry on then. Put the little rascals to work."

"I have some small tasks in mind." Jean-Paul said. He smoldered as he went back to his sleigh. He gave the boys the tongue lashing they expected.

"*Bandes de p'tits polissons.* You mischievous boys! Did you have to knock off a British officer's hat?" But he smiled to himself as he faced the road. "Giddap, Fabien."

The boys regained their spirit as they glided away toward the convent.

Ian also smiled to himself as he walked on to Place d'Armes. So he had finally met Jean-Paul Boisvert. A serious lad and adept with children. Already, he liked him. Now he recalled the night he and his fellow officers had passed in Beauport. Perhaps unwillingly, Jean-Paul and a Huron had helped water their horses at his father's direction. As he approached the parade ground he found it had been cleared of snow and it was mounded about the Place in a perfect square. There was no activity so there must have been a very early work party on duty.

When Ian entered the convent hall it was nine o'clock. The chapel bell rang. Was there an extra Mass this morning? He delivered Tante José's mysterious package to Mother de Bransac de la Nativite's aide, Sister Honorine.

"Ah, I believe it is the thread for the St. Andrew crosses. Oops," she put her hand over her mouth and gasped as if she had let out a great secret.

"You celebrate St. Andrew's?"

"*Mais, oui, Monsieur,* and all the saints that we know of."

"St. Andrew is our patron saint, we Scots. . . ."

"Yes, I know." There was an amused sparkle in her eyes as she reached for the package. Ian had the feeling she was hiding something.

Ah, well, these nuns would have their little games too. He went to chapel and slid in the very last pew. He avoided looking at the cloistered section. Usually seeing Marie-Louise at prayer was one of the highlights of his visit to chapel. He certainly did not want to encounter her eyes this morning. Those doe-like innocent eyes. Again, a little stab of pain went through him. To attend Mass this morning had never entered his mind in the last twenty-four hours. With mixed feelings, he stayed in a sort of stupor. What comfort could he find here now? He felt fallen from grace.

At Elevation, he saw the empty hole in the foot of the chalice as Father Resche raised it high for adoration of the congregation.

"My Lord and my God," Ian murmured. *"Mea culpa, mea culpa."* He rapped his chest with his fist and felt an ache that he would not receive communion. He asked forgiveness for the times he killed in battle. One of these days, as a matter of ritual, he would go to confession. Or would he? Like most humans, he wanted the best of all worlds. As the sombre altar boy shook and rang out the hand bell and the chalice was elevated once more, sunlight poured on it through the stained glass window. The gaping hole where the amethyst had been embedded in its stem irritated Ian. The other jewels sparkled.

He decided that he would go to the sacristy right after Mass and offer Father Resche the garnet in the hilt of his sword. The sooner the better. It could easily be placed in the empty opening. It would restore some of the lost resplendence to the chalice. It might even ease his soul.

Marie-Louise was not in the cloistered side of the chapel. Nor did Ian see her in the hall going or coming on some errand. Maybe, she was already in the sacristy folding away the priest's vestments. He hoped not. Maybe, she was in their new improvised private chapel upstairs. He knocked and entered the sacristy. She was not there.

"Bonjour, Father Resche." The chalice was still out on the armoire shelf with the wine cruets.

"Bonjour, Captain Lindsay." Father Resche finished buttoning his *soutane* collar. He enjoyed talking French with Ian. Though his English was adequate, it was hesitant.

"I've noticed there's a stone missing in the stem of this chalice for some time now. If you will accept it, I would like to donate this garnet from the hilt of my sword to replace the lost stone. . . ."

"Ah, yes, the missing amethyst," Father Resche stiffened. He was mindful of a few attempts from the conquering officers to suffuse with kindness, to help cover the unbearable blunders of two nations who would have to live together through a difficult winter. He was surprised at this sudden unexpected offer but he had been observant that Ian was unusual in some respects from other officers occupying the convent premises. He was bilingual because of his mother in far-off Scotland. He was among the few Catholic Highlanders who could not manifest his faith too openly, on

Murray's orders. Though in the embarrassing situation of carrying out duties and orders of an enemy occupation troupe, his conduct as an officer and a gentleman was above reproach.

Father Resche sighed. It was a simple, sincere gesture. "That is very generous but not necessary, Captain Lindsay. We intend to replace the stone, of course. Anaïse Médard has offered a choice from some of her aunt's jewels."

Oh, Anaïse again! Did it seem like some maudlin offer of expiation, a small thought in an aftermath to make up their destructive, imposing presence here. Ian hoped not. What was it exactly? At most, a prayer at the moment. Perhaps an expiation, yes, in part for the blood he had spilt on the battlefields. Nothing in the world would hardly be enough for that. But, at the very least, this offering could be a prayer that he would cease to see it flow in his nightmares.

"But let me, it would be a privilege, Father Resche. I have thought of it, really promised it as a special offering, if it's acceptable." Ian came up to the chalice and admired its simple design, simple in all but its ornate stem encrusted with five other gems, a ruby, a sapphire, a diamond, an emerald, a topaz and the gaping hole. Ian quickly unscrewed the garnet from his sword hilt with a small knife he had bought from an American Ranger. He placed the garnet in the opening. It was a little loose.

"Well, it might have to be adjusted by a proper jeweler." Ian looked up at Father Resche, disappointed that his gesture was not perfect.

"Jean-Pierre Massal who was married in this chapel September twenty-first is just the man." Father Resche smiled. There was nothing to do but graciously accept the Scot's impetuous generosity. He shrugged, and never mind what propelled it. "Reverend Mother will be pleased." He acquiesced.

"And you, Father?"

"And I, too, my son. I will be in touch with Monsieur Massal today. And perhaps the next time this chalice is lifted at Elevation you will see your gift raised up to the Lord."

"Thank you, Father,"

"It is we who thank you."

What would his father say? Would he approve? Of course, he would. Ian sighed with relief as he left the sacristy. He had intended to do this ever since he had noticed the damaged chalice. He had wanted to do this and now it was done.

Lieutenant McAlister met him at the door of his room.

"Hey! Quite a storm what? Did you hole up with John Knox last night? We saw your bed wasn't slept in. No yelling in the night . . . ."

Ian winced. They were good comrades, all of them, to supervise him through his nightmarish quirks. And if they believed he had stayed the night with John, so be it. He was covered beyond unnecessary explanation. He owed none. Only if General Murray had been looking for him. How had the men on the ships weathered the storm, he wondered?

"What are we about this morning?" He shuffled through a pile of papers on his writing table, still there since yesterday. War was paper work too.

"Pushing back all that snow, making paths so we can get on with our restoration duties. Did you ever see so much snow? Slows you down. . . ." McAlister put a comforting hand on Ian's shoulder. "We're lucky we have inside quarters. Found a few bodies by the ramparts. Stiff as boards."

Ian felt as if a huge stone fell on him. Men had died in the middle of the night and he had been cuddled.

"May they rest in peace," he murmured.

"Aye. Murray's called a meeting for ten."

"It's nearly ten now."

"We'd better hurry. See you."

Ian nodded. "See you." He had one more thing to do before he was in complete shift with the reality of his duties. He took a half rounded pebble from the stone jar by the window. It held a winter plant, a small yew. He had asked permission to bring it into his quarters out of the nuns' community room before it had been taken over for the General's meeting area. It reminded him of the plants in the great hall at home. With a bit of spruce gum, he cemented the pebble where the garnet had been in his sword hilt. That might do for now. Later, he would ask Bonhomme Michel in the convent carpenter shop for a bit of mortar to solidify it.

The heavy snow and how to work in it, and around it, occupied most of the meeting's agenda. The Canadians, well accustomed to heavy snow storms and the clearing of roads and paths, moved about as usual.

A memorial for the frozen dead would be held next morning. It was decided that the bodies had to be left buried in snow against the wall for the time being. Dr. Russell's report counted many men with frost bite.

Murray also had other worries apart from the state of his army surviving the elements. To continue to make an effective defense, he and his officers knew they must do much more than hold Quebec. To ensure the health of his troops he required continued access to the farms, along with the deliverance of goods up Côte de la Montagne from the ships that remained, he needed supplies of fresh provisions from the neighboring villages.

How to tighten control in three strategic areas was discussed. The British must control some areas of the forest to continue cutting large quantities of fire wood. To ensure further safety against marauding Indians and bonded Canadians sent by the French from Fort Jacques Cartier, in hostile scouting parties, it was necessary to increase security to occupy all the approaches and roads to Quebec. It was desirable also to control the south side of the St. Lawrence. Murray had been unable so far to throw a force across the river since Saunders had left with most of the fleet.

It was ordered and scheduled to send Captain Leslie out with a detachment of two hundred men to disarm the inhabitants wherever possible.

Ian observed his General more closely than ever at this assembly. Was he going to try to emulate Wolfe? If so, they would all be in for it.

Ian and his officers, all regiments left to guard the colony, knew that Murray was a tried soldier who had seen service in Europe, in the West Indies, and with distinction in the previous year at Louisbourg. Ian thought that he must be about forty now. He was ardent, high-spirited and fearless. He knew the art of war. He possessed a fine courtesy of manner and he extended this to the three Mother Superiors at the convent and the two hospitals. It was rumored that even the French thought well of him.

Murray, now become Governor to defend Quebec, was the fifth and youngest son of a Scottish peer, the fourth Lord Elibank. The first bearer of the title had held to Charles I during the Civil War and the Scottish peerage of Elibank was his reward. The loyalty of the Murrays to the Stuarts in the seventeenth century was continued in the eighteenth. Most of his officers knew him to be an especially zealous man. He had told some of them on occasion that he had served in every degree in the army but that of drummer.

It was not with undue concern that Ian observed and admired his General and now new Governor of Quebec. He had the feeling that by daring service he was going to be keen to emulate Wolfe who had been his junior in years. For all of them, Ian hoped that would not be his worst failing. They also knew him to be impatient of opposition and quick-tempered, but quick also to regret the hasty action or words of a moment of anger. An impulsive generosity was one of his most striking characteristics.

The tuning of violins with the plunking of a harp and voices of the nuns gathering in their newly devised community room rose above the business of the meeting.

"In recap and review, gentlemen," Murray shuffled through his papers as he emphasized the main points.

Outposts had to be maintained to keep the French army beyond the River Jacques Cartier. The less ambitious course continued to be the farthest outpost at Lorette, not on the plateau but in the valley, eight miles to the west. To keep the church fortified and by holding it to cut off the enemy from the most important road to Quebec, the one which led through Charlesbourg. The church at St. Foy, only five miles from Quebec, to be kept fortified. To check field-pieces and entrenchments. To place a force at Cap Rouge. These posts meant the control of the parishes in the immediate neighborhood of Quebec.

"Captain Lindsay, write up an order for the use of spruce beer for every soldier."

"Yes, sir."

"I'm still experimenting with the recipe and accepting all I can get from the farmers. It's rumored Amherst has the great original. Might not be a bad idea to bring his recipe back. I'm considering sending a volunteer excursion to his headquarters at Albany or Lake Champlain. I need to know what he's going to do next about this garrison and what his plans are for spring after the thaw breaks. We're deadlocked here for the winter."

"Aye, Aye," they all intoned, but none ventured to ask when the mission might start out.

"And ginger, we must get all the ginger we can. That's also good for scurvy. We might have to sell it, if it's too scarce."

Again there was a murmur of assent.

Murray concluded the review by especially pointing out that he wished to continue to provide for the administration of justice in these parishes by appointing Canadian magistrates. The officers assented that it was a good idea.

Then they all heard the most beautiful music. The round sounds of the harp, the blending harmonies of harpsichord and violins, the clear, bell-like, trilling voices of the nuns floated throughout the whole convent. A concert was in progress.

Lieutenant Malcolm Fraser leaned toward Ian. "If there is a heaven and angels in it, that must be what they sound like."

"Aye," Ian smiled. Was Marie-Louise singing too?

Murray was also smiling as he stood up at the conference table. "Gentlemen, the meeting is adjourned. Enjoy the music. I see Reverend Mother de Bransac is keeping up the morale of her nuns in spite of our being here. But remember the country is not won yet. All we have at the moment is Quebec and we are not absolutely certain of that. Winter is not our ally."

As Ian walked down the long corridor toward the library, he thought that any court salon in France, in all of Europe for that matter, would be proud to present the music he was hearing.

Before returning to his desk to post and execute the rest of the day's duties, he was allowing himself a few moments to find a book on Marie de l'Incarnation. Sister Honorine was doing duty as librarian. She helped him make a selection. There were only a few French publications. Another sister was working a tapestry on a frame in a corner of the vast room.

"You are not with the concert, Sister?"

"No, Captain. Sister Cécile and I are not musicians. Isn't that beautiful music they are playing?"

"Enchanting, Sister."

"It's fortunate you read French. We have no English work about Marie de l'Incarnation. Perhaps there are none at all. I doubt she is known in England."

"Well, my mother certainly knows of her. We visited your Ursuline houses in Vendôme and Tours during summer holidays."

"Ah, yes, Reverend Mother told us about you and your French mother," she smiled.

So, the nuns had their line of scuttlebutt. He returned her smile.

"Thank you, Sister," he waved the book at her.

On the way out, he stopped and peered at the tapestry that Sister Cécile was working on. She pulled gold threads through burlap and mixed them with woolen strands of many colors, then interwove with pieces of bark. The scene was a Huron village and the little four year old pensioner, Constance, stood beside Sister Cécile as she worked. Timidly, she looked up at Ian with large brown eyes.

"What is this?" Ian admired the tapestry.

"It's little Constance's village." Sister Cécile's artistic fingers fluttered back and forth, punching through the cloth with hook and gold threads.

"And does it look like your village?"

Constance nodded gravely as she caressed a row of brown bark wigwams on the tilted frame.

"She hopes it will be hung in her room."

"And will it?"

"It's for Reverend Mother to decide."

Ian thought Mother de Bransac de la Nativité was certainly keeping all her nuns busy. How did they find the time over and above the heavy laundries for the sick and wounded, the juggling in the cuisine to balance the food to feed all housed in the convent, and the housekeeping. The long corridors were always clean, the bannisters, the floors, the beams, all the woods were polished to a sheen. And they prayed, Ian knew that they prayed for and believed in miracles. His jumbled thoughts were interrupted with a call to Place d'Armes.

Finally late in the day he went back to his headquarters. He glanced out the round window in the hall. Myriad shades of blue had fallen on the snow as the close of a copper sunset lingered on the battered and repaired roof tops.

Now, the nuns were singing Vespers before the evening meal. He hummed the *Tantum Ergo*. At his desk, he felt sad as he wrote the names of the two men who had died in the storm and completed notes for the memorial. Maybe Anaïse was right, she seized every moment. Maybe, it was all they had. Was she the answer to his dilemma? If he applied himself to her good graces he might forget his obsession for Marie-Louise. He doubted it. The unexpected interlude with Anaïse had been physically refreshing. He could still feel the glow. But mentally, he brooded on the tragedies and misfortunes of war. The thought of Marie-Louise usually balanced him. He wondered what was she doing this evening? There were always tasks, never ending. When did they sleep these nuns? The reciting of the hours seemed to be the priority, the *belles heures*, his mother called them.

He touched the names of the two men he had just written down. Ah, they were out of it now. They were at peace. Were they with God? War was hell. Bloody hell.

"Are you out there, God?"

He looked out his window, a few stars appeared in the deep blue over the St. Lawrence.

Chapter Nine

In the process of rehabilitation in the grip of winter, each day encountered new obstacles for both sides in the garrison. A striving for routine sustained them all. The work-worn nuns in the two hospitals and the Ursuline convent relieved each other in round-the-clock schedules. The military drilled and carried out justice on the parade ground, weather permitting. Orders of the Day were issued from Chateau St. Louis and Murray's headquarters. Announcements were posted with directions where to apply for remedies for scurvy and frost-bite. Also lists of scouting parties who were sent out to reconnoiter the countryside outside the wall.

Ian had no doubt that blessed grace reigned in the convent and the chapels of the two hospitals. It was invoked every day in the continuing litanies of the nuns. There were lulls and moments when the good fortune to be alive could be considered, in a colorful sunset or a bowl of good hot soup. But on some days, in the midst of struggling routine, disaster followed disaster.

On the dark night of November 24, a French ship that had been anchored near Sillery tried to slip past the city in hope of gaining sail for France. The whole garrison poured fire and it was driven ashore on the south side of the river. It had come with several other ships on a fine breeze accelerating abreast of Cape Diamond. In the extreme dark, British gunners fired more at random than with accuracy but they grounded it.

The next morning, the French abandoned their ship leaving it stranded on the south shore. They also left a train of loose powder from the amunition room strewn about.

Captain Miller with his lieutenant and about forty men went aboard to inspect the empty ship. He gave orders to strike a light to see the extent of damage. Sparks falling in the loose powder caught immediately and blew up the vessel. Most members of the search party were killed instantly. The survivors were spread out in a deplorable condition.

Immediately after the explosion, a Canadian farmer ventured on board to seek plunder. To his amazement he found the Captain, the lieutenant and two seamen lying on deck in excruciating pain. He ran for help, sounding an alarm in his neighborhood. With the assistance of villagers, he brought the injured to his home where they were cared for with ointments and bear's grease.

In the afternoon, he crossed the river to give his report to Murray.

Murray praised him for his compassionate behavior and gave him twenty dollars and salt provisions. A crew was immediately sent to remove the dead and bring the survivors to the hospital wing of the Ursuline convent.

It was late that night when Ian finished writing the report of this disaster. Early in the evening he had seen Marie-Louise with the supper cart, then again later running to and fro on what errands he did not know. But her face was sad and full of worry. He sighed. He hoped she was asleep now in her cell. He wondered if she sometimes called out, "God, are you out there?" But no, he knew she held all the faith most of them no longer had in those beautiful, work-worn little hands, in her mind and in her heart.

Now, he must prepare a memorial for all of the dead to be held in the morning. These moribund lists were never ending. He sighed wearily.

War was not only hell on the battlefields. It was grim and tragic with stupid accidents. War was cruel, full of greed, starvation, want; it was boring, depriving, demanding, pressing and fraught with constant danger at every turn, even in its lulls. There were strange fellowships that bonded in war-torn situations.

When he worked this late at night, Ian's thoughts went into divided channels. At times, he dozed off over his work.

He no longer screamed in the middle of the night. Well, this night would have no middle for him. He was grateful the imagery of the bloody battlefields of Culloden no longer visited him. Was that the answer to his nightmare dilemma in this garrison, to sleep with a voluptuous woman? Was that the balm, the elixir to peace, while his heart yearned for a nun. A nun whose very innocence was erotic.

As he yawned and made ready for bed, he thought that in the midst of all the black deeds and senseless accidents of war, there was a spirituality that was never failing, that chased despair and he lived with it everyday, right here in this convent. It was the solemn procession of the nuns going to chapel.

In the midst of the tragedies and misfortunes of the garrison, the appearance of little pleasures exchanged from both sides lifted spirits and were balm for their weary hearts.

At the end of November, on St. Andrew's day, all the Highlanders were in good form. It was on that day that Ian learned what had been enclosed in the package he had brought to Reverend Mother from Tante José, a variety of colored embroidery threads.

In recognition of Murray's special protection of all the nuns, they were unsparing of courtesies to him and the Highlanders. Even in their troubled days they had found leisure for fine needlework to present to him and the Highlanders a set of stoles artistically embroidered with the cross of St. Andrew in honor of their Scottish nationality. In a corner of the field of each cross was wrought an emblematic heart expressive of that attachment and affection which every good man naturally bears for his native country.

Murray was extremely pleased. All of the Highlanders were happy to accept this gift of appreciation from the nuns for all the chores rendered. It made the day. A few Highlanders even did a Highland fling in the garden to the delight of the nuns.

There was a special service on the public side of the Ursuline chapel in late afternoon and Malcolm Fraser gave a short biography of St. Andrew. All the officers were in a light mood as they left the service.

"Sister Madeleine!" Ian met Marie-Louise in the hall. She was going toward the kitchen with a huge pitcher. "Did you work on some of those St. Andrew crosses, too? Here, I'll carry that."

She nodded and smiled, letting him take the pitcher.

"You made the day very special for us all. We thank you."

Marie-Louise blushed with pleasure as they entered the kitchen.

"Ah, Sister Madeleine, I need all the plates on that cart, please. *Merci*, Captain Lindsay," Mother Philomène took the pitcher from him.

There was a great steam in the kitchen, all was hustle and bustle. Other nuns in long white aprons were dishing up food. Marie-Louise gave Ian a farewell smile from the plate cart. He bowed and left.

December came in full force of the Canadian winter. No amount of clothing seemed adequate against the chill. Cold and ice grasped the town. Winds swept across glaring snow fields and piercing blasts scorched soldiers' cheeks like firebrands.

The nuns began the observance of Advent. The Christmas music was brought out of the choir's files and hymns were sung daily for the coming of Immanuel. There was a feeling of great expectancy throughout the convent.

On the third of December, Ian composed a special announcement in his Orders of the Day.

". . . As the sentries on their posts, and the soldiers otherwise employed on the duty of the garrison, may, from the severity of the weather at this season of the year, be exposed to frost-bite, Doctor Russell recommends that every person to whom this accident may happen should be particularly careful to avoid going near a fire, and to have the part frost-bitten rubbed with snow by one who has a warm hand, and, as soon as can be, afterwards put into a blanket, or something of that kind, that will restore heat to the part. This order to be read at the head of every company for six days following by an officer."

Some days were calm and serene, like today, with the sun sparkling on the snow, yet the bitterness of the season was relentless.

Ian worried about the men who were clearing the snow that was lodged under the scarp of the town-wall. Several had come back frost-bitten yesterday and some had even swooned away in the excessive cold. They were all completing a chain of block-houses which were to be erected from the Heights of Abraham, extending from Cape Diamond down to the suburbs of St. John.

Word came that Captain Leslie's detachment was detained at Point Levis church to watch the motions of some skulking parties of the enemy in that neighborhood. Three soldiers of the command at St. Foy were surprised and made prisoners by a body of French regulars who came down to reconnoiter that post.

Ian made two other brief notes in his journal. There was the matter of money. Murray had no money to pay the troops because the *Hunter* sloop of war, sent from Halifax with £20,000 on board, had set out too late in the season and had to turn back. Unfortunately, troops' pay was in arrears since October 24, 1759. There would be no issuance of paper currency and it was forbidden to use discredited French paper money with which Canadians were familiar. Murray and officers of the fleet had collected £4,000 before going away, which they lent to the army. Colonel Burton's notes and a loan from the Fraser Highlanders made up the difference.

Then he noted that there was a body of two hundred Indians skulking about the country, between the garrison and the most advanced post at Lorette. Extra precautions must be taken by soldiers who drove sleighs to the woods.

He remembered another note and scribbled new locations needed to be considered for garbage. He wondered where Jean-Paul dumped his cart load of refuse that he took away from the convent. He had noticed him go through St. Louis Gate and out toward the country.

Ian finished his paper work for the day. With another yawn, he thought of home and Christmas. He wrote a short, nostalgic letter to his parents, not knowing when it might be sent.

The light moments of St. Andrew's day passed too quickly. The nuns moved into an atmosphere of penance with the beginning of Advent.

But there was also an air of excitement and expectancy in all their hymns. The choir was preparing a special Christmas concert, the younger nuns were assigned to build a crèche and the art projects commissioned by the Reverend Mother were on-going in the sewing room.

In spite of all the preparations for this new forthcoming event on their calendar, continued extra work in the hospital wing and the persistent masculine traffic in the convent, Marie-Louise felt that the city itself was lonely now. As fatigued as she was when she went to her cell, on some nights she couldn't sleep. She felt the loneliness enter her cell, it mocked the walls with reminiscences of happier times. She crept from her bed, wrapping blankets about her to fend off the cold, and gazed at the city over the ramparts from her window. On moonlit nights she stared at what was etched of the ravage in the streets, on rainy nights, on nights of soft falling snow and on some nights she peered out the window even when the fog swept up the cliff from the St. Lawrence.

Her heart ached for the lost times when the routine was normal. When all they had thought about was their dutiful devotions of the day, the hours, the beautiful serene hours, *les belles heures*, their assigned work and when the Bishop would permit the novices, like herself, to take their vows. God had been at the center of everything. And now, she was appalled to admit it was General Murray who was at the center of everything.

She tried to keep a calm demeanor. She carried her duties out to the letter but inwardly she was worried about her mother, Jean-Paul, her father. . . . But in her secret heart, her most painful preoccupation was Captain Lindsay. Now, if she didn't see him every day, she suffered. And she was becoming attached to the children, the babies of the townspeople, especially Baby Joseph. If she didn't hold him in her arms every day, she missed him. They had been warned and lectured about attachments. What did this mean? She was changing daily. She had lost her girlish laughter. That in itself was not too surprising, so had all her sisters in the monastery and at the two hospitals. But even on good days, bright days when the sun sparkled on the snow, she continued to be moody. She blushed easily, she became flustered for no reason. More than once, she caught the Reverend Mother observing her at prayers. Certainly, she had not lost her fervor, but now she daydreamed. With mystifying awe, she admitted to herself that she spent almost as much time thinking of Captain Ian Bruce Lindsay as she did of God!

One day, after Mass, as she put the chalice away, a sparkle from the encrusted garnet in its stem caught her eye and she whispered, "Ian" as she touched the stone.

When Father Resche came in, she blushed hotly and quickly put the chalice away in the chamois bag.

"This has to stop," she told herself at prayers. She looked up at the sanctuary lamp. At least they still had their chapel even if they had to share it for the Anglican services. They were lucky to be alive. It was Jean-Paul's favorite saying. They had many blessings to be thankful for. But this was no time for her to be mesmerized by a Scot Highlander. One who spoke French and had a French mother in Fyfe. She was already promised and to Christ.

Her mind was also crowded with all the rumors Anaïse Médard brought to them. That the Ursulines at Trois Rivières wore red shoes until others could be procured and that they played whist all night.

"*C'est pas vrai!*" She whispered to herself. Incredible. What was their world coming to? She could well ask. Her thoughts always made full circle and came back to Ian. "*La Tête Rouge*", Mother Philomène had baptized him. Marie-Louise wondered about his home in Fyfe. Scotland was so far away. His mother's garden, what was it like? All these thoughts crept into her meditations.

"This has to stop." Or she would have to try and explain it to their convent confessor. But no, she would pray more fervently, work harder if that was possible.

She would send a note to Jean-Paul. When was his next visit to town? Maybe there was a side of meat hanging in their barn that could be spared to Mother Philomène's kitchen. Even when the fare was meager, the nuns observed some days of fast during Advent. On these days, Marie-Louise was hungry. She envisioned *tourtières* for Christmas. Maybe, Noël and Two Moose would go hunting again and bring something in? Please God.

Mother Marie-Anne Migeon de Bransac of the Nativity left the chapel as her nuns were finishing the closing litanies. She went straight to her study where her work table was piled high with account books, brochures and correspondence. This was the time of late afternoon when she worked best. Her quiet hour, *l'heure bleu,* she called it when the twilight was soft.

　　After the ravages of storms, on calm days, early winter twilight often inundated the whole city in a wash of slate blues after fiery orange sunsets. From the few houses still left standing intact amidst ruined darkened shells, candlelight glowed from their windows. Outside, the street lanterns cast golden patterns on fluffed up hills of powdery snow on each side of the narrow streets. Mother Migeon opened the latch of a leaded window just a crack and breathed the sharp air. But it was a mild cold tonight. She sat down, flipping her veil over her shoulders. Deep in thought, she propped her left elbow on the writing table and cupped her chin in a firm hand. She tapped her foot. Her feet were not cold tonight, they were warmly encased in woolen stockings and tightly bound in worn-out boots. For the stockings she blessed Mother Philomène and Mother Philippe. They would all be needing shoes soon. And where would they get material for new habits now that they were cut off from France? Mother Philomène and her delegated novices were knitting as fast as they could so that all of the nuns would continue to be warmly hosed. Over and above her head duties in the kitchen, Mother Philomène was also directing her delegation to knit underwear for the Scot Highlanders. She confided to Mother Migeon that they must be sliding down Côte de la Montagne on their bare behinds if they had not proper *culottes* under those plaid skirts. Mother Philomène could do anything. Before entering the convent, the eldest of their large family, she had helped her mother raise thirteen brothers and sisters.

　　Mother Migeon shook her head. Her main concern were her nuns, and now, even more so in the immediacy of daily war-time living with all this masculinity strutting about in her convent. All forty-five of them. But no, she sadly reminded herself. They had lost two nuns on September fourteenth, dear Mother Charlotte de Muy of St. Helene and Mary-Dorothy Jeryan of St. Joseph. And they were not even buried in their own grounds, but in the garden of General Hospital. And General Montcalm was buried here in their own chapel and not in the mausoleum of his beloved Candiac across the sea. These facts were the dictates of war.

"May they all rest in peace." She made the sign of the cross. So she had thirty nuns and thirteen lay sisters. Who knew when, and if ever, the novices could make their first vows. Monseigneur Pontbriand's health certainly was not improving and he had retired to Montreal.

Her gaze swept the mighty St. Lawrence dotted with the few remaining British ships anchored by Lower Town. Their lighted lanterns swayed and blinked in the descending darkness. The window shook a little, she heard the flip of the British standard in the breeze high above Chateau St. Louis. The red cross of St. George flew over Quebec City now. The *fleur-de-lis* on white silk was gone. Was it gone forever? Where was Levis, de Ramezay, Bourlamaque and all the other defeated French officers? Were they still thirty miles away planning yet another attack to recoup the walled city by spring, or had they all retreated to Montreal for the winter balls, licking their wounds, their heartbreaking shame and their lost pride? If there hadn't been so much rivalry between Governor Vaudreuil and General Montcalm. Would it have been any different? The French and Canadian leaders could only do their best in a war of snarled communications. And they had lost to greed and jealousy among themselves.

Mother Migeon sighed and closed the window. She sniffed. Well, they would have a taste of meat tonight. All of them, not much but Mother Philomène knew how to stretch and thicken whatever was at hand. Noël had brought in part of a moose from his village at Lorette. There was nothing left at the convent farms and stores in Charlesvoix, all had been pillaged and ravaged by both the French and English armies. Thank God for Jean-Paul, he had brought enough turnips in from Beauport to feed them part of the winter. This hardy vegetable would help garnish what the hunt and ice-hole fishing yielded.

Tonight, the soup would be full of nourishing red onions that had been found and gathered from bins of all the bombed-out cellars. It would be generously loaded with chunks of savory meat. It would warm the stomachs, hearts, and spirits of all who tasted this *potage*. It would help revitalize the sick and wounded.

Some supplies from the ships now came quite steadily into the convent and hospital kitchens. What was left of the Jesuit College continued to be the Commissary. The generosity of the British victors was two-pronged. To supply and feed the caretakers was just good sense and it was essential to put their soldiers back on their feet as quickly as possible. Conquest had many responsibilities and Mother Migeon had to admit General Murray was doing what he could for all of them. She had a conference with him once a week. They checked lists on the progress of priority repairs needed in the two hospitals, their convent and chapel.

Everyday, Mother Migeon corresponded with the other two Superiors in Quebec City, Mother Ste-Hélène at Hôtel Dieu and Mother de l'Enfant Jésus at General Hospital, also the Superior at Trois Rivières, Mother des Anges and Monseigneur Pontbriand in Montreal, these two by Indian runners. In ordinary times, this was not usually done when they observed the strict rules of their cloister. Except for conducting the business of the convent, there had been designated days for general letter writing. But now, it was a necessary line of communications for survival.

In the Ursuline chapel here, they were all keeping the faith in their own way. Anglicans took the space for their services twice a week. The townspeople housed in the convent followed their parochial worship on the public side of the chapel. The nuns continued their prayers and rituals on the other side of the grill. They also had a private chapel on the third floor where the last prayers of the evening were said. Would the *basilique* ever be restored?

Mother Migeon sighed again. At 74, she thanked God for her good health. She was still bright and energetic, she oversaw her establishment efficiently. Her handwriting was still correct and executed with a flourish. She worked untiringly for her nuns and she was well loved.

She had been asked to serve another term as Superior and she surmised it was because she had such good entente with General Murray.

There were noises beneath her window. What was going on in the garden at this hour of evening? Someone hauling wood for the officers quarters?

Mother Migeon went back to the window and opened it softly. She held her breath. She waited. There were muffled voices. Was that Sister Madeleine's voice? Marie-Louise? Who was she with? It was time to be in.

She had been concerned about her and more than usual lately. She had observed her chatting with Captain Lindsay, not only in the garden but in the hospital corridors quite often. What kind of friendship was developing between these two? Marie-Louise had nursed him through his injuries but he had long since returned to duty.

Should she talk with her? Marie-Louise was one of her younger nuns devoted and caring in all her duties but very worried and obsessed about her mother. Mother Migeon knew that Marie-Louise felt that all the prayers said for her mother, slowly dying in Beauport, were not enough.

Ah, but we might all still be killed, and very quickly, in this war drama, she reasoned. She turned from the window. There must be something light and entertaining tonight after supper in the community hall. Later she could resume her worries about Marie-Louise and what she might say to her. She thought of her escapade to be at her mother's side on September fourteenth. A very serious and dangerous infraction. As her Superior, had she let her off too easily? No, there had been no time or circumstance to do anything else when all bout them was exploding. Now with some restoration to routine, such as it was, yet was that poor, dear girl falling for that handsome Scot, *la Tête Rouge?*

Mother Migeon thought of all these things as she put a paper weight on her correspondence and left her study. She would ask Father Resche to expose the Blessed Sacrament. They would sing the *Tantum Ergo* loud and clear. They needed something to hang on to. They were ever grateful for the food gifts from the British commissary, they gracefully accepted every offer that came to Mother Philomène's kitchen door. But along with that, they still needed something special. They needed new inspirations, new hope to get them through the winter.

Early Christmas Eve, one of General Murray's Lieutenants came to Mother Migeon's study with a note. The General wanted to see her for a few moments.

She granted this request with a fixed time. It would be after the last detail was attended to in the chapel for the Midnight Mass.

Two subalterns accompanied Murray with a wooden locker. He was in full dress uniform. Mother Migeon knew there was a lot of celebrating tonight, on the ships as well as in the officers' quarters in the billeted wing of her own convent and throughout the city.

"What is this?" She folded and hid her hands within her huge sleeves.

"With your permission, Mother Migeon, a special offering of sherry. I learned from Mother Philomène that moose pie, she called it something I am unable to pronounce, is on the menu for your Christmas dinner tomorrow. This is an accompaniment for everyone housed in the convent."

"*Tourtière,* General, it's a meat pie. That's what Mother Philomène is baking. She has very deft fingers with spices, she sprinkles a little of this and that and something wonderful comes out."

"I can smell it. It must be delicious, this sherry will go well with it." He opened the locker and displayed the crockery bottles expansively.

Mother Migeon bowed graciously. She knew she couldn't refuse him his grand gesture. "We are grateful for your offering, General."

They both knew she had found the soft spot in his heart. He couldn't wish her a happy Christmas, nor could she, they couldn't exchange these jovial wishes. It certainly was not a happy Christmas. His army had invaded her city, her convent. But they could invoke the peace of Christmas.

General Murray had reached that moment of Christmas that comes to all mankind. It was that special moment he had to share with this formidable woman. And there was a style, not a submission, that she had. All the nuns had it. An indefinable air that even the angels in heaven, if there were such, could not match. What was it? This mysterious attribute of serenity that all nuns seemed to possess. Mother Migeon, this Mother Superior that he was working with, was never overly gracious or condescending yet her manner placed him, without doubt, of just where he stood. He could not cross this line. But he was a General, he reminded himself.

With a little smile, Mother Migeon accepted his moment of Christmas that he wanted to share with her, for weren't they going to rebuild the convent together? And at some moment on this magic night, Christmas came to every man, woman and child. It came and touched all hearts.

After the bowing and the closing amenities, Murray and his officers took leave of her. They went off to celebrate. The Anglicans would have their service in the convent chapel tomorrow.

As she glided down the hall to gather her nuns for the great feast of Christ, Mother Migeon thought, yes, she would allow the English sherry at Christmas dinner. Why not? They needed a little sparkle in their tired, cold hearts. The ornaments in the pine boughs that her youngest nuns had fashioned with beads and bark would scintillate in the community hall at dinner time.

But tonight, Midnight Mass would be the highest moment for them all. They would receive the Christ child in their hearts. They would all sing, "*Minuit Chrétien, c'est l'heure solonelle. . . .*" All over the world, it was the moment to forgive and be forgiven.

Early Christmas morning Marie-Louise prepared the chapel for the children's Mass. The few older children housed in the convent with their families had attended the Midnight Mass, the Mass of the Dawn and Mass of the Day following. Now, there would be a Low Mass at nine o'clock for all the younger children including the Hurons who usually came in from their village to visit the Ursulines on Christmas day.

Marie-Louise yawned sleepily as she smoothed the ceremonial altar cloth. The odor of incense still hung in the air. The English service would probably be at eleven o'clock. At three o'clock, Mother Migeon would take the Huron children to Vespers then there would be a light repast for all in the community room. That was the schedule.

As she genuflected at the main altar, she wondered how the Hurons celebrated Christmas in their village. From the polished floor, she picked up a stiff white paper box. She had sewed it together on all sides with thin gold thread entwined with red and green woolen strings. It was filled with maple sugar balls. All the nuns who had kitchen duty the past week had helped Mother Philomène make hundreds of the spiced sugar maple balls for the children. There was always maple sugar and syrup in the pantry, even when they were all starving for regular fare.

"*Baume du Canada*" Montcalm had called it when he had sent some home to Candiac.

In the hall, on the way to the townspeople's quarters, she met Ian.

"I especially wanted to greet you today, Sister Madeleine."

She smiled. "Yes, it's Christ's birthday. How do you keep Christmas at home, in Scotland?"

"We have a small chapel in our home, so we have Midnight Mass for my mother's sake. She usually invites a priest from France for the holidays. People from the surrounding countryside join us for dinner on Christmas day then we go riding with the dogs," he reminisced. He felt a surge of homesickness. Then he looked curiously at the festive paper box she was holding. "What do you have there?"

"Bon-bons, maple sugar balls for the children. Have one."

He hesitated. "Well, maybe one. I could hardly deprive the children of their treats."

"Have two, or more. Mother Philomène made a huge crock full. And even extras for St. Nicholas," she winked. She felt light and at ease with him this morning. She thought of other Christmas mornings, at home in Beauport with Jean-Paul.

Ian thought the wink charming and he envisioned her without her head coif as he gingerly scooped two of the sugary delicacies into his hand.

"The choir at Midnight Mass is the most beautiful I ever heard. You all sing like angels."

"I didn't see you."

"You were too busy," he smiled.

"Yes." She lowered her eyes.

"Sister Madeleine, Sister Madeleine, you're wanted at the parlor." The portress's voice was loud and clear.

"I must go." Marie-Louise fluttered away down the glistening parquet floor.

Ian stood looking after her with the gift of the sugar bon-bons moistening in his hand. Then he hurried to his headquarters and deposited them in his pewter rum cup. When would he eat them? He would save them forever. He smiled. There would be posted orders in the Place d'Armes today like on any other day. He must get to it. The Anglican service would be at eleven. He wondered where Captain Leslie's scouting party was at the moment, it was long overdue.

There would be extra rations of rum for everyone today. The fragrance of baking *tourtières* permeated the whole convent. Ian hoped the officers would be offered some. His mouth watered. He thought of his family in far-off Scotland as he wrote up the Orders of the Day.

Christmas day in the war-torn city passed rather well, Marie-Louise thought as she helped Mother Philomène put away dinner plates in the armoire. The kitchen windows were steamed with vapors rising from hot water in the copper tubs.

The aroma of the spiced *tourtières* still hung in the huge kitchen and down the halls. The accompaniment of General Murray's sherry gift had put them all in a light mood. "But please God," Marie-Louise whispered. "It's our first and last Christmas in war time." She was exhausted and stifled a yawn.

Winter had come to stay and held the city in its grip. The snow remained piled up to the roof tops. In spite of bitter cold, the sun was bright and its warmth at this time of late afternoon made some icicles drip.

When would they all return to normal routine? Marie-Louise shook her head pensively. There was no answer to that. There were other young novices like herself who had not yet taken vows. Now that their world had been turned upside down, the city bombed, their convent occupied, exactly when would that be? Not even the Reverend Mother herself knew. Their ailing Bishop was in Montreal for the remainder of the winter.

No one had gone hungry today. Thanks to Mother Philomène and her staff, they had worked long hours to produce the welcome abundance of meat pies. Everyone had been fed more than amply, the sick in the wards, the townspeople occupying the basement and gift pies had even been offered to the Highlanders.

Marie-Louise caught her second breath, she felt light as she prepared to go to evening prayers. Was it because she had seen Captain Lindsay, Ian, that morning? Long enough to offer him a few sugar balls. Where was he now? Celebrating on one of the ships? She blushed. He occupied her thoughts constantly. Was God going to strike her down dead if she continued to think of him? But no, of course not, she reassured herself. Nevertheless, he awakened emotions she didn't know about, didn't know she had inside her. Now, all these emotions were beginning to come out. They rushed alongside of her prayers, her vigils, her meditations. Was it noticeable? How was she to deal with this? The Reverend Mother must not be aware of this change in her. But there was hardly anything Mother Migeon de Bransac was not aware of. *Voyons donc!* Right now, the Reverend Mother's main concern was their lack of shoes and they were cut off from France for reorders.

At the close of evening prayers, Marie-Louise bowed her head in her choir stall. She asked God's blessing on all of them, on Quebec and the continued restoration of the city. After her meditations, she would go and visit little Joseph. That too would be part of her Christmas. She was becoming so attached to that little baby. An assault of homesickness swept over her. She thought of her mother, Jean-Paul, the whole family. What were they doing today at the Boisvert farm house in Beauport? *C'est Noël!*

The peace of Christmas day was broken when Captain Leslie's contingent finally returned. They stumbled into the convent foyer with the help of their fellow officers. They were exhausted and frost-bitten and were brought to the hospital ward. The nuns in charge bustled about and attended them immediately with every needed care.

Chapter Ten

The week between Christmas and New Year's day was full of activity, in the convent. Huron children came from Lorette and joined the children living in the townspeople's wing. The military clattered about as usual down the halls coming and going from their headquarters to the Place d'Armes. A break from serious committee meetings lent a holiday atmosphere. The children's voices heard throughout the convent corridors made every one smile. There were bursts of laughter, scales of music, giggles, whoops and hollers. They ran and glided on the polished floors between errands. Some of the Highlanders made a point to stop and talk with them.

In the downstairs work room, the older children's project was the making of small boxes with heavy colored paper. They sewed them together with gold thread. In the kitchen Mother Philomène was making large platters of maple *sucre à la crème* with her assistant cooks. Also, gifts came to the convent kitchen from those that still had something to offer. Yesterday, it was a side of pork and cream from a farm near Chute Ste-Anne that had been left unravaged and still operated. As a result, dozens of pork *tourtières* were baking for New Year's day visits. They were the traditional pies, more so than the moose *tourtières* that had been served on Christmas day.

"*Mon Dieu*, we're thankful for everything." Mother Philomène sighed with pleasure, having all the children about reminded her of happier times when classes were held. It was at this time of the year that she took out from her treasured armoire the last of the sugared lemon peel and the candied cherries. Under her direction, the children filled the gift boxes with an even, sufficient distribution of one each of these delicacies along with square pieces of the maple fudge.

After the midday soup and a visit to chapel, there was a molasses taffy pull out in the snow. "*De la tire, de la tire*," they all yelled happily as they pulled at luke-warm strands of taffy, threw them on the snow, cut them up in Mother Philomène's kitchen, then ate pieces of the delicious hardened candy. By late afternoon the Huron children left with calls of "*A demain*" and a quiet returned in the halls before the Angelus bell.

Ian thought the children's visit a happy intrusion. He was restless. As he was getting ready for mess, he contemplated the possible expedition that Murray was planning with some of the American Colonials they had in the regiment. It had been discussed among the officers. The Colonial Rangers knew the territory, they were cunning about slipping through the French lines to get into New England, then Albany. There were ways and routes that could be taken successfully even in winter. These rangers were like *coureurs de bois,* they knew how to travel the forest trails on snow-shoes and were clever in trading for canoes with the Indians who lived between questionable French and English territories.

There were marked depots where canoes could be picked up to use when rivers and lakes were navigable and where they could be left after use.

Since no rangers or *couriers* had been sent to Quebec from Amherst lately, Murray was anxious about getting news to the Commander-in-Chief of the North American campaign as to the state of the garrison at Quebec and what was in the works for the Commander's spring offensive. What was the coordinated plan before Levis' army returned pounding at the gate? Plus, if the mission was to be made at all, among other things, the original spruce beer recipe was needed. Amherst was noted for the original. Who had passed it on to him, Ian wondered. Why wasn't Murray satisfied with the one they were using now in Quebec. True, they were dealing with various local versions of it, some successful, some not.

Ian toyed with the idea of going. Why? To put distance between his obsession for Marie-Louise. And what kind of noble gesture was that supposed to be? How could he possibly do it when he revelled in seeing her each day. On the days that he missed, he contrived and schemed and was in a restless agony till the next time. Why? In good sense, this could go nowhere. Did he think he could blot her out by going off into the wilderness to meet every danger, even death? Hardly. At the moment, he felt she would be lodged in his heart for all time. So what *grande folie* was he contemplating here?

The hall clock chimed four. Too early for mess. He rose from his desk and decided to go to John Knox's stable apartment for tea and some of his Jamaica rum. He wrapped his tartan blanket about his shoulders then threw the French community cloak over this for good measure and let himself out. The air was crisp and the sunset magnificent. Down the street, he saw Jean-Paul in his horse-drawn *traineau* gliding on the hard packed snow. They waved to each other and went their separate ways.

Anaïse hailed Jean-Paul from her doorstep, clutching a shawl around her shoulders.

"Come in a moment, Jean-Paul, warm your fingers, have a cup of *chocolat*. I want to talk with you."

Jean-Paul jumped off his sleigh seat and landed on hard snow. The lingering sunset tinted the snow-clad streets and the stone houses that were still intact with their slate roofs in shades of pale rose and mauve. He tied old Fabien to an iron equestrian post in front of what was left of the Médard residence, then stomped up to the front door.

"You have *chocolat*?" Their breaths shot curly white plumes on the cold air.

"Come in, come in. I have lots of things from Couture's shop. That's what I want to talk about. Come."

"I hope you don't have rum, Anaïse. I would not want to see you stripped to the waist and flogged in the Place d'Armes by these so called authorities for selling it to their soldiers." He stamped his feet to shake off the snow. They went in through the double doors. Anaïse raised her hands.

"I have already been warned by Lieutenant John Knox and Captain Ian Lindsay. Spare me."

"*Bonjour*, Jean-Paul," Tante José called out. She sat by the fire in her *tonneau* chair.

Jean-Paul blinked, entering from the last glow of sunset, it seemed dark in the salon. *"Bonjour, Madame Médard."* He turned to Anaïse and shook his head in wonder. "You have *chocolat.*" He wet his lips in anticipation.

"Like I said, I have lots of things." She dropped her shawl on a blue satin Louis XIV chair and went to a side shelf jutting out from the stone fireplace. She lifted a large porcelain pot, poured a steaming cup of thick chocolate and offered it to Jean-Paul.

"And you have lots of things too, in Beauport." She looked at him meaningfully.

Jean-Paul sat by the fire to enjoy his hot drink. He relaxed. Every time he came he marveled that Anaïse had made this part of the house livable for herself and her old aunt who still refused to leave the city. The bombed off section was still in chaos and no one knew when it would ever be repaired.

"We are going into trade," she added.

"What?" He burnt his tongue but the rich liquid chocolate made his stomach glow. The delicate flowered china cup warmed his hands.

"You already are a merchant. Lieutenant Knox and Captain Lindsay eat your apples. . . ."

"Oh, that," he smiled.

"Yes, that's a beginning, Jean-Paul. We can keep our integrity, remain Canadians and still be merchants." She nodded with affirmation. "The British have things we need, we have things they need to survive, to live through this winter."

"This winter, this winter? All winters, *quel pays d'hivers,*" Tante José muttered. "I should have gone back to France with that ship load of so called nobility. . . ." She stared into the fire.

"Ah, but you had your chance, *chère Tante,*" Anaïse pointed a finger at her reproachfully. She poured another round of hot chocolate. "*Voyons,* you said nothing would budge you from this house."

"*Mais oui, mais oui,*" she nodded, the lace ruffle on her cap bobbed up and down. "It must be my age they're respecting, *ces Anglais,* by humoring me and letting me stay here in my own house."

"Yes, and we'd better not shake that. Don't rock the boat, *ma Tante.*"

"So," Jean-Paul set his cup down on a small gilt table. It had heavy legs that ended in lion's paws on the Chinese carpet. Here were a few treasures that hadn't been swept out of their hands, he thought. "We are going into trade and you need my help?"

"Yes, and you have already started as I pointed out. To the hospitals and the convent we give but to the rest we sell for the highest price we can get."

"What kind of money?"

"Ah, you're a sharp young man, Jean-Paul. We'll take all kinds, French while it lasts, English. . . . General Murray is going to have to come up with a system of new money very soon."

"But Levis," Jean-Paul interrupted, "Levis will come back in the spring and we won't need English money."

"Even so. Come with me into the foyer, I want to show you something."

"Levis! Where is Levis now?" Tante José called out.

"Fort Jacques Cartier or in Montreal, no doubt, preparing the next offensive. I hope you know that. Come, Jean-Paul."

Jean-Paul bowed in front of Madame Médard, his woolen *toque* in hand.

"*Tu es toujours un beau et grand garcon, Jean-Paul.*"

He bowed again and smiled politely. Elderly ladies embarrassed him. Well, they had to say something with their well-meaning compliments. Was he really a handsome and tall boy? He shrugged his shoulders. He followed Anaïse through a small door that had been hidden by a Gobelin tapestry. It blended into the thick stone wall that had escaped bombardment. He gasped with awe as Anaïse lit a candle. All around him was a well-packed store-room. He whistled softly.

"Did you have a devil's pact with Bigot? Did he leave you half his warehouse, that cheat?"

"Hush, *tais-toi,*" Anaïse put a finger to her sensuous lips. "Most of the merchandise I came by honestly. I connived a bit too . . . "

Jean-Paul nodded. She knew how to do that. He also knew how generous she was to the convent and the two hospitals. But who had she really negotiated with, what crafty French politicians had she cornered before they were returned to France as prisoners of war by the British?

"So, I'm going to re-open Couture's bake shop with a few changes after I wangle permission from General Murray. But I won't just be adding to the baked goods a few ribbons and *friandises.*"

Jean-Paul nodded again. "But we must be careful, Anaïse." He said it like a sage. Already he was into the proposed venture. Was it a serious commitment? What was he saying? What would his father say? His Uncle Guillaume? And first of all, 'Rie-Ouise?

And where was his guardian angel? They would chastise Anaïse. They would eat her alive and say she was luring young boys to her already questionable salon, never mind good honest trade.

"New England merchants will be coming up here," she predicted. "Let's do it for Quebec. For ourselves. We must keep Quebec alive, Jean-Paul. Not let them destroy the colony."

"How are you going to keep this *cachet* secret. If found, it will all be confiscated in a moment or taken away."

"But it's mine! *Doucement.* We'll be quiet. Besides, your sister and all the other Ursulines will pray for us."

Jean-Paul smiled and shook his curly head again. Anaïse was incorrigible.

"And the Augustinians and the Hospitalières and pray to God we don't end upon the scaffold in the Place d'Armes." Why, he thought, she was acting more his age than he. It was daring. Then he said, "Anaïse, we need more than prayers. *Merci pour le chocolat.*"

"For Quebec, Jean-Paul."

"For Quebec." He pulled on his *toque* about his ears. "*Bonjour, Madame Médard,*" he called out.

"Oh, for a boy you are so practical," Anaïse shoved him out playfully.

Outside Jean-Paul untied Fabien. The old horse had been patiently kicking at the hard-packed snow, his nostrils steaming on the sharp air. Jean-Paul rearranged the old blanket he had thrown over him and climbed up into the sleigh seat. With harness bells jingling, the sleigh slid smoothly down the street toward the Ursuline Convent. He felt he had become part of some counter espionage without even trying. She was something else, that Anaïse. His mother often said that. He threw his head back. He must tell no one; they would be very careful as far as the contraband was concerned. With Anaïse's facade shop a lot could be traded, bought and sold.

But now, as the sleigh sped down the street, his thoughts turned to Rie-Ouise and Mother Philomène and how delighted they would be when he arrived at the convent kitchen with the gifts of a goose and a capon. They were well wrapped in canvas, under boards in the back of the sleigh.

The whole city was awash in the blues of twilight. A few stars came out and the soldiers on duty were lighting the street lamps as Jean-Paul circled his sleigh into the back yard of the convent. "Whoa, Fabien!"

The kitchen door swung open throwing a golden light on the blue tinted snow. It was Mother Philomène in her long white apron.

"*Bonsoir, Jean-Paul.* You're just in time for hot soup. Hurry in and warm up."

At John Knox's *hangar*, Ian sipped hot tea with a shot of rum and warmed his hands in front of the small stove that kept the make-shift stable apartment cozy.

"Are you out of your mind, man? You don't have to go that far to get killed. You can accomplish that right here in Quebec, in the flash of a moment. Out cutting wood, you could get scalped on the trail or you could slip on the ice and splash your brains out."

"I know, I know. . . ."

"Let Amherst send his *couriers* to us and tell us what he's up to, what he wants done. It's all we can do to hold this place together for the next move." Knox shook his head as he observed his friend.

"Aye," Ian was pensive as he twirled his tin cup.

"You're restless, frustrated, vexed, stomped. Well, aren't we all, but some of us go up into the back country and meet a few brown-eyed *Canadiennes.* Also, there are a few French ladies left here still holding their salon on rue du Parloir. They must be bored, all the hand-kissing Frenchmen are gone and the Canadians that might be of any use to them are in Montreal. And you speak the language, *mon vieux. . . .*"

"Aye, John, you paint pretty pictures." He finished his tea.

"I'm trying to save your neck."

"Much obliged, dear friend." Ian winked good-naturedly. "You're certainly *au courant* of the local gossip, that journal of yours is going to be great reading one of these days."

"Aye. It's a *magnum opus*."

"Well, I must go."

"So soon."

"I'll check the scuttlebutt on the expedition, if any, at supper. I have some unfinished paper work this evening. We'll see what the new year brings."

"Aye. Keep the faith."

A few days after New Year, Murray assembled his officers for a private meeting. The agenda centered on the merits of planning a volunteer excursion to New York. Four directives were discussed. They were: to meet with General Amherst for much needed news and instructions for further sustenance of their garrison at Quebec; to inform him what they were doing to ward off the remaining French army now at Fort Jacques Cartier with Levis; to procure Amherst's plans to attack Montreal and where and when regiments from Quebec fitted in; and last, but not least, to also return with the original recipe for spruce beer. It was a preliminary meeting, a sounding as to who might go and what could be put together. Maps of the territory were thoroughly examined before they adjourned.

"I, for one, am not going out on anything that foolhardy," Malcolm Fraser commented.

"Aye, nor I." Lieutenant Hay joined in.

Ian was silent. He had not offered too many opinions throughout the meeting. He was thinking. He went out into the gray day. Dark clouds threatened, fierce winds swept up and down the St. Lawrence with extreme cold and powdery trains of snow curled along the streets of Quebec. He was just outside the convent wall when he saw Anaïse come toward him.

She looked strange in a long worn-out fur cape, moccasins over leggings, a woolen *toque* pulled down over her head, a heavy scarf wound about her throat and up to the bridge of her nose. Only her high cheek bones and flashing eyes were visible.

"Where are you going?" Ian walked up to her in the almost deserted street.

"I'm returning from Lower Town, I was delivering." She pointed to an empty tapestry bag over her arm. "Thank you for the carpenter help."

"How's business?"

"It's a beginning, *ça va*." She had just delivered cognac to one of the taverns.

"Don't be caught with liquor, Anaïse, or you'll be flogged." Ian thought, it might be well and good for whatever trade she conducted with Canadians, but he was concerned if she was selling liquor to British soldiers.

"I thought it was only the sutler women who followed your army. . . ., not Canadian women."

"Don't count on it." Ian stamped his feet on the impacted snow. Already, they were cold.

"Come home with me, *prendre un p'tit coup*, a little drink," she invited.

Ian smiled wanly and shook his head. "Thank you, Anaïse. I'm going to Lower Town myself to deliver messages to the ships."

Anaïse grimaced. "Later then," she insisted. "I have lots of rum well hidden."

He pressed her free mittened hand with beseeching urgency. "For God's sake, Anaïse, don't get caught. You'll be stripped to the waist and flogged and I won't be able to stop it."

"What a fuss about rum, liquor, whatever. It's what will keep the soldiers alive, it's winter."

They both knew that. But there was so much drunkenness of late, that General Murray had just imposed a stricter discipline over the use of spirits among soldiers and officers.

"We'll buy ginger."

"I have a little ginger. Spruce beer you can get from the farmers but it's scarce right now, even at Lorette."

Ian looked at her with tenderness and compassion. She was practical, even to the point of being caught red-handed with precious stores of liquor. He'd have to trust her on that. "Did Cadet leave you one of his warehouses? And where do you keep the stuff?" Now cynicism overtook his compassion.

"That I can not tell you." Anaïse didn't want his compassion. She wanted more than that. She wanted to relive the love-making they had shared that cold, bitter, stormy night. Was it only a few weeks ago? Hubert had receded in her thoughts since then. As a *coureur de bois,* he came and went. No one knew where he was. Now, he was probably with Levis preparing for the spring offensive. Even in ordinary times he was never on the scene when she needed him. She had accepted that, taken it in her stride. But now, she wanted more.

"Be careful," Ian's concern was genuine and caring. He raised her covered hand to his frosted lips. "Come, I'll walk you home."

Ah, it isn't there, she thought. He's not attracted to me. She bit her lip. Well, she'd ignore that. He would need her again. She'd melt that stone. This stoic with the red hair, "*La Tête Rouge.*" He was pining for someone else, that was evident. It was rumored he was smitten with one of the nuns. Was that so incredible? And who was she? Did *la pauvre* even know it?

"Tomorrow," she invited again beguilingly. "Come tomorrow then, there will be a warm fire, rum, soup."

They were now at the Médard house.

"If I can." How could he refuse, yet he knew even such warmth would not assuage his yearnings for the one who was unattainable. "Hurry in before we both freeze on the spot."

She quickly went in through the double doors with the huge brass knobs etched with fleur-de-lis.

Ian hunched into his cloak as he retraced his steps and went down Côte de la Montagne. He was cold. Clothes to keep warm were really a problem now. Most soldiers' uniforms were in disarray. They were wearing whatever they could find as extra covering. Even some of the white coats of dead French officers were in use. Deer skin vests had been found in the wardrobes of demolished houses. They were great buffers against the cold. Ian wore one today. He blessed the nun who had knitted the warm gray scarf that now coiled twice about his neck.

Marie-Louise had observed Anaïse and Ian talking together by the garden wall in mid afternoon. When she saw them walk off together an uncontrollable and new emotion seized her. She thought she also saw a little demon of jealousy laughing at her in the glass of the circular window in the front hall. It was half-way up the stairs, at mid-landing across from the banister railing. It was not only the Reverend Mother's favorite look-out but also that of several other nuns whenever they had a free moment coming and going. Marie-Louise looked again in the shining glass and reddened. Yes, that was definitely a demon laughing at her. She was beside herself.

What scheme, what wiles was Anaïse playing now? Everyone knew Anaïse at the convent. She and her Tante José were great benefactors from way back. The Reverend Mother not only tolerated Anaïse, she loved these two women. She said they all needed each other, more so now than ever. Why was she trying to find fault with Anaïse? It was, no doubt, a friendly encounter. Ian had seemed very courtly, very attentive. And why shouldn't he be.

Marie-Louise didn't walk sedately to the kitchen in her usual manner. She almost ran, seething in her little rage. What was the matter? Calm down, she told herself. She started clattering utensils in a busy frenzy until Mother Philomène came and put an affectionate hand on her arm.

"What are you doing, Sister Madeleine? I really don't need help this afternoon."

Marie-Louise looked up at her. She bit her lip and tried to hold back on-coming tears.

"Sit here, Sister. I will get you a cup of tea, a mixture of new herbs Noël brought us. We need a little *"medecine douce"* ourselves once in a while. We are all so over-wrought we need to take care of our own health too."

Marie-Louise nodded dumbly. A great sigh escaped her.

Mother Philomène put a steaming cup of the medicinal tea in front of her.

Marie-Louise sipped obediently. It soothed her.

"Thank you, Mother Philomène." Her composure was restored.

After Marie-Louise left the kitchen, Mother Philomène shook her head. "That poor child is in love," she murmured to herself. "In love with that *Tête Rouge* and she doesn't even know it yet." Surely, the Reverend Mother was aware of it. Well, she'd keep her counsel for the moment.

"Poor child," she repeated. And her mother hanging by a thread in Beauport. Thank God for Jean-Paul, and Baby Joseph. Even though Marie-Louise was becoming too attached to the baby. Ah, there were just too many attachments flourishing all over in their convent she reasoned as she took down her jar of greasy stock. She would make a thick soup. A thick soup? Well, she might as well throw her heart in it. They were all hungry. And it was bitter cold but in spite of it she opened the window a crack and let a blast of fresh air into the steaming kitchen. Toward Côte St. Geneviève she heard shouts from soldiers changing guard. She breathed the pure air. Her feet hurt. What were they going to do about shoes? The Hurons couldn't supply them with moccasins forever.

All this masculinity stomping around in armors of self-importance. It was too much. How could they survive it? On a calmer day, she would invite Sister Madeleine to knead bread with her. That would be an occasion to have a talk. If and when Jean-Paul could scrounge another sack of flour for them. Bless his heart, he knew how to juggle provisions.

When Ian returned from Lower Town, he found a map on his desk outlining the garrison of Quebec as they held it and the British Colonies to the south. There was a Memo attached from MacKellar. He studied it carefully. It was not an impossible venture at all, he thought. Well, it looked plausible on parched paper. He pushed the map aside and thought of Marie-Louise. He had not seen her today. If he hurried to the library he might find her there. There was still a little time before the Angelus. At the commode, he splashed water on his face, combed his hair and tied it neatly at the back.

Ah, there she was quietly reading in a corner by the window where he usually stopped and exchanged a few words with her.

They greeted each other and talked softly so as not to disturb two other nuns who were working on illuminations.

"Here is part of a letter Marie de l'Incarnation wrote to an Ursuline in Paris." Marie-Louise passed the book on a small table for him to read.

Ian smiled and went over it carefully. The date was August 12, 1653.

> *Vous me demandez des graines de*
> *fleurs de ce pays. Nous en faisons venir de*
> *France pour notre jardin, n'y en ayant pas*
> *ici de fort rares ni de fort belles. Tout y est*
> *sauvage, les fleurs aussi bien que les*
> *hommes.*

"They cultivated a garden of flowers then, even as you do," Ian marveled. "Her answer to the Parisian Ursuline is interesting. That they sent to France for seeds having no rare or beautiful flowers here then. That all was primitive, and uncultivated, flowers as well as men."

"And the winters were probably even more severe than now."

"Oh, I doubt it. This is the most rugged winter I ever experienced and we have some pretty cold ones in Scotland. My mother is always happy to see the start of spring."

"And she has a garden?"

"Oh yes, and spends many hours in it."

Marie-Louise walked over to the window and he followed her.

"See there, in that corner, we have *roses des Indes*."

He leaned with her over the window sill and looked down in the snow covered garden. It was delicious to be this close to her and he almost put his hand over hers. Instead, he withdrew.

"What are your favorite flowers, Sister."

"Oh, I love them all, all that we can grow here. But when I was a child, I used to go to Orleans in the summer and run in fields of butter-cups and daisies, they were wild and we'd bring home big bunches of them, Jean-Paul, Geneviève that is Sister. . . ."

"How delightful." They were back at the table now and he helped her stack the few books that were strewn about. Just then the Angelus sounded.

"I must go." She glanced at the two nuns at the other end of the library. They were putting their quills away. In a flutter, part of her veil fell on his arm.

"Perhaps tomorrow," he stammered.

"Here," she offered him the book they had read from. "I hope you enjoy these letters as much as I do."

"I look forward to reading all of them. I already have a good start, Sister Madeleine. Your interpretations help a great deal."

They all left in a processional walk and he was alone in the library. He sat down at the little table and sighed. If only they were different people somewhere else, in another country where he could say to her, "Let's go for a walk by the river." Or if he could come and visit with her a whole evening, to touch and hold hands, embrace. He knew how he felt but he didn't know how she felt.

On some days he felt she reciprocated with a glance or a smile that told him she was as entranced as he was. Or was that just his imagination in his wildest fantasies. He had to do something. But what? There was nothing to do. They were in an impossible situation. There was nothing to do about it and nowhere for them to go. Unless she didn't take any vows. How could he approach her on that? Did he have any right? What was he to do? If only they were in a place where they were two individuals who loved each other, who were the whole of life to each other, who could declare that to each other, where nothing else on earth would matter.

Suppose it were so. But it wasn't. If he declared himself, if she felt the same way and would even consider another state in life, if he asked her hand in marriage, whom did he ask? The Reverend Mother first then her father and what about Jean-Paul? There were other people to consider. Did a novice need a release from the Bishop? He himself would need military permission to marry from Murray.

To declare himself outright might soften his sufferings. "Please, God," he whispered. Or was he to hold his silence and get on with his life and leave her to what she had already chosen. There was nothing much for it and everything against it. "Let it go," he told himself. "Let it go."

When he came back to his room he still radiated with warmth. He felt as if he and Marie-Louise had sat in a garden talking about summer flowers in spite of the winter outside. She herself was like a delicate flower. What were her thoughts, he wondered, when she returned to her cell at night?

He would live in the now. Even if his love could never be accepted, Marie-Louise brought sweetness and light to his life in this winter-set garrison. He would live in the now. That's what the Canadians were doing. Home and Scotland seemed at the ends of the earth. There would be no letters from home until late spring. And no one knew whose ships would appear first on the St. Lawrence, the British or the French.

Chapter Eleven

A few days before the Feast of the Kings, Jean-Paul, ever a magician to provide, found a bag of flour in a burned-out barn up above Chateau-Richer. Mother Philomène was the happy recipient of it. An added portion came from Hubert just recently arrived from Jacques Cartier. He brought it in by dog-sled with a farmer delivering a few supplies to Murray. It was his camouflage.

"We'll bake as many loaves as we can. We may even bake a few *galettes des rois.*" Very pleased, Mother Philomène delegated duties, one batch of loaves would rise over-night. She kept part of the next afternoon open to bake another batch. She would signal out Marie-Louise for a *tête-à-tête.*

Most of the next day, the smell of bread baking rose and floated from the convent kitchen to mesmerize whoever walked the pristine halls. In mid afternoon, Marie-Louise answered Mother Philomène's summons with her mouth watering. She could hardly wait. She helped knead dough into small loaves. Her duties elsewhere all attended to for the day, she welcomed and indulged in this culinary distraction. It would help balance her obsessive thoughts of Ian. She secretly scolded herself, before Ian, it was God who had consumed her thoughts. By now, the whole convent must surmise her secret. Certainly, no longer a secret to the Reverend Mother. Not much could be kept from her. Marie-Louise blushed.

"I was in love with a man once," Mother Philomène confided as they both kneaded on the large oak table dusted with flour.

"You!"

"Yes, me," Mother Philomène smiled blandly. "*Ma très chère Soeur Madeleine. . . .*" She loved the young Boisvert girl and her friend, Geneviève. She remembered the day when these two Beauport girls had entered the novitiate.

"Tell me about it then," Marie-Louise looked at Mother Philomène with new awe. She knew this older, wrinkled nun, in charge of the kitchen had a heart bigger than her huge body. She was especially good with children. She had helped her mother raise thirteen. Nothing phased her, she was known to tackle any task. But now, what was this strange unknown story out of her past? And she was going to tell her about it. Was this to be a lesson in counseling?

Marie-Louise threw her head back bravely. Her veil flew and caught the corner of the pitcher shelf. As she carefully untangled it, she promised herself I'll forget him. Here again was a new, perhaps futile promise.

Sensing her wistful secret thoughts, Mother Philomène offered, "I'm praying for you. . . ."

"Thank you, Mother Philomène."

"Remember spiritual vision, Sister Madeleine."

Marie-Louise nodded. She brightened up. "There'll be smiles at supper tonight with our usual pea soup with not too many bits of salt pork in it but with this good bread. . . ."

"Well, let's keep that smile on your face, dear child. Let's have a hot slice of it ourselves, right now." Mother Philomène pulled out the loaves that were done. She sniffed them euphorically as she gave them a tender pat.

"Do we have some maple butter?"

"I have some in my *cachette*."

"You've been hoarding!" Marie-Louise accused with delight.

"Ah, yes, another of my vices from way back."

"I'll make some tea." Marie-Louise's mouth watered with anticipation. There were plenty of herbs from Lorette, usually shared with the pharmacists at the hospitals. Also, the nuns cultivated a general supply in their own kitchen garden. They carefully blended Huron herbs with their own to brew strong, medicinal and restorative tea as well as other concoctions for their "*medicine douce.*"

Ah, Mother Philomène thought as she broke two generous pieces of hot bread, love. All the fantasies of young love, all that emotion, joy, sadness, doubt, fierce affirmations. It comes and it goes. No one knows where it comes from when it hits or where it goes when it's all over. It picks you up and whirls you around. No one knows where to run to. It made one love-sick. Yes, there was that, too. She remembered. She looked at Marie-Louise. And now, for her to find out that being a nun was no safeguard against it, this human love. She wished she had a cure for this young novice besides prayer, hot bread and maple butter. Maybe, she could even invoke the shaman of Lorette village.

Marie-Louise rummaged further in Mother Philomène's armoire compartments. There was a cupboard within a cupboard lined with stone. She ignored a porcelain container and brought a medium size crockery jar back to the table.

"So tell me, what happened? This man you were in love with?"

"*Mon histoire,*" Mother Philomène winked. Her wrinkled face broke into a broad smile. "About half of the convent knows but not you young nuns."

"I feel privileged," Marie-Louise poured hot water into the tea pot to brew the tea and set cups out for their collation.

"Love and justice is working for you. . . ."

"Oh, Mother Philomène, I pray." Her voice quivered. Her hand shook as she poured the steeped tea.

"You can go through these things, your soul and body can be ravaged with indecision, pain, when what is true and enduring seem to leave the surface. All these things penetrate the heart of every person at different times in our lives. But keep spiritual vision, keep your dignity, Sister Madeleine. There are many ways to save one's soul. Love and justice is working for you. Believe it."

Marie-Louise took a sip of tea. It was hot and soothing, the bread was delicious. She felt better but inexplicable aches were still there.

"But this war. . . . All the dead, what good can come of it? There's only Montreal, Fort Jacques Cartier and Levis left. It's unfair. Why did they ever come here?" Marie-Louise was tearful again. She drank more tea pensively but left the rest of the bread untouched on her plate. "And I. . . . , and I. . . . "

"And you love one of them. And you feel guilty. Well don't." Mother Philomène finished her tea and slathered a last bite of bread with maple butter. "I would like to believe that the best spiritual vision we can keep, Sister, is that God never leaves us no matter what seems unfair." Was all this nun's talk realistic to a young girl in love? Mother Philomène rose from the table and went to the oven to pull out the last batch of bread loaves. How was the Reverend Mother weighing this? There were some redeeming factors. Captain Lindsay was a Catholic, he had a French mother and Marie-Louise had not taken any vows. But the Bishop was still writing furious letters from Montreal about all the mixed marriages that had taken place in Quebec since last fall. And now if a nun departed. . . . It was unthinkable!

"*Mon Dieu!*" Mother Philomène felt a blast of heat from the oven as she pulled the rest of the loaves out.

"There is a greater good?" Marie-Louise wanted to know. She cleared the debris of their light repast.

"That's what we have to believe. The colony could have been destroyed."

"Yes, we are alive. We are here to take care of the living and the dead." Marie-Louise also thought of all the mixed marriages, thirteen it was rumored.

"And on most days," Mother Philomène added with understanding. "You are glad that he is here too, this Captain Lindsay, even in these circumstances?"

"Yes." In her secret heart she added, "Oh, yes!" She lowered her eyes. "If you don't need me, I'll go to chapel now." She no longer understood herself.

"It's quiet and comforting there." Mother Philomène nodded as she brushed the excess flour off the table. Dusk was falling over Quebec. Soon the lamps would be lit on the streets. The Repentigny sanctuary lamp was always glowing in the Ursuline chapel. The war had not snuffed it out. All the nuns with kitchen duty would come in a few minutes to help dish out the supper that would feed the sick and convalescing wounded and then their own evening meal.

Mother Philomène tightened the mended apron about her large waist. She thought how badly they needed new materials and they could no longer get them from France. She sighed. And on matters of the heart? What more to tell this poor girl.

"We are not going to resolve an argument of possession that's been going on between France and England since Champlain came to these shores, not today. Great wrongs have been committed on both sides, my father said that often, he was a politician. Wars, Indian raids, treaties not worth their parchment. . . . When you have lived as long as the Reverend Mother and myself. . . ."

"It's difficult for me, for Geneviève, Sister Philippe, all of us novices to accept everything the way you and Reverend Mother do."

Mother Philomène smiled. She recalled Marie-Louise's escapade from the convent the day after the battle of the Plains. Her flight home with her brother to be with their critically ill mother. She was certainly different. It would not be surprising at all if she realized, as Reverend Mother might have already pointed out to her, that her true vocation might be to marry this *Ecossais* and raise a family whether in Quebec or Scotland. Nothing surprised Mother Philomène anymore. But she also knew that if the Reverend Mother was going to lose one of her nuns that she would rather marry her off to a *seigneur* of the countryside.

"There are some good men in the world. Not all sell their country up and down the St. Lawrence. Not all break women's hearts. Not all are governed by greed, thank God."

"War does strange things, people do strange things. Some of us become different people." Marie-Louise caught herself with a little gasp. She, too, recalled her escapade home the day after the battle of the Plains. Yes, we all change, she thought.

"La Friponne, all that was stolen and stored away in the warehouses of Bigot. Anaïse told me and Jean-Paul about that, she knows everything the politicians know. . . and more."

"Ah, yes, she's very clever and she's on our side."

"She's very good to the convent."

Mother Philomène nodded. "She grabbed what she could for all of us. She knew that Madame la Pompadour directed many decisions for the fate of New France, along with Voltaire not entirely to our best advantage."

"There are good women, too." Marie-Louise evaluated. "We all have our roles, our place, our vocations. . . .," her voice faltered, "to help balance good and evil."

"You speak with more wisdom than I sometimes gather in my great age, child. I like to believe that we are here to keep the sanctuary lamp glowing. Our convent is a fortress. I would like to believe it will still be standing with all our traditions when this terrible war is finally over, when you and I are long gone."

"*Ainsi-soit-il.*"

"Unless Levis liberates us, Murray will have to get us some materials." Mother Philomène smoothed her voluminous mended apron. "We will be at the end of everything by next winter. Reverend Mother is very worried about shoes."

"I know. Rumor has it that the nuns at Trois Rivières are wearing red shoes even, perhaps the only ones available on the last shipment. Of course, they were ordered for *les grandes dames de la ville.*"

"Do they really play whist all night? Our sister Ursulines at Trois Rivières?

"That I don't understand. Reverend Mother would not permit that here." Marie-Louise shook her head. "Let's get back to your story, Mother."

"He was from a *seigneurie* near Montmagny. He was busy with the trade routes of that time. All the closest routes, not only by ship up and down the St. Lawrence into Albany but the *coureurs de bois* routes established through forests, by rivers and lakes. He went to Montreal often. These routes established an innuendo entente of necessary commerce. Hard to get articles were exchanged from both sides in this New World trade long ago, long before the Seven Years War started. He went to Montreal once too often. He went to a grand affair there one night and met the belle of the ball."

Marie-Louise gasped. "And. . . ."

"*Coup de foudre* for both of them. I credit him with the bravado to come and tell me immediately."

"What did you do?"

"I ranted, raved, bit my fists, hated. . . . I was a mess, I locked myself up in my room. My parents could do nothing with me. I made myself ill, I nearly died."

Marie-Louise shook her head incredibly. "And your intended?"

"He married the belle of the ball, of course. Then I came back to my senses. My parents went out of their way to invite all the eligible young men of the region. I think it was in spite, in desperation that I permitted one of them to court and become attached to me. In a very short time, we became engaged. Just spite, I think, on the rebound."

"Yes?"

"Well, my dear child, it was never meant to be. We had a fierce fight, we broke up just over where the front door of our new home was going to be installed."

Marie-Louise giggled. "Mother Philomène you're impossible."

"At times, I wonder that the Reverend Mother let me in the door here. But in the end everything worked out. My first intended, with the very fine woman he married, raised a family of girls right here in Quebec City and I taught them some of their culinary classes."

"You did? How could you?"

"Yes, me. By that time their poor father had died. His wife, their mother was very courageous."

"And what did bring you here?"

"A tragedy in our village, an epidemic, a great loss of lives, especially among the children. That showed me how short, how fleeting and fragile life is. I thought a lot about my own mortality. I had calmed down a lot by then."

"That brought you here?"

"Yes, I came to help the nuns at first. I wanted to be of service, to expiate, to regain myself. I've been happy here ever since, these many years. It's my place."

"What a great story!" Marie-Louise exclaimed. "Like a novel."

Mother Philomène nodded as she shook her apron.

"No wonder you are so wise."

"At the very least, wisdom should come with age."

Marie-Louise questioned herself in silence. Would she want to teach Ian's daughters if. . . . If what? A pain stabbed her and she touched her bib. She thought of Madame de la Peltrie, of Marie de l'Incarnation who had left a son in France to come and establish a convent, to educate young girls, to convert the Indians, *les sauvages* as they called them then. Could she leave a son behind to go to the ends of the earth? She thought of little Joseph. What sacrifice! What really was a true vocation? She recalled the Reverend Mother's words, in counseling, during a closed retreat telling them that some of them did not have to become nuns to save their souls. Did they all understand that? What was she to do? She suffered in pained indecision. She was another person since they came. They? The British. The Highlanders. Since she met Ian. He was Ian in her most secret thoughts, no longer Captain Ian Bruce Lindsay. Ian, it was his presence that changed her. And they had come to conquer, to kill and to burn their homes, this enemy. Ian was one of them. That was the most painful injury.

"Oh, God! Are you going to strike me down dead if I love this man, even at a distance?" During sleepless nights, these were her cries from her anguished soul. It was rumored that he cried out in anguish too during the night. He had fought at the end on the Plains and still carried the guilt of killing at Culloden.

It was some weird trick of fate that he had first seen her in her mother's old red dress. That volatile day, that wild *élan* that surpassed all bounds and had brought her to her mother's sick bed in the borrowed clothing of unsuspecting Michel, the convent handy-man.

Only the war that hung over them all since had been excuse enough to permit the Reverend Mother's forgiveness. There had been no time to mete out necessary punishment with severe and enforced discipline. Time was too precious, too many hands had been needed for whatever task of emergency.

"There's something out there in this universe, and here in Canada, in this convent. . . ." Mother Philomène's soothing voice broke into Marie-Louise's thoughts. "Maybe, there's something else for us to do beyond this convent, but I hope not beyond our prayers. No one really wins in a war. We all have to rebuild, not only what is materially destroyed but ourselves as well. Sometimes, I wonder even at my age, dear child. . . ."

"But this vast land, there should be enough for everyone."

"The wars deny this."

"What about love?"

"Ah, love. Love was wanting in the hearts of some of our rulers. Greed consumed them. Montreal is a questionable last chance in my poor nun's opinion."

Marie-Louise folded a rumpled dish towel. The bell rang sharply.

"Reverend Mother is calling all of us to the community room before chapel," Sister Angelique announced as she breezed in on their quiet *tête-à-tête*.

"It's time to dish up supper, it must be a very short meeting." Mother Philomène brushed flour off her nose. They all left the warm kitchen and hurried down the corridor in a flurry of their heavy skirts.

Marie-Louise didn't like their make-shift community room on the fourth floor. She missed her favorite place. Governor Murray and the Fraser Highlanders still occupied their original community room on the first floor. How long would they stay? Yet, they were so helpful with all the chores, and they'd miss the help with food. Was it true they might all be out of the convent by June? She almost stopped her dutiful hurry as she realized how much she'd miss Ian when he would no longer be under their roof.

Down one hallway, a blast of cold air from outside cut across the lingering smell of baking bread. Marie-Louise wondered would she, one day, be like Mother Philomène? Would she work in that same kitchen and confide in a young nun, a novice who had fallen in love. Would she tell her that she too had loved a man. If Ian returned to Scotland and if one of her wildest fantasies didn't occur? A wild fantasy indeed, that she would probably leave the convent to marry him, and that they would live either in Quebec or Scotland as tour of duty dictated. Why, they didn't even know each other.

"*Mon Dieu!*" She wrapped her thoughts in prayers. What was the answer to her dilemma? She didn't know. With all they had gone through since last September anything was possible.

In the midst of all the preparations, meetings and discussions for the expedition to Albany, Ian felt swayed. He reassured himself of the duty and purpose of the expedition. Then, in either a moment of weakness or of strength, he decided to join up and volunteered. It certainly would put distance between himself and Marie-Louise. Not what he really wanted. It was almost in a "what's the use" attitude that he was removing himself from the scene of "*status quo*" with no solution to the mounting, pent-up passion that he couldn't express or put a name to, except that he was in love with her. It had nowhere to go, they had nowhere to go, and he didn't even know how she felt or if he even had a right to know. It was an impossible situation. He couldn't afford to make an outright fool of himself. It would be the least disturbance to everyone around if he made himself scarce and got on with his life. And let Marie-Louise get on with hers. That would be best.

In mid January, some changes evolved. The number of patients decreased in the convent wards. Soldiers returned to duty and some families in the townspeople's wing were leaving to live with relatives in the country. Mother Migeon announced a new division of duties with all due respect to her nuns' few leisure hours dutifully spent on the commissioned arts project. A schedule of classes would be resumed. The Reverend Mother pointed out that since they still had some facilities to teach, a trial program would be put in motion and that schooling for the remaining boys and girls should no longer be neglected. True, it would be different from their normal times when they had taught only girl day students and boarders. But nothing was normal anymore. Marie-Louise and Geneviève were both assigned to teach a class.

Marie-Louise looked forward to it. Both she and Geneviève had been teaching trainees when they first entered the convent. She had missed that work since last September. As she walked up and down the garden in a light rain the next day, she was already planning her class. Yes, it would be different with both boys and girls. She wanted to go over the curriculum with Geneviève but she had the uneasy feeling that Geneviève, of late, was keeping her distance.

Why was Geneviève avoiding her? They hadn't exchanged words except the morning and evening salutations on the way to prayers since the Feast of the Kings. Marie-Louise was puzzled. What was wrong? She knew she had been busy helping the three pharmacists making lists of supplies to be exchanged between the convent and the two hospitals. Geneviève was also busy with the convent gardener and plans to repair the potholed areas.

When one nun had asked, "Do we have a garden this year?"

"Yes, yes!" They had all answered. Surely, now more than ever, for morale. And so the planning of the garden also fell into the arts project. They'd nurture what they had and add new things from the country. One nun had even suggested a few new trees.

The Reverend Mother had emphasized how they must all put forth their best, the extra concerts, the art work, the upkeep of the convent as if Murray and his Highlanders were not living in their house. And so they all were, Marie-Louise thought as she heard the faint strumming of violins from the music room.

A mild day for January. Marie-Louise lifted her face to the light rain, if it was steady for a few days it would wash most of the dirty snow away from the city until the next storm. It would be good to have a class of children again. She must go in. Where was Geneviève? But instead of looking for her childhood friend she had a sudden desire to see Ian. Perhaps he was in the library.

She entered the library shaking the rain off her cape. Ian was not in his usual corner but Geneviève was there cataloguing books. She went directly to her.

"Sister Philippe, Geneviève . . ."

They were the only two there. Outside a soldier lit the street lamp on rue du Parloir and it beamed into part of the library.

Geneviève looked up. Her usual, ready smile was missing.

"Have you had more bad news from home?"

"How can you be so amiable to him all the time, always looking for him. . . .," she hissed.

"For whom?"

"Captain Lindsay, you're always looking for him, here in the library, in the garden. Well, he's not here."

"Geneviève!" Marie-Louise turned red. Hurt to the quick, she backed off as if a piece of Côte de la Montagne had slammed down between them.

"They came here and burnt most of our homes, our barns, maybe not your parents', they took part of our cattle. They're living in our convent and you make pleasanteries with one of them as if he were courting you. We may be at their mercy but we only need to be civil. Why don't you remember who you are?" Geneviève sat down, her outburst left her weak. She gripped the books she was working with.

"Geneviève!" Marie-Louise trembled like a leaf. She was in shock. She, too, sat down at the library table and faced her malcontent colleague. Never had Geneviève ever raised her voice to her. Was her budding friendship with Ian that apparent? But, of course, it was there for everyone to see. She steeled herself, she must not lose composure now. Two other nuns were coming in. They were talking about the new music for Sunday's concert.

"Good evening, Sisters."

Marie-Louise and Geneviève both nodded.

Still shook and ashamed, Marie-Louise rose quickly. "Geneviève, we'll speak later," she said weakly. She left the library with a semblance of dignity. When she gained the hall, she ran to her cell, flung herself on her prie-dieu and burst into tears. Her sobs were heart-wrenching. Oh, where was Mother Philomène?

Finally, she rose from her cramped position with a heavy sigh. Enough tears, enough, enough. She took off her veil and wimple, sponged her face at the wash-stand, put on a fresh wimple and shook off residues of rain on her mended habit. With her woolen cape wrapped about her, she went back to the wet garden. It was almost dark. There was still a little time before the supper bell.

Ian found her walking rapidly up and down the path.

"Sister Madeleine."

"Captain Lindsay!" Ah, she was glad to see him. Her voice told him so. They fell in step.

"I wanted to tell you myself. I am leaving on an expedition South. . . ."

"To the Colonies?" Her heart skipped a beat. What startling news! He was leaving. She stopped walking and looked up at him in the rainy twilight. She hoped he didn't notice her puffy eyes. "For how long?"

"At least six weeks, two to three months. . . ."

"Six weeks! Three months! When?"

"Tomorrow morning, after Mass. Two of us will be at Mass."

"Tomorrow!" Why did he have to leave Quebec? She didn't want to believe it.

"I'll miss seeing you, Sister." After a short silence, he added, "Marie-Louise. . . ."

"And I you, Ian." Not to see him for weeks. Here was another blow. It was too much.

The supper bell rang.

"I'll walk you in." At least they deserved that much, he thought.

Unconsciously, she raised a gloved hand toward his face and he clasped it to his breast.

"I'll never forget you, all you've done for me, for us, my regiment."

She nodded and gave his hand a slight pressure as she retrieved her own to the folds of her cape.

Once inside the warmth of the foyer, she found her voice again and whispered, "Godspeed, then. I'll see you in the morning after Mass." She left him with that promise and didn't know how she found her way to the refectory.

Mother Migeon de Bransac read from the lectern during supper. As she looked over her community, she wondered why her two nuns from Beauport looked so different. Sister Madeleine was red-eyed and downcast and Sister Philippe seemed sullen and withdrawn. What's happened to those two, she wondered. She must look into it. In an even voice, she continued to read about Marie de l'Incarnation's special devotion to St. Joseph.

The menu was better than usual. Murray had sent a round of cheddar from the commissary to Mother Philomène, so there was cheese soufflé as well as a thick vegetable soup with pieces of *saucisson.* Marie-Louise barely touched her food.

After Complines, by the time she reached her cell, the rain had turned to snow. It was much colder. From her window, she watched the fat flakes fall and cover the garden with fresh snow.

Still limp with pain, she tossed back and forth on her small cot all night. She tried to reason with herself. Maybe, what was happening was for the best. This "fever", this obsession might go away with Ian. She would regain her old self if she didn't see him every day. Geneviève's harsh words hit her in the face. "Why don't you remember who you are?" It was possible that Ian was in as much turmoil as she was. Maybe he wanted to go to this far-off territory. The distance might cure their infatuation. Please God, have mercy. Toward dawn, she slept a little, just before the first bell.

At Mass, Marie-Louise saw Ian receive communion with his fellow officers. They were dressed in a combination of uniform and trail clothes. They looked handsome in their red brick tartans, purposeful, serious and dedicated. She observed them from her choir-stall on the other side of the grill. She offered her own communion for his travels and safe return along with her daily petition for the safekeeping of her family in Beauport.

Immediately after the service, she delegated her usual sacristan duties to one of the younger nuns and hurried to the front foyer. It was bold and impetuous but no way was she going to miss a last glimpse of Ian before his departure.

The whole main corridor was busy with officers from Ian's regiment gathered to see the small expedition off. There were no nuns in this traffic.

Marie-Louise went half-way up the staircase to stand just below the round window as the delegates of the expedition came down the hall. There were two American Colonials; Lieutenants Edward Pinkham and Joshua Brunswick; two American Rangers; Gordon Neal and Colin Paige and two Fraser Highlanders; Captain Ross Maclaren joining Ian. All good, strong men of undaunted courage who knew the trails and inspired Ian's confidence. When Ian saw Marie-Louise on the stairs he quickly detached himself from the group and came up to her.

"Good morning, Sister Madeleine. Please pray for us, we hope your prayers will follow us."

"Everyday," she smiled but her eyes were sad. "You know the hours of our prayers. . . . Your intentions will be placed at the altar," she directed this to him alone. Shyly, she offered her hand.

Ian took it eagerly. The enormity of his leaving descended on both of them. Why had he volunteered? There was so much he wanted to say, to explain. Why was he leaving Quebec? He would no longer see her every day. He would be tramping in the snow, perhaps living on pemmican until they reached New York. It was as if he saw himself in a half-dream. What foolhardy gesture was this? There was no revoking a military decision. Would he return? Would he ever see her again? Quebec? Yes, by God, he would.

Their eyes held. It was a moment of realization in which they made a silent declaration of love to each other. What was to come of it was a mystery but it was there for them to feel and to see. They gave it to each other. He could take the discovery, the knowledge, the gift of it with him on this journey against whatever odds.

Slowly, reluctantly, he released her hand. Above the din of everyone extending best wishes, he tried to brush away the pain of all the farewells.

"Adieu," he smiled. "No, it's au revoir."

"Au revoir. Go with God." This time she took in the whole group.

The door was open. A blast of cold air breezed into the foyer. Outside the sun was shining on mounds of new snow. They were all excited, exchanging last minute phrases, checking their back-packs and their snow-shoes. John Knox patted them all on the back as they went out in the snow covered street. Jovially with a certain nonchalance and bravado, they all clambered into two huge sleighs. The horses, stomping on the hard-packed snow, had been patiently waiting for the signal to take them as far as the opening of the major forest trail. Then they were off with a wave.

Marie-Louise looked after them until the sleighs disappeared into *rue St-Louis*. What other nuns, if any, had observed this departure? It was only important to her, she reasoned. The Reverend Mother was at her accounts. And Geneviève would be only too glad to see even a few of them gone. She climbed to one of the third floor store-rooms and wiped a small look-out window of accumulated dust with the edge of her petticoat. She was just in time to see the two loaded sleighs slide out of Saint Louis Gate at a fast trot. She sent blessings after them and watched until they became specks on the country road.

Chapter Twelve

The week dragged after Ian's departure. Days were long. Nights were long. Geneviève and Marie-Louise barely nodded to each other in their encounters on the way to duties. The strained feelings didn't go away.

At meals, Marie-Louise made an effort to eat what was presented. Her appetite diminished. Even when she was hungry, the food stuck in her throat. Especially when they had beaver. By some edict of the *faculté de Theologie de Paris* and the *faculté de Médicine* it was permitted to be used as fish on Fridays because it had a tail. Years ago, the decree had been principally for the benefit of the *coureurs-de-bois* out on the trail but the convent kitchen used it when the fare was meager. It was not Marie-Louise's favorite dish.

All her extra moments were spent in her choir stall after everyone left the chapel.

When the Seders family took their leave of the convent, she held Baby Joseph in her arms and kissed the top of his downy head. She knew she would see him again. His mother promised they would return to visit often. Their leaving added to her sense of loss. She prayed harder, invoking all the saints in heaven.

She tried to regain her old enthusiasm for the new classes. She had four students, two girls and two boys, ranging in ages between eight and eleven. They were apt enough but her heart was not in it. For some of them

, it was an opportunity that might not be presented again. It was an added responsibility for Marie-Louise to worry about.

The cold held. Another nor'easter storm whipped against the city and left more snow. Between storms, detachments of soldiers went out every day in sleighs drawn by tired horses and some by Newfoundland dogs. They went to the forest area of St. Foy. The soldiers cut and drew wood to the garrison for fuel. It was a never-ending task.

Letters were exchanged between Murray and Levis. Murray made it clear that if any attempt was made by the French to molest, to annoy or to interrupt these details during the winter, it would be met with the severity of his orders to destroy every house in town not actually occupied by troops and British merchants.

Levis complied and circulated announcements throughout his environs and among the Canadian and Indian forces that these detachments of wood cutters were not to be molested in any way.

Everyone, on both sides, took double precautions as this indispensable service went on in order to warm all establishments and houses in Quebec.

They were fed, they were housed and they were warm. It was something to thank God for.

By the end of the month Marie-Louise finally came to some sensible resolutions in her meditations and in her prayers. Though it was against all the rules, she had formed two attachments in a very short time. To be attracted, to become attached, to have special friendships, even polite relationships was forbidden. She had trespassed that line and proven how human she was.

No doubt, Ian in his travels would meet interesting colonial women. She had sent more than one guardian angel after him. He was in God's hands and anything could happen. Perhaps he would get a transfer to Boston or Halifax and that would be the end of it. So be it. But she had also sent her love with him. They had exchanged that with each other in one brief moment. She had never before experienced the warm, radiating sensations she felt when she thought of Ian. As if she would float out of her habit. It was different from the crushes she had felt over the few Beauport boys who had come courting when she was fifteen. Her serious demeanor had scared them away. It had been easy to shut the door and enter the convent to offer her life to God. They had never awakened such feelings in her. But entering this monastery had not protected her from falling in love. To her surprise she was not immune.

What was it? An elusive magic that might leave her if Ian stayed away long enough? Would it puff away, disintegrate to the four winds like a faded dandelion? She hoped not. As a little girl she had blown away many faded dandelions when she had run bare-footed in the fields of Orleans. Though she tried to reason with herself now, the truth was, she didn't really want to let go of her entrapment.

The soreness of his absence would recede. She promised herself. She looked forward to his return. Little Joseph she would see again soon and that was always a positive. For the rest, here was another firm resolve, she would "let go and let God". She would take heart. She had to. Geneviève's words came back to her in her deepest meditations, "Remember who you are." She would throw herself into her work *à corps perdu*.

For her most fervent prayers now, her mother was the first priority. She bombarded heaven, yet her mother still hung by a thread. She wiped a tear. It was sad for all of them, her father, Jean-Paul and Uncle Guillaume. She was glad she had stolen that day last September to be home.

"Please, dear God, restore her to health," Marie-Louise sobbed in her choir stall, "or end her sufferings. Thy will be done."

By the first week into February, it was noticeable that Marie-Louise was losing weight steadily. Mother Migeon decided to call her in for counseling.

"As you know, Sister Madeleine, we are all praying for your dear mother."

Marie-Louise nodded. "Yes, I am very grateful for all your prayers, Reverend Mother." She wanted to add it wasn't doing much good but she kept silent.

"I am concerned about your own health. I'm proud of all of you, all my nuns, after what we've been put through here since last September. But we can't let go now."

Marie-Louise remained silent.

"I want you to make special efforts at table, Sister, to regain your appetite. We all work too hard not to eat well. We must sustain ourselves with the food we have, such as it is. Mother Philomène is worried about you too."

"I am sorry to distress you. I will try, Reverend Mother," her voice lacked conviction.

Mother Migeon refrained from mentioning Captain Lindsay. He was the real problem, her mother's turn for the worst didn't help. Neither did the absence of Baby Joseph. Then there was the new hurt, the malentente with Sister Philippe, Geneviève. She must talk with Geneviève too. But she had other suggestions for Marie-Louise first before going into her lecture about attachments and the premise that everyone who entered the Ursuline monastery was not necessarily cut out to be a nun. That was a last resort.

"I am going to relieve you from some of your duties."

Marie-Louise was going to protest but Mother Migeon raised her hand.

"No more hospital duty for a while, no more kitchen duty. . . ."

"But helping Mother Philomène is never a burden."

Mother Migeon nodded. "She's our mainstay. Nevertheless," she readjusted her veil, "one catechism and grammar class you may continue. What are your duties on the arts project?"

"Since I am neither an artist or musician, I help with the sheet music. I keep the paint brushes clean."

Mother Migeon nodded approvingly. "But you are an artist in your own right, in another discipline. You are an accomplished seamstress."

"I still mend vestments that are brought into the sewing room." Her mother had taught her to sew since she was seven.

"I know, I know. You do a great deal, perhaps too much. I have to remind myself, we are not in prison here."

"Yes, Reverend Mother." What was coming next?

"I'm going to ask you to do something you might enjoy and give you the time to do it." She didn't command it as an outright assignment.

Marie-Louise looked up. Mother Migeon was really worried about her. She was touched by this concern and that her Superior was trying to console and cheer her.

"Dear child, would you like to design something of your own? A new chasuble for Father Resche?"

Marie-Louise eyes sparkled with new attention. Why not? "Yes, Reverend Mother, if I can find the material."

"If we don't have it, we might ask Anaïse."

Ah, Anaïse, what was she up to these days?

"I'm sure Anaïse will find something for us."

They both smiled. A tightness eased off in Marie-Louise's chest.

"Then it's settled. And you will make more effort at table, Sister Madeleine?" She returned to formality of address.

"Yes, I will try, Reverend Mother."

"Remember, when we are making adjustments we sometimes have to change our goals day by day. But we pray for divine guidance to make these changes and adjustments. We do so knowing and believing we are taking steps in continuing growth. We are in a continuing growth process, Sister. God supplies us with the strength we need. I pray you gain new strength to achieve all your goals. Don't despair, dear daughter."

"Thank you for your counsel and concern, Reverend Mother."

"In your meditations today, I refer you to Isaiah. Chapter 40, Verse 31;

'But they who wait for the Lord shall renew their strength,

they shall mount up with wings like eagles'." Mother Migeon thought that was enough for today.

Marie-Louise knelt for her blessing. She went off in a lighter mood to the sewing room to rummage for material. Already she imagined a design on the drafting board. For the actual cutting, she would measure on one of the chasubles folded in the sacristy armoire or ask Father Resche to stand still a few mornings after Mass so she could take the correct dimensions.

That night before the last bell, Mother Philomène came to Marie-Louise's cell with a little porcelain pot of hot chocolate thick with cream and a matching cup.

"This delicious luxury should go to one of our patients." Marie-Louise tried to refuse it.

"Drink every bit of it, that's an order. Tonight, you are a patient. Good-night, Sister." Mother Philomène firmly closed the door.

Marie-Louise smiled as she sipped the hot beverage. In no time, she felt drowsy. She surmised the gift *tisane* was laced with cognac. She drained the cup to the last dregs, left the tray at the foot of her *prie-dieu,* slid into the cold bed flushed with warmth. In a few seconds she was sound asleep.

The next day, Marie-Louise found a piece of green brocade in the sewing room. A green to welcome spring, like the tips of new leaves sprinting from trees after fresh April rains, a color of hope. It had been part of a French lady's ball gown. She spread it out on the smooth pine table. Ball gowns were donated from time to time to the Ursulines, the Augustinians and the Hospitalières for the purpose of making church vestments when materials were scarce. It was an honor ladies vied for, to see part of their discarded apparel made over for rituals of worship at the altar.

Marie-Louise contemplated the folds of the bright green material. Where and how to cut it. What kind of moments had been enjoyed in the wearing of it, she wondered. What would she herself look like in such a gown?

"Ah, *orgueilleuse,*" she whispered and immediately erased this thought of vanity. Perhaps Ian would see colonial women in similar gowns in his travels. She didn't know what English women wore in the south. Something much simpler than Parisian styles, no doubt.

Marie-Louise took a few other left-over gowns out of the sewing room armoire. She inspected them carefully, a few dull reds, an iridescent violet and a faded white *peau-de-soie.* None of these would do, the green brocade still spread out on the table was the best. A few rolled up remnants in one of the throw-all baskets could be examined for lining material.

She consulted the church chart for the Division of the Proper of the Time. Green vestments were worn now until Saturday before Septuagisema, then it would be Lent and violet vestments would be worn till Easter. After the white and gold of Easter, green vestments would be resumed. A good red for the Masses of martyrs would have been a challenge to work with but there was no remnant of cloth or gown of a good enough shade for that. She certainly didn't want to work on black. She studied the church chart before she hung it back up on the wall. The Christmas section was divided into; Advent, Christmastide and the Time after Ephiphany. The Easter section was divided into Septuagesima, Lent, Passiontide, Eastertide and the Time after Pentecost. Ash Wednesday was almost upon them. Ah, she had a lot of penances to do this Lent. She caressed the green brocade. But first she must make a new chasuble for Father Resche.

Anaïse felt very much at home in the convent, most times she came and went as she pleased. *"Pas de ceremonie"* she would tell Mother Migeon when she came bearing gifts. She ignored that the Superior was trying to re-establish some of the cloister rules they had lost since the military was in the house. When she heard that Marie-Louise was making a special chasuble, she came straight to the sewing room to find her and deliver a remnant of cream watered silk for the vestment's lining. She also drew out of her tapestry bag a spool of lamé ribbon for trim and piping.

"You've lost weight!" Anaïse was shocked. "Are you ill? Aren't you eating? The whole country-side is sending food stuffs to your kitchen and Murray's commissary must still be giving supplies. . . ."

"Oh, yes. Everyone supplies us. We're very fortunate."

"Then what's happening to you? Are you fasting?"

"No, I'm fine. How is your store?" Marie-Louise sat down at the table with Anaïse. They unfolded the new acquisitions and spread them against the green brocade. "That's perfect, Anaïse. Thank you, thank you."

"I want to see the finished product."

"Of course, shall I get us some tea? And Tante José, how is she?"

"Remarkable for her age, in good health. Don't bother about tea, thank you. I must get back to the store and it's coming along. I need Hubert's help."

"Where is he now?"

"I suspect he's trying to join Levis' army."

"Jean-Paul would like to do that."

"Jean-Paul is needed at home to help your father to take care of your poor Maman. And I need him too, to help develop my trade whenever he comes to town."

"Maybe you should be in Lower Town."

"Yes, I know, that's where we've always had the markets, the taverns, and the merchants. Remember when we use to wait for the ships to come in from France with all the supplies. True, I'm in a lone location. Well, we'll see. I must get back and check my shelves for something to fatten you up."

Marie-Louise smiled. "You try to take care of the whole world, Anaïse. We're praying for you."

"I know I can count on that. To begin with I'm going to send over some port. I'll ask Reverend Mother to let you have a glass before every meal. That will whet your appetite. It'll make you eat anything, even beaver."

Marie-Louise giggled a little. "Oh, Anaïse, you'll make me a drunk. You can't go around debauching the nuns. You're impossible."

"No, I'm practical. And some day Quebec will thank me. And it's not me that's debauching the nuns."

They both refrained from mentioning the expedition or Captain Lindsay. But it was there between them.

"*Ah, la pauvre*," Anaïse thought as she left the convent, "she's pining away for that *Ecossais*, that handsome brute." And she, herself, no longer wanted to think of him. She needed to see Hubert.

Marie-Louise finished the chasuble in a week's time. It was a beautiful piece of work. Father Resche was grateful and proud to have it. Everyone admired him in the new finery to the glory of the church.

When Jean-Paul saw his sister again, in the chapel on the other side of the grill he, too, was shocked and asked for an audience with the Reverend Mother before he visited with Marie-Louise.

"Reverend Mother, I'm not only very worried about Maman but also Sister Madeleine, my sister, Marie-Louise. . . ."

"So are we all, Jean-Paul."

"I had hoped to go to Fort Jacques Cartier to join Levis now that most of the farm work is done for the winter but Uncle Guillaume is not that well either. . . ."

"Ah, but you can not leave your father alone with all these responsibilities. . . . And we are taking care of Sister Madeleine as well as we can."

Jean-Paul nodded.   He twirled a red woolen *toque* in his rough hands. He was embarassed that he had voiced all his concerns to his sister's Superior.

"If only Maman would get better. . . ." He didn't want to believe that she was, again, near death. She was in and out of a coma. He didn't want to believe that she might not recognize any of them before she died.

"We will all die in God's own time. Courage, Jean-Paul. You all need each other now."

After he left for his usual visit with Marie-Louise, Mother Migeon shook her head. She couldn't go back to her accounts. She was at her wits end. She had to make a decision, one the Bishop probably wouldn't approve of. After Complines she sent for her ailing young nun.

"Sister Madeleine, I've decided to send you home for a few weeks."

"Home? But Reverend Mother, I've tried everything. . . ."

"I know, dear child. But your mother is worse. This is very unsual. I would certainly not make this a practice. No one, as we all know, goes home for a parent's illness, or funeral. Those privileges were relinquished when you all enter the door of the monastery. But in this case," she repeated her stock phrase, "we are not in ordinary times. Your family needs you, you need them, you all need each other. You're wasting away before my eyes. There's nothing more we can do. " She rearranged her veil as she leaned over and looked at Marie-Louise with love and concern. "If you're to be of any use to yourself, to us, to your calling, you must be restored to good health."

"I have really tried, Reverend Mother." Marie-Louise fought back on-coming tears.

"I know you have, dear daughter in Christ. God does not ask the impossible. Go help and comfort your mother, support her in her final days. And be good to yourself. In this break away from us, ask God where he really wants you to be. Where you want to be. I pray you regain your strength in Beauport."

There was a long silence. Marie-Louise looked up at her Superior. This permission was incredible. To be with her mother while she herself was living in a pain she did not understand, dare not mention, would be the greatest comfort to both of them. If her mother did not regain better health, and that seemed unlikely, then she would be there to help prepare her for death. Perhaps, it was God's will.

"Thank you, Reverend Mother. I will go home." She knelt for her Superior's blessing.

"Go to chapel now for a few moments."

In the semi-dark chapel, the Repentigny sanctuary lamp glowed. Marie-Louise pulled out the kneeler from underneath her choir stall. As she knelt, her Missel fell from the shelf to the floor and a prayer card fluttered out of it. She leaned to pick them up and recognized Geneviève's handwriting on the thin card. "*La Paix du Seigneur*" was written in fine script below a well drawn figure of St. Francis of Assisi.

Marie-Louise clasped the card to her bib. "Yes, peace, Geneviève," she said softly gazing at the tabernacle. "Life's too short." She was going home to support and to be supported, to love and be loved.

Mother Migeon would explain her absence to everyone. She would see no one. No one except Geneviève, she would see her in the morning and make her peace before she left for Beauport.

Once home there were good moments. The snow held to the ground. There was enough food. The Boisvert men had been careful with the harvest even though Jean-Paul had brought many contributions to the convent. Marie-Louise made her mother as comfortable as possible. She sang and read to her when she would regain consciousness from her lapses. Uncle Guillaume took heart at having Marie-Louise about. He coughed a great deal. Marie-Louise made him take cherry bark syrup regularly. He spent their short evenings by the fire whittling. Jean-Paul took care of the animals in the barn and ran errands for the whole family.

"*Ah, chère enfant*, it was good of Reverend Mother to let you come to us," her thin hands would clasp her daughter's hand as she smoothed the sheets.

It was Hortense herself who asked for the last sacrament. The parish priest came. She revived a few days after that. She spoke of her vegetable garden, her gooseberries and raspberries. Jean-Paul drew a design for her and they bent their heads over it. They both laughed together that afternoon reminiscing over some of his boyhood pranks. Then she slipped away in her sleep with a faint smile.

"May she rest in peace," Jean-Paul sobbed. He was inconsolable.

They all cried at different intervals to heave out their grief. The villagers came to help. Joseph Boisvert made a slim pine coffin in the barn for his wife of forty years.

A procession of Beauport families took Hortense Boisvert to the little church of L'Ange Guardien in the parish's largest sleigh for the *Libera*. After the Mass, the funeral cortège all filed back to the house for more last respects. There would be no burial till the spring thaw. The slender coffin with Hortense's remains would be kept in the ice cold barn until she could be buried in the Beauport cemetery.

Neighbors came from as far as Ste-Anne-de-Beaupré with offerings of wine and hot dishes. Rosaries were said, love and sympathy was shared.

Though they were all exhausted, Marie-Louise slept fitfully. She prayed and thought of her mother in the cold barn. It had been a good death. They had always prayed to St. Joseph for that. One night she slept soundly all the way through, then ate a good breakfast. With a new vigor, she cleaned house. Mireille Le Conte came to help, it was like *"le grand ménage"* of spring.

With her new found energy, Marie-Louise sorted and mended clothes for the three men in the household, she cooked dishes that would preserve. In the midst of all these tasks on some days she missed the convent routine. She said her office daily from her Missel.

They managed day by day. They tried to adjust to the loss of Hortense. They all handled her things with love. Marie-Louise was especially tender with her father. Jean-Paul and Uncle Guillaume hovered over her. They poured cream over almost everything she ate. She regained her appetite. She even fell asleep a few afternoons.

"That's from sheer exhaustion," Mireille said with an approving nod. "That'll do you good."

Their eyes were still red and puffy from private sessions of crying. At intervals, they cried openly and embraced each other. In the quiet of the kitchen, while the men were at the barn, Marie-Louise said a few prayers for Ian. She wondered if he had reached Albany. And when? What was he doing?

Chapter Thirteen

At long last the Quebec expedition sighted Albany. It was a great wonder to Ian that they reached their destination at all.

The first cold days on the trail had been uneventful. They trudged into softer weather and made good time on their snow shoes. At twilight shelter was usually found under huge trees with low sweeping branches. One of the Colonials, Ed Pinkham, tended the camp fire and roasted whatever game was caught. The last of the spruce beer mixed with their meager supply of rum.

They by-passed Sorel. Part of the Richelieu River was navigable. Their two Rangers, Gordon Neal and Colin Paige led them to canoes left hidden for people on the trail. They also knew where to leave them after use for the next parties. One day they lost a pack of supplies in the river. After a desperate attempt to retrieve it, they all caught chills. The six of them huddled in blankets at their campsite in the quiet of the night. Occasionally, they heard wolves howling.

Ian counted the stars on fair nights. He saw Marie-Louise's face in the flames of their campfires. He remembered the chanting of the nuns. He wrote her imaginary letters against the sky, the snow and on the waters when they traversed smooth lakes.

They steered the Rapids between Fort Chambly and Fort St. Jean. After they passed through questionable American territory, they picked up two Caughnawagas, Chinnohete and Tontileaugo who were out hunting.

After some scary negotiations skirting the possibility of being scalped, on Gordon's recommendation the Indians were offered rum and money. They agreed to being hired as guides for the rest of the way. A fortunate coup, they all ended up in a village of Caughnawagas where they were sheltered against a storm that lasted for two days. To forget the weather and keep warm they got drunk. Colin Paige, Joshua Brunswick and Ross Maclaren developed dysentery.

"Better than frost-bite," Paige said grimly as he finished his rum.

In the vicinity of Ile aux Noix, they encountered a huge bear, an angry bear disturbed from hibernation. They ran from attack but not fast enough. Ed Pinkham had one of his arms mangled. Between their gun shots and swift Caughnawaga arrows, they all managed to fell the bear. The two Indians were adept at quickly binding Pinkham's wounds. Then they opened up part of the huge animal, his blood gushed crimson on the snow. Ten shots had gone through his chest and brain. They all dragged his remains under a large tree. They cut branches to shelter the carcass. A Caughnawaga sign was cut into the bark of the tree so the bear could be found by scouts from their village for the division of the meat.

Little progress was made that evening. Pinkham developed a high fever and had to be left at an American farm house the next day. Ian offered money to the Farnham family for his care. He wondered if these farmers would have to go all the way to Boston or Albany to spend it. One of their red-headed daughters, Emma, was designated for the extra nursing chores.

When the rest of them finally stumbled into Albany, it was nearly three weeks since they had left Quebec. A fast journey according to any *coureur-de-bois*.

"Ah, men, there's civilization!" Gordon was exuberant.

Though emaciated and half-starved, they shouted joyfully as they approached the English fort. With expressed gratitude they took their leave of the Caughnawagas. Gordon made an arrangement with them to be met in ten days so they could be escorted back as far as Fort Chambly.

In bedraggled exhaustion the five of them presented themselves at the military headquarters. They were welcomed and brought to Amherst's aides. Their credentials were checked. Pinkham's absence was explained. They were in a room where the walls were covered with maps. Ian was intrigued. He wished Patrick Mackellar was with them. Here was a great deal of information. Probably Amherst's contemplated routes to approach Montreal. Well, he was too tired to think of it now.

A Sergeant Chisholm appeared with officious salutes and assigned them all to bunks in barracks to sleep off their fatigue until they could be properly billeted to other quarters.

Ian dropped his pack-sack, his small sword, his snow-shoes and sank on a clean cot. He'd wash later. Before he fell asleep, he heard another sergeant down the hall.

"Billet these officers in some homes on State Street. We have to fatten them up before they start their trek back to Quebec."

"Aye, sir."

So there were some Fraser Highlanders here. Where was Monckton, Ian wondered. He fell into a deep sleep. He slept for twelve hours.

Ian knew he had definitely returned to civilization by the next evening. Freshly bathed, he was the happy recipient of a clean uniform complete with ruffled linen shirt borrowed from a Highlander. His companions were similarly attired so they could all present themselves at the Westbury residence to attend a dinner party.

"And that's where you'll be billeted next week, Captain Lindsay. The rest of you are assigned to different homes." Sergeant Chishom checked a list.

"Thank you, we're all much obliged, Sergeant."

"General Amherst will be there and will make an appointment to see you all tomorrow. You blokes are heroes. You'll be invited to all the parties in town."

The five of them were all together. They preened about and good-humoredly admired each other in their smart borrowed finery.

"Well, are you ready for a bit of petticoat, Captain?"

"I think we should pay respects to our generous hostess and have a good dinner first. We're lucky to be alive."

"Ah, well said. Let's go and meet this charming hostess. We're lucky to be invited. I could stand a drink." Gordon was eager to leave. "And don't worry, Captain, our own mothers would recognize us tonight."

They all left laughing and clapping each other on the back in informal camaraderie.

The Westbury residence on State Street was a large house of Dutch design.

"Here's a fine place to rest up your sore muscles, Captain Lindsay." Paige accepted a sherry from a tray held up by a passing black servant.

"Aye, it is that."

They all stood at the side-board admiring the party in full swing.

"Here's to Pinckham. Poor bloke," Gordon raised his glass.

"He'll be all right. You noticed that good looking red-head, the farmer's daughter, who came forth to take care of him. He's in good hands."

"Ah, yes. He should be all right," the two Rangers agreed.

"We'll pick him up on the way back." Ian put his glass down as Mrs. Abigail Westbury came toward him. He bowed over her hand.

"All you men coming from far away Quebec in so short a time! You're creating quite a sensation. Come and meet my daughters."

They were engulfed, crowded about, carried away and they enjoyed all the flattery and attention.

Music filled the double salons. Lovely, smiling, sophisticated women in gowns of beautiful materials, sparkling jewels and coiffed hair styles swayed about. Their attire complemented the men in colorful uniforms and enhanced their gallantry. Quite a contrast from the plain black and white habits of the nuns in Quebec. Yet, in the midst of this brilliant éclat, Ian thought of Marie-Louise as he had first seen her in a red dress in the lighted doorway of her home This far from Quebec, no day passed without his thinking of her. In his reveries, he saw her in the choir stall of the chapel, he saw her walking down the monastic halls, he saw her in the stair-way of the main foyer. What was she doing now?

"Captain Lindsay, General Amherst just arrived." Mrs. Westbury and her daughters whisked him and his companions away for proper introductions.

The dinner was delicious, served on patterned china at a huge mahogany table, the crystal and silver glowed in the soft candlelight. The wine poured at each course invited light talk and laughter. After dinner, the daughters of the house played the harpsichord to perfect the evening. Ian was impressed and awed. Colonial life in Albany had a particular correct and delightful society.

At the close of the *soirée* they were all pleasantly exhausted and after observing the amenities of responsible guests Ian and his men excused themselves. Early morning appointments were on the agenda for them at headquarters where they would be briefed and taken on tours of the fort.

Ian's old wound ached as he retired in the neat chamber he had been assigned. It ached more than it had on the trail. Pure fatigue. He had used up the last of his bear grease. The muscles in his legs still felt strained. Ah, they had been lucky. Without Chinnohete and Tontileaugo as guides they might have perished out there on the last part of the trail.

In the next few days, Ian and his fellow officers went from their billets to headquarters and were kept very busy. Ian was in awe of General Amherst. Monckton was in New York City and he was disappointed not to see him. He still moved slowly. They all did. He was like a man who had not eaten for days and had to be fed carefully, a little at a time. He was catching his breath. After being on snow-shoes, off and on for eighteen days, it was not surprising that his legs still ached. His daily routine was to assist with the aide-de-camp's correspondence and the dispatches that he would take back to Quebec to General Murray. In the evenings, he was glad to go home to the luxuries of the Westbury residence.

He was thawing out but he still shuddered and relived flashes of the bitter, excruciating cold they had all experienced on the long journey through the forests, across rivers and lakes. He took pleasure in the warmed bed at night. The Culloden dreams had not happened on the trail nor did they resurface here. But if he had thought that removing himself from Quebec could help to make him forget Marie-Louise he had been strongly mistaken. He thought of her constantly during the day and at night when all was still in the house, she was in his reveries and in his dreams.

Ian was grateful that he was housed in one of the best homes in the city. He knew that they were all being generously pampered before they hit the adventures of the trail again. Mrs. Abigail Westbury fed him well as she did all the other officers who came and went. Her two shy daughters, Heather and Esther, endowed with voluminous hair and moles on their chins followed the example of their mother's hospitality. They pushed a variety of foods on him, some he had never heard of before. Intrigued and affable, he was a responsible guest.

He learned that Mrs. Westbury had married into a Boston family but when she became widowed had displaced herself along with her two daughters to inherit and live on her father's estate in Albany. Since the war she had come back home to Timothy Eaton's house. Two black servants, Zita and Reo, a man and wife team, maintained the heavy work of the household. Ian had not seen many blacks. Nor had he seen Indians before he had embarked for Halifax and Louisbourg. Louisbourg seemed a far away place and a long time ago now. And Quebec, would he see Quebec again? Marie-Louise?

To make up for the loss of Boston's social excitement, it was apparent that Mrs. Westbury and her daughters had attached themselves to the military in their need of civilian divertissement. There were many socials. Ian had never eaten so many baked beans, thick brown bread and corn biscuits. He thoroughly relished all that was put before him. He appreciated the Westbury women's good care of him but tried to keep out of their way in the long hallways on the second floor and the little unexpected alcoves downstairs. He surmised secret places in their limpid, calculating eyes. They were different from Anaïse Médard. Anaïse was startingly direct. Was he some kind of eunuch? Here he was surrounded by English colonial women and all he could think about in his leisure hours was Marie-Louise. What was she doing now? Quebec seemed so far away, at the end of the world.

One of General Amherst's officers, Lieutenant Wayne Heatherington, was also billeted in the Westbury townhouse.

"What luck, old boy, we're in the best quarters in town for cold February nights," he winked knowingly at Ian. A heavy man, he was heard coming, his presence was felt. "Just checking to see you're settled in to warm yourself for a few days before you trek back to Quebec."

Ian smiled, nodded and shook hands. Trek back? He hoped the snow would be well packed all the way. On snow shoes, it could be almost straight-forward barring mishaps. He looked out the window. The snow was pale lavendar in the sunset. Candles were being lit in the house across the street.

"I think the ladies are favoring us with Indian pudding tonight." Lieutenant Heatherington winked again, patted his stomach and clicked his tongue.

"Indian pudding? Sounds very civilized after cooking whatever in an open pot in the woods. I've never had it."

"It's a New England concoction. Lots of things we've never had or heard of before, to be expected in the colonies. Where are you from beside the Quebec campaign?"

"Fyfe."

"I should have known with that Scot brogue."

A delicious aroma wafted up the staircase.

"Um-m-m, smells like we're having some kind of venison too, tonight. Amherst will be with us. Townshend go back to England in October?"

Ian nodded. He arranged the cravatte of his borrowed shirt as best he could. Which of the Westbury girls had laundered it for him? Or was it Zita? And there were mirrors in this house, many. Another unexpected elegance of colonial living. He had seen himself gaunt and spent in one of them. With all this food and drink, he would flesh out again but the journey back would keep him lean.

"Well, let's join the ladies, let's humor them. I could do with a glass of sherry. A snapping cold tonight. We'll hear trees split."

Ian shuddered involuntarily. But they were in a warm house, he reminded himself as they went downstairs. They would be dining by candlelight in the company of Bostonian women. The Commander-in-Chief of the whole North American Army would join them. For a fleeting moment, he thought of Wolfe. Had he now been interred in the graveyard of his home town church or had the victory of the Battle on the Plains merited him a place at Westminster Abbey? He thought of Marie-Louise again. What were they all doing now at the Ursuline convent? All the nuns and Marie-Louise with their veils flowing behind them as they glided to their many duties.

He bowed and greeted Mrs. Westbury at the side board. As she handed him a glass of sherry he imagined he saw Marie-Louise's face in the wine glass. It gleamed like a jewel. His legs still ached. He went to sit by Heather Westbury at the harpsichord. She smiled softly. What would these genteel women in this room think of him if they knew he was in love with a nun, a papist? That she lived in his heart and he was consumed with the thought of her.

Would one of these Westbury women come to his bed in the middle of the night while the wind was howling? Would he to one of theirs? He passed a hand across his forehead. "What wild delicious and erotic thoughts you have, *mon vieux,*" he muttered to himself.

But Marie-Louise triumphed in his heart across all this distance. His letters to his mother must have made this declaration even in the subtlest innuendo. Even yesterday, he had penned a letter home to be brought to Boston by the courrier. Ships sailed to England from Boston even in winter. He knew his mother would be sympathetic, rereading his letters in her sewing room. He wrote to his father separately about winter, the war and who was going to appear first up or down the St. Lawrence after the spring thaw.

Life was quite pleasant in Albany in spite of the piled up snow. He could envision a good life here. His wildest fantasy last night, before he closed his eyes, was to hurry back to Quebec with his pouch of dispatches to Murray, to propose to Marie-Louise and take her back to Albany. Escape, elope? Yes, that would be better than waiting, if she loved him as much as he loved her. Better than waiting hopelessly for approval from Murray, Mother de Bransac, her father and whatever dispensation she might need from the ill Bishop in Montreal. That wild fantasy had soothed him as he had fallen into a deep sleep.

With what reckless and noble gesture had he wished himself off on this journey? He had come in desperation because he thought it was better for everybody concerned. That it was better for him to be off and suffer alone, out of sight, without gazing everyday on the unattainable. Had it been that apparent, how love sick he was? John Knox had detected his foolish state and had offered good natured pats on the back understandingly as if matters of the heart during war campaigns were all of short duration.

A small miracle that he and members of the expedition had arrived alive and well in Albany, all in one piece, though stiff and brittle as icicles. All but Pinkham. Ian still couldn't feel all of his toes. His legs still ached at intervals.

During mess at headquarters, fellow officers told them how lucky they were that the expedition had escaped marauding enemy Indian bands. Yes, they were lucky. For days on end, they had the forests, frozen ponds, lakes and rivers all to themselves. The vast silence had been a retreat, an awareness of God. They had emerged on the borders of towns cleansed with a new sense of their souls. In some areas, skirting Iroquois territory, they could easily have been captured, scalped, their hearts torn out of their bodies and eaten raw. They had been doubly blessed to meet the two Caughnawagas when their strength was beginning to give out.

Ian thanked God, every morning and late at night. He thought of his mother's book of the hours, *les belles heures*, she called it. Of all the hours, Complines was his favorite. Was it time for Complines now at the Ursuline Convent in Quebec? Was Marie-Louise at chapel? He wondered.

He thought of the harpsichord played in the Westbury salon. Which girl played so spritely? Here all the graces of life were offered. The cold, winter and the passions of war were outside. Outside, for the moment, on the other side of the thick pine doors of this household.

Today, he had seen groups of children playing in the snow covered streets of Albany. Well fed children. Not like the children of Quebec he had seen sliding down Côte de la Montagne, hungry, thin and ragged, yet shouting with childish glee. They knew how to survive winter and even war.

The few shops of Albany intrigued him. If he brought Marie-Louise here, what would their life be like? Would they have children of their own? Would he ever go back to Scotland? He thought of the constant pot of pea soup in Mother Philomène's kitchen. The sherry was getting to him. His attention snapped back to the scene of the room. Above the harpsichord playing, he heard the officers and General Amherst's voices discussing the famous spruce beer recipe.

"An excellent cure for scurvy," Lieutenant Heatherington was explaining to some of the younger officers who looked as if they had never had need of it.

"Do you have many cases now in Quebec, Captain Lindsay?" General Amherst asked as he accepted another glass of sherry from Mrs. Westbury.

"Unfortunately, we do." Ian had been so involved with the study of maps, the copying and writing of dispatches that he hadn't gotten around to explain their need of the famous recipe. "General Murray made a batch of spruce beer shortly before I left, but he claims he does not have your recipe down pat and instructed me to return with an exact copy from you, sir, if you would be so kind as to furnish me with it."

"Of course, of course. It saves lives. I'm surprised the good nuns are not on to it."

"They are, we have different recipes from the farmers and Indians, we've tried them all. The good nuns also work with other prescriptions and solutions," Ian offered.

"*La medicine douce*," Heather said in perfect French.

Ian bowed and smiled.

The next day, the stark reality of war returned as he inspected the fort, military camps and parade grounds as a visiting officer

Late in the afternoon, in the aide-de-camp's office, he laboriously copied General Amherst's spruce beer recipe. He chuckled when he finished.

"Read that, Gordon," he pushed the sheet across the table where Gordon was pouring over maps. "That ought to cure anybody."

"Take seven pounds of good spruce and boil it well till the bark peels off," Gordon started to read aloud then repeated from the script in silence.

"Take 7 Pounds of good Spruce & boil it well till
the bark peels off, then take the Spruce out & put three
Gallons of Molasses to the Liquor & boil it again, scum it
well as it boils, then take it out the Kettle & put it into a

cooler, boil the remainder of the Water sufficient for a Barrel of thirty Gallons, if the Kettle is not large enough to boil it together, when milkwarm in the Cooler put a Pint of Yest into it and mix well. Then put in the Barrel and let it work for two or three days, keep filling it up as it works out. When done working, bung it up with a Tent Peg in the Barrel to give it vent every now and then. It may be used in two or three days after. If wanted to be bottled it should stand a fortnight in the Cask. It will keep a great while. "

Then he pushed the sheet back to Ian.

"Better strap that to your chest along with your dispatches. That'll take a good bit of cooking."

"I'll take it straight to Murray and I can see him now going to the kitchen to cajole Mother Philomène into whipping it up. She loves new recipes."

They both laughed. They were alone. Ian put all his papers in a neat pile.

"Come and take a good look at this map, Gordon, and tell me what you think."

"I think after receiving news of our victory at Quebec . . . ."

"I wonder when the General got the news."

"According to Captain Webster here, it was in October."

"That was fast. The local opinion is that it relieved him of the necessity of pushing ahead. There being no urgency and the season already late, he decided to abandon all military enterprises for the winter and retire to Crown Point."

"Aye, sensible, flanking operations by any considerable force could not be carried out through dense pathless forests, as we have just learned."

"From these maps, the water routes seem to be the only way to go at any time of the year."

"Isle aux Noix is still well defended by the French, the outcome of a successful attack there would be questionable. In the spring, maybe."

"Look here, Gordon, we'd better memorize this or make some sort of copy for future reference, permission granted."

Both men studied three outlined routes on the huge map. Montreal was the main objective. Three expeditions were designed to move simultaneously. One was to move from Quebec under James Murray, another under Colonel Haviland by way of Lake Champlain and the Richelieu, and the third under Amherst himself by Oswego, Lake Ontario and the upper St. Lawrence. All were to converge on Montreal at approximately the same time.

"How will an advance of three divisions that widely separated and without means of communication arrive simultaneously in the region of Montreal?" Ian whistled softly.

"Beats me. Any dates on that?"

"Still in the planning. Have to be early summer."

"Gentlemen," a Sergeant came in with four officers. "We have some militia troops here from New Hampshire, Massachusetts and Rhode Island. These gentlemen will be dining with you at Mrs. Westbury's this evening."

They shook hands all around. A hot rum was served as they exchanged news and got acquainted.

Ian continued to be amazed and thanked his good fortune that he was billeted in a household of lavish evening entertainments. Tonight an amusing little drama, a muscial, was presented after dinner by Mrs. Westbury and the ladies of State Street for the benefit of the officers. A pleasant finale was enjoyed, praised and critiqued over warm brandy. After lingering farewells in the foyer, everybody left in mellow spirits.

As Ian retired to his room, he heard the New England officers singing out in the street on the way back to the barracks. Snatches of song from the musical floated up to him. He looked out the window. Two of them made snow balls and threw them at large in pure pleasure. What a clear night, what a bright moon.

A most enjoyable evening, yet he felt a few lonely pangs. He was not as care-free as the officers throwing snow balls in the moonlight. He was in an impossible situation. He was almost sorry he had come. He would have been better left in Quebec with what he did not know. Here, he was feretting out future plans for the take-over of Marie-Louise's entire country. Yet, he wanted to ask her not to take any vows. He wanted to declare his love, to hope that she could love him too. He was unrealistic. How dare he even think of it?

Though he was relaxed with the evening's pleasantries, good food and drink, his mind was full of scattering thoughts. Was Levis still at Fort Jacques Cartier or was he now in Montreal? What was Vaudreuil doing to fortify Montreal while Amherst was planning his strategies of attack. And Bishop de Pontbriand? Was he still ailing? How was his health now? Would he return to Quebec? Would he be administering final vows to the Ursulines who were candidates, Marie-Louise among them. Where did that fall in the Ursuline Order's schedule. A schedule that could no longer hold firm since the disruption of war. He hoped the Bishop would be detained at Montreal indefinitely. Then he thought of France, Vendôme and his grandparents' glassblowing compound, his summer visits there. How long ago and far away were those memories from the here and now of the North American Campaign.

There were other more recent memories that lived with him at this distance. In the still of every night, he could hear the incantations of the Ursulines at chapel.

"Blessed be God."

"Blessed be his Holy Name."

In his mind he heard all the, "*Ora pro nobis*", the "*Kyries*", the "*Ite Missa Est*", the words from the "*Sanctus*", the "*Credo*" and the "*Hosannas*". Their voices came back to him in phrases of the *Magnificat*.

"*L'Ange du Seigneur a annonçé à Marie,*
Et le Verbe c'est fait chair."

Another sonorous phrase came to him, "*La paix du Seigneur soit avec vous.*" Yes, peace, would there be any peace when the lords of war had played all their games? How long would it take to pick up the pieces? To rebuild, to restore a quiet over all of the land from the Arctic down to Louisiana. An impossible dream, now that the ravage was on-going. It might take centuries to establish a lasting peace.

The nuns in Quebec went about their lives stoically because they operated on faith, sheer faith. They carried everything with assurance because they believed in God's presence.

Ian thought of the all-seeing eye of God carved in the stone of a feudal manor near Poitiers. He had first seen it as a child with his mother. It had assured him that God was, indeed, over-seeing the whole world. But he had lost the simple faith of a child. It was since he had crossed the ocean to the new world that he occasionally flung out his cry at the sky.

"Are you out there, God?" Was He out there in this frozen domain with only glimpses of summer?

The nuns believed it. They radiated the pure joy of God's presence. When he had seen this in their faces going to chapel, it had sustained him.

He thought of Anaïse. Anaïse had faith too. Anaïse and Jean-Paul, they loved Quebec with a fierce, strong love, a "never-let-go" love. No one would ever take Quebec away from those two.

He thought of the women in whose house he lived at the moment. What did they believe in? He wondered. Was he fulfilling all his responsibilities as a military guest? Or should he make the expected advances of the game to Heather or Esther? Spent from the trail, what charm did he think he still had to attract either one of them, or their mother. Was there time? Was it expected of him?

"Don't be a fool," he muttered. Even a dalliance wasn't that simple. He might be put squarely in his place. He could hardly put any of them or himself in any compromising situation. He was grateful for their hospitality, their company. That was enough. Even if he could promote or accept an interlude for what it was worth, it would not erase Marie-Louise from his heart.

He couldn't risk any fleeting, furtive or abortive attempt at even a dalliance. There was not time for the preambles of the social game. It was a take or no-take situation and the time for the taking had slipped by. He couldn't afford to lose his credibility. He had to protect not only his own integrity but everybody else's. True, at times, guests exchanged more than warmth in accepting hospitality. This wasn't one of those times, he decided. The women of Albany had no lack of military or civilian company. He was just another officer of the 48th of Foot, *en voyage*. A paramour would only be momentary escape and an added complication. He sighed. His thoughts ran a strange gamut.

In Quebec, he knew there was one place where his petitions were offered. It was at the altar of the Ursuline chapel. His gift, the garnet stone that now adorned the foot of the chalice that Father Resche raised every morning at Elevation was one small consolation. He was remembered in prayers at that moment, a consolation that soothed his most troubled moods.

And what a mood he was in tonight. At the small writing desk by the window, he sat down, took a piece of vellum, dipped a quill in the ink well and started to write a letter to Marie-Louise. It might assuage his loneliness. A letter that could never be delivered, a letter that she would never read. Of what use was it to pour his heart out, he crumbled it up and threw it in the waste basket. Would he ever be able to tell her how many imaginary letters he had written to her against the sky on the trail.

He heard swift footsteps down the hall, muffled laughter, the swish of silk. Ah, at least whoever it was who would make love tonight, they were dealing with reality, they could touch, they could talk. He envied them. Maybe, John Knox was right. He should seek a friendship, a relationship or a liaison that would make him forget Marie-Louise completely. But would it? He undressed and stretched out. The bed had been warmed before he came up by either Zita or Reo. What a luxury. He stretched out exhausted with all his longings.

If Marie-Louise were free, if she could be here with him, they might live in Albany indefinitely. Not only did he ache for a sight of her, he was homesick. He had been gone too long. Should he ask for a transfer to Halifax, then home to Scotland? Would that fix everything. Not that simple. So far nothing worked. He must get back to Quebec, safe and sound. Then see Marie-Louise again, no matter what. In the spring and early summer, according to Amherst's plans, all hell would break loose. And who knew where any of them would end up.

As he stretched out in the warmth of the comforter, he thought, "Enjoy it, *mon vieux.*" It would be rough on the trail going back. There would be less snow, less cold but more rain. The rivers and lakes would be more navigable, they would be rushing toward spring. He turned on his side and finally slept.

Chapter Fourteen

The whole countryside waited patiently for the first signs of spring. But winter never left Quebec in the month of March. A few more *poudreries* were expected to storm the city. Here it was the second Monday in March.

At sundown, the cold intensified. Anaïse puffed up Côte de la Montagne. At the top, she caught her breath then proceeded to pass the Chateau. She emitted a little snort of contempt. Incredible that this magnificent structure, partly damaged, was now occupied by British officers. She walked a little faster down *rue St-Louis*. At the corner of *rue du Parloir* she glanced at the convent.

The blues of twilight now washed into various hues of violet on the snow. Mother de Bransac's study light beamed from the dark recesses of the monastery. A sentry lit the street lamp at the cross section. His breath blew white swirls on the cold air.

"It's my blue hour, too," Anaïse murmured to herself. Her fingers, stiff in tight mittens, were stuck in an old fur muff for double warmth and protection. A woolen scarf wrapped around her beaver hat tied snuggly under her chin. Her quick steps crunched on the hard snow. Her feet felt like blocks of ice. They were well shod in thin moccasins and fitted into fur-lined boots laced up to her knees.

Mother de Bransac must be going over her accounts. How did she do it? How did she keep face with such calm and serenity when General Murray had been ordering her about in her own convent, her own fortress, since last September? And all those Highlanders occupying a whole wing. The Reverend Mother had a right to be worried about her nuns, especially the younger ones. Like Marie-Louise! Thinking about the Boisverts, Anaïse gasped with surprise. Was that Jean-Paul just now pulling up in his sleigh on *rue du Parloir*? What was he doing at the front door of the convent? He usually went to Mother Philomène's kitchen entrance. Anaïse peered in the dusk. Who was that with him? Jean-Paul was helping an elderly person disembark from the sleigh. But no! It looked like Hubert. Hubert? He never needed help from anyone. What was strange? What was different?

"Oh, no!" Anaïse stifled an up-coming scream in her throat.

The man hobbled into the convent hallway. He leaned heavily on Jean-Paul. It was indeed Hubert. Anaïse knew him well and now recognized him even at this distance. He was hurt. What happened? Some accident?

"Oh, no! *Mon Dieu!*" She shook her head. She didn't want to believe her eyes. She stuck one of her mittened hands in her mouth. "Not Hubert! Not him, Lord!"

The portress received them in the foyer. A shaft of orange light from the interior fell on the violet tinted snow. Hubert was minus his right leg! It was replaced with a wooden peg attached at the knee.

"Incredible!" Anaïse whispered. Her heart pounded as she stood in the dusk. What happened? When? Where? She leaned over the stone wall of the Maréchel garden. She threw up.

"God, you can't know what you're doing up there!" She wiped the bilge from her lips and wept. "We're flattened out with war and now, the best *coureur-de-bois*, the best *voyageur* in all Canada has only one leg!" Where could she run to? To him, now! But instinctively, she held herself from dashing to the convent door to confront them. Wait, another wretched instinct advised against it. Hubert would come to her in his own way, in his own time. What should she do first? The portress closed the door, the mellow light was gone. Anaïse stood alone in the soft dusk. She gasped, her warm breath blew out strange designs. It was freezing cold. She couldn't stay here.

"*Mon Dieu! Mon Dieu!*" She swept down *rue St-Louis* toward her own house, sobbing all the way. She must prepare Tante José, see to a hot dinner with whatever was available, warm some cognac, a lot of cognac. She arrived home all out of breath. The sentry patrolling *rue St-Louis* had not stopped her. It was too cold. She slammed the storm doors.

"Is that you, Anaïse?"

"Yes, yes, Tante José."

The warmth of the vestibule enveloped her as she dropped her heavy cape and wraps. How was she going to fortify herself, make herself presentable for the inevitable meeting with Hubert? What would they say to each other. No doubt, he had a well prepared speech ready. She invoked the Holy Ghost and hurried to the kitchen.

"I need a hot *tisane*, Anaïse. It's cold, even by the fire." Tante José's voice piped up.

Anaïse bit her lip, tears streamed down her cheeks. How irritating Tante José was when she issued commands from her *tonneau* chair. From a high shelf, she took down a casserole dish, in the cupboard she found a bowl with five eggs, collected a piece of cheese a bit green at the edges, a pitcher of milk, two onions, a piece of salt pork and a small syrup crock that now held the secret of a fiery cognac.

"I'm coming, Tante José. *Un moment.*"

First things first. Anaïse swallowed two large gulps of cognac. She felt the sting and fire of the liquid spread through her. With brusk vigor, she poked the logs in the kitchen hearth. After the casserole was organized and placed in the side oven, she would talk with Tante José

"Anaïse, I'm cold."

"I'm coming, I'm coming." Anaïse measured warm cognac in two silver cups. Why not? It would keep warm. She heaved a great sigh. Her heart ached. Her head ached.

The fire leapt and roared in the fire-place. The casserole started to bubble, the blended aroma of cheese and spices permeated the room. A good coup, she had shot a generous dash of cognac into the dish instead of wine, it would smooth the moldy edges she had not cut off the cheese. They needed everything. The aftermath of war and destruction would haunt the city for a long time. She silently complimented herself again for the hidden luxuries she had amassed.

And Hubert? Hubert, minus one leg. Anaïse trembled, pain shot through her heart. She set her tray down and leaned against the stone wall by the fire-place.

"*Esprit Saint,*" she whispered. "Mère Marie de l'Incarnation, what's to become of us all." A maimed Hubert! This was a new fear.

She steadied herself against the warm stone. A flash of the last five years ran across her mind. What had she done? Since her fiancé had abandoned her to return to France, and to whom? Perhaps she'd never know. Brokenhearted, she had changed. She had swayed with the politics of the times. She possessed hidden luxuries today because she had connived with Bigot and the rest of the politicians. In her hurt and rejection, she had become another person. She was no better than the traitors, the rest of the clever, greedy nobility that had been returned to France as prisoners. Too few had been the real nobles and she had fallen in with the borderline manipulators.

"Anaïse!"

"Yes." She yelled back. She decided she would go to Hubert. She picked up the tray and went to the salon. "And, I will bring him here," she muttered.

"Who?" Tante José took the warm cognac cup eagerly.

"Hubert, Tante José" Anaïse draped a shawl about her aunt's thin shoulders.

"Something's wrong," Tante José looked up at her niece with frightened eyes. "Another *malheur* in this terrible war?"

"Yes, Tante José, another *malheur*. Drink this and I'll pour you another."

"What terrible news that you're going to souse me for the hearing of it?" She sipped, then gulped and stretched out the silver cup for a refill. Her wary glance questioned Anaïse.

Anaïse set the tray aside, threw another log on the fire, knelt by her aunt and took her cold hands into her own.

Tante José sniffed, she was embarrassed. It was not too often that Anaïse was affectionately demonstrative but she always provided her with every care and respect accorded the elderly.

"What are you cooking?" As she felt the warmth of Anaïse's hands, tears sprung to her eyes.

"Sustenance for us all while it lasts."

"Ah, you have all kinds of hidden things, Anaïse. Who knows where?" She looked straight into her niece's eyes, demanding the news.

"It's Hubert."

"What about Hubert? He's here? In Quebec?"

"Yes, and he's had an accident. He's lost his right leg." Had she imagined the scene at the convent door.

"No! *MonDieu!*"

"He's at the convent now, with Jean-Paul. I thought it best to wait until they come to us. . . ."

"*Es-tu folle?* Why wait?"

"Now, I'm going to him. . . ."

"Bring him here."

"Yes, and he will stay with us for as long as he needs to."

"*Bien sûr!* Go get him. *Toute suite!* Don't let him get away to Lorette." Tante José disentangled her hands as she commanded and shoved Anaïse away.

"I was going to wait . . . ."

"Wait for what? We're too old to wait. Go to him. Now!"

Anaïse put the cassarole on the lower shelf of the oven. In the foyer she hurried into her cape and boots, locked the double doors and let herself outside into the cold evening. She ran to the convent. There she found Jean-Paul in the hall talking with Mother Philomène.

"Anaïse," Jean-Paul began, "Hubert's had an accident."

"I know, I know, I saw you arriving here. I didn't know what to do until you reached me. What happened? Where? How?"

"Come sit here." Mother Philomène took her to the hall bench.

Jean-Paul sat with her. "He was hoisting beams at Jacques Cartier, one fell on him."

"Oh, dear God! Where is he now?"

"In the chapel, I'm taking him to Lorette in a few moments."

"You'll do no such thing, take him home with me. I'll go tell him, he's coming home with me."

"Anaïse!" They both hugged her, tried to hold her.

She broke away from them and ran to the chapel. She found Hubert sitting in the back on the Reverend Mother's old bench. His eyes were closed, his lips moved in prayer as he fingered his rosary.

"Hubert! *C'est moi!* What's happened?"

They fell into each other's arms. No words came. They rocked back and forth.

"Never mind, tell me later. Come home with me."

He shook his head as he held her tight.

"Yes," she insisted. "Jean-Paul is waiting." She helped him up.

"Anaïse," he began. She didn't recognize his voice. It had changed.

"Come, dinner is waiting. We'll make you comfortable. You can tell us everything then." She held back her tears.

Jean-Paul came to help them and Mother Philomène saw them off in the sleigh.

When they arrived at the Médard house Tante José was waiting by the fire. She made a brave attempt to sound cheerful.

"Hubert! Thank God you're alive! What happened? Come sit with me by the fire. Come sit with people who love you and tell us all about it."

Hubert hobbled over to her, kissed her on both wrinkled cheeks and sat next to her in the largest chair. He lifted the pegged leg to the foot stool.

"You're alive that's all that matters." Tante José blew her nose. "Anaïse, get us some cognac."

In the kitchen, Anaïse poured three stiff cognacs and one cider for Jean-Paul. She gave him the tray to serve. They all sat about the fire, sipped and looked pensively at the leaping flames.

"It was a stupid accident," Hubert began. "We were repairing a wall."

"Ah," Tante José shook her head sadly. "What's going on there?"

"Getting ready for the spring offensive." He drained his cup and Anaïse poured more cognac. Then she sat close to him, put her arm about his shoulder and patted him.

Jean-Paul was silent as he sipped his warm cider. He was hurting for Hubert. He didn't know what to say.

"Well, it's only a leg. *Le bon Dieu* must have some future task for me to do without it. *Voyons, la belle*, I thought you brought me here for dinner."

Anaïse jumped up. "Yes, yes, it's ready. Come, Jean-Paul, help dish it up."

She poured more cognac and Jean-Paul followed her to the kitchen.

"Jean-Paul, there's no way you two are going to Lorette tonight. You'll stay here. I think I've given him enough cognac, he should fall asleep after dinner."

"But he'll insist. You know how he is. Oh God, Anaïse, why did this have to happen to him?" Tears were starting, he sniffled as he held the warm plates. Up until now he had tried to hold off his pent-up emotion.

"We'll get through this, Jean-Paul," she held him at arms length, the plates between them. "Let's get some hot food into him, all of us. Then, I'll put him to bed. We can talk later or in the morning."

Jean-Paul nodded and went off to set the table.

Tante José's voice rose above the clatter of the dishes. "Hubert, you'll stay with us for as long as you like."

"Thank you, Tante José. We'll see what it is I must do, or can do."

The dinner, simple, hot and delicious, took the edge off their shock. By the time Anaïse served a bit of goat cheese with gooseberry preserves, Hubert was dozing over the last of his cognac.

Jean-Paul helped him upstairs to Anaïse's room. He collapsed on the bed with a great sigh. Jean-Paul took off his one boot and tenderly pulled the comforter over him.

After Anaïse put Tante José to bed, she and Jean-Paul sat by the fire.

"I must get back to Beauport tomorrow, Anaïse. Even though Rie-Ouise is there helping with the chores, I can't be all over the countryside without the authorities questioning me, questioning us. And we're a house in mourning, people still come over to say the rosary with us. Mireille Le Conte has been a big help to us through all this. I can't be away too long."

"I know." She was tired, sad, mesmerized by the leaping flames in the fire-place. "Take him to Lorette then in the morning," she conceded. "It's only natural that he wants to be with his wife's people for a while. . . ."

"Tante José will put up a fight."

Anaïse nodded. "He can come back to us any time."

"Now that Maman is gone,. . . ."

"A dear woman, Hortense Boisvert, may she rest in peace."

Jean-Paul crossed himself. "Now that she's gone, I should be at Jacques Cartier."

"Not now, there's time for you to do that, after the sugaring. We have enough of one good man minus his leg. How is Marie-Louise?"

Jean-Paul smiled. "She looks better every day. We've all been trying to fatten her up. I put cream on almost everything she eats."

"Everybody should have a brother like you."

"It was good for Rie-Ouise to have this time with Maman before she died. I don't know when Rie-Ouise will be returning to the convent, but soon I think."

"It's unsual. I'm surprised the Reverend Mother let her go home at all."

"Yes, we all are very glad to have her."

They were both pensive. Jean-Paul started to bank the fire for the night.

"What will Hubert do now?"

"Ah, Jean-Paul, I imagine he'll still go to the woods once in awhile when several coureurs go together."

"No one will be able to stop him. That's where he can breathe."

"He can help me manage the store."

"And he should do his wood carvings. He gave Maman a beautiful statue of St. Anne. You should see it, swirls in the wood, he can do anything with that knife of his."

"He's a proud, stubborn man, Jean-Paul, we've got a task ahead to keep his spirits up."

"He has us. We'll get him through this." Jean-Paul hugged his knees and enjoyed the warm stone he sat on at the edge of the fire-place.

"Now, let's get some sleep. We have to pass this by Tante José in the morning, that he's going to Lorette."

"I'll sleep by the fire."

Anaïse lit a large candle, stuck it in a brass holder and went upstairs. In the cold chamber, she loosened her clothes before snuffing out the light and quietly laid down beside Hubert. She would keep watch in case he needed anything. He thrashed about and murmured in his dreams. She steadied him in her arms. She dozed off. In a semi-dream, she saw herself and Hubert. They were laughing and running, running in fields of daisies on the Island of Orleans. A soft summer evening in June, then they went dancing at a farm house in St. Petronille and later made love in the barn loft. She woke up with a start and saw where they really were.

Toward dawn, they were both awake.

"Is that a way to lure me to your bed, to get me drunk. You foolish girl, it'll never be the same again."

Had the liquor worn off so soon. It was no time for nonchalant bravado.

"To me you're still a giant among men. . . ."

"Ah, Anaïse, those nights we made love. . . ." He groped for her hands.

"We'll make adjustments. We'll get this behind you. You're alive, you're strong."

"Such faith I had a few weeks ago."

"You'll have it again," she assured him.

He buried his head on her breasts. She felt his warm tears slide down her cleavage. He cried like a child. She held him fiercely tight. Her lips brushed his hair. She caressed his brow. His sobs subsided. After a quiet interval, he fell asleep again. She carefully edged away from him so she might sleep a little too.

At six o'clock, the French clock in the hall chimed. She got up tired. Hubert was sleeping peacefully. She shivered, laced her bodice, put on a warm wool dress and went downstairs.

At the fire-place, she poked the banked embers.

"Good morning, Anaïse," Jean-Paul stirred sleepily. He was wrapped to the throat in a bear rug. "I'll start the fire."

"Take your time. I'm going to the kitchen to mix batter for *crêpes* before the rest of the household wakes up."

By daylight, sunshine poured through the house with promise of a good day. By the time everyone was dressed and at table, a cozy fire crackled. Anaïse served an allotted number of *crêpes*, there was plenty of maple syrup, and one cup of hot chocolate each. She had to be stingy with it until new trade policies were set up.

Tante José argued with Hubert but in vain.

After they left, Anaïse came back to the table exhausted. She tried to finish half a *crêpe* with a few sips of lukewarm chocolate.

"I don't see why he had to go to Lorette."

"They'll take good care of him there, Tante José. He wants to be with Thérèse's people. He can always come to us."

"Yes, whenever he chooses, he has a home here. I want my cane, Anaïse. I must walk a little today, even if it's up and down the salon."

Later in the day, Anaïse went to the store. She needed time alone. She made an attempt to go over accounts and inventories but her mind was full of Hubert. Well, she must make plans but she would be patient. She would wait for Hubert to come to her. Would he? Or she could go to him. On the way home, she stopped at the Ursuline chapel. She lit a candle at a side altar and prayed. There were a few nuns on the other side of the grill in quiet meditation. Marie-Louise's choir stall was empty and Anaïse missed seeing her there.

Torrential rains poured down on the city for the next three days. Most of the snow washed away, some patches remained to freeze again. All the gutters in Upper and Lower Towns carried off gushes of water. The air grew warmer and spring like but no one was deceived. It was not quite yet the exit of winter. Supplies were always low in the spring, even in ordinary times. Everyone was impatient, those without cellar gardens were reduced to eating smoked eels and frozen fish. Some of the ice in the river broke. Gray blocks of it crowded the shore. Ice hole fishing was held up till the next storm and freeze.

To Anaïse's surprise, Hubert reappeared at the Médard doorstep. He came in with a farmer delivering food to the convent. He was not empty-handed himself. He had gone hunting with Noël, they had shot a deer in the forest not far from Lorette. He brought a haunch of it to the Médard kitchen.

"And I brought you and Tante José some sassafras for tea."

"Good, I'll make some right now. Sit by the fire, we're going to talk." He looked good. She was happy to see him. She put a copper kettle to boil at the hearth and fluttered about.

"Where's Tante José?"

"She was picked up in a carriage for a short visit to Charlesbourg. She's with Mireille Le Conte and Jerome."

"That will do her a world of good."

The tea was hot and soothing.

"This is what they give sick people, Anaïse. How about something stronger in it, like *cariboo*."

"It's too early in the day." She said with a disapproving smile but got the cognac out and splashed some in his tea. "First we're going to talk about herbs. With your knowledge of what's growing in the forest and all about us, I could have a side herbarium in my store.

"*C'est possible.* Come here."

They embraced. He held her fast.

"I thought I was going to stay away, miserable fool that I am," he murmured softly in her hair, found her lips in a long kiss.

"I'm glad you didn't because we're going to have a courtship. You'll be coming once a week and after a proper length of time we'll publish bans and get married."

"*Es-tu folle?* Are you crazy!" He roared with laughter. "Why do you want to marry a man with one leg, a coquette like you?"

Anaïse stilled his lips with her fingers. "Because it's you. . . . between us, and in all this mess, we still have love and respect. We always said when there was no one left we might marry. . . . I think the time has come. It's now, Hubert!"

"For what purpose, *ma chère?*"

"We're alive, we're still whole enough to have children."

"For what purpose?" he repeated.

"For us, for Quebec, the future."

"*Tu rêves*, it no longer belongs to us, the future, Quebec, none of that. Even if you love me enough. . . . And when did you find that out with all that's going on?"

"*Imbécile,*" she had frightened him.

He released his hold of her for a moment but she ran a finger down his cheek, tweaked his dark beard playfully and snuggled back in his embrace. "You know something I don't know." Some of his old bravado was still in him. That intrigue and connaissance of the forest, that stealth that was ready to leap on the unsuspecting, on-coming predator. What did he know about preparations for the spring offensive. She wondered.

"Now, that is almost impossible, Anaïse. A conniver like you, outwitting Cadet even. Impossible." He laughed.

"We have to change our lives now, Hubert. We have to make changes, we have to go with what's happening around us. Leave the Huron village, it's time."

"And what do you propose I do to support a wife and family?"

"You can ply your art, it won't be by a fire in the forest, so be commercial like me. You can whittle and carve wooden figures, any articles that will sell. I'll run the store. And when the British bring their families here to live in this garrison as they call it, even their daughters will attend classes at the Ursulines. Everybody will need something. We'll be doing business with New England merchants. They're coming up already."

"Well, it isn't all over yet." Now he held her more tightly.

Ah, he did know something. She sniffed against his deerskin jacket, revelling in his embrace. She had a need of him. It had been too lonely.

"You think far ahead, Anaïse. Too far. . . . It isn't over yet."

"Maybe. Some of that stone left on half of our buildings will last, our flesh is in that stone. We won't forget those who died here but we have to start a new life." She sighed. Tired of coping, she was ready to start a new life under whatever regime, even if she knew it was all over, life as they had known it. But they were alive and the British could not get inside her mind or her heart. She'd run her own store.

She looked up at him with unabashed sincerity. How could she convince him. Her lips trembled.

"You're serious," he was filled with awe.

"Ah, yes." She unlaced her bodice and put his hand on her warm, soft breast.

His fingers slid down between both round breasts, they lingered and circled caresses. He bent down and kissed them tenderly.

"Let's see if we can still make love, then," he said huskily.

"Yes, oh, yes. We need each other." She was aflame with desire. In hot anticipation she thought of the love and passion they had given each other before. As she clung to him she felt and wanted him to believe it would not be any different now.

Chapter Fifteen

Early in March, Ian and his companions met again with the two Caughnawaga guides outside the military base and they left Albany. A fair day, soft winds rippled signals of early spring. But they were not deceived as they started for the trails to plunge into the freedom of the forest. More heavily burdened with provisions than when they left Quebec, they knew they were going back to the last of winter.

The five of them took a last look at Albany, a city of well-stocked Dutch houses along the Hudson. A welcoming city where they had been so well received and entertained, a city of unruffled conservatism and of tranquil picturesqueness. They took a last look at the military installation on the hill, headquarters of the North American campaign.

The Caughnawagas offered safety on the trail, they would be with them as far as the Farnham farm in the vicinity of Fort Ticonderoga and Crown Point. Then they would leave the southern boundaries to make good time on Lake Champlain, pass St. John and into the Richelieu River. It would be more navigable now than in January. Past Trois Rivières, they would be on the home stretch.

Ahead of them lay a broad tract of wilderness, shaggy with primeval woods. Inumerable streams would be crossed, rivulets that would gurgle beneath their shadows. They would be drenched with rains but dried out at campfires by gleaming lakes in fiery sunsets. The wastes between the questionable French and English lines were ranged by savage allies. Ian hoped they would encounter none.

The expedition into the colony of New York had toughened them all. But Ian could hardly wait to see the skyline of Quebec again. Away this long, he now realized that Canada had a vigor of its own. And the memory of Marie-Louise had a strength of its own. If he had thought the distance the journey put between them might help to forget her, so far it had not worked.

As they left the safety of Albany, Ian was still in awe of Amherst and all the forts that he was still working on, Fort William Henry, Fort Edward, and to the west Oswego, Fort Toronto and Fort Niagara, also the building of roads. It was no wonder he hadn't come to Quebec to join Wolfe. After Ensign Higgins had brought him the victorious news last October, there had been no need.

Now, Montreal was targeted for the next prize to solidify the possession of Canada for the British Crown. And he was bringing plan and map copies of the three-prong attack back with him along with the famous strong spruce beer recipe. When would it happen? What would Murray say? What next? They had better reach Quebec first. Anything could blow up in their faces long before the advance on Montreal.

They gave the Caughnawagas what they could safely part with, a few knives, belt buckles, most of their rum, they could get more at the Farnhams, a bit of laudanum and reluctantly one of their small swords. Ian thought they were lucky, treacherous atrocities had been committed even by friendly allies on both sides of this imaginable border. Parties of rangers had been cut to pieces in the vicinity of Ticonderoga for less. Ian and his companions were grateful for the trust and guidance of Chinnohete and Tontileaugo.

"We're lucky blokes that Amherst keeps the Indians in his employ well supplied," Paige commented relieved they had managed this far.

"Aye," they all agreed.

After tramping in heavy rain a whole afternoon, they arrived finally at the Farnham place like five drowned rats. They quickly dried out by the hearth. They were waited on and replenished with hot rabbit stew, good bread and rum.

Edward Pinkham, his arm still in a sling, hovered about them eager for every bit of news on what he had missed in Albany.

"You're looking pretty good, old man," Page gave Edward an affectionate pat on the back.

His arm was much better but he was still weak. Emma Farham was generous as she poured them all another round of rum. She lingered over Edward's cup.

Ian observed with a smile that a romance had blossomed between the two of them.

By next morning, even the last snow patch had been rinsed away by the heavy rain. They decided to dry out for another day, so did the country side. Fortified with another day of comforts, it was a good time to head back on the trail before another storm.

At breakfast, Ian and Gordon talked with Edward about a transfer.

"I could go back. . . ." he began. "I'll slow you up."

"Maybe, until you're a hundred percent, a transfer would be more sensible for the time being," Ian suggested cautiously.

"If I don't go back now and fulfill my duties of the expedition, I'm out here by myself. When are other couriers or voyageurs coming through that I could latch onto?"

"Good question. Who knows?" Gordon finished his tea. He was anxious to get started.

"But you'll save time without me."

"Might be easier for you to get yourself to Albany in another week or so. You could come back to Quebec with either Amherst's or Haldimand's expedition," Gordon advised.

"Amherst knows you're here. We'll write a letter. And I'll arrange for this transfer when I get back to Murray. Think about it for a minute." Ian thought a little more time for Pinkham to regain full health might be best.

They finished their strong tea, ham, eggs, corn cakes and talked about Albany, the forts, and the forthcoming attack on Montreal.

Edward Pinkham decided to remain at the Farnhams, then go on to Albany. After a round of farewells, the five of them left the hospitable

colonial family and Pinkham in their continued care. A dry day, full of
sunshine, they were eager to re-enter the forest and complete their journey.

Then heavy rains came and it was even miserable by their campfires.
At canoe caches, they sheltered under upside down canoes. They kept
themselves together with what they could track down in the woods and fish
in the waters. When they finally reached the Richelieu, there was no snow on
the ground, no ice floes in this part of the river. But it was cold and a new
freeze was expected. They traveled swiftly on the water, luck was with them.
They pushed hard even though they felt like their arms were going to fall off
their bodies. Finally they pulled themselves ashore to leave the last of the
loaned canoes in the appointed place for the next group of *coureurs*. Camp
was set up long enough for a midday meal of trout. After a quick clean-up
they marched toward Quebec in a jovial mood. The cold followed them.

When, at last, they saw the skyline of the city on the rock again, they
were ecstatic. They all shouted.

"Hip, hip, hooray!" They looked at it for a long moment from the
edge of the woods.

"Well, if we're not a group of the most bedraggled men anybody ever
saw," Gordon hurried on ahead of everybody.

They limped, walked faster, ran the rest of the way. They were met
by soldiers near the walls.

"Welcome back! Just on time for supper and grog." They were
relieved of their backpacks, medicine boxes, snow-shoes, and patted on the
back. Snow flurries started sweeping across the streets.

Once inside the warm convent, Ian went straight to the chapel. In
his usual place on the public side he said a prayer of thanksgiving for his
completed mission. A voluntary journey that had put all that distance
between himself and Marie-Louise. She was nowhere in sight. Two old nuns
were in their cloistered stalls with bowed heads.

"Oh, God! I'm so glad to be back." He went to his quarters. How
he had longed for that cell out on the trail, a cell kept pristine by the nuns.
Lieutenant Preston, a colleague of his regiment who had occupied the room
during his leave was now clearing out his gear. They shook hands.

"You look beat and no wonder! How is it down there with Amherst and the Conondagas?"

"He does things in his own way, slower than Wolf, very methodical. All those forts, huge lakes, different Indians. Monckton's in New York City, feeling better, very busy. We covered a lot of forest. I think I've become a ranger."

"You look like you need hot vittles. I was just going to mess."

Ian dropped his knapsack, short sword and bayonet. "I'll catch forty winks, freshen up and go straight to General Murray."

"He knows you're all back. He's scribbling away and waiting for your news. Let's chat later, you must know what comes next in this crazy campaign?"

"Aye, some of it. Smells like Mother Philomène has pea soup simmering." Ian's nostrils quivered. "I longed for a whiff of that out there while I was chewing pemmican."

"And there's molasses bread that'll satisfy your stomach, old man."

"I better get on with it. I think I'm too keyed up to sleep."

"You'll have leave to sleep all day tomorrow. See you later."

Ian collapsed on his cot. He dozed off and slept through the Angelus bell. He didn't even hear it. An hour later, he woke up with a start. He had to get to Murray with his reports. Where was Marie-Louise? He could hardly wait to see her again. Hot water had been left for him while he slept. Just as he finished freshening up, there was soft knock on the door.

He opened to an elderly nun who passed him with a tray of hot food.

"Captain Lindsay, supper is over. I was bid to bring you some sustenance. General Murray is waiting to see you and other members of the expedition after you've eaten."

"I'm famished. Your tray is very welcome. Thank you, Sister."

The meeting gathered in Murray's headquarters. They all delivered their letters. Ian's packet from Amherst, the precious spruce beer recipe and copies of maps for Patrick MacKellar. They smoked and went over the general scuttlebutt. Finally, they broke up with Murray's hearty congratulations to all of them.

Ian was exhausted, he could hardly keep his eyes open yet he ached for a glimpse of Marie-Louise. Where was she? He hadn't heard the bell for final evening prayers yet. He went toward the kitchen. Maybe, they were still cleaning up in there. He stationed himself in an unconspicuous corner of the hall as the final bell sounded. All the nuns who had been working in the kitchen left in their usual processional to go to chapel. Marie-Louise was not among them. Maybe she had been sent to General Hospital or Hôtel Dieu for special duty? He would see the Reverend Mother first thing in the morning.

Snow fell on the city with gusts of arctic winds. He retired to his quarters, it was good to be back. Heavy flakes pelted at the window, he removed his boots, slid onto his cot and fell into a deep sleep.

The next morning it was calm, new mounds of snow covered the city. A weak sun tried to come through a gray sky. After Mass, Ian went directly to Mother de Bransac's study and knocked.

"*Entrez.* Ah, Capitaine Lindsay, you've come back to us safe and sound."

"Reverend Mother," Ian bowed. He was happy to see her. "Sister Madeleine?" He cleared his throat and hung in the question.

"I sent her home," she said with finality.

"She's well?" A fear grabbed him.

"Alas, she was wasting away to a feather here these last few months. And ten days ago, her poor mother died. She's with her grieving family."

Ian gasped and bowed his head. "I'm so sorry to hear this."

Mother de Bransac nodded and made the sign of the cross.

"I must go to her, to the family, immediately."

"But Captain Lindsay. . . ." she rose from her desk. But Ian was gone. She couldn't stop him.

He went back to his room, breathless. He was beside himself. He must find a way to go to Beauport today, even if he had to walk. Then he calmed down and tried to think. He had made a bad exit with the Reverend Mother. He would have to repair that. He had tried so hard not to make a fool of himself. Now, he was doing just that.

Mother de Bransac sadly shook her head. She was very concerned about her young nun, Marie-Louise, and now she had an added concern about this worn-out captain who, at least, had returned from a dangerous voyage in one piece.

Ian had to reconsider. It was only after another restful night that he found a way to go to Beauport. He negotiated with a farmer from Sillery to borrow his horse and sleigh. He presented himself anew to the Reverend Mother in his freshened-up uniform.

"I was shocked with your news yesterday. I am off duty for a few days. I'm going to Beauport today with a fellow officer to offer my condolences to the Boisvert family."

Mother de Bransac nodded. She couldn't stop him. "Then kindly take this spiritual bouquet from all of us." She handed him a heavy envelope. "Whatever you can do will help. Jean-Paul is the solid mainstay to his father, to that family now. Sister Madeleine will be back with us soon. We will have a memorial mass said for her mother in the chapel when she returns."

She couldn't explain to him that it was very rarely that a nun left the convent. Not now, she thought. That in the case of Marie-Louise, it was extreme. That as her Superior, she had gathered what wisdom she could at the time and permitted the absence. She could only hope that what she had done was remedial to the restoration of Marie-Louise's ususal good health. What were the Captain's intentions? What was going to happen to these two young people? They must talk to each other now. She would pray, advise when asked and wait for the outcome. Would Marie-Louise be able to return with a firm decision on what she really wanted to do, must do, while she was still mourning, poor child.

The cold held, the sun refused to come out.

"I think there's another storm on the way. We'd best not stay too long on this condolence visit," Lieutenant McAlister said as they drove off to Beauport. They were covered with beaver rugs, they had woolen ear muffs over their bonnets and their warm breaths cut the cold air.

In mid afternoon at the Boisvert house, Marie-Louise started thinking about the evening meal. During this time at home she wore her full convent habit when visitors came. But she usually left off her veil and covered her habit with one of her mother's huge aprons when she and Mireille Le Conte were alone working in the kitchen.

They had just looked over Jean-Paul's plan for his mother's vegetable garden to be planted as usual this spring. It was to be one of her memorials. He was gone ice-hole fishing. Uncle Guillaume was off to an afternoon nap after taking his bark cough medicine and Joseph Boisvert was sitting somberly by the window smoking and looking off in the gray distance.

"*Tiens*," he said. "Here's Jean-Paul back with some fish. And some visitors coming up the road."

Marie-Louise quickly donned her veil. They all went to the door to welcome, to their surprise, the two officers and Jean-Paul.

"Monsieur Boisvert, Sister Madeleine. . . ."

"Captain Lindsay," Marie-Louise came forward.

"And this is Lieutenant McAlister." Ian introduced his fellow officer. He was full of joy to see her again. How thin and piquant her face, full of sorrow. "Our expedition just returned a few days ago. We heard your wife, your mother passed away." Ian directed his glance from Joseph Boisvert, to Jean-Paul and Marie-Louise. "We've come to pay our respects, offer our condolences and here's a message from the Reverend Mother."

Ah, he's safe and sound, Marie-Louise gave silent thanks, but thinner too. They all shook hands.

Monsieur Boisvert took over, bade them take their wraps off and sit by the fire. Jean-Paul went to a side table in the cooking section with the fish and took the wine out. Uncle Guillaume came downstairs to see what all the commotion was about. Introductions went around and since it was close to supper time, the officers were pressed to stay. Wine was poured. Mireille and Marie-Louise worked on the food. In no time, they added more red onions to the soup, cooked and creamed the fish and mashed turnips while the men sipped their wine.

At table, they all read the spiritual bouquet from the convent. A bonding spread through them. They talked as they ate and drank, considerate and sympathetic of one another. About seven o'clock the winds rose high, snow flurried gustily at the windows.

"Here's that other storm, we'd best leave," McAlister excused himself as he got up from the table.

Marie-Louise looked imploringly at Ian. So soon, he had just come.

Mireille got up too, picking up plates. "I'm just down the road but I have animals to care for. I should go too."

"I'm supposed to take Sister Madeleine back to the convent tomorrow or when the storm stops," Jean-Paul said.

"You could stay the night, there's plenty of room, the house is big," Joseph Boisvert invited the two officers.

McAlister looked at Ian. "You could stay and visit longer if you wish and if Jean-Paul is coming in tomorrow. But I'd best get back while the going is good."

"Thank you, Monsieur Boisvert." There was no hesitation. "Yes, I'll stay tonight and go back with Jean-Paul and Sister Madeleine."

Marie-Louise gave him a grateful look. She wanted some time alone with him. She needed that. Perhaps they could take a walk in the snow in the morning.

Mireille and Lieutenant McAlister bundled up and left in the on-coming storm. Jean-Paul went to the barn to check the animals for the night. A small chamber upstairs was assigned to Ian. Then they all sat by the fire with another glass of wine and remembered Hortense Boisvert. They lingered over good-nights when Monsieur Boisvert banked the fire.

"I'm glad you're back, Captain Lindsay," Marie-Louise placed her hand in his.

He held on to it for an extra moment. "I'm so sorry you're all going through this tragic loss."

"It was good of you to come." They hung on to this moment of reunion and observed again that they had both lost weight.

All was quiet in the great room after they retired with only an occasional sputter from the banked fire but the wind howled outside.

In the middle of the night, Ian woke with a start. The whole house was now cold as a tomb. Above the wind, he heard the snoring of the three men in chambers down the hall. Some of their spent grief, at last, now permitted them a deep sleep. He lay back for a moment. He could hardly believe that he was a guest in Marie-Louise's home, this place where he first saw her standing in the doorway in a red dress. Cautiously he got up. He stumbled about. A shaft of light came up the stairway from the last of the fire downstairs. He wrapped a gray woolen blanket about his shoulders. He had not undressed because of the cold. He was clad in pants, shirt and woolen stockings. Mother Philomène's handiwork, those warm stockings, he blessed her again for her concern of the Highlanders. He went down into the main room to stoke up the fire. Perhaps he could warm some liquor if he found any. With a few shivers, he made the fire roar in the great fireplace. He stuck one of the pokers into the red hot embers at the bottom of the grate. There was a jug of cider and cups on the sideboard. He poured a cupful and warmed it with the hot poker. The cider sizzled. He doubted that it would re-induce sleep at this point but it would tone down his shivers.

The wind whipped about the house in spurts and bounds. In a quiet interval, he thought he heard sobbing. Marie-Louise? It continued, heart-rending sobs. He found a candle in a pewter holder on the mantle, lit it from the fire and went toward the stairs to investigate. Which room?

Marie-Louise appeared at the top of the staircase. She had a huge blanket about her shoulders and a tiny, white cap on her head, tied securely under her chin.

"Marie-Louise!"

"Ian, I'm cold. I can't sleep."

He met her half-way up the stairs as she came down. He raised the candle to shed light on her tear-stained face.

"Come and sit by the fire then. I'll warm some cider." He put an arm around her. "My dear, I'm so sorry about your mother. All you've been through."

They went down to the fireside together. He settled her in her mother's chair and tenderly tucked the blanket in around her. He stoked the fire anew then he warmed two cups of cider with two red hot pokers. This time the sizzling and sputtering made him nervous. He hoped they weren't making too much noise.

"Here, drink this." He sat at her feet.

They sipped in companionable silence and gazed at the fire. In these unexpected, private, stolen moments, they revelled in being alone with each other. It was sheer bliss.

Marie-Louise thought this is the way it would be if they could be together. The cold left her, her whole body was aflame with desire and love.

"I'm so glad you came back to us."

"You were with me every day." He got up, took their empty cups and set them down on the hot bricks by the fire, then sat on the hearth bench.

The snores of Jean-Paul, Monsieur Boisvert and Guillaume were still heard faintly from the upstairs hall. Ian leaned toward Marie-Louise.

"May I see what you look like under that funny little cap?"

She smiled and untied the convent head-piece. It fell to the floor.

"Ah, you are lovely," he leaned closer and dared pass his hand in the short, blond curls.

"Oh, Ian. . . . What are we going to do? How are we going. . . .?" She hiccoughed with a small sob.

"Hush," his voice was low. "We mustn't wake anyone." He took her in his arms and held her close. "I love you. I know I have no right to speak or to ask anything of you, I don't deserve you. But please don't take any vows. I want you to be my wife. Think about this first. . . . I'll abide by whatever you decide." There it had all come out.

"Ian, I am already promised. Since you left on the expedition, I tried to live one day at a time at the convent. Reverend Mother sent me home and not only because my mother was ill and dying. . . ."

"The Church gives you time to change your mind. Take your time, I'll wait for as long as it takes."

She hiccoughed again and wiped tears away with a corner of the warm blanket.

"This is not the way I imagined proposing to you. I thought maybe it would be in the convent garden on bended knee, or here in your mother's garden."

Marie-Louise smiled. "We hardly had the occasion."

"We don't know how much time we have."

"No, we don't, life is short." She thought of her mother in her pine coffin in the cold barn waiting for the rituals of spring. "What's going to happen?" She whispered against his shoulder as he continued to hold her close.

"I don't know what's going to happen in the outcome of this war. But whatever happens, I believe God is giving us these few moments to help sort ourselves out. . . . Wherever and whenever we find these moments we should accept them."

"Yes." She clung to him. "I would like to believe that. Otherwise, I'm in a terrible state of guilt."

He re-arranged the blanket about her over the voluminous nightgown, retrieved the convent night cap from the floor and helped put it back on. "Now, you must try to get some sleep. I'll be down here by the fire if you need me. Try to sleep, if we're all going back to the convent tomorrow you must be rested. I love you."

She rose from the chair, held the blanket tightly about her. He kissed her forehead as he walked her up the stairs and held the candle high.

At the top she turned. "Ian," she said softly.

"Yes?"

"I love you."

"My dearest!" He set the candle down on a nearby hall table. He kissed both her hands, then her lips softly placing respect before ardor. "You have made me the happiest of men!"

"I don't know how to do this," her slender fingers caressed his face. "I owe the convent a lot. I would be letting everybody down, even God. I might be punished. We might be."

"Hush. No such thing. God loves you, I have to believe he loves us and that we can serve him in different states of life. I will not be the cause of any more of your unhappiness. Now, no more talk and whispers. You must get some sleep."

She nodded as she clung to him another moment then left him and walked down the hall to her bedroom.

Ian was filled with joy as he went down the stairs. He thought his heart would burst. At least, she was going to think about it, about him, about them and the possibility of their getting married. He could hardly believe it. Now that he knew she loved him, he promised himself he would not pressure her in any way. He would wait. He would temper his impatience. He went and sat by the fire. Outside, the wind continued to howl, moving snow drifts. At the windows, shutters slammed against the stone. The men in the other parts of the house slept on.

He yawned in the midst of his mixed emotions but he doubted he could go back to sleep now. He threw another log on the fire and it roared with new warmth throughout the house. What exactly were they going to do? What had motivated Marie-Louise to leave this comfortable home to become a nun? He had observed her with the children in the townspeople's wing, especially with the babies. She was so young, had she weighed very carefully that she would never have children of her own if she took religious vows. He knew he had sounded honorable, purposeful, organized. But what really could he do for both of them, for all of them? Jean-Paul, Monsieur Boisvert, Mother Migeon de Bransac, and most of all Marie-Louise? What was expected of him? Was it all up to him? Yes, it was. The responsibility was with him when and if Marie-Louise rendered a decision. He must decide what was best. Where would they marry? Where would they live?

Would Murray release him to return to Scotland? He longed to see his parents. No doubt, they had a marriage contract arranged for him for when he would return. And his gentle mother? What would she say if he told her, "I'm in love with a novice nun." Would she say it was an obsession of the war. Like Mother de Bransac, his mother was wise too. He poked the fire, nothing stirred in the rest of the house.

Above the arctic wind, Ian heard the lone cry of wolves from the north woods. Pitou answered from the depths of the barn. Would the simple verbal declarations he and Marie-Louise had made in the middle of the night seem as logical in the light of day? He wondered? What was he doing in this God-forsaken country where hungry wolves cried in the middle of the night just a short distance from civilization. He thought of the heather in the gardens at Lindsay Hall. He thought of summer, of the flowers he and Marie-Louise had talked about in the convent library. He thought of fields of them at Vendôme, the foundries, the glassblowing, the art on the crystal, picnics on the lawns by the forest, the rustle of silk parasols, his mother smiling in the sunshine as her lace fichu fluttered lightly about her neck. But especially, he thought of daisies, fields of them not far from his grandparents' work compound. And Marie-Louise had told him that she had run through fields of them as a child on the Island of Orleans.

What was he doing here, trying to win the heart of a novice-nun? The war wasn't over yet. Levis threatened to come back with his new offensive as soon as the ice broke in the rivers. Nobody knew what was going to happen. Nevertheless, Ian felt a certain peace now that he had declared his intentions. He prayed it would be the same with Marie-Louise. If the storm abated they could go back to the convent tomorrow to take up their respective routines.

The next morning Ian saw the world differently. The sun was shining through the kitchen windows. The whole country-side he had called Godforsaken in the middle of the night now scintillated. The snow sparkled, the sky was robin's egg blue, the wind had died down, everything was calm.

Jean-Paul came in from the barn with gusts of cold air. He set down a pail of milk. It still steamed from the cow's body warmth.

The fire roared in the great fire-place. Marie-Louise made *crêpes* and fried pieces of salt pork. She looked lovely and preoccupied in a billowing white apron over her habit. Monsieur Boisvert slathered *creton* on a slice of brown bread. They all rolled their *crêpes* in maple syrup and drank hot herbal tea.

Ah, Ian thought, as he ate the delicious breakfast, the Boisverts were better off here than in the city. That had been weighed back and forth. It certainly would not distract Joseph Boisvert from his bereavement and there was still a scarcity of food in Quebec. He was better off in his own house, on his own land with the memories of his wife. Moving to Quebec would not lessen his mourning. And who would take care of the farm? It was a well hidden place off the main road by the woods. A wonder part of his own regiment hadn't already ravaged it. He hoped it would continue to be by-passed.

"Here, you'd better put this on your head, it's cold out there. It's much warmer than that hat you *Ecossais* call a bonnet." Monsieur Boisvert offered Ian a beaver hat.

Ian took it gratefully, eagerly with a wide smile. Anything, he thought, to be accepted by this family.

"We'll miss you my dear," Uncle Guillaume hugged Marie-Louise. "But we know you're praying for us all there in that convent. It was good of the Reverend Mother to let you come home to us." He turned to Ian and shook hands. "I enjoyed reminiscing about Vendôme with you, *Capitaine* Lindsay."

Marie-Louise wrapped a woolen scarf over her veil, hooked her long cloak at the throat then embraced her father tenderly. Was it the last time she would have that privilege?

"Come, we have bear rugs in the sleigh, everybody will be warm," Jean-Paul promised. They all spilled outside.

"I have one more farewell," Marie-Louise said as she looked up at Ian.

"May I come with you?" He knew she was going to the barn.

She nodded. They both walked down the neat path Jean-Paul had shoveled, crunching the snow. He kept all the walkways open about the place.

The smell of hay and horse manure stung their nostrils as they entered the ice cold structure. It was as large as the stone manor. In a far corner away from the animal stalls, the simple pine box that enclosed the remains of Hortense Boisvert was surrounded with ice blocks.

Marie-Louise placed her hand lovingly on the coffin.

"I hope there'll be flowers," her voice faltered. "I hope there'll be flowers when spring comes, when they finally lay her to rest. . . ."

"Of course, there'll be flowers," Ian put his hand over hers reassuringly.

"I may not be here," a tear slid down her cheek. "At least I was here for the *Libera*."

He pressed her hand and nodded. "Come now," he said gently. He led her back out into the sunshine. There were more good-byes all around then they mounted the sleigh. Monsieur Boisvert and Uncle Guillaume fussed and tucked the bear rugs about them very snuggly. The impatient Boisvert horses spouted frosty clouds with their breaths.

Jean-Paul took the reins. He surveyed their country road that he and his father had cleared in the early morning. After each storm, every available Beauport farmer still left on his premises worked and shoveled to clear roads and paths to Avenue Royale along the river to make travel possible. They were ready to go.

"*En avant marche*, giddap," Jean-Paul clucked.

The horses trotted, the bells attached to the harness jingled as the sleigh glided down the road and swiftly passed the village of Beauport. Ian held Marie-Louise's gloved hand under the fur wrap as they sped over the snow. They were both silent. He thought the next time he would see her that they would be in their respective routines at the convent and if there were other people about, in the hospital ward, in the library, in the garden or in the kitchen, he would be addessing her as Sister Madeleine. But in his heart, she was Marie-Louise for all time now. They had exchanged something precious last night with their simple affirmations. A peace had come to both of them with the release of that admittance. They had given something to each other, something undefinable as yet, but something for the future. Would they have the courage to find the right solution, make the right decisions? Ian wondered as they arrived at the convent.

Chapter Sixteen

Ian and Marie-Louise returned to the convent and went to their respective routines as if they had never left. Marie-Louise went directly to the Reverend Mother to receive her blessing.

"Welcome back, Sister Madeleine. We were all very sorry to learn of your mother's death. Father Resche will say a Memorial Mass for her now that you're here."

"Thank you, Reverend Mother."

"You're looking well. Your family fed you better than we did."

"Jean-Paul is very good at hunting, fishing and in the kitchen."

They both smiled. The Vespers bell rang.

"We'll talk again later, Sister." They both rose to answer the bell.

It was as simple as that, Marie-Louise thought as she walked down the familiar hall, she was back in the fold. But her conflict was far from resolved. The time for a reckoning was not yet, not now. The dreaded talk for reassessment with all questions addressed. Then she must write to her father about her decision. When? *Doucement, doucement,* she told herself. One thing at a time. A small blessing that she didn't need to apply for the Bishop's release.

Ian attended a lot of meetings. He picked up the pieces on reports from a minor battle that had been fought at Lorette on March nineteenth. In the kitchen he tested Amherst's spruce beer recipe with Mother Philomène. Noël brought them everything they needed. They tried both the old and the new recipes, mixing and stirring. They made vats of it. The garrison surgeons continued to recommend it for scorbutic men. Again, Ian wrote memos to the commanding officers of all regiments to urge their men to drink it twice a day with their rum.

He carefully spaced seeing Marie-Louise in the library not to be too conspicuous. There were the occasional walks in the garden during the nuns' recreational periods when weather permitted. Sometimes she was alone. A glance or a snatch of conversation sufficed to carry him through. The memory of the few moments they had shared together alone at Beauport in the middle of the night appeased his troubled heart. He carried the knowledge of her love within himself, it calmed and sustained him. She seemed tranquil and serene. He knew she was doing a lot of praying and he was doing a lot of thinking. When the convent was quiet at night, he wondered just where her cell was. Was she sleeping?

Though they were at an impasse, Marie-Louise felt very much better. She threw herself into the busy routines of the convent. She took comfort in the fact that she and Ian were under the same roof. At various chosen moments, all the sisters came and offered her their love and sympathy. And when they sang the memorial Mass for her mother, she was deeply touched. Their beautiful voices soared in the chapel, Marie-Louise's heart lifted as the incense floated about her and the altar, it was balm and new solace.

These were her sisters in Christ, she thought. This was her home where she had come with Geneviève. Together, they had asked to be accepted in the novitiate, they had dedicated their lives. With new resolution, Marie-Louise thought she must reconsider everything. She had come here with sincerity thinking she had a true vocation. And now, she was sure of nothing except that she was in love with Ian regardless of who he was, a captain in a regiment that was part of the enemy that had come here to wage war on them. It was unreal.

She asked the protection of heaven for all of them. She prayed and meditated in her choir stall, her hour glass turned. The grains of sand dripped the moments away. What would time bring? They were teaching more classes. By next September some boarders would return, new ones might come, there probably would be no more need for a hospital wing to care for the sick overflowing from the two hospitals. It was hoped they would be teaching their full-time classes again. Would the war be settled and over with?

Everyone in Quebec looked forward to spring, the breaking of the ice in the rivers, the advance of Levis, yet dreaded what the outcome might be. Would it regain the city, return everything as it was, to what it had been? No one knew. They hung in a vigil loaded with uncertainty.

In her prayerful meditations, Marie-Louise knew that she had not only to talk with the Reverend Mother but also Father Resche in the confessional. She would hear their counsels but in the end she would have to make up her own mind. On some days, it was simple, especially when she remembered the touch of Ian's fingers on the nape of her neck. Many times she relived those brief moments they had been alone at Beauport. True, she loved him, undisputably, she knew that now. Was that what Mother Migeon had wanted her to find out? Now that she had been in Ian's arms, she wondered what it would be like to be his wife, to bear his children, their children, and put them to her breast? In a few moments, she had broken all the rules. What would the Bishop say? Already angered over all the mixed marriages, what would he say when he learned that an Ursuline wanted to leave the convent to marry a Scot Highlander in the British Army?

But now that she was back to her cell, her chapel, her convent, she might be advised to forget Ian. Could she do that? Or could she attempt to build the rest of her life on the few moments of happiness she had shared with Ian? Was this real or a mere fantasy?

She knew she had puzzled Mother Migeon greatly and that she weighed very carefully each nun's case of a vocation. There were some dividing days, when Marie-Louise didn't see Ian, she felt happy and at home again in the convent. This week she had the new duty of trimming the Votive Lamp in the chapel.

"*La lampe qui s'éteint pas,*" she murmured as she trimmed the wick. Yes, it was the lamp that never went out. Its twinkling flame was constant in the sanctuary. No matter what happened, she had such a flame in her heart and it would never go out. Did it burn more brightly for God or for Ian? Or could it fuse into one leap for both?

"To do God's will," Mother Migeon often said, "first you have to find out what is the will of God."

During her meditations, Marie-Louise asked the intercession of the two foundresses, Madame de la Peltrie and Marie de l'Incarnation. In her library periods, she looked up everything on their lives. Just yesterday, she looked up notes on Marie Madeleine de Repentigny, Sister Agatha, who had founded the perpetual memento of the Votive Lamp for their chapel.

In spite of disruption with convent routine by her recent absence, Marie-Louise found again the solitude of the monastery and embraced it. It cushioned her split, disturbed thoughts. She joined with full voice the chant of the divine office. When all the errands and duties of the day were over and the evening closed, she took strength in the spiritual silence that fell over all of the monastery. It was its greatest charm.

Marie-Louise had lost the old strengths she possessed before Ian came. Now, she needed new strength.

She remained in the chapel even after the first twilight shades descended, after the plaintive opening anthem of the Vespers Office, "O God come to my aid." She prayed fervently to the last "Amen" and whiff of incense about the altar. While the cold of the arctic winter still swept down the St. Lawrence, Marie-Louise with all the other sisters in the sanctuary of that chapel prayed not only for the dead but the living in Quebec. They prayed for Quebec. And Marie-Louise prayed for Ian and herself.

In spite of the war, Mother Migeon de Bransac had kept her nuns well organized and routines had been pretty well kept up. There was strength in routine. They were accustomed to having their days mapped out, each hour with its allotted occupation. The chapel was the core of their lives where they met eight times a day for matins and lauds, prime, terce, sext, none, vespers and complines. It all started with the bell at four o'clock, at earliest dawn. They all chanted their first prayers of the day as they went to chapel to refresh their souls. "To thee, O Lord have I watched from earliest light of day."

In between prayers, they worked all day according to their assignments interspersed with brief quiet intervals of recreation, conversations in community, walks in the garden, till the signal for retiring before nine in the evening. Then they all entered their cells as night fell about the cloister, and with all noises of the day hushed, they folded into the recesses of their own consciences.

April came with softer days and light rains but wreaths of snow and ice still clung to the city and a lull of apprehension reigned.

There was a lot of work on Ian's desk. On April 10, in the Orders of the Day, he repeated and added to a Memo on spruce beer.

"We've become a rum and spruce beer army," he muttered to himself as he wrote.

"The visible effects of the spruce, or hemlock-spruce, which has been given for some time to the scorbutic men in the hospitals, put it beyond doubt that it must also be the best preservative against the scurvy, and, as the lives of brave soldiers are ever to be regarded with the utmost attention, it is ordered that the regiments be provided with a sufficient quantity of that particular spruce, which each corps must send for occasionally; and it is to be made into a liquor, according to the method with which the surgeons are already acquainted; and commanding officers must be answerable that their men drink of this liquor, at least twice every day, mixed with their allowance of rum."

There was a note about some British merchants who had come up from New England after Christmas and had set up trade. Ian thought of Anaïse and knew she would most likely make it her business to get along with them. How was she getting on with her little store?

There was a note about newly gained intelligence from a deserter claiming that M. de Levis, at the head of an army of twelve thousand men, with a fleet of seven frigates and sloops under M. Vauquelin, *Chef d'Escadre*, was actually preparing, with all expedition, to execute the impending stroke the garrison had been menaced with for the last six months. It was stated that they had preserved sixty days' full allowance of provisions for the regulars of their army in support of this important enterprise. The rumors were that the

Canadians were refusing to serve until they saw what assistance France would send them, or which of the two fleets would first enter the St. Lawrence River.

On the strength of this information, Murray wanted the citizens to leave the city and after their departure some of the most insignificant houses in the lower town and suburb of St. Rocque were to be demolished and the timber to be applied to the use of the troops for fuel. Two large field-pieces, with a quantity of ammunition, were to be drawn out to Lorette. The roads were almost impassable for horse-drawn sleighs because they were covered with dissolving snow. An asterisk highlighted Ian's notes that soldiers should be assigned to clear them as best they could.

Ian knew there would be great protests to leave from those inhabitants that were still in the city. Was it really necessary? They would refuse. Ian sighed. He put his paper work in order, then decided to take a break. A walk in the garden, in the mist, would be refreshing.

Two nuns were at a far corner of the garden near *rue du Parloir*. They were trimming hedges. Ah, one of them was Marie-Louise. Ian walked up to them.

"Good afternoon, Sisters."

"Captain Lindsay, good afternoon."

Short capes covered their starched wimples. Their skirts were looped up almost to their knees. They stood in the mud in heavy laced moccasins. They looked comical without the sweep of their full length habits and long capes. Ian suppressed a chuckle.

"We're a sight!" Marie-Louise was embarrassed. "This is Sister St. Ignacious, one of our gardeners. She saw a robin this morning so we're starting to prune these old bushes here."

Ian bowed.

"There's a lot to do, if the last of the snow could be gone," Sister St. Ignatius shot a half-preoccupied glance in his direction.

Her French accent sounded strange and different. He wondered where she was from.

"We plant the vegetable garden by Mother Philomène's door. But here we have some flower beds by the hedges." Marie-Louise blushed with pleasure. She was happy to see him.

"You have hydrangeas here, too?" Ian noticed a spot of mud on Marie-Louise's nose. He smiled.

"*Bien sûr*," Sister Ignatius forgot her shyness. "They're huge and lovely. Oh, Sister Madeleine we're needing the larger clippers."

"I'll get them, Sister." Marie-Louise came up the path where Ian was standing. He walked with her toward the garden shed.

"She can hardly wait for June. Nor can I." She was flustered and trying to make conversation.

Nor can I, Ian thought, as he walked beside her. By then, he dared hope she might be back home so he would be able to court her properly. Had she started to apply for release forms? Did novices need the Bishop's permission? Should he ask? He had promised not to press.

She unlocked the garden shed door, it swung open shutting Sister St. Ignatius from view.

"Sister Madeleine, you have a spot of mud on your nose."

She giggled. "I have?"

"Allow me," Ian leaned toward her and softly wiped it off with a corner of his tattered tartan.

"Thank you." She smiled warmly and revelled in his concern. "Oh, here are the heavy shears. Bonhomme Michel must have rearranged tools in here for spring gardening."

"Let me," Ian took them from her.

"Ian?" Her voice took serious tone.

"Yes." He loved to hear his name pronounced in her attractive accent. He saw anxiety in her eyes, questions.

"We're looking for spring but what's happening? All the townspeople are evacuated. Not like in January when some families left for the country so they could be better fed. Everyone's gone. Even Anaïse and Tante José are leaving."

"Where are they going?"

"To Beauport, to my home."

"It's only temporary. You'll be safe here in the convent. Don't worry."

"Aren't you tired of this war?"

"Yes," he sighed. "I wish we were both in a place where we had nothing more serious to talk about then flower gardens, children. . . . "

"Oh, Ian, there is no longer such a place."

They walked back down the wet path in silence with the heavy shears.

"*Merci, Monsieur le Capitaine*, Sister Madeleine we can't be here too much longer. Let's just finish this corner."

"Good afternoon, Sisters." Ian left them and went back to his quarters with mixed feelings. The only assurance he had been able to give Marie-Louise was that they would be safe in the convent, no matter what kind of outbreak occurred. Murray's own headquarters were there and he had promised to protect them. And it wasn't much to have wiped a fleck of mud off her pretty nose but he was happy.

At ten o'clock on the morning of April 21, Ian posted the dreaded proclamation in all public places. It told the inhabitants still left in town that the enemy was preparing to besiege the city and that they must evacuate with their families and effects and not to re-enter until further notice. They fell into great confusion, commotion and discomfort. It was impossible for the Highlanders not to sympathize with them in their distress. The Canadian men prudently restrained their sentiments but the women charged Murray with a breach of the capitulation. They voiced that they had often heard "*que les Anglais sont des gens sans foi.*" Now, they were convinced of it.

They begged and tried to persuade Murray that it was not likely that Levis would come crashing through the city. If the Governor would rely on them, they would give the earliest intelligence of the motions of the enemy, and would submit to any restrictions whatever, if he would permit them to remain in their homes. Moreover, if they or any among them would betray the British guards, they would answer with the forfeiture not only of all their effects, but also of their lives.

Ian helped to dispatch these overtures to Murray but his excellency was not to be imposed upon, he said, "by any such bagatelles or Gallic rhetoric."

Numerous orders were being issued as fast as possible. A lieutenant of the 35th regiment, who was formerly in the sea-service, was appointed to the command of a schooner that had fallen down at Orleans and had to undergo some repairs and be fitted out for an express. The vessel was ordered to reconnoitre the river and proceed to Halifax to hasten up the British fleet in case they had not yet sailed and acquaint the admiral or commodore of the precarious situation at the Quebec garrison and the strength of the enemy's squadron in the upper river.

On April 24, the wretched citizens evaccuated the town.

Ian wrote an order to demolish the bridges over the river St. Michael near Cap Rouge and post a light infantry in that region to watch for the enemy.

Another order was written to raze the post at Lorette and for the detachment that kept it to fall back to St. Foy.

Caulkers were in great demand from regiments to repair sloops of war and small craft. A special note had come to Ian from the Governor, "They shall be well paid." Notices were posted. All the different fatiguing parties were to work from nine o'clock until noon, and from two until six in the evening.

With all that accomplished, things settled down. On the 26th, Ian caught up with the last of his paper work. At five o'clock, he slapped a snuff box as paper weight on top of the remains of his day's work. He felt the lull of apprehension over the whole town. Where was Levis? Somewhere between Fort Jacques Cartier and Montreal. When would he come with his attack? But it was not really expected until the big thaw, a real break in the weather, more ice had to dissolve in the river. A wind-driven rain rattled his window. He had heard Noël tell Mother Philomène when he brought in partridges an hour ago that it was hailing in the Huron village near Lorette.

He debated should he go to Lower Town for dinner on board the *Racehorse* at Captain Macartney's invitation. It would be a welcome distraction from the impending situation. Maybe the weather would abate, he'd give it an half hour. He went to the Ursuline library. He might see Marie-Louise. He was still reading the letters of Marie de l'Incarnation. He knew that Marie-Louise read them as well in her few recreation periods.

There was no one in the library. He found the volume where he had left off. He particularly enjoyed reading the foundress' letters to her son, Dom Claude Martin and to Dom Jamet. He marveled that this woman had not only written beautiful and interesting letters but also on cold winter mornings had compiled a French-Algonquin dictionary, an Iroquois dictionary and a catechism. His mother would have enjoyed these letters, he thought. At the initial start of the Ursuline monastery with the help of Madame de la Peltrie, how had they kept warm those cold winter nights in the 1600's, in their small wooden boxed beds? How did Marie-Louise keep warm now, did she sleep well in her cell?

The last of the embers shifted in the fire-place. Hail started pelting at the windows. He was the last one in the library. He had promised the Reverend Mother that if he left near six o'clock he would lock up. He walked down the cold corridor back to his quarters. What were they eating tonight? Some kind of soup and partridge? What would he have on board the *Racehorse*? If he got down there, at least he and Macartney could toss a few extra rums down the hatch. Well, why not? It was Saturday night, he had no desire to retire early, to ensconce himself and try to keep warm in the few blankets that lay neatly across his narrow cot. What nun had once slept on it, he wondered?

He should be able to make it back by curfew. In the hall, he picked up a heavy cloak hanging from a pine peg. "*La fameuse,*" they had entitled the community cloak, borrowed and passed around amongst his officers when any of them went out on single errands. He had found it in one of the better houses on *rue St-Louis*. A thick black wool, lined with beaver skins and there was a hat to match. He wondered what Frenchman had designed it as he swung its folds over his tartan. Where was he now, that Frenchman? Had he left with Admiral Saunders' fleet last October, to be repatriated to France? Or was he languishing in a Southampton or Bristol prison? He snuffed out his wall candle and let himself out by the main convent entrance.

The hail wasn't too bad, the cold air helped clear his brain and to *"prendre un p'tit coup"* as the Canadians called imbibing a shot of strong liquor would probably warm his love-sick heart. Ice and remnants of snow still gripped the side-walks. Ian shivered as he walked carefully down Côte de la Montagane to Lower Town. He stepped cautiously all the way down the hill. Fresh snow would probably make roads and walks safer if it was heavy enough but now it was hailing. He walked against the wind, huddled in the warm cape. On *rue Champlain*, lights from taverns glowed, fragments of song and mandolin floated on the cold air.

"*Au près de ma blonde qu'il fait bon, fait bon.*"

As he passed the last tavern bordering the square, a side door opened pouring light on the street and strong smells of ragoût. A strange odor, Ian decided it must be horse meat ragoût. They were half starving in Lower Town. It was said things were better at Trois Rivières. But here, there wasn't much merchandise left to carry on commerce, not even from the newly arrived New England merchants who were waiting for spring and new shipments, but they all still gambled. Gruff voices called out at *vingt-et-un* and *caviagnole*.

There were rumors that before Wolfe came, before the French politicians had sapped the Canadians, great fortunes had been won and lost in the flutter of cards. Some had been stripped down to their shirts.

Ian was saluted by the guard on the quai. A deck hand helped him climb into the waiting dinghy and he was rowed over the cold water past bobbing ice floes to the rope ladder hanging from the *Racehorse*. He was piped on board. Lighted lanterns gave Captain Macartney's cabin a soft and cozy glow. A crystal brandy decanter was already on the table with two goblets. Ian knew they were souvenirs from Dublin and he thought of his grandparents' glassblowing compound near Vendôme.

"Good evening, a wild night out there." Macartney poured two generous measures of the amber liquid. "It's just us for dinner." The crystal glass sparkled as it was handed to Ian. "That'll warm you up."

"Aye." Ian took it eagerly, gulped some of it and shivered. "Wolfe came with his new red coat and you came with your crystal. Your cabin's mighty cozy, Captain, sir." He winked.

"Aye, it is that." Macartney winked back. "But you'll hear the creaking on the left side of my ship against some of the packed ice. Poor Wolfe, where did they plant him in England, I wonder?"

"His own churchyard, no doubt. To Wolfe."

"To Wolfe."

Ian went to the port hole and looked out. He let his cape drop on a leather bench.

The steward came in with a steaming pot and a hard crusty bread. He dished up two plates and left them.

"What do we have here?"

"*Des fèves, mon vieux.*"

Ian tasted the hot beans flavored with generous chunks of salt pork. "*Umm, delicieux.* Where do you get such fare?"

"My cook here frequents a brown-eyed brunette in Sillery. They seem to have a secret larder somewhere with sides of pork and a few other things." Macartney poured another round.

Ian started to relax but he asked. "Do we have a strong guard out here on the dock?"

"Aye, all through Lower Town and alongside my ship. Levis won't come out tonight."

"Who knows? But we can't sleep on our laurels." Ian sopped up the last of the thick beans with the heel of the bread. "Very, very good."

Macartney pushed a small pewter bowl of maple sugar balls toward him.

"*Ah, baume du Canada.* I hear from the nuns that's what Montcalm called maple sugar and he even sent some to France, to his estate."

"Did you taste a tart, a sweet made with it?"

"Yes, I did at Christmas, from Mother Philomène's kitchen." Ian thought of the two maple sugar balls Marie-Louise had given him Christmas morning.

"Lucky you." Macartney smiled as they sipped another brandy. "Those nuns must take good care of you. And you have the added advantage of being R. C., you must be in great favor."

"Lucky you, yourself, pampered here with secret goodies from a *habitante Canadienne*."

They both laughed. The wind whipped about the ship making it creak and sway, the hail had let up but rain continued to slash.

"You may as well stay the night."

"I don't need a second invitation. It must be late, nearly two bells. . . ." As he leaned back in his chair, Ian thought he heard a plaintiff cry from the river, somewhere off the ice floes. "What was that?"

"What?"

The steward knocked, his head appeared in a slight opening of the door. "Begging your pardon sir, we think there's someone out there. . . ."

"Yes!" Ian got up. "Crying for help it sounds like."

"Lower a boat, see what's going on," Macartney snapped.

"Aye, sir." The three of them ran out on deck. A boat was being lowered as they peered over the rail.

"There's a bloke down there on a large piece of ice, sir."

"Get him up here."

Everyone labored to get the crying, shivering man up on deck in a rope swing.

"Egads, it's a French soldier. Bring him to my cabin immediately."

"Aye, Captain."

"We'll throw some whiskey into him, a blanket over him and find out where he comes from."

Everyone thundered to the Captain's cabin half-carrying, half-dragging the wet, delerious man as fast as they could.

Ian and Macartney wrapped him in blankets and made him guzzle a shot of brandy. The steward went off to the galley to warm up more.

"Who are you? Where do you come from? Ian, you talk to him, you savvy the language."

"We can't rush him. Let him catch his breath. Now that we've got him up, let's not choke him to death."

"Aye," Macartney agreed. "Easy does it."

"*Qui êtes-vous?*" Ian threw another blanket over him. The steward came back and handed him a tankard of hot brandy. "*Doucement,*" Ian fed it to him slowly.

They got the story piece-meal in between lapses of unconsciousness.

"He's Jean-Baptiste Begine, a sergeant in the French artillery," Ian addressed Macartney.

"What's he doing a way out here on a piece of ice?"

"He and six other men were put into a floating battery of one eighteen-pounder, his *bateau* overset in the storm, he supposes his companions are drowned."

"Good Lord!"

"He says he scrambled through numberless floats of ice until he found and clung to a large one, that he lay on it for several hours, the tide carried him as far as St. Lawrence's church on Orleans and then the tide brought him back here where we found him."

"Incredible!"

"He says a French squadron consisting of several frigates and armed sloops are coming down to the Foulon at Sillery."

"Keep him warm, keep him coherent. We've got to take him up to Murray immediately." Macartney snapped orders to bundle the unfortunate man in a hammock to haul him up Côte de la Montagne and sent a messenger to inform Murray.

"He might expire his last breath on the way," Ian protested.

"We'll have to chance it. Let's go."

With the help of a few deck hands, Ian and Macartney ascended the hill with their burden in the sleet and the rain. They entered the main foyer of the convent with great commotion.

"What's going on?" Mother de Bransac, fully dressed with hands folded over, out of sight, into her great sleeves, stood in the middle of the circular stair-way.

"We just found this French soldier on a block of ice." Ian explained.

"The poor man. Bring him to the hospital ward immediately." She directed.

"We're bringing him to General Murray first, Reverend Mother," Macartney said as they all passed her.

"He needs immediate attention." She disapproved of the detour. "We'll prepare a bed." She turned and hurried upstairs to awaken the Sister in charge of the hospital wing.

Murray had been reading and dozing late over dispatches and orders of the day when the messenger from the *Racehorse* had brought him the alarming news. He had catapulted over in his chair. Now, he was waiting at the door of his quarters for the rescue party.

"Put him here. Put him here." He commanded. "Here's some warm brandy and more blankets. Here by the fire. Where do you come from, my good man? Where is your regiment?"

When Murray had the whole story together, he was through with the gasping, shivering French sergeant and had him dispatched to the hospital ward. He had all the officers quartered in the convent awakened for an emergency meeting.

"Levis is out there and we're going out to meet him." He told them.

"But sir," Malcolm Fraser protested still in shock. "Would it not be wiser to defend the city from inside the walls?"

"We're going to nip this in the bud. Sound the alarm."

All hell broke loose as all regiments met on the Place d'Armes to await orders.

"It's do or die," Ian muttered as he hustled along with his officers.

"Then let's do it." They all echoed.

It was dawn. The gates were opened and they went off in the slush and snow to attack the on-coming French army. It was the Battle of the Plains in reverse.

Chapter Seventeen

The battle of St. Foy was a replay in reverse to the battle of the Plains of Abraham of the previous September. Murray, according to his officers, made the same mistake as Montcalm, giving battle when there was no need. The French, under Levis, carried the day with the bayonet but after their exhausting march through snow, slush and mud, then battle, the men were too weary to pursue the beaten foe. Murray and his men regained the sanctuary of the city.

There were many pieces to pick up in the aftermath, there was no guarantee that all of the fighting was over. Loose ends of paper work piled up on Ian's desk. He left these duties for the more pressing ones of checking a list of the sick and wounded in the convent ward. Then he went out to do the same at Hôtel Dieu.

"Ian!" John Knox called out from *rue des Remparts*.

"John!"

Happy to see each other on this chance encounter, brief salutes were exchanged. They fell in step crunching the crusty snow.

"Where are you going?"

"Hôtel Dieu." Ian punched one torn mittened hand into the other. Their breaths puffed on the cold air. "I just talked with Charles Stewart in his quarters. Now, I'm going to check on the rest of the poor lads. Most of them are not long for this world I'm afraid, our Scotties."

"I'm coming with you. What's Stewart got to say?"

Ian's smile was a smirk. "He says, 'from April battles and Murray Generals, good Lord deliver me!'"

John Knox nodded. "What a bloody massacre! Levis had the right idea of retaliation. They almost won!"

"Aye, I agree with Malcolm Fraser. Our General has every military virtue except prudence, trying to emulate bold, chinless Wolfe."

"And Amherst, our Commander in Chief of the whole campaign, won't he be fit to be tied when he gets wind of this."

"Runners are on the way. Lucky for Murray he's not here in these parts. Amherst's going to be slow and sure about whatever plan for advancing toward Montreal. Aye, slow as molasses."

Ian thought of the few soirées he had spent in General Amherst's presence in Albany. How carefully and responsibly he had transmitted even the spruce beer recipe to him for delivery to Murray.

"We need help now," he said. "Wonder where's Coleville?"

"It's about time he or someone shows up from Halifax. Spring is here!" John shivered. "But not enough ice is breaking up."

"Pitt's orders must have been for the *Commodore,* the *Northumberland* and whatever ships of the line left from the fleet going home last September to winter in Halifax. That's not so far away."

"His squadron should be appearing on the St. Lawrence anytime now."

"What a sight that would be!"

"Maybe first week of May?"

Two small boys ran past them throwing wet snow-balls. A gray day, there were no promising hints of sunshine. Ian thought of the well-fed, warmly dressed colonial boys he had seen in Albany throwing snow-balls during a brilliant sunset back in February. One snow ball had grazed his shoulder. He remembered their laughter. Raggedy boys didn't laugh as heartily in the streets of Quebec.

"Here we are." John went in first. They were admitted into the warmth of Hôtel Dieu by a small, thin *hospitalière.* A smell of strong medicine assaulted their cold nostrils. The nun bowed affirmatively at their request to see the wounded. Her dark, snappy eyes directed them down a long corridor. Her slight smile was benign. She left them at the door of a spartan cell.

"Well, you blokes!" Malcolm Fraser, pale, weak and propped up in a small bed was delighted to see his fellow officers. "We lost a lot of men."

"We know." They said in unison.

"I don't think Hector Munro is going to make it. He's in the next room with others."

John and Ian shook their heads sadly.

"And poor John Fraser caught a musket ball in his skull, was obliged to quit the ranks. . . ."

"Don't talk too much. Don't tire yourself," Ian touched Malcolm's shoulder. He was clad in a faded night shirt and clutched a tattered, black wool shawl. Perhaps some nun had given it up, Ian thought, for her patient's warmth and recovery.

"Damn it, Dr. Morrison wouldn't treat him. You know he had lately been exchanged out of our Highlanders to the Surgency of another corps. . . . In the end it was Dr. Badelard of the French army who cared for him. Damn decent of that Frenchie," Malcolm started to cough.

"Easy, old man," John Knox gave him a light pat on the back.

Another *hospitalière* came in with a tray of medication. With simple dignity, she handed a small cup to her patient. Fraser drank it in one gulp. "*Merci.*"

"*De la medicine douce,*" she informed the three of them. As she left the room, Ian noticed her sleeves, worn out but neatly mended, the black material of her habit had a greenish tinge. What have we done to these people, he wondered. How did they ever get through the winter? Would they all awake one morning in May, or June? And it would be spring. May was already here. May was tomorrow. May would steal over them and they would all still be in the slush and snow.

While John and Malcolm talked about Stewart, Ian went to the round window. He looked out at the snow mounded city toward the Intendant's palace. His eye flickered back to the pale gray wall, close to the window was a picture of Marie-Catherine de St-Augustin with the inscription, "*L'héroique amie des malades et des ames.*" He knew it was a gift from the Augustinians at General Hospital. He sighed, he was tired of counting the dead, the wounded, he was tired of battles and he was tired of winter, everybody was. Enough cold in the neck, icicles from the eaves, blizzards, mounds of snow. He thought of Mother de Bransac's fire in the Ursulines community room, a fire that hadn't gone out since last fall. And last fall, a fire had been lit in his heart by one of her nuns. He thought of Marie-Louise. What would his mother say, in cold Scotland, when she read his letter sent from Albany via Boston? It was as cold in Scotland as in New France. He thought of some of the winters of his childhood. There had been long icicles to the ground and rivers froze there too, from bank to bank.

"Good of you blokes to come, and thanks for the extra rum," Malcolm eyed the small crockery bottle John Knox left on the bedside table.

"Do everything the good nuns tell you so you can get out of here." John rose from the visitor's chair. "Come," he motioned to Ian. "I have wood-pile duty today."

Ian snapped out of his reverie and made his farewells. A smell of onion mixed with pharmaceutical odors followed them down the hall. Once outside they curved rue des Remparts to the top where it became Côte de la Montagne, then descended to Lower Town.

"Well, he doesn't look too bad."

"No. He'll make it." Ian prayed. "But he looked cold." He thought of the wood piles, all were much lowered in the yards of the Ursuline convent, Hôtel Dieu and General Hospital. The battle of St. Foy had interrupted their hauls. It was still a great danger to haul logs from the forest through sleet, ice and snow, past the wall into the city. True, the French Indians had retreated to exalt over an almost victory and lick their wounds in Montreal but other Indians were always there as well as winter. Winter was an enemy too. Everyone was ready for spring.

It was one thing to visit the sick and wounded to determine how soon they would be fit for duty but quite another task to list the dead.

As Ian made up the death list a few days after his tour of Hôtel Dieu, each name he wrote was a stab in the heart. Among the Fraser Highlanders they had lost the intrepid Captain Donald MacDonald. Malcolm Fraser. . . ., why he had just talked with him. They had joked about the extra rum he and John Knox had brought him.

Ian's pen was heavy as he continued to list names, Lieutenant Cosmo Gordon, 55 non-commissioned officers, pipers, privates. The list went on, Colonel the Honorable Simon Fraser, Captains John Campbell of Dunoon, Alexander Fraser, Alexander Macleod, and Charles Stewart. . . . He had chatted with him too, only a few days ago. He put his pen down for a moment and buried his face in his hands. He thought of all the letters that would have to be written to tell their families. He thought of the losses on both sides. He shook his head incredibly. It was too much. He grieved as he eyed each name. Some of the men had kept journals. Malcolm Fraser's was on his work table. It would be a study in sorrow to go through some of them, reliving their days when they were giving their best, in the end their very lives. They'd never see Scotland again.

General Murray's unsuccessful sortie remained an almost victory for Levis. The French artillery had bombarded the town night and day until the seige was lifted. Now, once more the garrison strove to repair the defences of the town.

Officers and men were working with barrow, pick and shovel. They were all lucky they had been able to gain their re-entry inside the garrison with the ammunition running short. Their expenditure had been reduced to 75 barrels of powder, 960 shot and 135 shells a day.

The big question to all now was what ship would appear on the St. Lawrence first, leading a saving fleet, French or English? The battle of St. Foy, victorious attempt though it was for the French, had failed to regain the colony for France. Hope folded for the Canadians, Levis and the French regiments. Now Montreal was the last stand, the last stronghold. What would happen next?

What would the summer bring? Everyone was busy, conquerors and conquered. New graves were dug for the dead at the edge of the Plains of Abraham. Fields had to be tilled and planted if any of them were to survive the following winter. Spring farming had to be done by whoever was left, whoever would do it. The nuns continued to take care of the sick and wounded in battle, to pray in their respective chapels, in the hospitals, in the

Ursuline convent. The clearing and rebuilding of the city was resumed in between straggled skirmishes outside the wall. But soldiers, nuns, artisans, farmers, tired seigneurs all knew that finally, slowly, surely, General Amherst would advance toward Montreal. How many French remained in Montreal? Would Levis and Vaudreuil be able to gather them all for one last fight to save New France? What were they doing? Still dancing? The winter balls were over. Would the conniving politicians that had been sent back to France last fall ever be brought to justice at Versailles?

Marie-Louise went about her duties with a stiff upper lip. She prayed, she worried, she stilled and steeled herself in the midst of extra hospital work. She hoped there would be no more battles. She did not see much of Ian. He was busy counting the dead. There were no more chance or contrived encounters in the garden or the library. There was no time to seek out the Reverend Mother to have that special talk to discuss how she would apply to leave the convent. How would she write to her father, tell Jean-Paul? In the quiet of her cell, she asked herself many questions. In the aftermath of this new battle, she asked herself why and how could she be in love with a man so involved with war and killing. How could she leave all that she knew and travel the world with him? But it was an undeniable truth in her heart that she did love him. Would she scandalize the Bishop and the whole countryside if she carried this out? The last rumor was that Bishop de Pontbriand was still ailing.

Mother de Bransac worried too when she saw her young, love-sick nun go about her duties. She pressed her lips. Should she break in or continue to wait for Marie-Louise to come to her? The battle of St. Foy was a *coup manqué* now. Would it affect Marie-Louise's decision. But she had already decided, hadn't she? Mother de Bransac sighed. She wished all of the British officers to be gone and out of her convent. In spite of her good entente with Murray and as helpful as all the Highlanders were with heavy chores, enough was enough.

As if he read the Mother Superior's thoughts, Governor Murray scribbled himself a memo that he would order all of his officers to move out of the convent by late June. He would keep his headquarters there, however, to have access to the Holy Family parlor for the distribution of justice.

Marie-Louise contemplated there were two ways she could leave. She could return home quietly and resume residence with her family with the only explanation that it was no longer her vocation to remain at the convent. Or she could wait for her father's permission and approval after writing him that the the real reason for returning home was to accept courtship with intention to marry. Would he welcome that? But she was still needed here. She would wait but not without anxiety. They were all counting time. Some officers would return to England in the fall. It all depended on what would happen in Montreal. Anything could happen. If she had faith to come to this convent, then she must have faith to leave it if her life beckoned in another direction.

Marie-Louise's hand trembled as she started drafting a letter to her father. Her hands were rough and sore. It was hard work to try to restore and regain routine after the havoc of battle. A few warm days came heralding spring and they had started washing outside again, at the brook. Crocuses were appearing in the garden in between last patches of snow. The tumultous business of the officers went on about them, up and down the corridors. Outside, bodies that had been stacked up against the wall of the city all winter were being buried as quickly as possible before they decomposed. Now, it was not only their chapel that was borrowed for continuing Anglican services but also space and ground in their catholic cemeteries, especially the one by General Hospital.

Finally, the interview with Reverend Mother took place. She tried to explain that the only thing she was sure of in her divided state was her love for Ian, a man in duty bound to carry out the duties of an officer at war. So how could she stay on in the convent? She wanted to be with him. Would God forgive her, bless her, guide both of them?

Mother de Bransac was serious, compassionate understanding, loving and sympathetic.

"I know how heavily this weighs your heart. But if this is your firm decision. . . . Dear child, you have a lot of love to give. You can save your soul as a wife and mother just as well out in the world if your time with us is over. Our prayers will go with you in your new life."

They both felt regret, the regret of leave-taking. She was young and untried. They both wondered what would be encountered in this new journey into the unknown.

The letter to her father would be dispatched to Beauport by Noël. What would he answer? He would need time. And when the ailing Bishop would hear of it in the clerical mail would he be shocked? Or was it a small matter in time of war? Would she gain leniency with all who knew her because she and Ian were of the same faith?

It wasn't all over yet. There was a new air of expectancy while they were all wiping up after St. Foy. And who would come up the river first, the French or the English?

Marie-Louise would stay on duty in her usual responsible position until she received her father's answer. But then what? How would she break this to Jean-Paul, her uncle, her friends and neighbors? How would she pick up her life at home so Ian could come and court her properly? Where would they marry? The ideal place would be her convent chapel with all her sister nuns about her and singing in the choir but it would be less conspicuous, more quiet in her own parish. Would that appease an ailing Bishop who was still writing angry, disapproving letters about mixed-marriages. So be it. She and Ian would marry where they chose. She felt she was doing the right thing in the eyes of God. The Bishop's absence from Quebec City had spread concern through the outlying parishes. Some pastors were no longer there. Was the pastor gone from L'Ange Guardien church? A neighboring priest had come for her mother's proper burial. Jean-Paul had brought her every detail with love. They had cried anew together.

Rumors continued to spread that Amherst was on his way to attack Montreal. Just when? Was he still at Lake George? Lake Champlain? Lake Ontario? No runners had come for days. Noël hadn't been seen lately. Had he delivered her letter safely?

Where was Ian? He, also, hadn't been seen for several days. Was he still counting and burying the dead, writing letters to families. Her heart ached for him. If only she could touch him. If only they could clasp hands, embrace each other for a moment.

"Dear God," she mumured. "Help us."

Marie-Louise knew that Mother de Bransac had a new worry, aside of one of her nuns leaving for the outside. It was also rumored that Murray would empty the convent of all his Highlanders by the first week in June. As much as the Superior would be relieved to see them gone with their daily commotions, there would be another concern. Would that mean that commissary help would be withdrawn from the nuns?

The Reverend Mother had not been told yet, not in so many words, but it was also surmised that Murray planned to take advantage of the good weather and move all the recovering patients to fresh air and the military hospital on the Ile d'Orleans.

There was a lot on their minds in the midst of their daily tasks. Marie-Louise found solace and strength in her private prayers. In the quiet of the chapel, in solitude when all the other nuns had recited the community litanies and left. She sat and stared at the sanctuary lamp. She restored herself for the next physical task. In the winter they had stacked sheets in the attic and other items they couldn't wash when stormy weather had reigned. Now, there was a frenzy to do them all and dry them outside in the garden on sunny days. These sheets would replenish all those they had lost to the emergency of bandages. Were the men at home, at Beauport, thinking of that. Juliette would remind Jean-Paul. Surely, her father would think of it, remember when her mother had started spring housecleaning at this time of the year. She had done some of it when she had been home on leave. Hard to believe her mother was no longer there. Changes, changes, and more to come. Well, thank God, they had all survived the winter. Now, where did their fate lie? With a Commander-in-Chief coming from the south with his Brigadier-Generals to force an oath of allegiance to the British Crown from all the inhabitants of the villages up and down the St. Lawrence, all those who had not already signed. He was coming to attack Montreal, to gain the whole country. Where was he now, this Amherst? Where was Ian? If she didn't see Ian soon, she would die of it. He must tell her what was happening outside Quebec. Murray was permitting some families back into the city to pick up their effects.

Anaïse had connived to keep Hubert at the convent as handy man help for Bonhomme Michel which gave him fairly free access coming and going. Aunt José was in the nun's infirmary. Anaïse had been permitted to stay to help the nuns which enabled her to keep a sharp eye on her store and the Médard residence. Amazing!

"I think Anaïse can do anything," Marie-Louise said to herself in the middle of her prayers. "Anything!" She pulled her black wool shawl about her shoulders. The clock chimed eleven. It was a cold, blustery morning with no promise of sunshine for the ninth day of May.

"A ship just appeared up the river," Geneviève flung at her from the door of the chapel and disappeared, her veil flying.

The clamoring of the officers was heard as they all went out. The nuns ran to the third floor with as much subdued decorum as they could manage. Marie-Louise ran too, but further than the third floor. She went up to the attic, to her round look-out window. It had gotten dusty again since she had come to watch Ian leave on his expedition last winter. She had only one good petitcoat left. This time she wiped the window clean with a forgotten ripped-off piece of sheeting. Breathless, she scanned the wide sweep of river. She waited.

Then she heard the sound of guns, cannons. She counted a twenty-one gun salute. The joy of the yelling troops, the huzzas resounded. Shouts and the thunder of the garrison's artillery shook and rent the air. The gunners continued to fire. Marie-Louise blocked her ears, leaned against the wall and slipped to the floor. So it was a British ship. And there must be part of a fleet following. Was Levis still on the ramparts of Cape Diamond? What would he do now? What were the defences at Montreal?

Ian where are you? "I am worried, so worried." The whole convent shook. Well, she couldn't stay here. She picked herself up and shook her habit free of the attic's dust. She would go help Mother Philomène in the kitchen and have tea. That's where all the news came, to the convent kitchen.

Cabbage soup was bubbling and steaming in the cauldrons for the noon day meal. Its rich odor came through the transom down the hall. Marie-Louise could smell the onion slices. She hoped it was laced with carrots and bits of salt pork too. A good day for hot soup, she thought, as she tried to shake the chill off her shoulders.

"Marie-Louise, Sister Madeleine!" Ian's voice stopped her short.

"Ian! Captain Lindsay!" She turned. There he was. She was so happy to see him she hardly realized that he was ushering her unceremoniously toward the library.

"I must see you."

She didn't protest, she went willingly. There was no one in the library.

The exhuberant shouts of the garrison soldiers still rang from outside. Their gun shots continued to split the air, cannons boomed.

Ian led Marie-Louise to the table where they usually talked. He saw all the consternation on her face, the questions in her eyes.

"For your sake, I almost wish that ship was French." His voice was full of concern.

She bit her lip, her smile was sad. He looked handsome. His hair was neatly tied back. His eyes gleamed a deeper blue today, his tartan was mended and pressed. A bolt of jealousy shot through her. Was he seeing someone? But no, he couldn't. They were secretly committed to one another. She shook herself. Now that he was before her she hardly knew what to say.

"Where were you?" Her voice trembled.

"Burying the dead." He saw the love in her eyes.

"May they rest in peace."

"I'll be gone for awhile, away from my quarters."

"Where?"

"South."

Ah, yes. That's probably all he could tell her. Everything would converge toward Montreal. She wanted to tell him that she had written to her father. But no words came. Their eyes held.

"I want to assure you that no harm will come to the convent."

"How long will you be gone?"

"I have no idea." He wanted to say that he hoped the next time he saw her she would be at her home to receive him. But he refrained, he had promised not to push. "I'll see you as soon as I return."

She nodded. A few shots still rang out. An uproar of jovial noises came from the officers quarters.

"I love you," he said simply.

"And I you." Oh, these furtive, fleeting, stolen moments in which they tried to say all and forgot most of what they intended to say.

At every leave-taking, he gathered more boldness. But still, as he must, he placed respect before ardor, he clasped both her hands, then raised one to his lips and imprinted a warm kiss.

"I wish I could take you in my arms."

She looked up at him, flushed, nervous that someone might find them in this tête-à-tête. "I pray we'll have such moments soon," she wanted to add in the eyes of God and all who know us but she simply said, "Take care of yourself."

"Captain Lindsay, Captain Lindsay?" His colleagues were calling for him down the corridor.

With an affectionate pressure, he quickly released her small work-worn hand and was gone. She slowly raised it to her mouth to savor the touch of his lips.

Though she presented a calm enough exterior by the time she reached the kitchen, she felt undone. But the flush on her face did not escape Mother Philomène's eagle eye as she handed Marie-Louise an apron and invited her to a cup of raspberry tea. The celebrating shots and noisy tumult outside finally died down. It had all started at eleven o'clock. It was now noon.

"We have to hang on, Sister Madeleine. It's the little things in routine that hold us together. Dinner will be at one o'clock today. Most of the excitement might be over by then. . . ."

"I doubt it." Marie-Louise burnt the tip of her tongue with a mouthful of tea. She still felt Ian's kiss on her hand and raised it to her cheek.

"Here, there's time to peel and cut these small carrots into the soup."

"Levis can't fight even part of the British fleet and that's what's coming up the river. Where is he? We're still picking up the fatalities of St.

Foy." Most of what she had wanted to say and ask Ian was now directed at Mother Philomène.

"The frigate *Lowestoft*, that's what came in with Captain Dean giving the garrison a twenty-one gun salute. They'll be strutting around for awhile. We still have our patients to care for, they're alive. We all have to eat. Do the carrots, Sister Madeleine."

Marie-Louise picked up a knife and a small bunch of shriveled carrots, they must be the last from the cellar bins. What kind of harvest would they have for next winter. What were they planting at home, in Beauport? The soup smelled good. She rolled her tongue on her lips in anticipation. Yes, they all had to eat to survive the next catastrophe.

The whole garrison celebrated for the rest of the day, soldiers, sailors and officers. It was only after the evening Angelus that Marie-Louise found tranquility in the chapel. In the middle of her prayers, she longed for Ian. In her fantasies, she saw herself at home in Beauport. She saw herself running to him to receive his embrace when he would come to call. They would hold each other in blissful warmth.

When she heard one of her sister nuns turn over the hour glass, she shook herself out of her day-dream. How could she be true to herself and God in this divided state? Now that she had written in confidence to her father, she felt a need to tell someone. Jean-Paul must hear of it from her first. They were close. What would be his reaction? Was he mature enough to handle this? And, of course, she would tell Geneviève. Her father might not know what to answer. He might forbid the whole thing.

Jean-Paul showed up the next day with the first maple syrup of the season from Beauport. He came to one of the parlors to visit with her. She was happy to see him and thought he needed a new *toque*. Wasn't Juliette knitting these days, she wondered. When she told him she had written to their father about leaving the convent, he was incredulous. He shook his brown curly head.

"At home, when we all learned this is where you wanted to be. . . . At first, we were broken up that you were leaving us, you know that. Now, I can't imagine you anywhere else."

She nodded. "I didn't know that once Geneviève, Sister Philippe and I entered here that anything else was possible. I didn't know. . . ." Her voice was tearful.

"Are you sure?" Ah, he did seem mature. Her little brother.

"Don't you think I've searched my heart, my mind, body and soul. Long nights, I couldn't sleep. I thought we had enough of the war to contend with."

"It'll break Papa up, to say nothing of the Bishop. . . ."

"We're both of the same faith, Jean-Paul. Maybe, I could just walk out. I'm not under a final vow," she flung her veil back. "But I wouldn't do that "

"No, you wouldn't, Rie-Ouise." He looked at her with all the love in the world. "Well, if you must walk out of here right into a mixed marriage and with Papa's approval I hope then I guess Captain Lindsay's the best of the lot."

Marie-Louise smiled. "You must be extra kind with Papa while he is pondering all this. Now I must wait till his letter comes."

Jean-Paul sighed but he smiled too.

"Where will you marry? Where will you live? You've talked this over with Reverend Mother?"

"Of course, no one in this convent does anything without her counsel."

"Well, maybe Mother Philomène."

They both smiled.

"I would like to be married here in the chapel but considering the circumstances. . . ."

"Yes, considering the circumstances and the possible further wrath of the Bishop. . . ."

"It might be better arranged at L'Ange Guardien."

"Anaïse is getting married. Did you know that?"

"She is?"

"That's what Tante José told me. I just visited with her." He twirled his *toque*. "Anaïse and Hubert are finally going to be together."

Ah, so it was Anaïse who was to be wed in her beloved chapel first. She was jealous.

"When, Jean-Paul? This is news!"

"Soon, in June Tante José said."

"That soon. June is upon us."

"And you?"

"I am waiting for word from Papa and how I can properly leave here."

"I want you to be happy, Rie-Ouise." He rose to go. He was offering that he wanted to understand. He loved his sister. He looked up to her.

"We are not always in control to predict the future or what is going to happen to us, Jean-Paul."

He nodded. "No wonder Papa is so withdrawn. And Uncle Guillaume . . . . They've kept this from me. In time we will get use to the idea. . . . We will all be happy for you. If you need me. . . ."

"We all depend on you. You're strong, Jean-Paul, strong as the rock Quebec is built on."

Later, alone in the chapel, Marie-Louise cried softly. Now, she would have to tell Geneviève in some quiet moment, maybe during a walk in the garden. Then, she would count the days for her father's answer. Mother de Bransac thought that it would be a favorable reply since she had taken no vows. And that news would be the first she would give Ian when she saw him again.

Chapter Eighteen

The sight of the British flag flying from the man-of-war, *Lowestoft*, its steady advance amid a twenty-one gun salute and final anchor in Quebec Basin had greatly depressed and deployed Levis' forces. Nevertheless, at the eleventh hour, he thought there was still a chance. Even though he knew that no enforcing French fleet would arrive now, he tried another valiant assault.

The huzzas from towers and parapets still lingered and buoyed the defenders of the stronghold. All Highlander regiments, soldiers and sailors augmented their vigorous efforts to hold the fortress.

Under fierce fire, Levis made his final attempt for yet another attack to capture the garrison. French batteries opened again upon Quebec on the eleventh of May. One was opposed to Cape Diamond, a second against the citadel and a third, the Ursuline bastion.

But when more British men-of-war arrived and dashed at the French frigates driving them up river with heavy loss, Levis saw that the game was up. He raised the seige on the evening of the sixteenth abandoning forty guns. He began retirement to Montreal. He dropped garrisons as he retreated, at Pointe-aux-Trembles, Jacques Cartier, and Deschambault.

There was a calm over Quebec the next day. Hubert was quietly fixing a prie-dieu in the convent's carpenter shop when Anaïse breezed in.

"Mother Philomène invites us to moose ragoût."

"Sounds good." Hubert sighed. "But, oh, *ma vieille,* I wish I were on my way to Montreal with Levis to lighten his black mood, to help him write those bitter letters to Paris."

"Of what good now. You're here. We're alive. We're going to get married, *mon vieux.* Someone has to stay here, stay behind to pick up the debris after the last gun shot. Montreal's out there, they didn't go through what we experienced here. . . ."

"Yet!"

"Some of us have to remain, to rebuild on this rock."

"*Tu as raison.* You're right." He encircled her in his huge arms and hugged her. "But even one frigate from France would have saved the day and perhaps Canada for another year. *Quel malheur!*" He shook his head.

"Whatever help was coming from France must have been intercepted in Baie des Chaleures to prevent any entrance into the St. Lawrence. The *Lowestoft* or part of its following squadron could have demolished any of our ships and supplies."

"You think like a general." He placed a tender peck on her forehead and released her. "Come, then let us fill our bellies so we can work around here."

"Yes, you big bear, we have a lot to do."

There were still a few English patients to be gotten down to Lower Town and on a ship to transport them to Orleans. This traffic was going on between infirmary and the main hall of the convent when Marie-Louise saw Ian again.

"Captain Lindsay, I thought you were gone." She was surprised, happy to see him. She came down the stairs with an armful of sheets.

"Sister Madeleine," he bowed. "Someone else was sent on that mission and I am retained here to transfer the last of our patients to our makeshift military hospital on Orleans. The fresh air there will help recuperation."

He and two of his lieutenants were helping a man on crutches.

"Here," he directed them. "We'd better take Sergeant Brodie down Côte de la Montagne in a hammock to go down to the ship. . . ."

"No, no," the young sergeant protested, glad to be on his feet. "I can make it, I can make it in slow stages."

"Well, try then. I'll go see who else is left and catch up with you later."

But instead of going directly back to the infirmary, he led Marie-Louise out into the garden.

"I'll miss my quarters in the convent," he said wistfully. "I'll be cramped back on a ship." He hadn't entirely moved out yet.

"We'll miss you. I'll miss seeing you up and down the corridors. I thought you were gone for awhile. . . ."

"You're never really going to get rid of me." He smiled confidently.

Two young nuns fluttered by them with freshly picked bouquets of daisies, irises and white lilacs. They were giggling and bowed slightly as they passed.

"What's going on? I mean beside the grand cleaning to sweep us out."

Marie-Louise laughed. "They're trying things out with various vases for design and effect. We're preparing the chapel for a wedding."

"A wedding!" Ah, he wished it was theirs. When would that be?

"Anaïse and Hubert are getting married."

"Anaïse?" He recovered his surprise. He would always be grateful to Anaïse. She had probably saved his life and with more generosity than he deserved. "I've heard of Hubert," he was about to add politely that he must be a fine fellow but he really didn't know that. What he had heard was that when he wasn't in the woods, he lived between Lorette and Jacques Cartier and was possibly a spy. What was he doing here?

"They have courage those two," Marie-Louise rearranged her veil. "In spite of the loss of his leg. He has a pegged leg. They're going ahead with their plans."

"I wish them both every happiness." So that was why Hubert was still in Quebec. A *coureur de bois* with one leg. But he must be a match for Anaïse or she wouldn't be marrying him. What would they be up to? Not much for the war was nearly over. From day to day, Murray waited for the directive from Amherst telling him when to leave Quebec City with all troops for Montreal. He was very impatient. What kind of opposition would Levis have time to prepare with Vaudreuil?

"Anaïse and Hubert have known each other for years."

Ian thought of Scotland, his parents. Were they even now trying to arrange a marriage for him with someone he had known for years, since childhood? But the one he wanted to marry was here sitting beside him on a garden bench in this unexpected, stolen moment.

"Sunshine becomes you, Sister Madeleine."

She blushed. "You were gone before I could tell you the other day. I did write to my father about us, about what I want to do."

"You did!" He was jubilant. He leaned toward her but she held up her hand. He caught it and lightly kissed her fingertips.

She withdrew it demurely and placed both her hands in the folds of her large sleeves, nun fashion. He understood. They were in everyone's view here. He stole from heaven what tid bits he could.

"I remain here on duty until the answer comes."

"Will it take long?"

"Who knows ? He needs time to get over the surprise, the shock. He may be hurt. I'm asking to return to my life at home so you can approach him properly."

"You must get word to me as soon as you know. I'll be assigned living quarters on one of the ships anchored near Lower Town."

Her eyes sparkled. Neither one of them doubted that the answer would be anything but favorable.

"I'll find a way to send you news immediately."

"In spite of the chaotic situation in which we live, you have made me the happiest of men."

"We are in God's hands, Ian." The way she whispered his name fell on his ears like a caress. "Come, I'll help you and the *infirmière* ready the other patients for transfer."

"I'll go check on Sergeant Brodie's descent down the Côte with my lieutenants first. See you shortly." Overjoyed with the news she had just given him, he ran out of the garden.

June came with a burst of color in the convent garden. Some families began to trickle back into the city to regain their delapidated homes and to care for their unkept gardens.

The convent was being emptied of all the Highlanders. There was the hurrying and bustling of moving out. Though relieved to see them go, Mother de Bransac knew that she and all her nuns would miss them. Especially her younger nuns who had gotten used to their help, gallant manners, joking, pleasanteries, even the innocent flirtations. There were promises that they would call to see them. Mother de Bransac hoped not too often. Marie-Louise's involvement was more than enough to cope with.

The moving of all the English patients from the hospital wing had been a major maneuver. Everyone had helped. It was understood that Governor Murray, though he was moving into Dr. Arnoux's residence, would keep headquarters in the convent and use the Holy Family parlor for the dispensing of justice. A few days after they had all left, Mother de Bransac ordered a general housecleaning and an airing of all the floors in the convent. Finally, things fell into place and some tranquility reigned.

A bright spot and new excitement came when Mother de Bransac gave final directives for the chapel to be ready for the wedding of Anaïse and Hubert. The fresh air of warmer weather buoyed them up. They flitted on special errands and were all unsparing in giving each other considerate little attentions.

"My mother always said it was lucky to help for a wedding." Geneviève was giving the golden vases a wipe in the sacristy as Marie-Louise folded some of Father Resche's vestments in the armoire drawers. She hung his cloak on the door hook. He was hearing confessions in the chapel at the moment.

"Yes, my mother said that too." How soon would they all be preparing like this for her own wedding?

"May she rest in peace, your dear mother."

"Amen." Marie-Louise locked the armoire. Here was a good moment to tell Geneviève.

"Geneviève, I have written to my father to receive me back home and I told him why. The Reverend Mother, of course, Jean-Paul and now you are the only ones who know. . . ."

A long silence hung between them. Then Geneviève nodded solemnly. "Ah, I will miss you."

"I don't love God less, Geneviève, a different love came to me. In this new, unexpected love perhaps I can love God more. I can have children of my own."

"If you were telling me you are leaving to marry one of the boys we danced with in Beauport, I would understand that better. . . ."

"I know, I know."

"I've watched you suffer through this."

"I didn't know this could happen to me."

"You don't really know this man. He came here with his regiment to destroy us."

"Regardless of the war's outcome, we want to be together. We are both of the same faith. I want to be home to receive his attentions so I can get to know him better. I am torn but I believe I no longer have a vocation here, Geneviève."

"And the Reverend Mother?"

"I will go with her blessing."

Geneviève nodded again. "We'll miss you," she repeated. "It'll take a while for your father to put this together."

"I'll be here in my usual duties in the meantime." She hoped it would make up for her absences from the convent.

"What if your father disapproves? You might have to leave on your own. Where will you live? And the Bishop is still writing scathing letters to his clerics about all the mixed marriages since last winter, not to mention the increase of pregnancies among our young Canadian girls with not only French soldiers and officers but now the English. We have a scandal in our own Beauport. A mother and daughter are *maitresses* of two Highlanders. Don't hold your breath, *ma pauvre*." Geneviève delivered her words with concern.

"There will be many more mixed marriages if they win the war. A fact of life we'll have to live with. Who are we to judge that some of those marriages won't be blessed."

"That's true. You're much more practical than I am. I will pray for you both, you and Captain Lindsay."

"Thank you." Marie-Louise smiled. Their bond of friendship was still there. "But I am holding my breath. I need all the support I can get." She shook her head. "And I will not be a scandal, Geneviève, I'm trying to do this in good faith."

"I know, I know."

"Where do you get all that gossip?"

"It comes in from all sides."

"It's good that we're all busy preparing for Anaïse's wedding. . . ."

"Who knows, perhaps your answer will come sooner than we think. Your father will receive you with open arms and we'll, no doubt, be preparing for your own wedding as well. Maybe a fall wedding."

Marie-Louise blushed. So Geneviève was not going to condemn her after all. No matter what the outcome, she had her blessing too.

Anaïse and Hubert exchanged their vows in the Ursuline chapel on a soft, golden day in the first week of June. At high noon, the event transported and suspended everyone present above and away from all the problems of war. It was as if they had all floated into another era for a few brief hours.

Anaïse was demure in a light blue dress with a smooth collar of white silk. Her dark hair piled high was secured with a crown of daisies neatly tied at the back with a bow of white ribbon and streamers. Hubert was solemn, serious and loving in a gray coat with navy cravat. From time to time, he gazed critically at a small wooden statue of our Lady he had carved and presented to the Ursulines as a gift on his wedding day.

Father Resche, the celebrant, was resplendent in rich gold and white vestments. Perfume from huge bouquets of late white lilacs overflowing in the gold vases spread throughout the chapel. Tall tapers flickered orange flames. The voices of the nuns' choir soared gloriously at various parts of the nuptial Mass. Organ, violins and harp concerted in the background.

Anaïse and Hubert pronounced their vows loud and clear. Tante José cried. Elegant in a plum colored dress, she was seated in a special chair by the altar. A filmy pink fichu was pinned at her throat with a mauve cameo brooch. Her lace cap was askew. The dresses she and Anaïse wore today had been pulled from a wardrobe of a more affluent and stylish time and had been neatly mended for the occasion.

The few invited guests had all gathered in their Sunday best, sponged and pressed. Jean-Paul came and explained to Marie-Louise that their father was not feeling well. Uncle Guillaume hobbled in on his cane. The Seders family came in from the country with Baby Joseph. Mireille Le Conte, Jerome Leduc, Noël and all Hubert's friends came in from Lorette. They had all brought what they could to add to Mother Philomène's menu.

The only shadow on the bright day was Joseph Henri Boisvert's absence. Marie-Louise had looked forward to a few words with her father, a brief exchange. It was a new worry that he wasn't well. Was that why he had not answered her letter? It must have upset him greatly. In the midst of the festivities she had to hide the stab of disappointment.

Baby Joseph gurgled, cooed throughout the ceremony and occasionally shouted little cries of joy. After Mass, they all spilled out into the garden. A buffet table was set. There was pork, chicken and moose *tourtières,* carafes of wine, apple cider, spruce beer and spice cakes. A small dais was set up by the purple lilac bushes for two violinists and a mandolin player.

There was laughter, toasts and the clinking of glasses. The whole garden splashed with color, warm breezes rippled through jonquils, daisies, irises, the grass was emerald. Below at the edge of Lower Town, the St. Lawrence sparkled in the sunshine. Puffy white clouds in a cerulean sky crowned the whole day with ambiance.

Marie-Louise was misty-eyed as she helped replenish the table and pour the wine. If only Ian could join them. Where was he today? If their wedding could be like this. Ah, there was a great chain of love here. Mother de Bransac and all her nuns had been unsparing. Mother Philomène with her young aides had baked till the last minute. They well remembered their benefactoresses, Anaïse and Tante José, with the opportunity of such a happy occasion.

Baby Joseph was brought to Marie-Louise for a final good-bye before all the guests left. She held and admired him. In his seventh month, he had grown sturdy in the country. Almost reluctantly, she put him back in his mother's arms. By late afternoon everything was back in place. The garden was empty but the music lingered on. The newlyweds left for a visit to the chapel at Hôtel Dieu and then the privacy of the Médard residence. By the time the Angelus rang, the nuns had regained their usual routine.

Hubert and Anaïse walked back from Hôtel Dieu hand in hand in a glorious sunset. The Upper Town was quiet. All the activity was in Lower Town and at Orleans. Murray had sent a few ships in Levis' wake to see what he would be up to on his way to Montreal while he himself waited impatiently for Amherst's final orders. He had already moved into Dr. Arnoux's household. There were no sentinels out on the street yet. It was as if they had the whole upper city to themselves.

At the Médard entrance Hubert lifted Anaïse over the threshold. They laughed as he swayed a bit on his peg leg.

"Tonight, we go across the threshold of this house that is dear to you, but one day I will build you a house. . . ."

"In the meantime, we'll finish repairing this one." She gently disentangled herself and went to the kitchen. A soft breeze blew in and swayed freshly starched curtains at the windows. The house had aired all day. On the marble top side board there were buffet left-overs, *tourtière* halves, quarters of cakes, and a jug of wine. Mireille had brought a bouquet of white lilacs from the chapel and had also left a bowl of fresh eggs with a piece of cheese and a small bunch of parsley from her farm.

"*Mon mari,* how would you like an omelette and some of your favorite cognac for our wedding night supper?"

"*Ma vieille, ma femme, Madame Carrier,* it is I who will do the cooking tonight. You sit here." He came up behind her and sat her in the first available chair. "Are you hungry?" He tilted her chin and lavished her with tiny kisses.

Anaïse laughed. "Not really. I just want you." She extended her hand and proudly looked at her ring.

"And I you, *ma chère,* but nevertheless, I'm going to fix us a hot supper. So where's your *tablier?*"

"I can't wait," she giggled as she pointed to an apron hung behind the door.

He hummed as he prepared a fire in the kitchen grill. He set a small table then measured, mixed and cooked. Finally, he presented a fluffy omelette with a comical flourish.

After the first mouthful with a sip of wine, Anaïse was pleasantly surprised.

"Bravo! You could cook at Versailles with the best of them."

"Eat."

"Oh, I forgot to tell you, in the midst of all the preparations. Yesterday, Tante José gave us most of her jewels for a wedding gift."

"Where are they?"

"In the convent in a safe cache."

"There are a lot of things in a safe cache in that convent. Whatever are you going to do with them? We no longer have any occasion for you to wear them here now."

"We are going to build our business, our trade with them. And we'll start with New England merchants until we know the outcome of this war."

"You never cease to amaze me. You want us to establish a business, raise a family. Woman, what faith you have."

"Better than thinking of going to Montreal. Quebec needs all the rebuilding we can muster. . . ."

"I know." He reached across the table for her hand. "But I must go to Montreal. I want to be there for whatever happens. I must find a way to get there."

"Yes," she said wistfully. She gave his hand a squeeze then finished her wine. "I don't know why I understand this . . . . Just make sure you keep out of the way of stray bullets or arrows. Montreal is not the forest."

He laughed softly as he got up from the table and came around to gather her in his arms. "Ah, if you understand me, we are well matched, *ma vieille.*" He started to unlace her bodice.

"Come," she shivered with desire and pulled him gently toward the stairs. "I went by tradition and designed a special night gown for tonight and a night shirt for you. I made them out of old sheets."

"*Merci*, but we will have no need of them till winter."

A late blue twilight washed over the city and entered the house. Anaïse lit a few candles in the bedroom.

When Hubert saw her in a voluminous draw-string night gown there were tears in his eyes. Part of her breasts showed round and inviting. She pirouetted for him, smiling. He caught her in his arms.

"You're so beautiful," he whispered huskily. He undid her hair, slowly, tenderly. It fell in lush strands over her shoulders.

They were standing by the bed. He loosened the draw string of the gown and buried his head on her soft breasts. "Ah, I must have done something good to bring us to this moment, that you marry a wreck like me."

"You did some remarkable things, Hubert. You're a very unusual man and today you made me an honest woman."

"It's amazing that we end up together after all we went through alone, all we went through together. . . ."

She silenced his lips with a long kiss. The gown fell to the floor and she started to help him undress. They lay on the bed and touched each other tenderly. Full of love, Anaïse felt strong and confident that they could give each other something no one else could. The happy tiredness of the whole day overtook them and they fell asleep holding hands.

It was only when a rose-hued dawn appeared at the windows that they awakened. They started to make love, tenderly at first, in the ways that they knew but there was also something new and thrilling as their passion mounted. They gave each other every pleasure.

With a happy sigh, Hubert dozed off again. In the cool of the morning, Anaïse remained in the circle of his arms, against his beating heart. She pulled a single sheet over them as she stretched and snuggled against his warm body. She hoped it was the beginning of their family.

Several days after Anaïse and Hubert's wedding, the convent received the mournful announcement that Bishop de Pontbriand had died at the Sulpician monastery in Montreal at three o'clock in the afternoon on the eighth of June. This official notice directed to all clergy and religious houses came from Etienne Montgolfier, Superior of the Sulpicians and the Bishop's executor. It requested all parishes and institutions to sing a solemn high Mass to his memory. The letter further explained that after a *Libera* Mass at Notre Dame of Montreal burial followed immediately, a necessity in the hot weather, due to the scarcity of spices for embalming.

It was also announced that only four canons, Briand, Rigauville, Resche and Poulin already in Quebec would attend a meeting, at the convent, to discuss election of a new Bishop. Montgolfier would come in from Montreal.

Upon receipt of this news, Mother de Bransac summoned all her nuns to the chapel for prayers. Then she went to the kitchen to consult with Mother Philomène as to what they were going to feed the priests and clerics who were coming in for the meeting. A few Huron children had brought blueberries in bark containers early that morning and she was grateful. There was a dessert that Mother Philomène concocted with boiled blueberries, steamed dumplings and a brown sugar maple sauce that piped up meager dinners to the full satisfaction of any stomach, and mourners had to be fed.

Along with her sister nuns, Marie-Louise was crushed by the news of the Bishop's death but somewhat relieved that now he would never learn of her defection. Who would replace him and write the weekly letters to the convents? Who would help Montgolfier take care of the shuffle of paper work that usually followed an ecclisiastic's death?

On July second, after a Mass of the Holy Ghost the meeting of the canons followed. The results reported to the Reverend Mother and messages sent to the two hospitals were that Briand would remain with the government of Quebec, Perrault was assigned to Trois Rivières, Maillard a secular priest was assigned to Acadia, Forget du Verger to Illinois and the Jesuit Baudouin to Louisiana. Briand was already vicar-general of Quebec. Montgolfier would remain in Montreal.

The Bishop's death now gave Murray more power over the church in occupied territory. But he was now involved and impatiently awaiting Amherst's instruction as to when he should join Haldimand to converge on Montreal. He was far too busy to worry about the next Bishop at the moment.

In the first week of July, the Ursuline chapel was draped in black, an honorary coffin was placed in the nave with a black velvet covering, tall tapers flickered in gold candlesticks and a *Libera* Mass was sung for Bishop Henri Marie Dubreuil de Pontbriand. Consecrated bishop in Paris before he left for Canada, he was now buried in the Sulpician cemetery in Montreal. He had died a long way from France, a long way from his beloved Vannes. After the last prayer was said a deep silence reigned in the chapel and all who attended the memorial left somberly, quietly.

Marie-Louise remained in her choir stall. She prayed for their dead Bishop and for the election of a new one to be held as soon as possible. Who would it be? How long would it take? Maybe the next Bishop would be more lenient toward mixed marriages but she doubted it. Maybe in one of her reports the Reverend Mother might have mentioned she had a novice with a lack of vocation for her to remain at the monastery. She might even have said that her young nun would better serve God by marrying and raising a family. She trusted that she certainly wouldn't have mentioned a Highlander. The sand in her hour glass ran out. Instead of turning it over for more prayers and meditation, she decided to go to the kitchen to help Mother Philomène. She made a brief sign of the cross and left the chapel.

Chapter Nineteen

A runner brought news that Amherst had left Albany en route for Oswego on June twenty-first. But there was no direct message to Murray yet as to when he should leave Quebec. This omission added to his impatience. He decided not to wait any further and launched preparations for his part of the expedition toward Montreal.

Troops intended for this maneuver were encamped about a quarter of a mile from town. Some men, recovered and fit for service, came in from Orleans. All those unfit for duty were left in charge of Colonel Fraser to be sent to England and to be recommended for Chelsea Hospital at the earliest opportunity.

Ian and John Knox were busy expediting the baggage of the troops on board the transports.

"The weather's good but this might not be a pleasure cruise, lad. It's not just Wolfe's victory on the Plains that's winning this war." John's shirt was damp with perspiration. He squinted at the hot July sun.

"Aye." Ian continued counting supplies. "But don't forget your journal."

"It's those Richelieu Rapids I worry about."

"I went by them last winter, not so bad."

Ian stayed behind to attend Mass before he left on the second embarkation. Two of his Catholic lieutenants came with him. Marie-Louise was in her choir stall. Their eyes met in an arc from across the cloister to the public side of the chapel. At Elevation, rays of sunshine filtered through the stained glass windows and sparkled on the jewels in the foot of the chalice.

"My Lord and my God," Ian murmured as his closed fist rapped his chest. "I am not worthy to receive you but say the word and my soul will be healed."

As Marie-Louise lifted her head, he caught her eye again. They both smiled on this breath of adoration to their God. He knew they both prayed in their respective requests for each other, their growing love, their individual commitments, their future and for all the people of Quebec and Canada. He also prayed for his regiment, for Murray, for the Brigadier Generals and he even murmured a short prayer for Amherst.

"Oh, God, I am only a speck in this war. I pray for justice, for peace for us all." Again guilt assaulted him for the men he had killed under rules of war. The best solution would be that they all pull out and go home. Be satisfied with the prize of Quebec. But he knew that was not going to happen. The die was cast. With slow-butt Amherst in charge they were all going to go out and imitate Wolfe's do or die.

Marie-Louise managed to be at the garden gate as Ian and his companions came through. They had stolen this time to come to Mass. They all exchanged "Good mornings."

Ian stopped and let the lieutenants go on. "That was a beautiful Mass. I have to believe there'll be a time when we're not always saying good-bye."

She smiled and nodded. Ah, he looked so handsome this morning, so full of purpose. She came toward him.

"We leave between five and six today."

"Then I'll be thinking of you especially at the Angelus."

"And I will think of you." Before he could say anything else, several nuns spilled out into the garden. He gazed at her with love, bowed and hurried on to join his officers.

He and John Knox sailed with the left brigade at five that afternoon. The right brigade had left at five that morning. Over all, the embarkations went well.

They passed Jacques Cartier about nine in the evening and anchored at the village of Chambaud in about ten fathoms. The inhabitants on the north and south shores were awed and terrified to see so large a fleet. There were thirty-two sails, besides floating batteries, with a number of flat bottom boats and *bateaux*. At low water, some boats went to sound the Rapids of Richelieu.

A detachment of the enemy encamped at Chambaud fired a gun but with little effect. The next day, Murray disembarked. With some rangers and a company of light infantry, he scouted several miles up the country. Fifty-five men of St. Croix and seventy-nine of Lotbinière took the oath of neutrality. Murray's pompous proclamation to the Canadians against the clergy was having its effect.

"Who can carry on or support the war without ships, artillery, ammunition, or provisions? At whose mercy are your habitations, and that harvest which you expect to reap this summer, together with all you are possessed of in this world? Therefore consider your own interest and provoke us no more." Then turning to a priest, he subjoined, "The clergy are the source of all the mischiefs that have befallen the poor Canadians, whom they keep in ignorance, and excite to wickedness and their own ruin. No doubt you have heard that I hanged a captain of militia; that I have a priest and some Jesuits on board a ship of war, to be transmitted to Great Britain: beware of the snare they have fallen into; *preach the Gospel*, which alone is your province; adhere to your duty, and do not presume, directly or indirectly, to intermeddle with military matters, or the quarrel between the two *Crowns*."

Ian had heard this proclamation before.

The troops re-embarked that evening. It was ordered that they would pass Chambaud when the wind was fair. The men were ordered to keep below and not expose themselves on deck. There was new intelligence that a body of Indians had been sent to the south side of the river to annoy and pick off men in the fleet.

Murray immediately dispatched a flag of truce to M. Dumas, commanding officer at Chambaud and assured him, "That, if these savages are not instantly recalled, or any barbarities should be committed upon our troops, they shall have orders to give no quarter either to regulars, or others, that may fall into our hands; and that the country shall undergo military execution, wherever we land."

The battalion corps and grenadiers landed alternately without further orders the next day to set up a market under proper regulations for the benefit of the fleet. Army salt pork and salt were exchanged for fresh eggs, salad greens and butter. Ian got off his ship and lingered at a farm woman's booth, she had flower bouquets and maple sugar. He bought a wax paper cone of sugar balls and she silently stuck a huge daisy in it. Her eyes matched the soft brown of her dress. He smiled and thought of Marie-Louise and wondered what this farm woman was going to do with the English coin he gave her. They were all British subjects now. He wondered when and how she would spend it. And how Murray would resolve the money problem.

There were deserters on both sides. A spy was caught, a sergeant of the French regulars, disguised in the apparel of a Canadian farmer. Under penalty of death, he gave information that two battalions of regulars with a body of Canadians and Indians were posted at Isle Royale, Isle aux Noix, Isle Galot and that the remainder of the French army was cantoned between Trois Rivières and Montreal.

All through the slow progress of the advancing fleet, Knox recorded the beauty of the countryside. Most of the inhabitants had given up their arms on order but they were on the alert. The Canadians knew by now the outcome would not be to their advantage. It was treacherous going. There were bands of lurking Indians in pockets of the forest ready to pounce at a given signal as the might and armament of the fleet advanced menacingly.

The parish of St. Antoine gave up their arms and took the oath of neutrality. The men stood in a circle, held up their right hands, repeated their own name and said:

"Do severally swear, in the presence of Almighty God, that we will not take up arms against George the Second, King of Great Britain, or against his troops or subjects; nor give any intelligence to his enemies, directly or indirectly. So help me God."

There were a few quiet moments late at night in the lush July heat on the St. Lawrence. Some soldiers and sailors slept fitfully in their ships' hammocks. On Ian's ship, John Knox wrote in his journal in a cramped officers' cabin. Beside him, Ian read from a small leather pocket book.

"So what are you reading, old man?"

Ian looked up. He levered himself in his bunk closer to his lantern. "My mother gave me this before I left. Excerpts from *La Chanson de Roland*, my mother's favorite of a very few. Just the right size *livre de poche* for a *chatelaine*."

"Umm. . . ." John wrote on.

"I think I'll give it to Sister Madeleine when we get back. I miss the convent library."

"You did spend a lot of time there."

Ian sighed. He missed the convent. He could hardly wait to see Marie-Louise again. Soon now they would be at the three-point meeting. And what would that be like? They were all nervous in spite of their stiff military exteriors. He yawned.

"We need our forty winks, John. Let's stop burning the mid-night oil."

"Aye. It's stuffy in here. And the mosquitoes!" He slapped one on his neck. "I'd like a walk on deck."

"Better not. We're too close to shore and the Indians are all mixed up. We no longer know who they're allied to."

"Aye." John closed his book. "Good night then."

Before Ian slept he thought of his home in Scotland, of his maternal grandparents in Vendôme. He had left for the North American campaign in a great spirit of high adventure. Now, he was subdued to a feeling of great responsibility. He longed for all this to be over with, he longed for peace, to marry Marie-Louise, to find a small seigneurie in Beauport, or be transferred to England. What was in store for them all? What was to be decided in Montreal? How would Marie-Louise's father answer her letter? Once she was home how would he be permitted to court her and ask for her hand?

In the quiet of the Ursuline chapel, Marie-Louise prayed for her father's answer. She went about her convent routine. They were washing outside again. On hot, sultry days, she thought of Beauport, of Orleans and how she would like to show Ian where she ran in favorite spots on the island as a child.

Now that the Highlanders had vacated the convent, in the tranquility of their repossessed space, Mother de Bransac led her nuns back to the stricter routines they had observed before the war. Without the distractions and traffic of men residing in part of their convent, little by little they regained their serenity and their chapel on the ground floor.

Marie-Louise did not sleep well during these hot July nights. She tossed about on the thin mattress of her wooden plank bed. The warm summer breezes came through her barren cell window. All the panels that boxed the bed in winter for warmth were now neatly folded at its foot. She missed seeing Ian in the corridors and she felt lonely now that the townspeople were gone. She had grown fond of them, especially Baby Joseph. It had been difficult while nursing some of them to keep the no touching, no hugging, no kissing, no matter who rule.

Marie-Louise felt she had broken all the rules when she relived the night she and Ian had sat by the fireplace in her home in Beauport and they had committed to each other. But she was trying to make amends to leave in good standing, to prepare for her new life with Ian as his fiancée, and eventually his wife and mother of their children.

"Oh, bring him back safely to Quebec, to this convent, to me," she whispered on these sleepless nights. She still felt his tender kiss on the nape of her neck and she blushed hotly in the dark of her cell. She stretched her young body in the long white regulation night gown. Warm tears wet her lashes, she murmured little prayers until finally she slept.

Now, all the nuns prayed in silence again behind a lattice of black iron bars. They were returning to only two hours a day conversation with a fellow nun and one visitor a month. Marie-Louise agonized over this. How would she manage that with Jean-Paul. He had the run of the convent with his cart load of occasional provisions from Beauport. They had always been able to receive letters but they were going to be allowed only a number of responses and these would be inspected by the Reverend Mother.

They were in full season for keeping the gardens weeded and they worked hard at it. They scrubbed the refectory and corridor floors. They repaired Stations of the Cross brought to them from the chaos of burnt-out churches in the countryside and they made wooden rosary beads.

In this new quiet there was some deep soul searching. In silence, Mother de Bransac carefully reviewed her nuns. Among her postulants, after all they had gone through in the last nine months, did they still have the same sense of vocation? Was it only Marie-Louise who wanted to leave? They all seemed as dedicated as when they had first entered the heavy doors of the monastery. She was especially worried about the nuns who had completed their five year trial and were due to take a final vow. That ceremony would have to wait for the election of a new Bishop.

Hubert joined a few Huron friends and *coureurs-de-bois* shortly after the fleet left Quebec and together they followed a land route along side of it with the least detection possible. But after a few days of hard traveling he gave up. In a black mood, he had to admit to himself and to his generous companions that he was too much of a burden to put up with. He requested Noël to report back the news of whatever transpired. He returned to his new home and his bride. Tante José had left the convent infirmary and was now re-installed in her residence. She and Anaïse were happy to have Hubert back. They said not a word. There was plenty to do in the city. They prayed and anxiously waited for the outcome at Montreal.

Ian's ship arrived at Point Champlain on the twenty-eight of July. Here they were overtaken by sloops from Quebec with news of the arrival of two battalions from Louisbourg, the 40th and the 22nd.

July folded into August and on the fourth they reached Trois Rivières.

"Ian, we're not going very fast on this cruise." John muttered. He took out his spy glass.

"Umm. . . . But we're picking up oaths as we go along."

"There doesn't seem to be as much poverty in these small parishes along the river as in some of the Quebec neighborhoods." John inspected the south shore in the eye of his glass.

Ian agreed. "Their farms are neat and well kept. Here, let's have a look. What a beautiful morning!" He admired the countryside. "Their gardens are yielding. Did you stop long enough to see all that produce at the market the other day?"

"Aye, and they bring us salad greens, good exchanges for our salt. Yes, and they're all becoming British subjects, they're taking the oath. . . . They'd better."

Ian handed back the spy glass.

"True, but we don't have to burn all their habitations down to get them to do it. Enough is enough."

"Bloody war, Ian."

"Yes, bloody war since Wolfe climbed the cliff. It's them or us. The French military will have to go back to France if we win the war. But I tell you, John, these Canadians don't give a damn who is going to own the country now, French or English. They know who really owns it and might still when we're dead and gone, not King Louis or George the Second. They're across the pond and write treaties at Versailles about who gets what. They don't work and nurture the land, make it grow. The Canadians do. First the Indians held it sacred. Who knows where they came from. The French came and colonized it, those who stayed became Canadians in the process. And here we are, we're going to govern them better than they have been. Let's hope we don't botch it up. We fought a war for land neither nation owned in the beginning."

"That's quite a speech." John Knox smiled. "Think I'll go below and write some of it in my journal."

"Aye, do that."

"Next you'll be telling me that in years to come we'll have a few Jean-Pierre MacDonalds, Antoinette MacKellars and Paul-André Macduffs. You'll probably end up raising a family here yourself, old boy." He gave Ian a speculative look with a twinkle in his eye. "Little Canadians wearing kilts."

"That I would be so blessed. Go write your journal, it might become a best-seller in London when this bloody war's over."

"Aye, they'll get used to us, these Canadians. And we will govern them better than they have been. We have no Voltaires to advise us. We'll spread the British influence for good. . . ."

"The good they'll take. We'd better be wise. But *tu rêves, mon vieux,* if you think it's going to be easy even though we have the might and force at the moment."

John shrugged.

Later, they were both sent out in two armed boats up to the three rivers to sound and contrary to their expectations, discovered a channel along the south shore. It was so close in to the shore they expected to be shot at. Above them on the heights, a group of Canadians drew up with their arms. But they were not molested.

"What water have you, Englishmen?" A Canadian voice called out in broken English.

"Sufficient to bring up our ships and knock you and your houses to pieces," an officer of Lord Rollo's equipment called out. "If you dare molest us, we will land our troops, burn your habitations and destroy your country."

"Let us alone," they replied. "And you will not meet with any annoyance." One spokesman bellowed, "If your officers choose to come ashore and refresh themselves, I will be answerable for their being at liberty to return when they so desire."

"Well, none of us are going to accept that tricky invitation," John snickered.

"I think it's sincere," Ian said.

"You would."

Two canoes came up along side of their ship with a quantity of greens and salading.

"It's acceptable, John. They're unarmed and we need the greens."

Another group of inhabitants off the south shore came on board without fear. They had vegetables, poultry, eggs and other supplies for exchanges of salt, pork and beef. They had great need of salt to preserve eels and other fish for the winter.

On the morning of the eighth, Ian's part of the convoy passed Trois Rivières. He and John observed in their spy glasses about two thousand French lined up at their different works. They were clothed as regulars, except a few Canadians and about fifty Indians, their bodies were painted a reddish brown and their faces with a variety of colors.

"That's as close as I want to see any of those." Ian whispered in awe.

"Aye," John agreed. "But the French light cavalry seems well appointed, all in blue, faced with scarlet, the officers in their white uniforms."

"And look, those are all fair-looking houses situated on the banks of this delightful river."

"It's this clear, pleasant weather that makes everything look so green and inviting. See that verdure, those well-kept fields. Aye, I could live here. It's beautiful country."

"You're right John, no doubt, some of us will settle here." Ian agreed as he admired the countryside.

That evening they anchored at Lake St. Peter. A runner came to the fleet while they were at mess with the news of Amherst's and Haviland's progress.

A feeling of nervous precaution rippled through part of the fleet when the officers found out that half of the men of the town of Sorel were absent with their arms.

On the twenty-second, at one o'clock in the morning, Lord Rollo and the regiments under his command, with the rangers, got into their boats and rowed off. At two, they landed a mile below Sorel, burned many houses and laid waste the greatest part of the parish.

Ian was appalled at the burning of Sorel. He thought it too extreme a measure, unnecessary. He could hardly contain himself when he had to make copies of Murray's letter to Pitt. The words floated in his mind.

"I found the inhabitants of the parish of Sorel had deserted their habitations and were in arms; I was therefore under the cruel necessity of burning the greatest part of these poor unhappy people's houses; I pray God this example may suffice, for my nature revolts when this becomes a necessary part of my duty."

Ian reasoned to himself that Murray had a difficult role and it shifted in some instances between being a father governor to the inhabitants and then a tyrant who burnt their houses in punishment if they didn't sign the oath of fidelity.

On the twenty-third, they came to an anchor off Contrecoeur. Various accounts came in from prisoners and deserters of the armies under Amherst and Brigadier Haviland.

Murray dispersed manifestoes to all the neighboring parishes stating that if they would surrender and deliver up their arms, he would forgive them. If not, they knew what they might expect from the examples which he had hitherto reluctantly given them. He further added as for such Canadians as had been incorporated in the battalions of regulars, if they would surrender he would not only reinstate them in their settlements and lands, but likewise enlarge and protect them. But if, after all, they would still persist, they must expect to share the fate of the French troops and be transported with them to Europe.

These manifestoes had the desired effect. That evening, four hundred of them, belonging to the parish of Boucherville, came to Varenne and delivered up their arms. After taking the customary oaths, they asked Murray to give them safeguards for their parish, which was granted. A sergeant's party was sent off with them to protect them from the Indians allied to the British.

Eight Sachems, of different nations, recently in alliance with the French came to surrender for themselves and their tribes to General Murray. They stepped out to the beach opposite Montreal, flourished their knives and hatchets, rent the air with war-hoots and intimated to the French that they were now allied to the British.

On the 6th of September, Amherst's army passed from Isle Perrot to the island of Montreal; on the following day Murray's army made a like movement from Isle Teresa and landed on the lower end of the island and marched toward the town. The enemy came out from everywhere to meet the troops with refreshments. The advance was slow because of all the broken bridges. Finally after much maneuvering, the city of Montreal was surrounded on all sides. Three considerable armies had advanced on different lines widely separated through hostile country, two of them at least having exceptional difficulties to be surmounted, Amherst's force covering some three hundred miles from Oswego; Haviland and Murray covering each about one hundred and fifty miles from Crown Point and Quebec respectively. Each force for that time being cut off from its base, and relying solely on the supplies it carried, yet all three had arrived at the rendezvous almost simultaneously. Amherst, Murray and Haviland complimented themselves that thus far they had accomplished a fine military movement.

"This is quite a town, John."

"Aye, so this is Montreal where all the French officers, Governor Vaudreuil, his aides and their paramours cavorted at all those balls last winter, according to our military scuttlebutt."

"And where the ill Bishop took refuge with the Sulpicians." Ian added.

"You learned a lot about ecclesiastics living in that convent."

Ian smiled as he thought of Marie-Louise.

The town was a long narrow assemblage of wooden and stone houses, one or two stories high, above which rose the peaked towers of the seminary, the spires of three churches, the walls of four convents, with trees of their adjacent gardens, and at the lower end, a high mound of earth, crowned by a redoubt, where a few cannons were mounted. The whole was surrounded by a bastioned wall, made for defence against Indians, and incapable of resisting cannon.

"It's amazing that we all converge here pretty much on schedule. We're probably going to be errand boys transmitting letters between Amherst, Vaudreuil and Murray."

"We and a few others, John. We made this critical junction of our three armies in the space of forty-eight hours. It took us about five weeks to cover approximately one hundred fifty miles. Amherst left long before us and Haviland after. What do you think their mileage was?"

"Roughly, Amherst must have covered three hundred miles and Haviland approximately the same mileage we did."

"I hope Amherst is going to keep the Indians quiet. It's a toss-up now as to which ones are allied to us or the French anymore."

"He's good with them. Sir William Johnson, his aide, knows how to handle even the Iroquois."

Amherst had encamped above the place the night before. Murray's part of the fleet had landed to camp below it. Governor Vaudreuil, looking across the St. Lawrence, could see them and the tents of Haviland's little army on the southern shore.

Vaudreuil called a council of war. It was resolved that since the militia and many regulars had abandoned the army, and the Indians allied to France had gone over to the British, further resistance was impossible.

Fifty-five articles of capitulation to be proposed to the English were drawn up and unanimously approved by the council.

Amherst had communicated that the whole garrison of Montreal and all other French troops in Canada must lay down their arms and not serve during the present war.

The French were to be denied to march out with the honors of war. Amherst was inflexible on this point. Upon hearing it, Levis was incensed that his troops should lay down their arms of war before the capitulation was signed. He made a formal protest in his name and that of the officers from France. He insisted that the negotiation be broken off. He sent his note of protest by M. de la Pause. He asked permission of Vaudreuil to withdraw with the troops of the line to the Island of St. Helen in order to uphold there on their own behalf, the honor of the King's arms.

This suicidal proposal was rejected as he knew it would be. He was ordered to conform to the capitulation. He burnt the French flags on St. Helen's Island the night of September seventh. Instead, two stands of British colors that were taken from the late regiments of Pepperell and Shirley at Oswego, in the infancy of the war, were restored.

At six o'clock the morning of September the eighth, Vaudreuil sent word that he accepted the British terms and later in the day he signed the capitulation with a heavy heart knowing full well that he gave away half a continent, the vision of New France along with the wretched reality of Montreal.

Levis did not attend the ceremony.

Next day a column of redcoats entered Montreal through the Recollets' gate, and wheeled into line on the square of the Place d'Armes. The French trooped into the square without flags, drumming or trumpeting, sullenly dropped their muskets and marched away to a camp assigned to them on the ramparts. They now numbered barely two thousand, since hundreds more had deserted.

The British flag replaced the lilies of France on Citadel Hill. Major Isaac Barre took a fast ship for England to tell the King and his minister that the war in North America was over. He carried Amherst's official dispatch to Pitt and also a letter to a friend that revealed his private satisfaction that all had been executed without loss of life.

Order was maintained during the occupation of Montreal. A red coat found looting would be hung immediately. The Iroquois were sent home with thanks and presents; four lace hats, 119 pounds of wampum, 242 pounds of silver trinkets, 600 cords of birch bark and 44 anchors of brandy. Amherst was glad to see them go. And also the Canadians were glad to see them go, they had feared a massacre and were immensely relieved. Some of the Indians went away grumbling because there had been no uprisings with opportunities for scalping. Small groups detoured in other directions.

The refugees who had come to Montreal went back to their farms and the town began to settle down. According to the surrender terms, the French troops and all officials who wanted to go would be shipped to France within fifteen days.

During these days, relations between the armies were correct, but bitter. During the two sieges of Quebec, the opposing commander had exchanged gifts of wine, spirits, rounds of cheddar and other delicacies for their tables. Levis had even sent spruce beer, *sapinette,* for Murray's men and braces of partridge. Now they refused to meet.

Vaudreuil gave a dinner party for Amherst and no French officers showed up. Major Malartic had to get special permission from Levis to visit Murray, with whom he had often dined at Quebec.

In the midst of occupation duties, Ian and John looked the town over. In a leisure moment, John made a confession.

"Ian, I'm going to ask Amherst's permission to go back to Europe, and Murray's indulgence to repair to Quebec immediately to settle some affairs preparatory to my departure. . . ."

"You surprise me!"

"I would like some men to attend me in a flat bottom boat so as to really see the country. We should be provided with a quantity of sugar, salt, tobacco and pork in order to traffic with the Canadians for poultry, pigs, whatever."

"Sounds like a lark. Wish I could join you but I'm assigned to return to Quebec with Murray, same ship we came on. He's writing letters like mad. He too wants to leave as soon as possible."

"Aye, there's a lot to be done for Amherst's visit to Quebec."

"He'll be following on our heels. And there's still some of the French to be packed off."

"Well, I'll either be ahead of you or behind you. Too bad about the flags. What a trophy to bring home if we could have put our hands on even just one of them."

"Amherst accepted Levis' explanation."

"I swear to you, I did see one on the Plains. If the cloud of smoke after the general fire had vanished half a minute sooner, I would actually have possessed myself of one stand. They were a white silk with three *fleur de lis* within a wreath or circlet in the center part, and two tassels at the spear-end, all of gold."

"Deprived of the honors of war, the rumor that Levis burnt his colors at St. Helen's Island is believable."

"Aye, too bad, Ian. Well, I'll be off."

"Bon voyage then, John, see you in Quebec."

Chapter Twenty

Forty-eight hours after the capitulation of Montreal, Montgolfier, the Superior of the Sulpicians engaged Noël to deliver the clerical mail to Quebec City and announce the military news. It was assumed he would arrive there before the return of Murray's fleet.

Noël and three Huron companions canoed most of the way, making good time. They were wary and nervous of the Iroquois and Mohawks who had not left to go home at Amherst's direction. Some of them were still out there roving the countryside. At Beauport, Noël left his escort who continued on to Lorette. He walked and ran the rest of the way in the close of a golden September afternoon. He slackened his pace after entering Quebec by the Palace Gate. On his back he carried three pouches of letters and dispatches, one for General Hospital, one for Hôtel Dieu and yet another for the Ursuline Convent. How would he tell Father Resche and the three Superiors that they were now all British subjects, himself included. Father Montgolfier had emphasized parts of Murray's treaty with the Hurons before he and his group left Montreal. No English or party was to molest or interrupt them from returning to their settlement in Lorette. They were to be received on the same terms with the Canadians in being allowed free exercise of their religion, their customs and liberty of trading with the English garrisons. And it would be recommended to officers commanding these posts to treat them kindly.

There was a crystalline chill in the air. They had been lucky, good weather had held through most of the journey. Noël and his companions had admired the countryside, especially the leaves bursting with vivid colors. The greens of summer had turned to pale yellow, tawny orange, brown and crimson. He was alone now back in his territory. He shifted the mail bags. What was in them? He did not know. One of them contained all the correspondence duly signed by Bishop de Pontbriand shortly before his death last June.

Noël's mouth was dry, the fatigue of the journey overtook him, he was hungry and thirsty and he had cramps in his legs. He wondered what Mother Philomène might offer him in her warm kitchen. He decided to stop at Hôtel Dieu first and not linger there.

At the convent, Mother de Bransac thanked Noël for his delivery.

"Montreal capitulated on the eighth. We are all British subjects now." He spoke to her in French, very solemnly.

She nodded slightly and, as he knew she would, sent him to the kitchen. She went back to her study to read the contents of the Montreal mail. She had received this expected news stoically enough without much expression except a few nods. She sighed heavily. Among Montgolfier's letters she was surprised to find many signed by Bishop de Pontbriand. He must have experienced a surge of energy before he died to have tied up all the loose ends of his paper work. "God rest his soul," she murmured as she knelt at her prie-dieu. She prayed for a proper treaty of peace to be drawn, for the French returning to France, for Quebec and Canada. She would have to assemble all her nuns in the community room and tell them that they were now, all of them, British subjects. After the Angelus, that would be time enough. She sighed again and passed her cross under her head ban. She sent up a few prayers for Levis and Governor Vaudreuil. Were they already on their way back to France? What would this peace be like? In December, her extra term as Superior would be over. Who would replace her in this unenviable position? She thought of Esther Wheelwright, *Mère de l'Enfant Jesus*, an Englishwoman. She had been brought to the Ursuline convent as a little girl after an Indian raid on her village in New England and she had stayed to become an Ursuline. Politically, Mother de Bransac thought, she would be an excellent choice. Not too young, not too old to take the post.

Now, her next thought was that they must have the convent ready for General Amherst's visit. The mail told her that he would arrive any time. Murray, no doubt, would appear in Quebec first to spruce up the delapidated city, in this state by their own hands. Would the returning fleet with the Commander-in-Chief of the whole North American Campaign expect them to sing a *Te Deum* in the chapel?

"Please God, not that," she whispered. "But for peace, Lord God, be praised."

An hour later Mother de Bransac also received two other letters by local courier from Beauport. They were from Joseph Henri Boisvert, one addressed to his daughter, Marie-Louise and the other to herself. She read them both. His tone was sad but the language was full of love and groped for sympathetic understanding of Marie-Louise's decision. He wanted her to be happy. He would welcome her home and offer his counsel when needed.

Mother de Bransac made a copy of her own letter for the religious archives. Then she went to Marie-Louise's cell to leave the longed-for patriarchal answer on her writing table with a note that they would talk later.

After placing fresh bouquets of chrysanthemums at the chapel altars, Marie-Louise returned to her cell and found the copy of her father's letter with Mother de Bransac's note. She read them with a leaping heart. *Merci, bon Dieu!* All these past weeks, she thought how she must have hurt and distressed her father with this decision out of the blue. That he might shut her out and where would she have gone? That she would scandalize the family, the whole countryside. Now he understood that she wanted to do everything right. She clutched the precious document against her wimple and ran back toward the chapel.

"*Quelle épouvante!* What's your hurry at this hour?" Geneviève stopped her at the door.

"Ah, Sister Philippe, Geneviève, it's come, it's come!"

"What? What happened at Montreal?" She asked fearfully.

"I don't know but my father's letter has come!" Marie-Louise waved it at her. "I'm going home. He's trying to understand."

"Ah, bonheur," Geneviève broke into a wide smile. "I'll come in and say a short prayer with you, then." She was genuinely happy for her friend.

They both went to their choir stalls to pray and meditate on all the changes that were about to take place.

In the convent kitchen, Noël wolfed down two large bowls of pea soup. His legs were still tired and he was very sleepy.

"So what happened in Montreal?" Mother Philomène placed a cup of strong tea in front of him.

"We're all British subjects now. Vaudreuil capitulated. There was no fighting, no bloodshed and we are to look forward to peace. . . ."

Mother Philomène nodded seriously over the soup cauldron. She knew he had brought in the mail pouches and they would all get the official news from the Reverend Mother. "Poor Levis," she murmured to herself.

"Where's Hubert? Is he here?"

"Yes, he's in the carpenter shop late today."

Noël found Hubert busy polishing the back of a mahogany hall bench. He gave him a full account of the capitulation as he knew it.

"Ah, *mon ami,* I feared as much. After St. Foy, the game was pretty well up for us. Come home with me, you'll stay with us tonight. You can deliver the pouch for General Hospital on your way to Lorette tomorrow."

Noël ate again with Anaïse, Hubert and Tante José. Generous portions of caribou stew was served, it was hot, rich and delicious.

"Peace!" Tante José exclaimed between mouthfuls. "Really, Hubert, *c'est vrai.* And how do you think they'll treat us?"

"At this point, *chère Tante,* it's to everyone's advantage that they treat us well and we all make the adjustments to survive together."

She grumbled and went off to bed.

Hubert stoked up the fire. An early September chill settled on the town. With the candles and lanterns lit, it was cozy inside. Not new to Médard hospitality, Noël pulled a bear skin nearer to the great kitchen hearth, stretched out and instantly fell asleep. Anaïse threw a woolen cover

over him. Then she and Hubert went into the small parlor to talk and sip brandy.

"So, the great General Amherst will be here in a few days."

"*Ne te casse pas la tête.* It's too late to worry." Hubert built a fire in the small metal stove by the chimney with bits of kindling. He tended it as he sipped his brandy.

"Well, we have something much more important to get ready for."

"What's that, *mon ange?*"

"Hubert, I'm with child," she said softly.

He set his goblet of brandy down, swept her in his arms and rocked her back and forth. "*C'est vrai?* It's true! You're sure?"

She nodded, nestled against his chest.

"But what a time to bring a child into the world, a little British subject."

"This child is for Quebec, no matter whose subject she or he will be. And you, *mon vieux*, are going into politics if we're now all British subjects." She disentangled herself and kissed him lightly.

"*Es-tu folle!* We're going into trade and now politics?"

"I'll run the store. But we have to know how we're going to be governed. You've got a good mind, you're going to use it."

"You have no fear."

"Neither have you. We were duped under the French regime. Now, we have to be clever enough to see that the orders of the capitulation are carried out and what kind of new government will be formed. We're fortunate to be able to keep our language and our religion. . . . We'll have to keep abreast, study law, whatever it takes for the rest, to live and breathe with this new peace."

Again, Hubert said solemnly, "You never cease to amaze me. Well, *petite mère* to-be, it'll take time for a peace treaty to be negotiated, written, signed and sealed. I'll have to be a very clever man to please you." He took her into his arms again.

"You are clever, Hubert." She nestled in the warmth of his embrace. "You know as well as I do, we have a lot of work to do, to continue to rebuild. We will look forward to living in this peace. . . ."

"Yes," he said seriously. "To raise our family. I know your heart is set on having more than one child." He placed a light kiss on the nape of her neck.

"If God permits." She snuggled against him. "In our ordinary roles, Hubert, we can accomplish a lot. Quebec is not going to fade away."

"That we should all have your faith," he murmured against her swept up hair. "Well, *voyons,* I have a small errand to run in Lower Town for Mother Philomène."

"Now?"

"Yes, now. There's a lot to do. Murray's fleet is about to return at any moment. This town is going to be bustling with added traffic to get everybody that's going back to France and England properly packed off."

"Then away with you. I'm going to draft a letter to Murray to find out what kind of goods we can expect as British subjects from England and New England."

"Ah, you're always calculating," he smiled, kissed her soundly and left.

At the sound of the vestibule doors closing, Tante José woke up.

"What's going on? What's going on?" She called from upstairs. "Anaïse, it's cold. We need a fire. Where's Hubert?"

"The heat will be coming up in a few moments." Anaïse encouraged the fire in the stove, then went to check the kitchen hearth. It was warm and comfortable. Noël was snoring with the mail pouch for a pillow.

Several days later, part of Murray's returning fleet was within sight of Jacques Cartier.

"Ah, at last." Ian finished a series of letters, put his coat on and went up on deck for fresh air. John Knox's *bateau* was not far behind them this morning. It was a fair day with light rippling winds. He could hardly wait to see Marie-Louise. He wrote her a love note against the blue sky. He breathed the good air. It was dangerous to stay on deck too long. He turned to go back below.

Suddenly, out of nowhere a group of Indians on horseback, yelling and hooting, galloped alongside the fleet on the south shore. They were not alone. It looked like there were a few French and Canadians deserters with them. They flung arrows at the ships. Ian caught one in the chest and fell on the deck floor.

"Man the guns!" A lieutenant screamed. Everybody scuffled and fell too. Shots rang out, cannons boomed.

All in the puff of a moment, it was over, they were gone, swallowed up in the far reaches of the forest. Ian groaned in pain. A sailor sprawled out next to him moaned.

"Permission to come aboard?" Ian heard John Knox's yell, loud and clear.

There was running and scrambling about on deck. He felt himself being lifted and brought into the captain's cabin. He heard Murray's voice.

"What the. . . . ? We've just dictated Amherst's very words, no incident or bloodshed at the capitulation. Now this!"

"Bloody hell! Must be malcontents from Amherst's tribes who have not gone home as they were told, and no doubt a few French and Canadian deserters among them. Who will ever know? Get the Doctor here on the double." The Captain looked at Murray. "Do you want to send out a scouting party?"

"I'll see to it. Take care of Captain Lindsay."

John Knox came on board in a sweat of anxiety, ran past everyone to get to Ian. He knelt by him while one of Ian's lieutenants cradled his head.

"Ian! Ian! You're not going to die on us now. We've come this far, we have the whole of Canada in the palm of our hands. Don't die! You're not going to leave with a bloody arrow stuck in your chest. We hardly knew you. Where's the ship's doctor?"

"Here's the doctor. Make way everybody." Another lieutenant hovered over Ian. "He'll be all right. We'll be at Lower Town in a few hours."

"We'll have to get him to Hôtel Dieu, there's no longer a hospital ward at the convent. The *hospitalières* will take good care of him. Make way for our doctor." Lieutenant McHardy took charge.

"Where did the rest of those bloody savages go? Just one stray arrow out of the whole howling lot and Ian had to get it. Damn!" John Knox cursed.

Another volley of cannons boomed for good measure. Then only the traffic noises of the crews on board the moving ships filled the air.

Ian was unconscious of the racket around him. The doctor pulled the arrow out clean. Then he wiped, medicated and bandaged the wound.

"There, he should be all right. Let's get him and the wounded first mate to the hospital."

"Worse luck," John muttered.

"Captain Lindsay's tough, sir, he'll pull through." Lieutenant McHardy didn't want to consider anything else.

"Please God! There's Quebec bursting out of the rock, there's Lower Town right ahead. Let's fall to lads, and get them up the hill as quick as we can, right to the hospital."

"Aye, Aye."

Ian moaned. John bent over him. "Hang on! Hang on! We'll get Sister Madeleine to take care of you."

"Marie-Louise," he whispered. Pain surged through his whole body then lodged in his chest. Everything went hazy again.

At Hôtel Dieu, Ian grasped John's hand. He regained a lucid moment. "Get Father Resche and ask Sister Madeleine to come if the Reverend Mother gives her leave."

"Yes, yes." John assured him.

Ian fell back exhausted. He drifted away into a dream world. He was back home. He thought he saw Sergeant Thompson coming in from Tain, proud in his tartan. He had just signed up to join the great North American Campaign. Then the scene shifted. There was a lot of light, golden sunshine. Marie-Louise was sitting with his family on the lawn at Vendôme near the *brûlonnerie*. In the same red dress she wore the first time he had seen her in Beauport. His father, in kilts, was smiling and talking with her. It was a picnic, all the ladies had their parasols. There was wine and fruit on a long table and beyond there was a path of brilliant light that

led right through the forest. Marie-Louise got up and beckoned him to join
her. Everyone was smiling. They started walking in the lighted pathway. It
was bordered with heather like in the hills of Scotland. Marie-Louise held
him by the hand. They seemed to bounce lightly down the walk as if they
were floating. Then he knew no more.

"The trip up the hill was too much." The doctor closed Ian's eyes.
The *hospitalière* shook her head.

"Oh, no!" John sobbed. He picked up Ian's *La Chanson de Roland*
with its ragged tartan book mark. He gathered sorrowfully with Ian's
lieutenants. They left Hôtel Dieu to find Murray who was by now back at
his headquarters in the Ursuline convent. They would have to complete
arrangements right away. There was enough going on with the formal
dispatches of getting the French and their baggage back to France and on
what ships without this erupting tragedy of what to do with the remains of
one of their officers.

John Knox grimly decided he would be the one to give this heart
breaking news to Sister Madeleine, Ian's beloved Marie-Louise. How would
he tell her? Before he went to the *parloir* of the Holy Family with his fellow
officers, he stopped in the quiet alcove of a long corridor and he sobbed like a
child. After he composed himself he decided to go to the Reverend Mother
first. Later, it was she who broke the news to Marie-Louise.

"Dear child, if you need me. . . ."

Marie-Louise couldn't utter a word. She left in silence, her veil
fluttering, and went directly to her cell.

A little later, Geneviève knocked three times at Marie-Louise's door.

"Sister Madeleine?" Several novices passed by in the hall.
Cautiously, Geneviève opened the door. "Marie-Louise, I looked everywhere
for you. Aren't you going to walk in the garden?" The recreation bell had
just rung. Outside, the whole town was inundated in golden September
sunshine.

Marie-Louise sat by the window, her hands folded over her rosary.
Geneviève placed a small vase of marigolds on the window sill. A thin blue
silk ribbon encircled the container ending in a perky bow.

"Aren't they lovely? Part of the fleet's back. When are you going to tell Captain Lindsay that you are going home?"

"I'm never going to be able to tell him, not in this life." She rediscovered her voice, it was a strange low whisper. "He died at Hôtel Dieu, this morning."

"Oh, my God!" Geneviève collapsed kneeling at the prie-dieu. She pressed her hand against her mouth. There was a long suffering silence between the two of them.

"*Requiescat in pace*," Geneviève finally murmured. She made the sign of the cross. "He already knows," she added softly. "And he knows that you love him very much."

Marie-Louise nodded as tears rolled down her cheeks.

"Shall I send for Reverend Mother or would you like to go to her?"

"No."

"You want to be alone?"

Marie-Louise nodded.

"Marie-Louise, he already knows what you wanted to tell him. He's with God."

She nodded.

"And he knows that you love him very much."

Marie-Louise nodded again.

Geneviève took both of Marie-Louise's hands in hers and pressed them hard. "Oh, *ma pauvre* Marie-Louise, God will give you strength. I'll be in the chapel if you need me."

Again, she nodded.

At six o'clock when the Angelus rang, Marie-Louise was still sitting by the window in her cell. Jean-Paul came to her with the Reverend Mother's permission. When she saw her brother, she got up and they embraced.

"Jean-Paul, Jean-Paul!"

He felt the pain in her heart. "The funeral's day after tomorrow, can you go? Shall I ask Reverend Mother if you could go with me, if you. . . .

"No, will you please go for me?"

He nodded.

"I will always remember Captain Lindsay, Ian, as I last saw him in the garden. Ah, *mon p'tit frère*, life is so fragile." They clung together."

"I'll stay in town at Anaïse's then, in case you need me."

"I'll go to chapel now." She sighed with excruciating pain.

"I'll come with you."

A silence reigned in the chapel. The prayers of the Angelus had been recited and all the nuns were now at supper. Soon it would be time for Complines. Marie-Louise sat in her choir stall. Jean-Paul found a place in the public section. From force of habit, Marie-Louise turned her hour glass over.

It was unbelievable that Ian's life was over. That she would never see him walk down the corridors, smiling at her, looking for her in the garden or in the library. One day she would have gone to the ends of the earth with him, another day she was divided about her long ago commitment to the convent, to Quebec. Now the decision was no longer hers to be made, even though she had made it with sacrifice. It was out of her hands. It was all taken away. All she had of him to look at was the garnet stone he had donated and was now placed in the foot of the chapel chalice. And her life? How long was it for? O my God! She shivered. She lifted her eyes to the sanctuary lamp. Then she looked for Jean-Paul. He was in his usual place with bowed head. She knew he was praying for her, and Ian, he was fond of Ian, even though he had not been in total approval of her marrying him and leaving Quebec for England, France and finally Scotland. And Jean-Paul always prayed for Quebec.

When all the lights were out, all the prayers said, Mother Philomène came to Marie-Louise's cell that night with a hot *tisane*. After a few hard swallows, Marie-Louise burst into long, heaving sobs in Mother Philomène's comforting arms.

The next day, Marie-Louise was called to parlor by Reverend Mother to receive Lieutenant John Knox. She left them alone.

"Sister Madeleine," he began hesitantly. "I took the liberty of bringing this. I feel Ian, Captain Lindsay would want you to have it. In fact, he told me he was going to give it to you." He placed the small leather copy of "*La Chanson de Roland*" on the parlor table. The torn piece of tartan spilled out of the gold edged leaves. He picked it up and put it back in place.

Marie-Louise didn't know what to say. Finally, she said. "Thank you, Lieutenant Knox." Sensing his grief and trying to control hers, she asked, "At what time is the funeral set?"

"At noon, tomorrow. Then I leave for England and Scotland. I will be the bearer of this tragic news to his parents."

"I will pray for your safe journey and for Captain Lindsay's family. . . ." She couldn't go on.

"Aye, Sister, I will need all the prayers you send to heaven for me."

"There will always be prayers here for all of you, for whoever enters Quebec." What strange inane things people said in grief. Strange because she had wished many times against heaven that the English fleet had never come there.

"Governor Murray, all of us of the garrison, you have our deepest respect for your order. We think you are the most wonderful women. . . . Some of us wouldn't be alive today but for you."

"God be with you." Again, she said the usual phrases nuns used. Was she going to be able to resume her role as a nun that effortlessly? She doubted it. She was eaten alive with pain.

The next day at noon, Marie-Louise stayed in her cell at her prie-dieu. It was a lush Indian summer's day with all of the convent windows open. Over the sounds of the usual monastery routine, she heard the muffled music of the bagpipes' laments from the Plains, the gun salutes. She prayed for Ian's soul. She mourned and wondered how she might have acted differently. Traffic noises from the docks in Lower Town came up the hill. She went to the window to see part of the English fleet getting ready to leave the basin with French prisoners. Was Governor Vaudreuil, Madame Vaudreuil, Levis, Cadet, Bigot and the Penisseaults finally leaving? Amherst's schooner had been lent to the Vaudreuils. Not all were leaving. It was rumored that one third of the fleet, since last September, had married Canadian girls and were staying in the garrison. Artisans and merchants of France were returning to the mother country with their families, some

Canadian officers who had served in the Marine were also leaving. But most of the Canadian population refused to leave their ancestral land.

"But you, Ian, you're staying here in the soil of Quebec. Quebec has claimed you." She broke into fresh sobs. "Adieu, Ian." What lost chances had slipped by their abated passion in the middle of that freezing winter night by the hearth fire in her Beauport home? She relived those few tender moments of love when they had committed to each other.

Jean-Paul came at two o'clock to tell her about the funeral.

"You're going home, now?"

"Yes." He wanted to ask her what she was going to do but he didn't. It was too soon. Let her be, he thought.

"Give my love to Papa and Uncle Guillaume."

He nodded and twirled his woolen *toque.*

Cannons boomed from ships that were picking up anchor in the basin and the garrison saluted them as Jean-Paul left the convent. He went and stood at the top of Cape Diamond and cast a critical eye on the exodus. What did the future hold for Quebec now that they were all British subjects? No one knew. Whatever the fate, he knew he would never leave Quebec. He wondered what ships would be left with the garrison for the winter. He lingered a few more moments, then came down the hill. He was walking home today. He crossed town and went out by the Palace Gate. At the close of September, it was a bonus day, a day like summer. Along Avenue Royale, he kept his gaze on the ships as they passed Orleans. The delicious aroma of pickling spices and of bread baking floated on the air. He thought that Mireille Le Conte might be baking in her outdoor oven for one last time before winter set in. He would stop by for a moment then he would go on to Juliette's. He hadn't seen Juliette in over a week. He knew she would offer him a bowl of soup and they would visit. His heart ached for Marie-Louise. Ah, what would he do if anything ever happened to Juliette? She was always there.

Marie-Louise sat for most of the afternoon in her cell. She knew no duties were expected of her. She could barely function. Ian's book with the tattered tartan bookmark was on top of her father's letter. She touched them tenderly. Doors and windows began to close, the balmy day had grown chilly. She felt cold and numb. The pleasant odor of Mother Philomène's soup wafted down the halls. What was it tonight? Fresh vegetables from the garden. The Angelus started to ring, nuns appeared from everywhere to go toward the chapel.

Marie-Louise rose from her stupor and joined a file of novices in the corridor. For now, she would go and sit in the glow of the sanctuary lamp, the Repentigny lamp, the lamp whose flame never went out.

About the Author

Irene Landry Kelso, of Acadian heritage, is originally from Moncton, New Brunswick. In early years she emigrated with her family to the United States and was educated in bilingual schools in New England.

A former Rhode Islander, she was a newspaper reporter for The Pawtucket Times. She later combined fiction writing with historical research and travelled to Canada, France, England, and Spain compiling data for two novels.

She has a degree from the Henry Jackson School of International Studies - Canadian Studies, University of Washington.

She lives in Seattle, Washington.

ISBN 155212414-2